I0831806

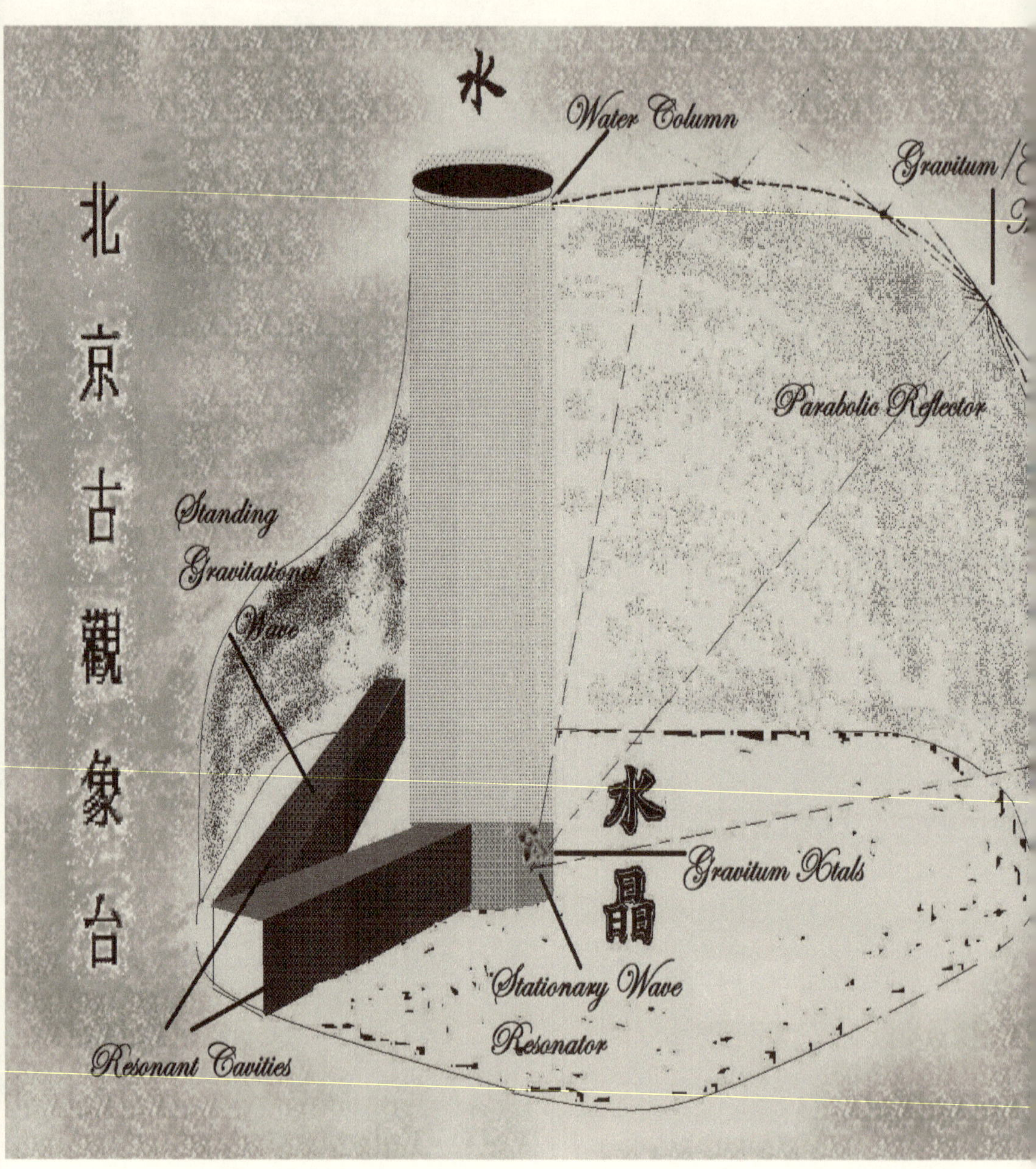


**Design of Gravitational Wave Rectifier**
**by Kuang-hsien Xu**

# MATTER
# OF
# PERSPECTIVE

First Published in Great Britain by Wise Grey Owl Limited 2010



ISBN 978-0-9561574-4-7



Published by Wise Grey Owl Limited

www.wisegreyowl.co.uk

Farthings, Main Street, Staveley, Knaresborough,

North Yorkshire, HG5 9LD

Publish@wisegreyowl.co.uk

# MATTER OF PERSPECTIVE

**David C. Fletcher**

*Illustrated by the author*

A Wise Grey Owl Publication

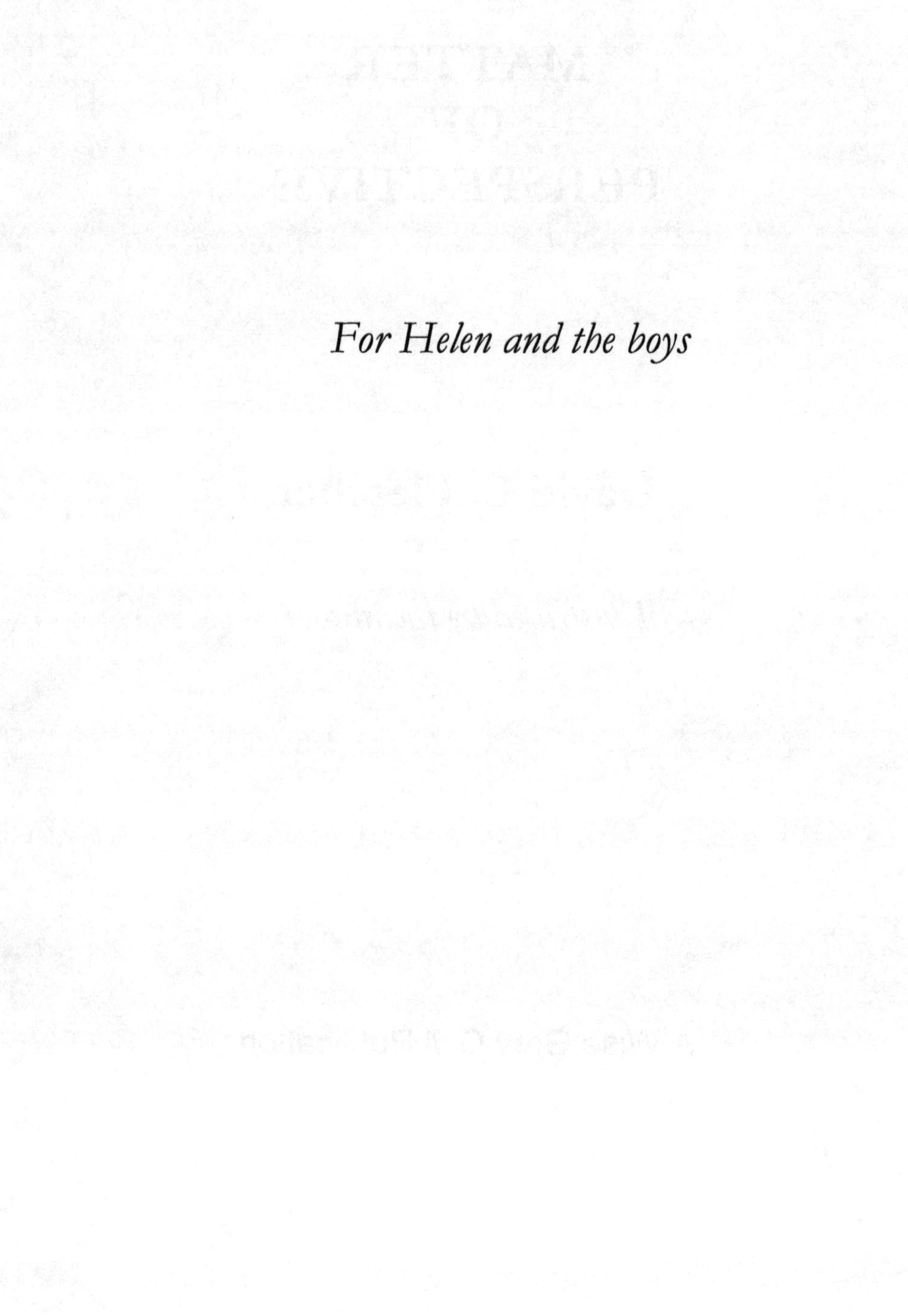

*For Helen and the boys*

# Author's note

I would like to express my thanks to my wife and sons for tolerating my withdrawal into the fantastical world of gravitation. In addition I am truly grateful for the support of those who read my first novel and encouraged me to write the sequel. In particular I'd like to thank Judy and other friends for helping me to sweep away so many typos.

I would also like to thank you for buying my book. I hope you find it entertaining. Although it has been created out of my imagination, I have tried to make the science and the storyline as plausible as possible. In the last analysis the book is a novel. All the protagonists are made up and so is gravitum. However, much of the other science and engineering is not. One day someone may discover a substance that behaves differently with gravity. If they do, who knows what may happen?

# Contents

# Part 1

# Rocking and shaking

# One

## Escape

'EeeOoo EeeOoo EeeOoo' screamed his computer terminal.

Even though Hitzubishi Mitzuko was already alert, the noise startled him. He had not expected the tamper alarm to sound.

'Kuso!' he cursed. 'It must be that interfering Aoki san, baka!'

He had been sitting with the keyboard on his lap waiting for the conditions to be right for the most important experiment of his life. With just a few keystrokes he could set the apparatus into action remotely. Mitzuko would then take his place in history as the engineer who really changed the world.

'Damn Aoki; he will ruin everything,' said Mitzuko out loud. 'Why can't he leave things alone?'

Mitzuko tapped a few keys on his keyboard.

'Imi imishe Kuso!' he shouted, as he hit the enter key.

His computer monitor responded with a message, 'System pressurizing – Danger.'

'That will fix them,' he thought.

But the computer had not finished.

'Servo malfunction – Control system failure!' it said.

'Kuso!' he cursed again.

Mitzuko had deliberately chosen to operate the system remotely so the researcher would be safe. As he was the designer and only researcher, he considered that this was the most sensible approach.

'Now Aoki san had put everything at risk because of his weakness and paranoia,' he thought. 'Aoki had probably disconnected the control circuitry.'

He could feel the anger and frustration well up from the pit of his stomach. He fought to control his emotions.

'I must be calm,' he thought. 'That is the samurai way.'

He could not be a samurai any more. The class of ruling warriors had been outlawed after the battle of Tabaruzuka, but Mitzuko came from Kagoshima where one of his ancestors had died following the code, so it was in his aging blood.

With gargantuan effort he became calm. Mitzuko focussed his mind on creating a strategy to recover his experiment.

'I must go to the laboratory and confront him,' he thought. 'It may be dangerous, but there is no prize without risk.'

He made his way to the roadside outside his small suburban house where his pick-up was parked. He paused, alert.

'Was that a rumble through the concrete road beneath me?' he thought. 'It's starting.'

He looked at his watch, concerned. It would take him an hour to get to the Tokyo Academy of Geosciences. It would be tight, but he could do it. He had better hurry. Mitzuko was nervous, even frightened, but after years of discipline these were other emotions he had learned to control.

****

Aoki Hideo was not a samurai either, neither were his ancestors; they were hinin, the lowest social class. In past centuries his ancestral class had been ranked four levels below samurai. In fact it classified his forebears as non-human. This could be quite damaging to a person's ego but at that moment none of this mattered. Class was the last thing on Hideo's mind, besides he was too young to care about ancient history and he had more immediate concerns. With the help of Prama, a foreign scientist seconded to Osaka University and her friend Claire they were desperately trying to load a large stainless steel machine into the back of his car. This was no ordinary machine; it was the core component of his boss' laboratory experiment.

'The vibration is getting worse,' he said, anxiously eying the shiny cylinder.

'Yes,' said Prama, tensely.

'The gravitational wave radiation is getting stronger, just as Anil predicted,' said Claire, with signs of panic in her voice.

Anil, Paul and Jacques were sitting around a telephone in England anxiously waiting for an update. Anil had run computer simulations of intensified gravitational wave radiation incident on the Earth. The UK team was tracking two binary star systems in space that had combined to increase the intensity of gravitational wave to a billion times more than the ambient background. This normally benign radiation was about to pass over Tokyo. Hideo's boss's machine, designed to react to the incoming signal, was already responding violently. Anil hoped desperately that they could quickly move the machine away from the huge population centre and Hideo would keep Prama safe.

Back in Tokyo, Hideo was concentrating on the problem in hand.

'We must concentrate on getting it into the car and then out of the city,' he said, using his last reserves of self-control to calm and focus them. 'We only have a few hours before the beam reaches its maximum.'

Hideo and his companions were well aware that they must get the device out of the city before it caused seismic vibrations; vibrations that would allow the Earth's tectonic plates to slide over each other. The experience from a similar experiment in the UK had been bad, very bad. And England was not in a major earthquake zone! Hideo knew nothing about gravitational waves, but he knew an awful lot about earthquakes. He knew they were in danger.

'You're right. We're running out of time,' said Prama. 'One, two, three, push!'

'It's no good,' said Claire, her panic rising further, 'it's too heavy. We can't get it over the lip of the boot.' Claire's mind cleared. She knew the only way out of this was to use her brain. Panic was not helping. 'We need help or lifting equipment,' she said, more calmly.

Claire looked around the car park for inspiration. She knew that if they did not think of something quickly, the thirteen-storey building above would collapse on top of them. All her instincts told her to run, but nowhere was safe. She saw some scaffolding and loose poles in the corner.

'Look,' she said, 'over there; scaffolding poles. Could we use them for leverage?'

'Brilliant,' said Prama.

Hideo said nothing. He was already on his way over to the stack of poles. He started to carry a pole back to the car.

'Stop,' said Claire. 'Take the car to the scaffolding. The apparatus is still on the trolley. Prama and I can wheel it.'

In a few moments the car and trolley were in position, next to the pile of metal poles. It took them half an hour, thirty precious minutes, to rig up a tripod and levers to lift the device into the back of Hideo's hatchback. In that time the vibration had become more violent. Shock waves seemed to be impacting on the solid surfaces in the basement car park. The longer scaffolding poles were starting to resonate. Suddenly a small block of concrete fell from the roof in front of the car. It missed the bonnet by inches.

'We've got to get going,' said Claire.

She moved to clear the debris away from the front of the car. Hideo and Prama got in and drove the car past her, toward the exit. The passenger door was obstructed by a pillar. Claire could not open the door to get in. She started to move around the back of the car.

'Go,' said Prama to Hideo. 'Leave her, she'll be safe now.'

Hideo gunned the engine and sped up the ramp out into the street. Claire, standing alone, stared at them first in disbelief and then in horror. Tears started to roll down her cheeks. Her knees gave way and she slowly sank to the floor. Claire took out her mobile. There was still no signal. She looked about her. The pillars of the building were damaged. She must leave quickly, before the building collapsed. As if in a trance, she stood up and made her way into the street and then a park.

Claire did not know how long she had been walking. She sat down on a park bench and looked at her phone again. The signal was back. She called her husband, Paul.

'They have gone Paul, they've gone.'

'I know,' he said softly. 'Prama has just phoned Anil.'

'What are their chances?' she asked.

'Not good, I'm afraid. We've lost contact with them. We think the device is still interfering with their mobile telephones, so we can't even track them.'

Claire was no longer listening. Her emotions were focussed on the loss of her friend; a friend who had just saved her life by leaving her behind. In her subconscious she heard Paul's voice say something.

'You must get out of there.'

'It's alright,' she said in a trance. 'I'm in the open; in a park.'

****

Mitzuko Hitzubishi arrived at the Academy of Geosciences in time to see Hideo and Prama driving out of the basement car park. Hideo's Datsun was a hatchback and Mitzuko could see by the depressed rear suspension that it had a heavy cargo in the back. He strained his eyes to look through the rear window. He could just make out the large stainless steel cylinder in the rear compartment.

'Kuso! They have stolen the gravitational wave rectifier, interfering idiots!' he exclaimed. 'They'll kill themselves.'

His instinct was to confront them, but he was too far away to cut them off. He decided to follow. The street was empty. It was still dark; just a few hours before dawn. He would have to be careful not to be seen. Mitzuko dimmed his lights and moved off behind them. Mitzuko could see that the back of Hideo's car was vibrating.

'They won't get far,' he thought. 'They will be soon forced to stop. Then I will take control.'

****

'We need to find a way of reducing the vibration,' said Hideo. 'I can hardly control the car.'

He was too focussed on the challenge of driving to notice that they were being tailed.

'If only we could de-pressurize the cylinder,' said Prama. 'Paul said that's what makes the crystals sensitive to gravitational waves.'

The crystals that Prama was referring to were the key component of Hitzubishi's device. Hitzubishi, Hideo's boss, had confiscated them. Originally they were part of a meteorite fragment that had been found at the bottom of the East China Sea. Inside the meteorite there were several translucent blue stones of varying sizes. Hideo was one of the seismologists responsible for the find and it was he who had extracted four blue crystals from the engulfing rock. Realising the crystals were something special, Hideo enlisted Prama and Claire to help analyse the samples. He explained that he suspected that the meteorite had caused seabed vibrations so powerful that his team had detected seismic vibrations in Tokyo, nearly one thousand miles north east of where they found it. Prama's colleagues in the UK knew that the crystals were sensitive to gravitational waves and dangerous when pressurized; particularly in an earthquake zone. Unfortunately, before Hideo could take them to a safe place, his boss had installed the crystals in the device that was now vibrating in the back of his ancient, or as Hideo preferred to call it 'classic' Datsun.

Prama started to climb over the front seat in to the rear of the car.

'Be careful,' said Hideo. 'You know how heavy that cylinder is. If it rolls on top of you it'll crush your arm'

Prama laughed.

'We are trying to save Tokyo from a disastrous earthquake and you are worried about me hurting my arm! I'm more likely to hurt my leg with these on my feet.'

Hideo glanced at her designer shoes and then her long legs. He returned his gaze back to the road embarrassed that his glance had been longer than it should. Prama kicked off her shoes.

'That's better,' she said. 'Don't worry I'll be careful.'

Prama started humming a song about shoes as she searched the surface of the cylinder; she found music helped her relax. The tension eased.

Hideo continued to struggle with the steering wheel.

'Can you see anything useful?' he asked, finding that he had to raise his voice above the noise of metal banging against metal.

'Nothing obvious,' shouted Prama, no longer humming. 'How much further to open country?'

'We will be out of the city in about another twenty minutes. Then we have to drive for about seventy kilometres to Chichibu-shi. I used to go there for walks with my parents. It is a deserted area.'

'Is it seismologically active there?'

'It's difficult to find anywhere around here that isn't,' replied Hideo, 'but it's the best place I could think of within the range of this car,' he paused. 'That is if we are not shaken apart before we get there.'

They had been driving for over forty minutes and they were still in the suburbs of the city. Prama was starting to wonder whether they were travelling towards the most dangerous part of the gravitational wave radiation. Hideo's phone rang.

'Can you take the phone please?' he said.

Prama took the mobile and pushed the send button.

'It's the UK team,' she said, relieved that they would tell them what to do next.

Prama explained where she and Hideo were and asked to speak to Anil. He should be able to tell them where they could dump the cylinder safely.

'Hello Anil,' she said. 'Hello, hello…. hello.'

The phone went dead – no signal.

The noise and vibration in the car was getting worse. She put Hideo's mobile down and examined hers. There was no signal either.

'Which direction is Chichibu-shi?' screamed Prama, over the increasing noise whilst her eyes scanned the cylinder for a valve or switch that might reduce the internal pressure.

'It's inland, northwest of Tokyo. Why?'

'If I could talk to Anil, he would be able to tell us where the focal point of the gravitational waves is.'

'Why does that matter?'

'That will be where the gravity radiation is strongest. We need to be as far away as possible from the maximum field strength. At the moment we don't know whether we are travelling away from the peak intensity or along with it. It could be following us,' she added.

'Oh,' he said, also shouting. 'Why don't you call him on your mobile?'

'I've tried, but I think the cylinder is affecting time and space for all objects around it. This means that my mobile is tuned to a different radio frequency from the cellular transmitters nearby.'

'Are you still speaking in English?' he asked. 'What does that mean?'

In spite of their fear, a smile was exchanged.

'It means the mobile will not work unless it's a long way away from the gravitational wave device.'

The car was now starting to zigzag along the road. Fortunately at this time in the morning there was virtually no traffic; just the occasional delivery vehicle. Its driver would put Hideo's unusual driving style down to the demon drink from the night before. They were now entering open country. Fortunately the police were not particularly attentive either because in such a law-abiding country, cameras and constant patrols were not considered necessary.

'We must pull over, so I can check with Anil that we are not heading towards a high intensity spot,' said Prama, above the noise. 'If we are driving in the right direction the vibration will abate as we move away from the peak strength of the invisible gravitational wave beam.'

'And if we are driving the wrong way?'

Prama did not need to answer; he could see her eyes in the rear view mirror.

'Oh that good,' he thought.

'I'll pull over as soon as I can,' he said, hastily.

The road headed into a cutting, with steep embankments on either side. They were approaching a wide section with a lay-by. With great difficulty Hideo pulled in and drew the car to a halt. Stationery or not, the car continued to vibrate and shake like a wild thing. The sun was just below the horizon and the sky was beginning to lighten a little.

'You should get a signal up there,' shouted Hideo, pointing to the steeply rising hill at the side of the lay-by. The noise was becoming deafening. 'See if you can make your call, but do it quickly. The vibration is getting worse.'

Prama had already slipped her designer shoes back on and was halfway out of the car. She glanced back at the apparatus on the back seat.

'It looks like the peak intensity has been following us. Now we've stopped the vibration is getting worse.'

Not waiting for Hideo to reply, Prama quickly made her way towards the hill, watching the signal-strength icon on her phone.

'I'll blow the horn if the vibration becomes too bad,' he shouted after her but she had disappeared into the half-light. She did not hear him. He gazed towards the path where he had last seen her. He tried to remember the song she had been humming. Perhaps it would calm him … something about shoes… Suddenly he felt isolated, alone.

Occasionally losing her footing, Prama climbed the steps that had been cut into the embankment. The path was steep but she moved as quickly as she could. As she made her way to the top, her head was starting to spin from the exertion. She could see the lights of Hideo's car below her.

'I've got a signal!' she shouted, but Hideo could not hear.

She dialled a number.

Obscured by the embankment a pick-up truck had pulled up near Hideo's dishevelled car. Prama did not see it. She heard a ring tone in the mobile earpiece.

'Allo, c'est Jacques,' came the reply.

'Jacques, it's Prama. We're in the countryside. I'm ok. Is Anil there? I need to speak to him urgently,' she said keeping the panic out of her voice. After a few words from Jacques, Anil came on the line.

'Anil thank god, it's you. I love you too, but I need your help,' she paused. 'We are travelling northwest from Tokyo. Are we moving towards the focus or away from it?'

As she was concentrating on Anil's reply Prama did not notice the pick-up that had parked near Hideo's vibrating car. The driver and Hideo had moved to the back, opened the tailgate and reached inside. Suddenly her subconscious noticed that the vibrating noise had stopped. She peered through the murk towards the car. She could see the vehicle more clearly. She was only half concentrating on the scene below, focusing her attention on the dialogue with Anil.

'What towards it?' asked Prama, starting to assimilate what she was hearing. 'So we must travel southwest, not northwest!'

'Thanks,' she said. 'We have to change direction then.'

She looked again.

'He's gone!' she said. 'Hideo's gone straight into the path of the radiation. Oh my God!'

****

'Get out, idiot!' shouted Hitzubishi, pointing the gun at Hideo. 'And walk round to the back of the car.'

Hideo jumped at the sound of Hitzubishi's voice. He slowly opened the door and climbed out. He was shaking, not sure whether it was from fear or an after-effect of sitting inside of his vibrating car.

‘Open the tailgate,’ barked Hitzubishi, pointing his gun towards Hideo’s head.

Hideo opened the tailgate. The cylinder was now banging violently against the wheel arches of the car.

‘Slide back that panel,’ he shouted, indicating a steel plate recessed into the surface of the cylinder.

Hideo reluctantly put his hand on the surface of the moving cylinder. With difficulty he slid back the panel, revealing a keypad.

‘Key in six three nine seven one,’ snapped Hitzubishi.

‘I can’t,’ said Hideo. ‘It’s moving too violently.’

‘Just do as you’re told!’ ordered Hitzubishi, above the din.

Concentrating very hard, Hideo reached inside the car and keyed the number into the moving panel. There was a hydraulic sound and the vibration started to decrease. The noise stopped.

‘Close the hatch and move to the front of your car,’ said Hitzubishi, quietly.

Hitzubishi followed him round to the front. He ordered Hideo to hook his car to a towing bar on the back of the pick-up truck. Hitzubishi san made him fit a device to the Datsun’s steering wheel, so that the front wheels locked in line. After a few seconds the job was done.

‘Get in,’ he said, pointing at the driver’s door of his pickup. ‘We’re going to tow your wreck. You’re driving.’

Hideo got behind the wheel.

‘Now drive.’

‘Where to?’

‘I’ll tell you,’ snapped Hitzubishi san. ‘Now just get going.’

They moved off with the dawn sun breaking through the thick clouds behind them. A prisoner at gunpoint, Hideo had to do as he was told. Although the cylinder had stopped vibrating, he was sure that it was still dangerous. The device was isolated inside his Datsun towed behind. For all he knew it could be starting to shake again. He was conscious of a normally benign powerful gravitational beam bearing down on them from above. He could almost feel it. But in reality the feeling was fear. Hideo knew how devastating the beam would be if it activated the sensitised gravitum inside Hitzubishi's device. If he had heard Anil's words to Prama he would have been more worried, because they were driving towards the peak intensity of the radiation. But he knew nothing of Prama's revelation; he just had a strong feeling of foreboding.

# Two

## The Beiping Ancient Observatory – Winter 1827

Kuang-hsien Xu belonged to a group of low ranking mandarins who, after many years of service, never quite achieved the elitist standards expected of Han-Lin Academy graduates. Many years before, as a young man, he had passed all of his exams with distinction but his personality was too reserved, introvert and, even worse, somewhat nihilist. These characteristics had prevented him from becoming the senior official that his family had hoped for. His interest in astronomy, although profound, was a singular activity that made him quite happy in his own company. This had not helped him with the many interviews he had attended for the more traditional posts in government service. As was normal with Xu he was alone again. At nearly fifty feet above the ground, on top of the Ziwei Palace in Beiping, Xu had a wonderful view of the heavens from the Beiping Observatory. Unusually for him, he was not focussed on the sky, instead he was gazing south at the main road through the suburb of Liang-hsiang. He was expecting a package from the Governor of Hunan province; a package containing fragments of a meteor. He was impatient and excited at the prospect of holding a bit of the heavens in his hands. He hoped it would arrive before it was too late. It was still early, the hour of the dragon, and he hoped that the messenger would arrive today; he was already a week overdue. He looked up at the position of the sun. The day before Xu had kept his vigil for over fifteen hours, until the hour of the rat. He hoped the consignment would arrive soon; he was not sure how much longer he could wait.

He thought back to the evening, over a hundred days ago, when he had seen the star fall out of the sky. It had been a wonderfully clear night and the beauty of the display was imprinted in his brain. Through the French telescope, he had tracked the falling star. He had even seen the bright flash and dust cloud following the impact with the ground. He reported the phenomenon to the observatory's mandarin. At first the Commissioner of the Observatory did not believe him because no one else had seen the collision, but Xu was insistent. He did not dare admit that he had used a barbarian telescope to enhance his sight. Eventually other reports came from the southern provinces closer to the impact. The Commissioner, still doubtful about Xu's incredible eyesight, reluctantly accepted his version of events. So Xu was given permission to instruct the governors of Henam, Hubei, Hunan and Guangdong to return to the Beiping Observatory any fragments of the meteor that they had retrieved for official Imperial investigation.

The largest fragment of the meteor had been found in Guangdong Province. The governor of that province, Viceroy Pao Teng, had been a student with Xu many years before. Unlike Xu, Pao was not a gifted academic. However he was street-wise and in striking contrast with his erstwhile friend Xu, Pao's career blossomed in the service of the Emperor. Xu and Pao were no longer friends, in fact theirs was mutual dislike. Towards the end of their formal education, an incident at the academy had caused Xu to lose respect for Pao. Ironically Pao's particular character flaw was perversely a positive benefit in his career as a politician. Xu was not particularly surprised when he heard that the envoy sent to deliver the Guangdong meteorite fragment became entangled in corruption and political intrigue. The fragment had been dispatched by sea only to be stolen by a barbarian pirate. In the attack, the pirate was responsible for the death of the son of a mandarin from Guangdong. This was reported to Beiping in such a way that the Imperial government became outraged by the barbaric act. The incident caused a diplomatic rift between China and the foreign trading powers of Britain, Russia, France and America.

Xu did not understand, or care about, any of these political manoeuvrings. As far as he was concerned Pao Teng had lost an important artefact. Xu wondered whether Pao had organised the whole plot to irritate him. Xu was an astronomer not a politician, he did not realise that Pao did not care about him at all. Pao had moved on. On the other hand, Xu's mind worked differently. To him every event had meaning. He had been taught the teachings of Kong Qui, but as he grew older his Confucian education had given way to a deeper belief in "The Way". He rarely discussed his ideas with his colleagues; he feared that they would not understand. Some of Qing elite had already noticed Xu's many visits to the White Cloud monastery, in the suburbs of Beiping. If they found out that he had Taoist friends in Korea, an inferior foreign country, they would probably think him insane. Although, Taoism and Kong Qui teachings were equally important to the Chinese people, administration was dominated by confucism. What could a Chinese mandarin possibly learn from foreigners? Except for his long dead parents, Xu did not seem to care what other people thought. For the time being, his main concern was to get his hands on a fragment of the meteor. This was an object from the Universe beyond the Earth. To a neo Taoist like him, it had great philosophical and alchemical importance. With the loss of the Guangdong fragment, there was only the consignment from Hunan province left. He prayed that it would be delivered safely to the Observatory.

As Xu peered out over the tiled rooftops to the South, he realised that the road was sliding out of focus.

'I must rest,' he thought, as he straightened his back painfully.

He decided to return to his room and relax for a few hours. I'm sure they will call me when it arrives.

'A little Kuo-Hsiang meditation will do me good,' he thought. 'I will return when I'm refreshed. If the rock is delivered while I'm away, I'm sure it will come to me.'

A few minutes later Xu was sleeping on a small cot in the corner of his room. As an official of many years seniority, his lodgings were located in a stone building adjacent to the observatory. Although he had only one room, it was spacious. The haphazard nature of the furnishings, were more about Xu's unconventional lifestyle, rather than a lack of generosity from his masters. The entrance to the room was through a stout oak door, opposite which was a large window facing south. At that time of day the sunlight through the window illuminated the room brightly. With a different occupier, the room might have been warm and comfortable, but Xu's tastes were somewhat more spartan. The room resembled a workshop or laboratory rather than a cosy retreat. In the centre of the room was a large wooden table, or workbench. Arranged at jaunty angles were various scientific instruments; some of Chinese manufacture, others of European origin. Spot-lit by the Sun's rays from the window was a large, partially constructed device, made of brass. Xu was clearly constructing a mechanical device based on the technologies scattered about him. It was an orrery, a mechanical version of the solar system, showing the position of the planets as they rotated about the Sun. Against the walls of the room were many cupboards containing the writings of ancient sages, treatises on alchemy and astrology. Where there was space there was shelving, with bottles containing different coloured substances and more scientific instruments.

There was a knock at the door. Xu did not stir; he was dead to the world. The visitor lifted the latch and peered around the edge of the door. He looked across and saw that Xu was asleep.

'That's typical of low ranking mandarins, sleeping the booze off when everybody else is working,' he said to his companion, sweating under the weight of a heavy packing case. 'Let's put the crate over there by the wall and leave him to his dreams.'

They struggled through the door way with the heavy burden and dropped it in a corner underneath some shelves displaying a row of Swiss, French and English clocks; all ticking loudly. Xu slept on, oblivious to the fact that his meteor had been delivered.

****

Many years after Xu was sleeping peacefully in his cot, a lone samurai knight was making his way across the mainland of Japan. Okuba-sama was not aware of any connection between his journey and the antics of a middle ranking Chinese mandarin who had waited for the delivery of a rock twenty years before the samurai was born. What ever had happened in Beiping, the young Okuba-sama did not care. He was tired and hungry, and the esoteric effects of general relativity meant nothing to him, not yet anyway. He had a mission and his samurai training did not allow him to flinch from his duty. He was trekking over open country to a meeting place on a plateau west of Choshu, in the south. Although not on horseback, he was a samurai of high rank, a "mounted Samurai" from the southern province of Satsuma. Under normal circumstances this would have given him many privileges, but after his daimyo, or lord, had committed suicide. Okuba had become a masterless wanderer; a ronin. This status did not make him any the less dangerous. He was a man with a mission who would take revenge on the Bakufu officials who had tricked his master into committing seppuku.

****

It was three o'clock in the afternoon. There was a loud knock at Xu's door. This time the noise woke him from his reverie.

'Who is it?' he called out, sleepily.

'It is Lihua,' replied the intruder.

'What do you want?'

'I do your room at the Hour of the Tiger.'

'Please go away,' he pleaded.

She was already sweeping, paying no attention to his whining.

Lihua was Xu's servant, responsible for the cleanliness of Xu's room. She was a bright, headstrong eighteen-year-old, modelled on her formidable mother who had served Xu for twenty years up to her death. Lihua had a passion for her work and given the opportunity she would have ensured that Xu's corner of the Qing Empire was spotless. However Xu was congenitally scruffy and when she had inherited the job two years earlier, she followed her mother's approach of bullying Xu into tidiness. The approach had not worked for either Lihua or her mother. Even though Lihua's mission may have been impossible, this did not stop her trying to do her duty; besides for all her surliness, she loved her master dearly.

'Mr Kuang-hsien,' she said, getting his attention.

'Yes Lihua,' he replied, with weariness in his voice.

'What is that mess in the corner,' she asked, outraged that he had brought more junk into the room.

'What mess?' asked Xu, rubbing sleep from his eyes.

'This dusty box,' she replied, eyeing the muddy crate suspiciously. 'It looks as though it has been dragged through a rice field. It's filthy.'

Xu's eyes came into focus. His demeanour changed instantly when he realised what it was.

'How did that get there?' he said, more to himself than to her.

'What sir, it's not yours? I'll get it removed immediately,' she said heading for the corridor.

'No, stop. It's mine alright,' he said. 'I've been waiting for this for weeks.'

'Oh dear,' she thought, 'something else to clean.'

She looked around the room at the gadgets of different shapes and sizes. There were hundreds of them, or so it seemed when she tried to clean them. She knew that some of them were fragile and should be handled carefully. Badly made, she thought, but who was she to say?

'I suppose you're going to make more mess unpacking the box,' Lihua said accusingly.

'Possibly,' he said a little frightened of his servant; the females of Lihua's family resembled his own long-dead dragon-like mother. 'I'll start now,' he continued, impatient to see the contents. 'You can tidy up the waste as I unpack.'

'If you insist, sir,' she said, pronouncing the "sir" with the tone of a maiden aunt tolerating an errant child.

Xu took a metal bar from the corner of his room and started to lever the lid off the crate. He removed some straw packing that was immediately below the lid. He paused apprehensively. He had thought he had seen something unusual through the layers of straw.

'Did you see that?' Xu asked, staring into the crate.

'What?' Lihua asked, peering over his shoulder into the crate.

'The blue light.'

'I can see nothing except filthy straw,' she said curling her lip in disgust.

'There through the straw and against the wood of the crate.'

She peered into the opening. She could see a blue glow shining against the shaded side of the crate.

'Sir, it's on fire!' she said, rising alarmed. 'I'll get some water.'

'No it's not,' he said. 'The box is cold.'

A cloud obscured the Sun for a moment, darkening the room. The glow appeared to get brighter.

'The light seems to be coming from below,' he said, digging into the next layer of straw packing and scattering it around him. Suddenly he stopped digging and stared at the object.'

'Ai!' she exclaimed, nervously. 'What is it?'

He cleared the remaining straw away from the object. They were looking at a roughly shaped oval block of grey stone, about four times the size of an adult human's head. Embedded into it were blue crystals that were emitting the light that Xu and Lihua had seen projected on the wall of the crate. Two crystals, about the size of large birds' eggs were shining particularly brightly. These were located a few inches apart. To Lihua, they looked like eyes.

'It's the head of a demon!' she screamed, hysterically.

'Stop it! It's harmless,' Xu said sharply, not really convinced but it seemed to be the right thing to say.

Lihua became silent. He was impressed. He never expected Lihua to do anything he instructed; her acquiescence had taken him by surprise. Xu's attention returned to the crate.

'It is a rock from the heavens,' he said. 'It fell to Earth many days ago. I saw it fall.'

'It fell from the sky, and you say it is harmless!' said Lihua, calmer, her doubts about his sanity confirmed.

'Well, I think it is,' he replied, tentatively poking the rock with a chop stick he had found lying on his table.

'You think! Mr Kuang-hsien, You think!' she exclaimed.

'Well I've shared a room with it for nearly half an hour and it hasn't eaten me yet,' he said, his tone not reflecting the confidence of his words. 'So let's not worry. It's only a rock.'

Lihua, never the healthiest of colours, went pale at the word "yet". She stood back and watched from a distance as he withdrew the chopstick and examined the end. It looked undamaged.

'Yes, it's safe,' he said, more confidently.

'A magical rock that glows,' she observed. 'A rock not from this world with glowing blue eyes and he says "it's safe",' she added, shaking her head.

'Yes, interesting isn't it?'

She looked at him exasperated and started tidying up an area of the room as far from the crate as possible.

Xu had cleared most of the straw away and was trying to lift the rock out. It was too heavy. He moved over to a stool next to his workbench and studied the crate at a distance.

'I'm going to need help to examine that,' he thought.

Lihua, becoming braver, went over to the shelves above the crate that held a number of barbarian clocks. She started dusting them.

'Mr Kuang-hsien.'

'What?' he said, still concentrating on the contents of his crate.

'I thought you said that these machines had pointers that told you the time,' she said, gently dusting one of the clocks whilst holding a puzzled expression on her face.

'Yes, the short pointers tell you which hour it is and the long pointer fractions of hours,' he replied distractedly.

Lihua listened thinking what a stupid idea, why would anyone want to know how far through the day they were when they could look outside. She brought her mind back to her conundrum.

'They're a waste of time,' she said, her pun going straight over her head. 'How can they tell you the how far through the day you are when they're all mixed up like this?'

'Uh?'

'Well, why does each machine have the long pointer showing a different direction? Are they all broken?'

'What?' he asked, only half listening.

'Look, Mr Kuang-hsien,' she said, getting his attention. 'The machines on the top shelf show a different time to those on the bottom shelf. I told you that these barbarian devices were useless.'

Xu looked up at the clocks. Lihua was right they were showing different times. The clocks at the bottom were slow. He had checked them this morning and they were all the same. He looked down at the crate then back up to the clocks. I wonder…, he mused.

# Three

## Knights in White Linen

'The barbarians insult us. We cannot allow ourselves to become weak like the Chinese,' said Okuba-sama.

He was addressing a small group of Shinto acolytes and samurai who called themselves men of spirit, or Shishi. Most of the samurai were lower class and master-less ronin. They were disenfranchised members of the Japanese ruling class. This meant that although they were able to use their formidable fighting skills as they wanted, they were desperate to find direction and purpose. The acolytes came from a nearby Shinto monastery. They were meeting in a cave in the limestone of the Akiyoshi-Dai plateau in the secluded west of Honshu. Okuba, addressing the whole group, was outraged by the presence of an American sea captain who was demanding trade relations with the Japanese authorities. Okuba and most of the gathering saw Japan as superior to other nations. They did not need any relationship with foreigners, especially barbarians with uncouth manners and appalling arrogance.

He continued, 'We are the superior nation.' There were nods of agreement. 'The Tokugawa government and the weak shogun dishonours us by taking tea with them. This is our Devine Land, founded by the sun goddess. We must never kow-tow to these non-humans. The barbarians must be expelled, the shogun defeated and the Emperor restored.' Okuba's eyes were alight with fury. 'Revere the Emperor!' he screamed. 'Sonno-joi!'

There was a shout of affirmation from most of the group, excited by the passion in Okuba's speech; the noise made more spectacular by resounding off the walls of the cave.

There were about a dozen of them in all. The samurai were distinguished by their informal white jackets, kobakama trousers and pairs of daisho swords. The latter were thrust into sashes around their waists. The group were squatting in a circle around a crackling fire. Those without the katana and wakizashi swords included three Shinto monks. Clad in white but without any weapon, one of the figures seemed to stand out in the flickering light from the flames.

'Okuba-san, you speak well,' he said, 'but you must learn patience my son.'

When Yoshida Shoin spoke, the group became still in a respectful silence. He was the Sensei; the Teacher. He had neat long dark hair, was cleanly shaven and was clothed in a simple kimono. Although a samurai by birth, he did not wear the double swords or the triangular, black eboshi hat worn by the other samurai. He looked around focussing on each warrior in turn. These were provincial knights, faithful to Nature, Shinto and the old values. They dropped their eyes as he looked at each one.

'I agree that the Tokugawa shogunate has shown weakness in the way they have handled the barbarians, but they are not so weak that we can restore the Emperor immediately. The fruit is not ripe enough to be picked.'

There were murmurs of obedience around the more restrained of the assembled group. The respect for the Sensei was unanimous, but not agreement. Okuba-san could sense this and was careful before he spoke his next words.

'Yoshida-sama, as always you speak wise words, but when will the time be ripe? Surely we cannot allow ourselves to be slowly eroded like the feckless Chinese?'

All eyes returned to the Sensei. He rose to his feet. As he stood before them, he had an indefinable presence that demanded attention. Although not tall, or powerfully built he emanated authority. They listened intently.

'Our Chinese neighbours are indeed "feckless",' he said, his eyes appearing to glow in the light of the fire. 'It may be hard to believe that they were once a worthy opponent, but even now, they are not stupid. The barbarians are reducing our once great Chinese enemy to mere slaves. The barbarians have the cunning of wild beasts. We must understand these beasts before we take action. Just as the samurai fighting tradition mimics the nature of predatory animals, we must use stillness and learn how to circle the enemy without them knowing when and where we strike. The Chinese once had experience in this. They have now become soft, but my spies tell me that the knowledge is still alive in other places.' He paused, the bait planted, 'Have any of you heard of Doseon-sa - The Tao gathering monastery?' No answer. 'The ancient traditions are still performed and the monks are skilled enough to untangle the barbarians' magic.'

'Where is this monastery?' asked Okuba-san, with a cynical edge in his voice. He was becoming impatient. He wanted action and the discussion about Tao monasteries seemed irrelevant to him.

'It is built on the sacred Samgak-san Mountain in Korea,' he replied. 'I have been there.'

One member of the group gasped. Japan had been a closed society for many years and unofficial contact with foreigners was forbidden. Other members of the group were impressed by the Sensei's defiance of Tokugawa rule. He was clearly not to be subjugated by anybody, except the Emperor.

The Sensei continued, 'If the Confucian authorities had listened to Taoist advice then China would not be in decline. As it is, we can learn from their mistakes.' The group was torn. They had been brought up to believe that they were superior to any foreigner and that there was nothing that could be learned from China, Korea or anybody. However underneath they knew that much of their history was closely tied with their neighbours who were not barbarians.

'I believe that these Korean monks know many of the secrets of the Taoist elixir.'

'You mean the elixir of immortality?' asked Okuba, reflectively.

'Yes, they know how to slow down or speed up time itself. They believe they can leave our time and return when they are ready.'

'I don't understand,' said Okuba, becoming increasingly cynical.

'Imagine you planted an apple pip in your garden. How long would it be before you could eat the fruit?'

'I don't know,' said Okuba, 'maybe ten to fifteen years.'

'Imagine if you could step into a box, or drink a potion that made only one day pass for you, but when you returned to the tree twenty years had gone by, what would you find?' asked the Sensei, looking at Okuba.

'A tree full of fruit and plenty to eat. You would never go hungry,' replied Okuba, thoughtfully, 'but the idea is too far-fetched,' he continued, realistically. 'These monks could never have discovered such a thing; if they had, they would rule the world.'

'You would have thought so,' replied the Sensei, 'but these are Taoist monks not Samurai. They are not interested in ruling the world. They have a childish desire to understand things and nothing else. They are secretive and reclusive. They want to keep their secrets to themselves.'

'They are weak,' commented Okuba.

'Maybe,' said the Sensei, 'but if it is true then a discovery like this could be a powerful tool in our fight.'

The rest of group was no longer torn; they were in a state of agitated anticipation. Most of them had not understood the dialogue between Okuba and the Sensei, but they were caught by the excitement. They had all heard about the Taoist search for the elixir of eternal life but this was mystical stuff of the ancient world. It was certainly not the kind of thing a low ranking samurai or acolyte would normally be exposed to. Could it be true that a monk somewhere in China or Korea had discovered the magic of eternal life? They did not really care about the details. The idea of using something magical against their enemies had whetted the appetite of the small group of frustrated warriors.

On the other hand Okuba did care about the details. His mind was racing. If there was such a thing, then the possibilities were endless. He and his allies could live forever. They could build their resources in a fraction of time and when they had an overwhelming advantage, they could destroy their enemies with ease. They could pick the time and place for all their battles. The knowledge from the monks would be a tremendous weapon against all their enemies, he thought. From Okuba's perspective, it must be true and it was fate that he would learn the secret.

'Sensei, if this elixir exists, then shouldn't we take the secret from them? Could we use it against our enemies in our battle to restore the Emperor?' he asked.

'Yes and yes,' said the Sensei, then addressing the whole group. 'True or not, we must send a party to the monastery. The opportunity is too great not to try to employ it in the service of the Emperor.'

'Surely, they will not give us the secrets of the elixir willingly?' asked Okuba rhetorically.

'Again Okuba-san is very astute,' said the Sensei addressing the whole group.

The praise made Okuba's chest fill with pride; Yoshida knew how to manipulate his followers – even the most arrogant.

'Our party will have to be prepared to break down any resistance,' continued the Sensei. 'But it will not be easy. The monks are schooled in Hwarangdo martial arts, which are the forerunners of the Samurai tradition. The monks will not be cowed easily. My plan is to assemble a group of our best samurai. They will protect two monks who have been trained in "The Way". The monks' task will be to learn about the elixir and how to use it.' He paused looking around his audience, who were now hanging on his every word. 'If the Korean Taoists do not release the information willingly, the samurai will persuade them.'

Okuba and the other samurai liked the sinister way in which the Sensei made his last point.

'Are you the warriors who will serve the Emperor to death?' asked the Sensei, raising his voice.

'Hai!'

'Are you willing to risk everything for the elixir?'

'Hai!'

'Will you take the secrets from the foreigners to restore the Emperor?'

'Hai!!'

They came to their feet as a unit.

'Sonno-joi,' they shouted in unison.

# Four

## Quite bunkers

Hideo's mind was churning as he drove along the road to Chichibu. For the first time Hitzubishi san had stopped pointing the pistol at him and was examining a map on his lap. He placed the pistol by his side as he turned over the page.

'Don't even think about it,' said Hitzubishi san, glancing at him. 'I've got eyes in the back of my head. One mistake and I'll blow your brains out.'

Hideo was at least twenty years younger than Hitzubishi. Hideo considered his options.

'Don't worry Hitzubishi sama. I'm not going to jump you,' said Hideo, more calmly than he felt. 'I'm just curious about where we're going.'

'That's your problem, Aoki. You are too curious. One day it will kill you.'

Hitzubishi san returned to his map reading.

'Turn left here,' he ordered.

Hideo manoeuvred the vehicle from the twisty tree-lined track on to a major road.

'But this is the main two-nine-nine,' exclaimed Hideo. 'There's residential housing all along this route. We must get away from populated areas!'

'Let me worry about what we must get away from,' said Hitzubishi san, menacingly. 'You just follow the route I give you.'

Hideo glanced in his mirror and saw his Datsun was behaving itself. There was no sign of the vibration or the noises of before.

'At least the device is behaving itself,' he thought.

He looked up and saw a signpost.

'We're coming in to Nishiagano,' he said. 'We're not far from the Shomaru tunnel. It will be dangerous to go underground with our cargo.'

'Baka, I'll decide what's dangerous, not you. Just drive.'

'Look what happened to the underground car park at the Academy,' said Hideo, defiantly. He no longer cared that he was talking to his boss; Hideo was probably fired anyway. He continued, 'The cylinder almost destroyed it.'

'No almost about it,' said Hitzubishi san, smugly. 'It did destroy it and the building above.'

'What the whole building collapsed?' exclaimed Hideo.

'What happened to Claire?'

'Who?' Hitzubishi san paused, 'Oh, your little foreign friend. I expect she's dead, flattened.'

'You're mad!' said Hideo, now trembling with anger, not fear. 'You would have destroyed most of Tokyo with an Earthquake caused by your insane experiment.'

'No, I'm not mad. You're stupid. If you had left the Gravitational Wave Rectifier alone, the building would still be standing and your friend would be alive.'

Hideo took his eyes off the road and looked in horror at Hitzubishi's mirthless smile.

Hitzubishi san continued, 'The device was perfectly safe until you tampered with it. It was designed to absorb the vibrations. It wouldn't have damaged a single brick in Tokyo's buildings.'

'Rubbish,' said Hideo. 'The cylinder nearly shook my car apart and we were nowhere near the strongest gravitational wave signal.'

'I have never seen you so confident,' he replied, with an edge to his voice. 'I'm almost impressed, that weak little Aoki has spirit after all. It's a shame you are always so fundamentally wrong.'

Hideo looked puzzled and then alarmed.

Hitzubishi san continued, 'Whilst it was in my laboratory, the rectifier was suspended on special mountings. They were designed to insulate the device from its surroundings. It was perfectly safe until you and your friends removed it from the academy.'

'If it was so safe, why did you decide to control the experiment remotely?' asked Hideo, hotly.

Hitzubishi san did not answer.

Hideo continued, 'I'll tell you why, because you were prepared to risk the lives of millions of Tokyo inhabitants, but not yourself.'

'Just drive,' snapped Hitzubishi san, his neck starting to redden.

The traffic was building around them. It was the start of the morning rush. They stopped talking as they entered a tunnel; neither of them keen to pursue the earlier line of dialogue. Hideo put on his headlights and looked carefully at the tunnel walls as they drove past. There was no sign of cracking or vibration.

'Maybe Hitzubishi san does know what he's doing,' he thought.

'Looking for the tunnel to collapse?' asked Hitzubishi san, with a smirk. 'If you want, I could arrange it. The gravitational wave beam should be at its peak about now.' He looked at his watch. 'In fact it should be right overhead.'

'Then we must get out of here! There must be hundreds of cars in this tunnel and a mountain of rock above us.'

'You think you know so much my dear Aoki,' he replied. 'Now stop the truck by that service tunnel.

'We can't stop here!' said Hideo, confused. 'We're in the middle of the tunnel and there's too much traffic.'

'There's a service road on the left. Pull on to it and stop.'

The underground road widened for a hundred metres or so. There was space for Hideo to park the truck and its payload. He pulled up as vehicles behind streamed past his right shoulder. In front of him was a dark service tunnel. A few metres inside the entrance, he could make out steel shuttered doors sealing it off to the public.

Hitzubishi san reached across and took the ignition keys. He opened his door, stepped out and stuck his head back in. He opened the glove locker and took out a torch.

'Stay here,' he said.

'What are you going to do?'

'Just do as you're told!'

Hitzubishi san switched on the torch and made his way towards the closed gates. He stopped a few feet in front of them and shone his torch on the left hand wall. He was looking for something.

'What's he doing?' thought Hideo. 'He seems to be looking for something.'

Whatever it was Hitzubishi san had found it. Hideo watched as he selected one of his keys from his key ring and inserted it into the wall. The shutters started to roll upwards revealing the opening behind. Hitzubishi san removed the key and an illuminated panel appeared a few centimetres from the keyhole. He tapped a few of the buttons. Hideo's eyes were adjusting to the darkness and as he peered through the windscreen he noticed movement on the left hand wall behind the gates, at right angles to the main service tunnel. Straining his eyes he could make out a camouflaged concrete panel that had been slid to one side to reveal the black mouth of another tunnel.

'Go past the gates and take a sharp left into the auxiliary tunnel.'

Hideo jumped, he had not seen Hitzubishi san return to the passenger seat.

'I said…'

'I heard what you said,' interrupted Hideo, 'if you want me to drive you need to give me the keys.'

Hitzubishi san handed the keys to Hideo. He glanced at them briefly, noting the two rusty keys that Hitzubishi san had used to open the tunnel doors. He started the engine. As he turned the truck towards the entrance, the headlights lit up the auxiliary tunnel entrance. It was just wide enough for the pick-up truck to pass through. Remembering the Datsun behind him, Hideo had to take a wide swing to get both vehicles into the entrance. There was a screeching noise as his car was dragged along the side wall whilst the combination was straightening.

'Be careful,' said Hitzubishi san. 'If you damage the GWR any more I may have to shoot you after all.'

'I don't care about your cylinder anymore,' he said, defiantly. 'That's my car behind. I hope you'll pay for the paintwork job.'

'What for that wreck?' Hitzubishi san laughed, 'It's falling apart. The journey from Tokyo nearly shook it to bits! If you had left the GWR alone it would still be the rusty heap it was before.'

Hideo let the comment pass. There was nothing to be gained by provoking him further. He concentrated on his driving.

The walls of the tunnel were matt, dark rock and there were no tunnel lights. His headlights seemed to disappear into the darkness all around him. Hideo drove gently, but he could not avoid scraping his car along the walls. As he peered into the darkness in front of him, he thought he could detect bands even darker than the surroundings.'

'Shit,' he said, 'it's a gate!'

He slammed his foot on the brake pedal.

'What the fuck are you doing?' exclaimed Hitzubishi-san. 'Keep going, it will open automatically.'

As if obeying an order, the gate slid open into a recess in the tunnel wall. Hideo drove through the opening and he was immediately aware that the walls on either side had disappeared. Everything went to a different kind of black.

'Stop,' ordered Hitzubishi san.

Hideo re-applied the brakes and felt the combination slide to a halt. Clearly the ground underneath was smooth and polished.

Not bothering to speak to Hideo, Hitzubishi san stepped out of the car taking his torch and pistol. He walked towards the back of the Datsun where the tunnel had opened into a large cavern. He shone his torch on the wall and found a control panel. He threw one of the switches and somewhere in the distance Hideo could hear a generator start up. After a few moments the cavern was lit up by harsh orange flood-lights. Hideo gasped. He stepped out of the pickup and looked around him. The chamber was huge. In the distance, on the other side of the cathedral-like gallery, water was dripping through the roof trickling down huge stalactites hanging from the roof. The only stalagmites were at the edge of the cave. The floor of the cave had been levelled and concreted over and there was a drainage channel around the outer perimeter. When he looked down, he saw that the ground around his feet was dry. Puzzled, he strained his neck, looking for signs of a waterproof shelter above him. Although the lights were dazzling, he could see that the ceiling immediately overhead was smooth. There were no stalactites. This part of the cave appeared to have been plastered and amazingly, it was bone dry. He shielded his eyes against the flood lights so he could get a better view of the roof. Perhaps it was a trick of the light, but he thought he could see flecks of fluorescence in the rendering. Trying to avoid being dazzled, he ran his eye across the roof until he returned to the damp part of the ceiling. In contrast with the rough stalactites, the plastered area appeared to be shaped into a smooth curve. They appeared to be standing underneath a semi hemisphere.

'Why would anyone build that in a cave?' he thought.

He lowered his head and readjusting his eyes to the lower light intensity, moved his gaze to Hitzubishi san.

'What is this place?' he asked, his voice echoing off the walls and ceiling of the cave.

'It's an old military bunker,' replied Hitzubishi san.

'I've heard about those,' said Hideo, 'I thought most of the World War Two bunkers were south of here.'

'Oh you've learned some history,' said Hitzubishi san, condescendingly. 'Caves like this were built all over the country for defensive reasons. This one is much older. It was built in the eighteen nineties.'

'During the first Sino-Japanese war?'

Hitzubishi ignored the interruption, 'Anyway, the entrance to this one was found by the Americans just after the last war and they dynamited the entrance. The outside world forgot about it,' replied Hitzubishi san. 'We improved access to it when the road tunnel was built in the nineteen-sixties.'

'We?' asked Hideo.

Hitzubishi san ignored him and walked to the back of the Datsun. Hideo looked around again. His only experience with secret criminal laboratories was in a score of Hollywood movies. He knew what they should look like. Except for the bizarre ceiling, this bunker was as similar to his sleek, polished ideal as a camel is to a cheetah. He was disappointed. The cave was cold and musty. The floor was littered with rusty tools and machinery. The air was beginning to smell of diesel exhaust. He could see entrances to other small tunnels. Like disused mines in a gold rush western, they were partially shuttered by planks of wood. Across the chamber, slightly to his left and under the damp stalactite area, there was a wooden shack. It had a leaky outlet tube running into an opening in the cave's ceiling. From the noise and the exhaust, the shed appeared to house the generator. By the smell, the diesel engine had not been serviced for some time. To the right of the shed, some fifty metres away, stood a cylindrical stone tower. It was positioned away from the far wall, was about six metres in diameter and almost ten metres high, spanning the space from floor to ceiling. At the base was a small doorway sealed by a rusty steel door. From the door, his eyes traced the circular wall of the tower until they came to a stone tube. This ran behind the shed between the tower's outer surface and the cave's perimeter. The tube appeared to be a tunnel or corridor, between the tower and the cave wall. It exited the tower about one hundred and twenty degrees around the circumference.

'If it is a tunnel,' he thought, 'the occupants of the tower must be dwarfs.'

The tunnel was less than a metre high. He could see another tunnel symmetrically positioned on the other side of the tower. These ran behind the tower in straight lines until they disappeared into the rock face.

He gazed at the construction trying to imagine what it was for.

'Ah I see you've found the Mark Two GWR,' said Hitzubishi san, appearing quietly behind him.

'I do wish you wouldn't do that!' said Hideo, startled.

'What?'

'Creep up behind me.'

'That's the least of your worries,' he said ominously.

'Anyway, what do you mean "the Mark Two GWR?", ' asked Hideo, returning his gaze to the tower. 'That building is ancient; far too old to be using gravitational wave technology.'

'As I said earlier Hideo, you know very little about my work,' he replied, in a friendly voice that unnerved Hideo even more. 'Gravitational waves were proposed by Einstein in nineteen-o-nine. That device was built later. Its predecessor, the Mark One, was damaged in a raid by our enemies.'

'At the end of the war?' asked Hideo.

'Yes,' said Hitzubishi san, not saying which war or which enemies. 'It was built many years ago and then damaged in a rock fall. Very few of the original brotherhood survived.'

'The brotherhood?'

'I need you to help me with the Mark Three,' continued Hitzubishi san, glossing over Hideo's question.

'So you are telling me that the cylinder in the back of my car is the Mark Three?', asked Hideo, incredulously.

'Helping me now would be good.'

'Then that means, that gravitum was discovered over sixty years ago!'

'You could say that,' replied Hitzubishi san, starting to enjoy Hideo's confusion. 'In fact the Mark One was quite a lot older.'

'I knew it; you are mad!' exclaimed Hideo. 'If gravitational wave energy conversion had been discovered before, the whole world would have known.'

'You'd be amazed how much ancient knowledge has been kept secret,' said Hitzubishi san, condescendingly, 'and a good thing too. There are some ideas that low ranking people should never learn and that includes the properties of the blue crystals.'

'Low ranking people?' asked Hideo, outraged. 'You mean like me!'

'If you say so. I haven't got time to stand here chatting,' said Hitzubishi san. 'Now help me unload the Mark Three,' he said pointing his gun threateningly.

'Why should I? I'm not your slave,' he responded defiantly.

'Maybe not, but if you want to get out of here, I advise you to help.'

Hideo glanced at the gun and then at Hitzubishi san.

'Ah that spirit again! Go ahead,' said Hitzubishi san, reading his mind. 'You should know that the doors to this cave are secured by electronic keys and computer controlled locks. If you shoot me it could be a hundred years before anyone found our bodies.' He paused, to let the thought sink in. 'At least my death would be quick,' he added.

'I could take the gun anyway.'

'Pointless really. It's not loaded! You are free to go.' He paused, casually lowering the pistol. 'But you won't do that will you?'

'Why not?'

'Because you are curious. You want to know what my work is all about,' replied Hitzubishi san smugly. 'And you'll never get another chance if you leave.'

In spite of his anger, Hideo knew his ex-boss was right.

****

A few minutes after Hideo had left with the gravitational wave rectifier, Prama realised her situation. Once out of the city, Hideo and Prama had avoided populated areas as much as possible. They had turned off highway two-nine-nine and followed a series of minor country roads that twisted alongside the major route. They had successfully managed to avoid civilisation. Prama could not remember seeing any traffic, a house or a building for miles. She remembered that the main road was to the North, but she had no idea how far. Hideo had left with the map and all her other possessions save the mobile and the clothes she stood up in. In short she was stranded in the middle of nowhere without a map and in range of a device that was likely to cause a devastating earthquake. However Prama was a resourceful person. She was not prone to panic. She looked at the battery life on her mobile and decided to phone a friend.

'Thank god it's you,' said Anil. 'Where are you?'

'I wish I knew.'

Anil stopped to collect his thoughts.

'What local dialling code is displayed on your mobile?'

'Code? It's just a picture of someone,' she replied, not elaborating the details of her screensaver.

'Ok, how much battery power have you got left?' asked Anil, preparing the ground.

'Plenty,' she said.

'Great,' he replied, 'But let's not waste it. Stay where you are and do exactly what I say.'

'But what about the earthquake?' she asked.

'Hideo must have done something to the device,' he replied. 'After he left you I checked on the seismology website for p and s wave activity. There was nothing unusual.'

'Oh, that's wonderful,' she said relieved. 'Have you heard from him?'

'No but please stop asking me questions and let's get you out of there. Your battery won't last forever.'

Anil gave her instructions about how to find the code for the cellular repeater closest to her phone. Then he disconnected. She sent a text to Anil with the details. A few minutes later her mobile rang. The picture of Anil was replaced by his name as her phone identified the incoming caller.

'Hello, handsome,' she said.

'Now behave yourself and listen,' he said, with a smile in his voice. 'You are in the countryside north of Hanno city.' He paused, as if checking something. 'You are on one of two minor roads. I don't know which one. Can you get to the top of a hill?'

'I'm sitting on one thinking about you next to me,' she said flippantly.

'Good for you,' said Anil, trying to control the situation. 'The sun should be south east of you. Look to the north east. Can you see any buildings?'

Prama peered into the distance. She could not see the sun. It was becoming overcast with rain clouds moving rapidly across the sky. Visibility was not good. Suddenly there was a patch of light and she could see the outline of the sun.

'I've got my bearings,' she said. 'It looks like it's going to rain.' She turned round and strained her eyes towards the horizon, now merging with the sky. 'No I can't see anything but mist,' she said and then, 'yes I can make out some buildings,' she said, excitedly.

'Well, let's hope that's Agano. It's about four miles away as the crow flies. What kind of shoes are you wearing?'

'Why?'

'I'm afraid you've got a long walk. Take the road towards the east and phone me when you reach a T-junction. You should go left.'

'They're high-heels. In spite of the mud, they're rather sexy actually. But they're not the best footwear for a ramble.'

'Oh,' he said.

'You said "as the crow flies". I can't see any birds to give me a lift, so how far is it as Prama hobbles?' she asked.

'You don't want to know,' said Anil apologetically, 'probably twice as far.'

'What in these shoes?' she muttered.

'I didn't catch that,' he said.

'Oh nothing,' she replied.

'What happens when I get to Agano?' she asked, applying her best positive mental attitude.

'You can get a train back to Tokyo from there.'

'Ok, but I've got no money, only my phone.'

'Oh shit,' said Anil uncharacteristically.

'Now that's not very polite,' she said teasing.

'Sorry,' Anil was at a loss. 'Let me see what the rest think.'

There was a discussion in the background. She could hear Jacques' voice.

Anil came back to the phone, 'Paul is speaking to Claire now. She will get the train from Tokyo and meet you at the station. Don't worry my darling, we'll get you home.'

'I know you will. I'll call you soon. I love you,' she said cheerily and hung up.

Humming a Kirsty MacColl song, Prama took off her shoes and made her way carefully down the embankment towards the road. When she reached the bottom she took a large rock from the verge. She admired her beautiful shoes for the last time, broke off the heels and put on her new fell walking shoes. The song popped back into her mind.

'So I'm sitting at a bar in Guadalajara…..,' she sang.

# Five

## Alchemy and Curiosity

Over the weeks following the delivery of Xu's crate, he had been busy investigating the rock's effect on the instruments around his room. Xu was an excellent record keeper and had collected a wealth of information documented in exquisite calligraphy on scrolls of paper. Although the rest of his room appeared chaotic, his document filing was punctilious in the extreme and Lihua knew that cleaning there was off limits. However being an inherently nosey person, she wanted to know what he was up to.

'Master, what's in those scrolls?' she asked, pointing at the filing system on the other side of the room.

'Nothing that will interest you,' Xu replied, knowing it would not rest there.

She took a step towards them and raised her duster in a threatening manner.

'Please don't dust them, Lihua,' he pleaded. 'They're not dusty.'

'I need to make sure everything is clean,' she said, resolved to grind him into submission.

She moved closer.

'Alright,' he said. 'Why do you want to know?'

Being a direct, forthright person, Lihua would have preferred a question with "what" not "why", but she shrugged.

'You've been playing with that demon's head for weeks and written down everything you've found out,' she said emotionally. 'I want to know whether I should find another master before you are possessed.'

A tear formed in the corner of her eye.

Xu was surprised.

'Is she worried about demons or my safety?' he wondered.

He decided to try the latter.

'I didn't know you cared,' he said gently.

'I don't,' Lihua replied, swiftly wiping the tear away. 'I just want to make sure you don't get us all bewitched with your toys and demon rocks,' she said without much conviction.

'I see,' he said, smiling. 'Then sit down and I'll tell you what I've discovered. It's rather interesting actually.'

Lihua looked at him suspiciously.

'That's the kind of attitude that gets the silly old fool into trouble,' she thought.

She sat down on a stool opposite him.

'Do you remember the two blue eyes you saw on the first day the crate arrived?'

'How can I forget?' she said. 'It still makes me shiver when I think about them.'

'Well, I took a small hammer and chisel and removed them from the stone.'

'Mr Kuang-hsien, you did what?' she exclaimed. 'You took the eyes out of the demon's head. He'll go wild,' she said with panic rising in her voice. 'Do you know what you've done? You'll cause the palace to fall around our ears!'

'Where do you get these ideas?' asked Xu. 'The thing in the crate was not a demon's head. It was a rock and the eyes are blue gems.'

'You must be wrong, Mr Kuang-hsien. I have seen my fortune teller.'

'Ah,' he said, 'that's where your ideas come from.' He paused trying to decide the best way to proceed. For her mother's sake, he did not wish to patronise Lihua. He knew that she had been brought up well and was intelligent. Lihua was often too sharp for her own good, but for his own reasons, Xu tolerated this. She was certainly a formidable character; obviously inherited from her mother's side, he thought. Xu had considered enlisting Lihua to help him before. Like so many of the people in Beiping she was very superstitious; a character flaw that could get in the way of Xu's experiments. However this was his opportunity to enlighten her. Besides he knew far more about superstition than anybody, as he was responsible for collating the official almanac.

'Let me show you something,' he said, taking one of the scrolls down from the shelf behind him. 'This is a map of the Purple Forbidden Enclosure.'

Xu unrolled the document on a table next to his filing system. Lihua pulled her stool closer so she could see it.

'It looks like a painting of the night sky,' she said, casting her eyes over the document. 'What's that star in the middle?'

'That's Tou Mu. The Europeans call it the pole star. They used to think it was fixed in the sky, but it isn't. This map records the position of the stars when something strange happens.'

Luhia had never seen a star map before and was absorbed by the exquisite beauty of the calligraphy.

'Did you make it?' she asked.

'Make what?' he asked, absentmindedly. 'Oh the map, yes,' he said, 'and my predecessors produced many more like it.'

'So what's special about this one?' asked Lihua.

'Before I answer that, let me show you something.'

He moved across to a small chest in the corner of his room and removed two objects.

'Are they what I think they are?' asked Lihua, nervously.

'I expect so,' he said, amused. 'These are the eyes as you call them. Personally I prefer to call them Sky and Earth.'

'I don't understand you, master.'

'You will,' he said, enigmatically.

Xu walked over to a large round table that much to Lihua's irritation he had recently acquired.

'Something else to dust,' she thought.

'Come over here and help me lay the table,' he said.

'Why, are you going to have a meal?'

'No, we are going to arrange my instruments for an experiment.'

'So you're going to play with your toys again?'

'Do you want to know what I've found out or not?'

She moved over to the table and stood next to him.

'The chart I've just shown you depicts the position of the stars when something strange happens to my crystals.'

'Earth and Sky?'

'Yes.'

He handed her one of the crystals.

'I don't want it, Mr Kuang-hsien,' she said, shrinking back. 'Please take it away.'

'Go on,' he said kindly. 'It's harmless.'

Reluctantly she took the stone in her hand. It was cold and smooth, but it did not turn her into a monster, so she became curious and examined it more closely.

'You're holding Earth,' he said. 'I named it that because it is the darker of the two stones.'

'It is so smooth and soft to touch,' she said.

'I had it shaped to resemble an egg and polished by an ivory carver in Liang-hsiang.'

'He's done a wonderful job, master,' she said, admiring the perfect shape. 'Oh I see you've carved the ideogram "Earth" on it. Is that so it doesn't forget its name?'

Xu could not decide whether her last words were from superstition or she was just joking. He decided to ignore it. Instead he asked, 'Have you noticed anything else about it?'

'Oh, you mean it's not glowing like last time,' she said. 'Well that's not surprising, given you've gouged the eye out of the demon's head. You've probably killed it.'

Xu bit his tongue.

'She's as stubborn as ever,' he thought.

'Ah! But it does glow, with or without "the demon's head". It glows when the stars are in the position shown on my chart.'

'You mean the stars were in that position when we opened the crate?'

'Yes.'

'But it was daytime. The stars weren't out,' she exclaimed, thinking she had found a flaw in his argument.

'They were there alright; it's just that you couldn't see them. The sunlight hides them from view.'

He looked across the room at one of his clocks.

'Come on Lihua. Are you going to help me or not?'

'I suppose I've got nothing else to do,' she said, handing Earth back to him.

He placed the stone in the centre of the table. He pointed towards an array of small carriage clocks on the shelf next to his document file.

'I'd like you to take some of those clocks down from the shelf, make sure they all read the same time and arrange them in a small circle around Earth. I'll make a similar circle of clocks around the edge of the table.'

'Mr Kuang-hsien, I don't understand what that will prove?' she said, doubtfully.

'I believe that when the stars are in the right place, the crystal will start to glow and the inner clocks will read different times from the outer clocks.'

'So what?'

'It means that time moves differently depending how close you are to the crystal. Another way to think about it is, if you kept Earth close to you, in your pocket for example, than you would age less than me.'

'I'll never age as much as you, Mr Kuang-hsien,' she replied, flippantly.

'Alternatively, if I carry the stone and not you, then I'll stop aging and you'll catch up.'

'That's ridiculous!'

'Let's do the experiment and I'll prove it.'

They laid the table out exactly as Xu had described. Earth was in the middle surrounded by two concentric circles of clocks. They waited until the time Xu had predicted. There was no sign of Earth glowing and an hour later the clocks all read the same time.

'There I told you, Mr Kuang-hsien,' said Lihua. 'I win. Your experiment doesn't work.'

'It doesn't work every time,' said Xu, crestfallen. 'There must be some other astronomical pattern that I can't see.'

'Master, I think your clocks are usually faulty and for once they worked properly. The Earth blue eye has nothing to do with the different readings on the clocks that we saw earlier.'

'We'll see,' said Xu defensively. 'According to my calculations the next cycle will coincide with the full moon, about four weeks away.'

'Sir, I still won't believe it even if the clocks record different times. I bet you'll adjust them just to prove yourself right,' said Lihua, becoming bolder as she began to understand the experiment.

'An old friend is visiting soon. I'll ask him to judge whether I'm tampering with the clocks.' Then remembering that she was supposed to be his servant, he said, 'In the meantime I'd be grateful if you would clean up the mess around here. I want it spotless for our next experiment.'

****

A few weeks later Xu was disturbed by a knock on his door. He had been going over his calculations again and again but he could not find an astronomical configuration that correlated exactly with the times when the Earth and Sky glowed blue. He was becoming quite frustrated about the whole enterprise. He was not looking forward to Lihua's reaction if his experiment failed again. He stood up and made his way to the door. He opened it and there in front of him stood a face that he had not seen for nearly twenty years.

'Hao Jiahou! You haven't changed a bit,' said Xu.

'Nor have you, old friend,' said Chin.

'You are right, we are both still congenital liars.'

They laughed as the twenty years had had a similar effect on both their appearances, but not their sense of humour.

Chin had been a fellow student at the Han Lin Academy. Xu and Chin were members of a trio of friends who had studied together. Chin had been a foreign student from Korea, who was accepted into the Academy when China was trying to increase its influence over its neighbour. As a Confucian educated official in Korea he was likely to become a long-term ally. As is often the case with young men, the friends had rebelliously become interested in Taoism. To Chin this was natural, as Taoism had remained strong in Korea but Xu was supposed to be a Chinese official and such ideas were unusual.

'Have you heard about Pao?' asked Chin, after they had settled down with a glass of rice wine.

'You mean the Governor of Guangdong who lost my meteorite?' said Xu bitterly.

Pao Teng was the third member of the inseparable trio. Xu had fallen out with him after he had copied some of Xu's answers in an examination. The examiner realised what had happened when he found that the pair shared both correct and wrong answers to the intricate questions. So the copier was not only a cheat but also inept. Unfortunately for Xu, Pao had persuaded the examiner that Xu had copied from him. Xu was forced to retake the examination and he passed easily. Although the examiner realised he had misjudged Xu, he did not admit it and the incident remained a black mark against Xu's character.

'Well he became Viceroy Pao Teng and he has just been replaced by Lin Tse-hsu.'

'What the Governor General of Kiangnan and Kaingsi?'

'Yes the same,' said Chin.

'He was just below us in the Academy.'

'I remember Lin. He is a good man but I don't envy him his new assignment.'

'Why not?'

'It's rumoured that Pao was heavily involved in the opium trade and because of it piracy in the region is out of control. A few months ago the son of a senior mandarin was killed at sea by a barbarian pirate.'

'How do you know all this?' asked Xu, curious that his friend, a foreigner, was better informed than him.

'Korea has had its troubles with barbarians as well,' Chin replied. 'We have informants everywhere but I shouldn't tell you that should I?' He grinned mischievously.

'Oh politics, I'm glad I'm out of it,' said Xu, disdainfully. 'So Pao was disgraced because of opium trading?'

'It seems that way,' said Chin. 'It appears the barbarian pirate ship was sunk by another foreigner, either that or it was consumed by a tsunami tidal wave.'

'A tidal wave?'

'Yes it devastated Japan and our south coast. We think there was an undersea earthquake somewhere in the Great Southern Ocean.'

'When was this?' asked Xu, suddenly making a connection to something else.

'In the middle of last year.'

'I wonder,' mumbled Xu to himself.

'What do you wonder old friend?'

'I wonder if it was the same barbarian ship that stole my original meteorite sample.'

'I don't follow.'

'Last year, I sent an official instruction to Pao telling him to send me a piece of a falling star that had been recovered in the north of his province.

'What happened?'

'The fragment never arrived. He sent it by sea and it disappeared around the same time.' He thought for a moment, 'I suspected Pao of stealing it but I suppose the rock is at the bottom of the sea now.'

'Was the fragment important?'

'I thought so but it's not important now. I managed to get another piece from Hunan province.'

'So what's so special about this falling star?' asked Chin.

'I believe it changes how time passes,' Xu replied, in a matter of fact way.

Chin lent forward, 'Now I am interested,' he said. 'Tell me more.'

Xu and Chin drank more wine whilst Xu talked about his experiments with clocks and rocks. As they drank, their reminiscences and ideas became as silly as their slurred words became incomprehensible. Too late, Xu remembered that the day after was his next opportunity to do the clock experiment.

'Oh well, I'll have to do it with a headache,' he thought, just before he passed out.

****

Xu and Chin were slumped over the round table snoring loudly when Lihua arrived to clean Xu's room. She slammed the door closed and smiled as Xu woke with a start. His friend was still asleep.

'He's making a noise like a sow on heat,' she thought.

'Master, shouldn't you get ready for your next experimental failure?' she asked, taunting him.

'What?' he asked.

'I told you a demon would possess you,' she said as she peered into Xu's bloodshot eyes. 'You'd better sober up. It's nearly afternoon and the experiment is not ready.'

'I didn't think you were interested,' Xu moaned, thinking he'd never drink again.

'I want the opportunity to prove that you are wrong, Mr Kuang-hsien,' she said, baiting him.

Chin uttered a low moan and moved his head into a more comfortable position.

'Mr Chin is not dead then?' said Lihua. She looked pityingly at Chin, then returning her scrutiny to Xu. 'You look awful, Mr Kuang-hsien. You should know better at your age,' she added. 'I'll get you some rice porridge. That will make you better.'

She left the room slamming the door behind her for the second time. Xu winced. His friend let out another moan.

'I wish she wouldn't do that,' Xu muttered lamely.

He looked at his friend, surrounded in earthenware bottles that once contained wine.

'Surely we can't have drunk that much,' thought Xu, looking at the empties. 'I'm too old for this.'

'Come on old friend,' Xu said, a little louder then was good for him. 'I need your help. I don't know about demon rocks. I've got a demon servant. We've got an experiment to do before she makes my life a misery.'

'What did you say?' said Chin.

'Oh, nothing,' said Xu, quietly so that his head did not explode. 'You're drunk and I need to sober you up.'

'You can talk,' said Chin, and fell back to sleep.

****

In contrast to Xu and Chin, Yeon-gi was, like the statue that stood behind him, stone cold sober. As the master monk of the Doseon-sa Tao gathering monastery, he would not have shared Xu and Chin's hangovers. However he would have understood them; in fact he had a deep understanding of most humankind and their foibles. At that moment his thoughts were elsewhere. He was trying to take his mind beyond the three-dimensional world of Xu, Chin and the valley below. He had just explained to a group of acolytes that only when a person is beyond these dimensions is he or she really cultivating Tao. He knew this was true, but was having self-doubt. Was **he** really beyond the three dimensions, he wondered, or was it an illusion created in his mind? He hoped that his friend Chin would help him find an answer. In the meantime he would take his own advice and look for truth through meditation.

****

After much protestation, grimacing and grumbling Lihua had managed to force a foul smelling medicinal brew down the necks of her two charges.

'Mr Chin, Mr Kuang-hsien, you have brought it on yourselves,' she said in a matronly tone. 'If you will drink those foul concoctions, you deserve everything you get.'

'Is this supposed to make us better or kill us?' said Xu, wondering what was worse, the headache or the medicine.

'Well, if it kills you, you won't have a headache anymore,' she replied, cheerily. 'Anyway, I thought you wanted to show that those stones aren't evil magic. If you don't, it'll prove I'm right that they're demon eyes.'

For the first time Chin opened his mouth as if to speak. Lihua looked at his cup, still half full with her noxious brew and glared at him. He diplomatically remained silent and took another sip. His face contorted.

'I see what you mean about making life a misery,' he mumbled peering at Xu through bloodshot eyes.

'What did Mr Chin say?' Lihua asked Xu.

'Nothing important, I suppose we'd better get ready for our experiment,' Xu replied, changing the subject.

He stood up slowly, being careful not to move his head too rapidly.

'I feel better already,' he said shakily.

'That's a pity,' said Lihua, believing that their punishment should go on for longer.

The dialogue continued in this way for the next few hours and after many mistakes with the clocks and even more pints of cold tea, they had arranged the round table to Xu's plan. By late afternoon the experiment was ready. By then Xu and Chin, although not completely recovered were sober. They started to work together reviewing star charts and preparing blank documents on which to record their observations. In spite of herself,

Lihua could not help admiring the two old alchemists working together in unspoken harmony.

'When will it happen, Mr Kuang-hsien?' asked Lihua.

'When will what happen?' asked Xu, absentmindedly.

"'When will the eyes glow?' she asked.

'By our calculations the crystals will glow just after sunset,' replied Xu, stressing the word "crystals".

'We don't know exactly,' said Chin, protecting his friend from possible embarrassment. 'It could be any time up to midnight.'

'Precisely so,' said Xu.

'Doesn't sound very precise to me,' said Lihua, sarcastically.

Chin looked up sharply.

'Why does Xu tolerate this insolence?' he thought. 'Oh well I'm sure he has his reasons.'

Chin let the comment pass.

Lihua looked around the table at the array of ticking clocks arranged in concentric circles around the goose egg sized blue crystal.

'With all these magical barbarian watches and clocks, I would have thought you'd know exactly when the eyes will glow,' she said, pausing to pick up one of the gold watches that was located in the outer circle.

'Don't fiddle with them,' said Xu irritated. 'It has taken us all afternoon to put them in their right positions.'

'Don't worry, Mr Kuang-hsien. I'll put it back,' she said defiantly. 'I want to make sure there is no trick in it.'

She examined the intricate engraving on the outer case.

'It's beautiful,' she said, as if noticing the workmanship for the first time. 'Are you sure it's the work of a barbarian?'

'That one is Swiss. Here let me show you,' he said, holding his hand out for the watch.

To his relief she carefully handed the delicate instrument to him. He laid it in the palm of his left hand and with the nail of his right hand index finger he levered the back open, to reveal the gold plate that covered the mechanism. The panel had two holes; one for winding and the other to adjust the hands. There were several lines of a strange calligraphy engraved in the gold.

'This is foreign writing,' he said. 'You can work out how to pronounce the words by the arrangement of the characters. It's written in French.'

'That's useless,' said Chin. 'The Qing administration can rule a country of many languages, because the ideograms can be interpreted whatever language you speak.'

'It's a different way of looking at things,' said Xu. 'We have thousands of ideograms that take many years to master.'

'Some calligraphy is designed to stop poor people like me ever understanding it,' said Lihua, bitterly.

They let the comment pass.

'The Latin script has fewer than thirty symbols. It is easy to learn and can be used with many languages, but you must learn the language to understand it.'

'I told you it's a magic spell, written by barbarians!' she said, stepping back.

'Don't be silly,' said Xu. 'Let me show you.' He pointed at a series of characters in block capitals. She reluctantly peered over his shoulder. Also becoming curious, Chin came up behind her.

'It says TOBIAS; the maker's name,' Xu explained. He pointed to a line of symbols above the central winding hole. 'It says "Trois Leviers et Trois en Rubis". This means three levers and three with rubies. The words describe the watch's mechanism.'

Xu used his fingernail to lever the plate open, revealing the exquisite workmanship inside. Earlier, under Xu's instruction, Lihua and Chin had each wound up a number of the clocks and watches through their keyholes using the keys Xu had given them. However they had never seen the miniature machinery inside. They both gasped as they saw the beautiful filigree work dotted with tiny ruby bearings. They became transfixed on the tiny balance wheel rotating backwards and forwards edging the other gears and cogs around.

'There is so much movement in such a tiny box,' said Chin. 'It looks as though it's alive.'

Lihua just stared, uncharacteristically dumbstruck.

'It's not alive,' said Xu. 'There is a tiny spring coiled around a drum just here,' he said pointing to the mainspring. 'It stores the energy from when I tightened the spring this morning. That's why we had to wind up all the clocks.'

'So, if we hadn't wound them up the clocks would not work?' asked Chin.

''That's right,' Xu replied, then looking at Lihua, 'so you see magic is just something you don't understand. That's why I want to understand the stones.'

'So if you understand everything, Mr Kuang-hsien, then there will be no magic,' said Lihua, disappointed.

'Possibly,' said Xu. 'But it will take more than my lifetime to understand everything. In the meantime it's wonderful to try to find things out.'

A light sparkled behind Lihua's eyes. It was as if she had had a revelation; an insight. She waited for Chin and Xu to be silent and having collected her thoughts asked, 'If it takes more than one lifetime, then why are you mandarins so secretive?'

Both men gazed at her speechless.

She continued, 'If clever people like you shared what they learn with more normal people, knowledge would grow and people like me would not have to fall back on magic. The empire would be so much better.'

'That's what the academies are for,' said Chin coldly, amazed at her impertinence.

Lihua looked down and fell silent. She thought that maybe she had gone too far.

'I think Lihua could be right. Perhaps the academies are for the elite only and rooted in the past,' said Xu, surprising his companions. 'I must find a way of passing on my fragments of understanding so that it does not die with me.'

'There he goes again,' puzzled Chin, 'tolerating her insolence.'

The room became quiet as the three of them retreated into their private thoughts. Finally Lihua brought them back. She took the gold watch from Xu and placed it back in the outer circle on the table.

'Mr Kuang-hsien, Mr Chin,' she said, 'are we going to do this experiment or not?'

# Six

## Back to the Plan

It was summer eighteen-seventy-three and eight years had passed since Okuba-san had met his Shishi brothers on the Akiyoshi-Dai plateau. Since that meeting, Japan had been involved in a terrible civil war and the Shishis' objective of reinstating the Emperor had been achieved, but at what cost? They had lost their battle against barbarian infiltration and the old ways were dying out in favour of modernisation. Japan was copying foreign ways; the samurai were disappearing as their way of life became consigned to the history books along with their stipends of rice. Yoshida Shoin realised that his plan to obtain the Taoist elixir had been sidelined by petty battles and vendettas between the various factions, always present during a civil war. Slowly but surely, through death in combat or persecution, the original group had dwindled to half its original size. Soon there would be no one left to execute his plan. In short his action-orientated band of samurai and monks had been distracted and their raid on the Korean monastery had stalled. In desperation he had approached an old friend Saigo-sama to use political influence to provoke a military invasion of Korea. This would allow him to gain access to the monastery under cover of a war with one of Japan's old enemies. Unfortunately Saigo was betrayed and his fall back plan fell through. Yoshida Shoin was now under house arrest.

'I must return to my first plan,' he thought.

It was at this point he started to draft his instructions to Okuba-san.

****

The sun had set and Xu's room was lit by oil lamps. The three of them were seated silently in a triangle formation around the round table; guarding the perimeter as if they were making sure it would not escape. Although Lihua had taken Xu's words about knowledge and magic to heart, she was still a little nervous about demons and for this reason she held a kitchen knife clasped behind her back, just in case. Except for the background ticking of clocks the room was silent and Lihua's concentration was so intense that the slightest noise from outside caused her to jump. This contrasted with Xu and Chin, whose drinking bout the night before was still the dominant factor in the efficiency of their brains.

'Mr Kuang-hsien, what was that?' asked Lihua in a loud whisper.

Xu and Chin's eyelids slid open as Lihua stood up.

'I saw something,' she said. 'I swear the stone moved.'

'It hasn't moved Lihua,' said Xu. 'It's not time yet. It must have been a trick of the light from the lamps.'

'There it did it again. Look Mr Chin,' she said, enthusiastically. 'The Earth crystal started to glow and seemed to come closer and then move away again.'

'I tell you, it's the oil lamps,' Xu said, not prepared to admit that her younger eyes may have seen something that he could not detect.

'Let's douse the lamps,' said Chin, suspecting that she may have been right.

'We'll see nothing then,' complained Xu, feeling that he was losing control of his experiment.

'Go on you old fart,' said Chin. 'She may be right. Let's find out.'

'Alright,' he replied dousing one of the lamps.

Chin and Lihua did the same with the others.

Then as their eyes became accustomed to the dark, they could see it; a slow pulsating blue glow, emanating from the Earth stone. Out of the corner of his eye, Xu saw something else. He glanced over to the shelf where he had filed the other crystal. Sky too was glowing; an eerie fluorescence ebbing and flowing in exact harmony with the radiation from Earth.

'It's happening,' he whispered, more to himself than his companions.

'Amazing,' said Chin.

Lihua said nothing; her eyes wide open, staring at the slowly pulsating blue light.

'You were right, master. The crystal glows when you said it would. It's beautiful,' she said, incredulously.

It was the first time she had not used the word "eye" to describe the crystal. She was hooked on the search for knowledge. She would no longer dismiss a difficult puzzle as magic. She wanted to understand. Xu was proud of her. He was proud that she had said, without sarcasm, that he was right. He had won her respect. Chin could see Xu's pride. He did not understand why Xu should care what his servant thought.

Earth and Sky began to glow more brightly so that the fluorescence was evident even when the lamps were re-lit. Xu and Chin began to move from clock to clock taking and recording the readings, and replacing the instruments back to their allotted point on the table. Occasionally Xu disappeared outside to check his star charts against the night sky. Like a sponge, Lihua absorbed everything she saw.

They continued with their measurements and observations well into the twilight hours. Finally all three were exhausted and needed to rest. Lihua went to her bed for a few hours and returned with a tray containing two cups of her mother's herbal tonic and some rice cake. Chin and Xu were already awake pouring over the results of their experiment. She placed their breakfast on the packing case in the corner.

'Mr Kuang-hsien, Mr Chin, are you hungry? Some food,' she said. 'You need to eat.'

'Place the food on the table,' said Chin, with authority. 'We've been up for a long time. We'll eat shortly.'

She put the tray down and waited. Chin expected her to go and turned to Xu. She held her ground.

'Thank you, Lihua,' said Xu, pleased that she was taking an interest. 'Is there something you want to know?'

Chin rolled his eyes.

'Mr Kuang-hsien, what have you found out from the clocks?' she asked.

It was Chin who replied; he did not know why.

'It seems that most of the clocks in the inner circle are slower than the ones outside,' he said, subconsciously accepting her as an apprentice alchemist.

'So you will live longer if you are near the stone?' she said, surprising them both with her insight.

'Yes,' said Xu, impressed with her powers of deduction. 'Only by a tiny amount, maybe a few days over the whole of your life, but yes you would live longer.'

'Xu, have you noticed that some of the clocks around the outside of the table are not consistent,' said Chin, picking up one of the gold watches.

'Which clocks were those?' asked Xu.

'The ones furthest from the window,' said Chin, looking around the room. 'Perhaps it was the Sky crystal that interfered with them.'

'No, Sky is on the shelf next to the window,' said Xu, puzzled.

'It's the crate,' said Lihua, quietly.

Neither Xu nor Chin heard her.

'Perhaps Sky works back to front,' said Xu, clutching at straws. 'Perhaps it speeds up time.'

Lihua moved over to the crate.

'It's the crate, Mr Kuang-hsien,' said Lihua more loudly.

'What?' said Xu.

'There must be more crystals in what's left of the meteorite,' she said. 'Whatever causes time to change must travel though the walls of the crate,'

'and the crust of rock that they are encased in,' mused Xu finishing her sentence for her.

‘So you’re saying that there must be more crystals inside that crate,’ said Chin, interrupting Xu’s train of thought. ‘But you didn’t know they were there because they were hidden inside a rock.’

‘Yes,’ said Lihua, smiling.

‘If we have more of the crystals, perhaps we can make time go even slower,’ said Xu to himself. ‘There are so many experiments I could do, but there’s no time.’

‘Is that meant to be a joke?’ asked Chin, looking at Xu’s expression.

‘Clearly not,’ he thought.

Chin continued, ‘What do you mean?’

‘I do not have long left,’ said Xu. ‘There are many more experiments to do and I don’t have enough time before I die.’

‘What do you mean you’re as strong as a horse,’ said Chin outraged. ‘You are the same age as me.’

‘That’s true but hadn’t you noticed that I look twenty years older than you. I’m ill,’ he said. ‘I suppose it’s because of the late nights and too much drink.’

‘Master, you’re not dying,’ said Lihua, a tear rolling down her cheek. ‘You can’t be.’

It was the first time either of them had realised how attached they had become to each other. At that instant he realised that Lihua was turning from a petulant adolescent into young woman. Difficult, but he loved her just the same.

‘I’m afraid I am my child,’ he said. ‘Don’t cry I’m old and tired. My time has come.’

‘Rubbish,’ said Chin, unsympathetically. ‘You always like melodrama. You’re just a bit run-down that’s all. You’ve got twenty years left.’

‘I don’t think so,’ Xu replied sadly. ‘Whatever happens, we have learnt something wonderful from our experiment. I don’t want it lost when I die. I want you to take the knowledge with you to my Taoist friends in the Doseon-sa monastery. They will continue my work.’

‘Well I won’t do it,’ said Chin defiantly.

'Yes you will,' replied Xu, 'and I want you to take Lihua with you. She is only a young girl but she is determined and clever.'

'Headstrong and insolent more like,' said Chin.

Lihua, now in floods of tears rushed over to Xu and for the first time he embraced her as he should, given she was his daughter.

****

Before Chin finally agreed to take Lihua with him back to Korea, Xu told him about Lihua's true relationship to him. Although Chin could now understand why Xu tolerated her manners, he was still displeased.

'Does she know?' asked Chin.

'No,' said Xu.

'Are you sure?' he said. 'If not, what else is going on in her head? She seems a little headstrong for just a servant girl.'

'She's like her mother,' replied Xu, his eyes focussed elsewhere. 'I suppose I indulge her too much.'

'You do,' Chin replied, 'and she will become a real handful if she isn't tamed.'

'I know,' said Xu, weakly. 'I've never been good with discipline, especially with women. That's why I want you to take her back to Korea.' He paused thoughtfully, 'But don't tame her, just teach her how to respect others. Her wildness and curiosity make her what she is.'

'I will, but I will not promise not to teach her better manners. That is my condition.'

'I agree,' replied Xu, reluctantly. 'I know you are right.'

Chin spent the next few days preparing for his return to his home near Hanseong. Lihua spent her time fussing around Xu, ignoring his instruction that she should leave with Chin. Finally Chin lost patience and told Xu to put his foot down and tell Lihua to prepare for her trip. Two days after the experiment, Lihua came to see Chin.

'My master said that you wanted to see me,' she said sulkily.

'I need you to start packing your things for the trip. We need Xu's notes and the left over pieces of meteorite.'

'I can't. My master is ill.'

'You should stop worrying about your master,' he said. 'There's nothing wrong with him.'

'You're so cruel,' said Lihua. 'He's dying.'

'No he's not,' Chin replied. 'He's play-acting. He'll outlive me! Anyway he wants you to go to the monastery to help the Tao alchemists.'

'I can't, I'm a girl. They only let men live there!'

'He has already got permission,' he replied, showing her an official looking document. 'You should obey his wishes.'

Lihua went back to Xu and tried to get him to change his mind. Unusually, he did not budge, so she knuckled down and started to work with Chin.

****

The Doseon-sa Tao gathering monastery was located on a sacred mountain just outside of Hanseong. Being something of a VIP, Chin had quite an entourage and it took several months for his party to make its way cross country to their destination. His servants carried the crate containing the remaining fragments of the meteorite along with numerous items of luggage that he loved to carry with him. Lihua's belongings however were far more modest. Just as Chin had expected, Xu had exaggerated his illness and within a few weeks was much better. News of this reached them by special messenger along with further results from his continued experimentation with the Earth and Sky.

'I told you he was play-acting,' said Chin, smugly.

'Yes you did, Mr Chin,' replied Lihua. 'You are right. He has always enjoyed drama, but it is only now that I realise how much I love him. Since my mother died he has become the closest thing I have to a parent.'

Chin did not reply. He wondered whether this was the time to tell her about her father. He decided that if Xu had kept it from her, then it was not Chin's place to tell her. Over the months of their journey, he had seen a change in Lihua. She was growing up to become a shrewd young woman who was learning to think before she spoke. As Xu had wished, she was not tamed but in Chin's company she had learned to control her mouth. No longer a surly servant, she had become an intelligent companion. He had tried to teach her as he would his son. But she was more; she was intelligent with a brain that seemed to absorb everything.

Finally they were near their journey's end and the master monk, Yeon-gi, looked down over the valley beneath the monastery. He saw the entourage picking its way up the steep mountain pass.

'That's typical of Chin,' he thought. 'He goes on a trip to see our friend Xu and carries a mountain of useless material things up a mountain. Why does he do it?'

He scanned the group to see if he could make out Xu's daughter. He had corresponded with Xu for many years. Some time ago, Yeon-gi had written to Xu encouraging him to come to the monastery so that they could work together on the elixir. Xu had said that he was too old and would not survive the journey. It was then that Yeon-gi had asked Chin to go and persuade him. But before Chin had arrived in Beiping, Xu had written to say he would send his best student, a girl. Although the master was surprised, he agreed to Xu's suggestion. It was whilst Chin and his entourage were making their slow return, that Xu's next letter came explaining that "his best student" was in fact Xu's daughter.

It took the party the best part of the day to make their way up to the gates of the monastery and the master was waiting for them as they entered. Immediately Yeon-gi could see Xu's likeness in her.

'I wonder why he didn't tell her that she is his daughter,' he thought. 'She must have guessed.'

As Chin and his fellow travellers got closer Yeon-gi could see something else in Lihua's eyes. In spite of the tiredness of the journey, her manner displayed an exceptional intelligence and curiosity. These must have been inherited from Xu but the master detected another, more subtle facet.

Lihua had a bearing that displayed a determination and purpose not common in young women of her age. This had clearly come from her mother. In an instant he decided that Lihua would be a great asset in their search for the elixir.

That assessment of Lihua's character was one of the most important judgements the master ever made and after Chin, his servants and luggage had left for his home in the valley below, the master immediately put his misgivings regarding her sex to one side. He immediately involved her in the alchemists' work, already underway in the monastery. As Lihua had predicted, the meteorite fragments contained several more blue crystals and over the next few weeks she showed the monks how to extract them without damage. They were quickly able to reproduce Xu's time experiment. Very soon she became a central fixture in the day-to-day alchemy of the monastery.

# Seven

## Enlightenment

Lihua applied herself to her new challenges and although she never saw Xu again they were in constant correspondence and it was this acquired knowledge that made her become an enigma to those around her. Although she lacked one of the essential characteristics of a Taoist master monk, she was female; Lihua became the next best thing. She was an essential personality in the search for the elixir of eternal life. Lihua guided many of her acolytes through scores of complex experiments that were designed to reveal the secrets of the blue crystals.

By the time she had reached her early twenties she had been given her own lodgings. These were carved out of the mountain rock at a respectful distance from the monks' quarters. She had one room set aside specifically for experiments on the blue crystals. This laboratory was a facsimile of Xu's quarters in Beiping's old observatory, except it was much tidier. One morning in early spring, Lihua had calculated that later that day the stars would be in the right position to cause the crystals to glow. She gathered a small group of novice monks around her. They were eager to see her perform her famous experiment.  There was a sharp tap, tap, tap as ice and water trickled down from the snow capped mountainside above her lodgings. Tense in expectation, the noise made one or two of the students jump.

'Don't worry,' she said. 'It's only the snow melting on the ledge above us. It happens this time every year.'

The group relaxed. She pointed to a clock on the wall.

'The stars will not be in position until the big hand is at the bottom,' she said.

They all looked towards the clock hand, willing it to speed up.

'Over the years,' she explained. 'I have made small improvement to Xu's original experiment.'

They dragged their eyes away from the clock to listen to her.

'In the centre of the table, I have four crystals that are held in position in a strong wooden frame. In addition to the clocks that Xu had in concentric circles in the plane of the table, I have more clocks above and below the table. They are all set to the same time.'

'Excuse me,' said one of the students. 'Why do you need the extra clocks?'

'The original experiment was only conducted in two dimensions.'

'The plane of the table,' suggested the student.

'Yes, if you remember your teachings we want to move beyond our three dimensions. The extra clocks are held in a metal framework so we can measure time in a sphere around the central focus.' She continued, 'This experiment is in four dimensions; three in space and one in time.'

'Thank you, mistress,' he said, at ease. 'I understand.'

More ice fell on the roof above them, startling the students again.

'Not long now,' she said pointing at the clock. 'The star…..'

There was a sudden bang as something fell on the roof. This even startled Lihua.

'What was that?' she asked.

Nobody answered.

Suddenly the whole room was in pandemonium. Everything went white and then dark. An avalanche had slid from the ledge above and fallen on the building and the massive weight of snow crushed almost everything beneath it.

It took many hours for monks from the monastery to dig out the survivors. Amongst them was Lihua who, by some miracle, was almost unharmed. The next morning she went back to the pile of snow that had once been her home and she discovered one of the most important properties of the mysterious stones. Like many great discoveries it arose from an accident; an accident that almost killed her.

****

Back in Beiping, Xu continued to look at the stars and play with his clocks, and blue Earth and Sky stones. He continued to write to Lihua every month to give her ideas and tips that would help her with her work. In none of his letters did he mention that he was her father. He did not have the courage.

****

Lihua and a group of supporters took nearly two days to dig out the remains of her experiment. Amazingly some of the smaller clocks were not damaged by the deluge; having been protected perhaps by a joist or shelf of rock. The blue crystals however had been under the full weight of the snow and this had applied immense pressure to their surfaces. The time differences on the working clocks were far greater than any measurement she had ever taken before. It seemed that the pressure on the stones had made them more sensitive to the stars' influence. It was at this moment she realised that she knew how to make a machine to extend life!

****

After the accident Lihua made the connection between pressurising the blue crystals and their increased sensitivity to the heavens. This was key to the design of her next experiment. When she explained her ideas to the Master, he allocated her a secure spot outside the monastery walls where she could build her experiment and new lodgings. He assigned a team of five young monks to protect her and help with the construction. She was now able to build the machine she had dreamt about. Her experiment consisted of a robust stone building with one room. The walls, floor and ceiling of the room were plastered with a mixture of gypsum and a secret ingredient. A set of four blue crystals were placed inside a water-tight, stone chimney that extended a quarter of a mile up the mountainside. This was filled with water, placing the crystals under immense pressure. She found that when the stars were in the right place, clocks inside the experiment ran much faster than clocks outside. Lihua's living quarters were built next door against the wall furthest from the chimney and the blue stones. She soon noticed that the clocks in her lodgings went slower than those in the monastery and slower still when compared with the clocks in the room where she did her experiments.

As she tried to understand, Lihua discovered that she could make clocks go faster or slower, but she could not make them go backwards. The monastery gained a great deal from her discoveries. The monks found that they could store perishable food in the slow-clock room (her lodgings) in the spring and it would still be fresh two summers later and they could germinate seedlings twice as fast in the Fast Room. The monks however noticed one strange change in Lihua; she had developed an incredible capacity for sleep. After a full day assigning tasks to her acolytes, she would go to her lodgings at night and sleep for over thirty two hours. In time she learned to give them enough to do for two days.

By her fifty-seventh birthday a young-looking Lihua realised that she would never be able to make time go backwards. For her this would have been the ultimate elixir – eternal life. She had taken her research as far as it would go. On that day Chin, at nearly ninety years old, made a special trip to bring her more bad news.

'I'm very sorry,' he said, sadly. 'Xu died peacefully in his sleep two months ago. I received the message through the diplomatic courier.'

'He said he wasn't well, forty years ago,' she said, her eyes filling. 'He must have been right after all.'

'Yes,' said Chin, chuckling, 'and I was wrong. I said he'd had twenty years left in him. He managed forty!'

'And you out-lived him,' she said, wiping a tear away from her eye. 'You said you wouldn't.' She paused realising what she had said. 'Oh, I'm sorry I didn't mean that how it sounded. I just wish I had seen him before he died.'

'I know,' he said sympathetically, 'but you had the next best thing, you exchanged letters every month.'

'I suppose that's true. Anyway he had his wish. His work lives on in me,' she said brightening a little. 'I'm just not sure I can do any more without his advice.'

'You can. You must. He was very proud of you, you know,' he said. 'You were his only child.'

Although Lihua had realised that she was Xu's daughter, Chin had never explicitly spoken of it before.

'I suppose I must carry his work on to the next generation of alchemists,' she said.

'But you have,' he said. 'You are still.'

'Yes, but the problem is that every time you hand knowledge to the next generation, you lose something,' she said, reflectively. 'If only he could have lived longer he could have put my students back on the right track without any errors.' She paused, 'He was the original source of so much learning.'

'You know that the barbarians have a phrase "Chinese whispers" for such errors', he said, enjoying his joke.

'Well he and I were Chinese,' she said, smiling.

'But you are a Korean now and well known for your knowledge of eternal life,' said Chin. 'It is a bit late for Xu and me, but you can be the continuity.'

Lihua did not know that her reputation had moved beyond the walls of the monastery. More importantly, she was not aware that her work had caught the attention of a band of Japanese freedom fighters. It was at this time when Sensei Yoshida Shoin, Okuba and the samurai, soon to become fugitives from the Japanese authorities, were meeting in a cave on the Akiyoshi-Dai plateau to develop their plan to steal Lihua's secrets.

# Eight

## Betrayal

Lihua had been hit hard by his death and now that the Master had confirmed that Xu was her father, she was desperately sad that she had not been kinder to him. She was in this state of mourning when the Shishi arrived. However, unknown to her the Tao monk's web of intelligence had tracked them from their bridge-head in Gijeon region to the foot of the sacred mountain on which the monastery was built. Okuba Sama had managed to pull together an assortment of twenty samurai whom he felt would be good enough to defeat the inferior Korean foreigners. He had also brought along two young Shinto monks who were non combatants and although they were there for their brains, he had ensured that they had had at least some basic training.

The band's objective was to kidnap Lihua and steal any samples of the elixir that they could find. The plan was to retreat to their boat, moored in a quiet spot twenty miles south west of the monastery. From there they would sail around the southern tip of Korea back to Japan. They had decided not to land on the eastern shore of Korea, because they would be spotted by the enemy if they took the long cross country route across Korea. Okuba had not realised that his band had been tracked since they left port in Japan and if he had marched across land he could have beaten the messengers to the monastery. As it was, the Master had had many weeks to prepare his defences.

When the attack came, the Taoist monks were ready for them. Okuba had completely underestimated the martial skills of his enemy and he paid the ultimate price. After the battle only four of the samurai were left alive and they were given the option of committing seppuku or remaining prisoners; an unacceptable disgrace to the Japanese warrior class. All but one of the samurai performed the ritual suicide by slicing their bowels open with a ceremonial knife. The Shinto monks and the disgraced samurai were absorbed into the monastery to take harsh instruction from the Master. The monks knuckled down and took their punishment without dissent. They knew that there would be no one to save them and for better or worse the monastery was their new home. The remaining samurai however was not so easily cowed.

Although their target had been Lihua, she did not care about the battle and it was not until she received a number of items from Beiping, that she started to emerge from her dark period of mourning.

Two weeks after the abortive raid, the master made a visit to her lodgings.

'Lihua,' he said. 'Before Xu died he expressed a wish that you should have some of his belongings.'

Lihua brightened at the thought that her father had sent her something and then after a short pause she looked into the master's eyes.

'You know Master, I am not interested in material things and keep-sakes that remind me of Xu will make me sad,' she said, imagining Xu had sent trinkets. 'I would rather you dispose of the things as you wish.'

'I have confused you,' he said. 'The observatory authorities have sent two carts, full of his devices and equipment. I'm not sure how much has survived the journey, but I'd like you to decide what we should keep.'

Without a word she stood up and started towards the door.

'There is another thing,' said the Master, stopping her in her tracks. 'He sent you a letter to be delivered on his death.' He pulled a scroll from his sleeve and continued, 'I think you should read it first.'

Lihua took it from his him, and turned it over in her hands. She looked at the red seal that had been put there by her late father. She realised that it was probably one of the last things he had done for her. She ran her finger tenderly over the smooth surface of the hard, shiny wax. A tear formed in the corner of her eye. The Master turned to leave.

'Come and help me with the carts when you are ready,' he said turning towards her and gently touching her on the shoulder. She nodded silently as he stepped out into the winter chill.

Lihua sat down on a wooden stool and read.

*My Dear Daughter,*

*It is to my lasting regret that I did not call you that earlier. My friend Chin and the Master chastised me often that I never told you about your mother and me. I did not want your love for this old man to halt your learning. Would you have gone with Chin if you knew you were my daughter? Possibly, but I did not want to take the risk.*

*But now I can tell you. Your mother and I were very much in love but, in the eyes of our betters we were not compatible. We ignored them and had a happy life for many years. When she died, I became absorbed in my work and I did everything I could to draw you into it. I was the proudest man in the world when you took my work on. I never want you to stop.*

*If you are reading this letter, I must be dead. The observatory will have sent you some of my devices. Amongst them you will find some copies of diagrams and ideas for experiments. The originals are in the Palace library.*

*Among the devices, you will find a barbarian device for looking at stars. I want you to examine this very carefully. It is called a Newtonian telescope. I think that the invisible energy that makes our stones glow is like light and we should be able to control it. I have copied the explanation of my diagrams also. Please read them and continue my work. My dear Lihua please remember how proud I am of you, even now I am gone.*

*Your loving father, Xu*

Lihua, stood up wiping the tears from her cheeks. She rolled up the scroll and placed it in a drawer, tenderly, as if she were putting her baby to bed.

'I don't know what I should do,' she said to herself, confused. 'My father's alchemy should go on. He has told me what to do. I'm not sure I can do it.'

She stepped out of her lodgings in a daze. It was cold and windy. Snow was flying horizontally across the paving stones in front of her. The visibility was so poor that she could barely see the pathway to the main gate of the monastery. She pulled her quilted coat tightly around her shoulders. Not even a blizzard could tear Lihua from her thoughts. She ploughed on through the settling snow using her instinct and an automatic memory of a walk that she had done a thousand times before. As she stepped under the archway of the main gate, the blizzard eased a little. The walls of the courtyard were providing some shelter. Outside the walls she had been walking into a perfect mass of blinding white, now inside she could make out the shadows of the two carts. As she got closer she saw that someone was unloading them. She could make out two or three monks carrying items through the doors into the divine hall. Shivering against the cold, she moved closer to one of the carts and looked inside. There was no sign of Xu's telescope. 'Perhaps it's already been unloaded,' she thought. Startled at a crunch in the snow, she turned quickly and collided with a man carrying a large box on his shoulder. Already unstable under the weight of the box, he slipped and fell on top of Lihua. The box slipped away under the cart.

'Kuso!' he cursed.

'That's Japanese for shit, isn't it?' she said, lying on her back, with his full weight on her.

'Yes Miss Lihua,' he said, embarrassed. 'Sorry Miss Lihua.'

Lihua was lying in the snow, pinned to the ground but with the warmth of his body it was not unpleasant.

'Are you going to get up?' she asked, smiling.

'Yes Miss Lihua,' he said, struggling to his feet and then helping her up.

In the shelter of the cart, she could see him more clearly. He had a strong chiselled handsome face. She felt a warm tingle as he returned the examination, holding her eyes in his. Unlike the other monks, he did not drop his gaze. She had not met anyone like him before. If she hadn't been standing in a snow-storm, she would have blushed; it was her turn to be embarrassed.

'You are one of the Japanese Shishi aren't you?' she asked, slightly flustered.

'Yes, we get all the hard jobs,' he said, 'They call me the disgraced samurai. They think I deserve it.'

She looked about her.

'Do you?' she asked.

He did not reply.

'We'd better get inside,' she said. 'We'll freeze to death out here.'

They walked together towards the entrance. He opened the door and let her in and immediately turned back to resume his unloading.

'Thank you,' she said quietly to his back, but he did not hear.

****

The Master received Lihua in the Taoist living room. He was waiting patiently, sitting cross legged on the floor. He remained still as she entered. She moved in front of him placed her hands together and gave him a formal bow. He glanced up and smiled.

'Sit down, my daughter,' he said.

She knelt down, resting her weight on the backs of her calves. He sat silently as she relaxed.

'Have you read your father's letter?' he asked.

'Yes,' she said, succinctly.

He waited silently for her to continue.

She looked away from him and went on, 'I now understand why he sent me here.'

She paused for a reaction. There was none.

Lihua continued, 'When I was with him in China, he never acknowledged that I was his daughter. At the time it did not hurt me, because I assumed that my father had died long ago. In my early years I was cruel and disrespectful to him and he didn't seem to mind. I thought him weak and silly. But after meditating here I started to suspect his secret and became angry with him. It is only now that I have read his letter that I can understand him.'

'And forgive him?' asked the Master.

'That may take some time,' she said, 'but I think I will.'

She cast her eyes to one side, considering the question again.

She continued, 'My father must have known that the monks at this monastery had special knowledge of the blue crystals and for some reason he could not travel here himself. I realise that sending me here in place of him was the greatest honour he could have paid me and now I am ashamed that I behaved as I did towards him.'

Again Lihua's eyes started to fill. Her chin fell towards her breast to hide the tears from the Master. She was having some difficulty continuing. The Master waited for a moment before speaking.

'You were just a child,' he comforted. 'and like many children you were headstrong and unable to see things through older eyes. You should not chastise yourself. It is perfectly normal.'

He reached forward, took her chin in the fingers of his right hand and gently lifted her head.

'There is no need to cry Lihua, he loved you and wanted you to work on his legacy. Will you do that for him, for me and for yourself?'

'I will,' she said.

'Then go back to your lodgings and sleep. When you are rested we will help you with your new experiments.'

Lihua gave the Master another formal bow and moved towards the exit.

'By the way, Lihua,' he said. 'You will see a small box of papers by the door. Please take them with you. Your father wanted you to have them.'

****

Thirty two hours later, Lihua emerged from her living quarters fully rested. The snow was lying deeply outside. The snow-storm was over. The sun was shining. It was a beautiful morning. Xu's equipment was laid out in the divine hall waiting for her to sort through it and as she scanned the neatly stacked crates, the Master came up behind her.

'Are you rested?' he asked.

'Yes thank you Master.'

'I have allocated the Japanese to help you,' he said, 'Do you mind?'

'No,' she said, 'that is fine.'

'I'll send them over in a few moments,' he said, turning to go. 'If you have any trouble with them, tell me and I will deal with them,' he said over his shoulder.

The three surviving Shishi arrived in the divine hall and stood meekly behind her waiting for instructions.

Lihua told the two Shinto monks to open a group of packing cases ready for her to examine the contents. She was keen to find the Newtonian telescope. The third Shishi remained waiting in position for instructions. Suddenly he built up the courage to speak to her.

'I did not see you yesterday,' he said.

'I was in my lodgings,' she replied, trying not to encourage his forwardness.

'Have you been ill?' he asked, concerned.

'Just sleeping,' she said, surprised that he would care.

'For thirty-two hours?' he said, becoming bolder.

'It doesn't feel like that to me,' she said, suddenly realising that they were entering into a conversation. 'Time goes slower in my room.'

'How can that be possible?' he asked, his curiosity getting the better of him.

'It is because of the experiment,' she said, saying more than she intended. He was still looking at her, waiting. She did not know why, but she felt the need to bare her soul to this man. She prudently decided to give him something to do. 'Can you start unpacking the items out of that packing case?' she said pointing at the box that one of the others had just opened.

'Of course, Miss Lihua,' he went to the box and started unloading, carefully arranging the items on a clear area of the floor.

Lihua watched him and could not stop herself.

'What's your name?' she asked, knowing that she should not encourage him.

'I have many names,' he said, 'it depends on my situation.'

'What an odd answer,' she thought becoming curious.

'What's your name in this situation?' she asked.

'Jiro,' he said. 'I am the second son.'

'Where is your elder brother?'

'He is dead. He died in the raid,' he replied simply.

'Oh,' she said.

She did not know whether it was because they had both lost loved ones, or something else but she was feeling too much of an affinity for this young samurai. He reached inside the crate to pull out another device. It was a large tube mounted on a tripod.

'It's the telescope,' she thought.

'Will you bring that device over to my room?' she said. 'I want to examine it more closely.'

'Yes, Miss Lihua,' he said, smiling, his eyes twinkling. 'It will be easier if I carry it in the crate though.'

'Yes good idea,' she said. 'Put it back in the crate and bring it over when you're ready.'

Lihua left the room. She wanted to get out of there quickly. Ignoring the deep snow, she hurried back to her quarters, virtually running. Her heart racing she knelt on the floor, frightened of the emotions that were overwhelming her.

'I have your box,' said his voice at the door.

She stood up and after taking a deep breath opened the door to let him in.

'Put it over there,' she said, pointing to the corner next to her bedding.

He carried the crate to the spot and gently lowered it to the floor.

'Would you like me to unpack it?' he asked.

'Yes,' she said, watching him.

He started to take the telescope out of its box. Handling it with utmost care he placed the tripod on the floor next to her cot. She continued to watch him silently.

He looked up from his work and smiled as he caught her eye. She looked away, but returned her gaze as he started to return the straw packing into the empty case.

'I've worked something out,' he said, not looking at her.

'What's that?' she asked breathlessly.

'I understand why you look so young and beautiful,' he said.

'Why's that?' she said disappointed but glowing from the blatant flattery.

'Because you are young and beautiful,' he said.

'And by that you mean?' she asked, wondering if he was as shallow as he seemed.

'If you sleep thirty-two hours every time you go to bed and your body thinks it's only eight hours, you are the same age as me.'

'How old are you?' she asked.

'I have seen twenty-four summers,' he said. 'You have seen more summers but almost the same number of days and nights as me.'

'You are cleverer than you look,' she said standing up and walking towards him.

He stood up to meet her, their bodies very close.

'Do you want me to make love to you?' he said.

'Yes,' she replied.

****

At eighteen months, Lihua's pregnancy was the longest in human history. Her son was born about one year after Jiro had escaped from the monastery and returned to Japan with many of Lihua's secrets. Although she was angry she soon got over his betrayal. He had gone and that was that. She knew that she did not love him; her feelings were sexual and little else. Lihua named her son Quon. From that point onwards all her love was shared between her child and alchemy.

By the time Quon was fourteen (or twenty eight, depending on your point of view) he had become the image of his father, and he had the brain-power of his mother. He was clever and just as head-strong, but not as outspoken as Lihua. He had inherited some of his father's cunning ruthlessness. He had learnt from conversations with the monks that his father had been Shishi, a patriot, a samurai. In his imagination Jiro was a hero of Japan, an exiled knight who would defeat all about him to restore the Emperor. Quon longed to follow in his father's footsteps. His mother could not shift him from this dream. By the beginning of the year eighteen-ninety-three, Lihua was becoming concerned about her son's character and education. She wanted him to mix with children of his own age, learn a little of Confucian values. He needed to be tamed just as Chin had tamed her years before. She felt he needed to have male role models who were a little less wild than his father. There was another worry. The atmosphere at the monastery was becoming tense. Across the whole country there was a feeling of impending disaster. Japan and China were rattling sabres at each other over control of Korea. It seemed inevitable that if there was a war it would be fought on Korean soil. Lihua was convinced that the Japanese would return to the monastery with a big army and her protectors would not be strong enough to fight them off. Her other worry was that Quon's father would arrive at their head and drag his son and Lihua's remaining secrets back to Japan with him. She tried to put the worry to the back of her mind reasoning that Jiro did not know enough to build "preservation" and "incubation" rooms like those at the monastery. Jiro had missed a vital ingredient; he had not managed to steal any blue crystals. By then he would have been in his late fifties; a little old to join the modern Japanese army but she could not be sure. With all these factors weighing on her mind, she decided to take a decisive step before it was too late. She arranged to send Quon back to his grandfather's academy in Beiping and place him under the protection of the mandarins in the Imperial Observatory. Although Lihua had been three years older when she had made the reverse journey, she felt that Quon was stronger and better prepared.

****

Less than eighteen months after Quon's departure Japanese troops entered the monastery and set about razing it to the ground. Lihua's worst nightmare came true and Jiro was indeed in the army and in his full glory as a general at the head of his troops. He loaded Lihua, all of her equipment, documents and stocks of blue stones on to a cart and took them back to a battleship waiting off the west coast of Korea. Jiro had learnt about his son through the network of spies. For weeks, he interrogated Lihua ruthlessly about Quon's whereabouts. But it did not matter. By then Lihua knew that Quon was safely in Beiping.

Showing little sympathy for the emaciated Lihua, Jiro, pressed her into service to build Xu's final device in an underground bunker in Japan. Working as a slave in the dark, damp conditions played badly with her health and she died without finishing the project, taking some of her secrets to her grave. Having failed in his task, Jiro fell foul of his masters and was executed. The remaining workers were set free and after the cave-in, the cave was sealed up. As far as the rest of the world was concerned, the whole programme of Japanese research never happened; that is except for one person, one of the young Shinto monks who had been involved with the original raid. His experience in the bunker had shaken him. He felt as though all his earlier sacrifices to restore the Emperor had been futile. Just like Lihua had been betrayed by Jiro and his mother country. He no longer felt that he belonged to Japan, Korea or anywhere else. He had become a stateless international wanderer. His name was Mitzuko and it was a fortuitous reunion in Hong Kong with a young graduate of Beiping's Han-Lin Academy that laid the foundations of one of the most secretive companies in the world.

# Part 2

# Jacques and the buddleia stalk

# Nine

## The Storm

To most people a torrential downpour would be at best an inconvenience but to the bearded driver it was useful. It gave him extra cover; the kind of cover that men in his profession crave for. He was behind the wheel of an armoured truck that was designed to transport money between banks. However on that day there would be no visit to a vault, because the role of this stolen vehicle was entirely different. The beard applied slight pressure to the brake pedal, causing his vehicle to fall back from the car in front. He did not want to be remembered for rampant tailgating. He smiled to himself and glanced at the sign on the lorry in the adjacent lane.

'How am I driving?' it said.

The beard chuckled out loud and thought about the sign on the rear of his van that read, 'Police follow this vehicle.' He certainly hoped they did not. He enjoyed the irony of stealing a security company's lorry that was supposed to be under police protection. Over his career the beard had turned his talents to many things and he took pride in being able to perform any task that was assigned to him; the more difficult the challenge the better. On this job he had already disabled the feeble tracking system so he could now go wherever he wanted and cause whatever havoc was necessary to achieve his objective. He was surprised how easy it was to build a traffic camera jamming device. Even he was impressed at his own ingenuity. His invention generated powerful broadband electromagnetic pulses that were transmitted from the roof of the van. Any device using semiconductor components within four hundred feet would simply pick up white noise.

'Brilliant,' he thought.

He was amused to think that in a country where the authorities thought they could watch everybody doing perfectly normal things; he would be invisible doing very bad things. The beard's thoughts came back to his primary goal. He continued to keep his quarry in sight, always two cars ahead. He did not need to be any closer just yet; the opportunity would present itself soon. The beard had followed the car all the way from the address he had been given in Altrincham. He had checked and rechecked the registration and was absolutely confident that he had the right mark. The traffic drew to a halt.

'This could be a problem,' he thought. 'I'll need momentum.'

****

Jacques was excited and impatient to get to the restaurant. He had spent weeks organising the anniversary dinner. Timing was critical and Amaury's plane was late. That was not unusual and Jacques was kicking himself for not allowing a larger contingency. He knew Francine would have done just that. She was the best project manager he knew. He smiled to himself proudly.

'Hi Dad,' said a familiar voice, waking him from his reverie, 'let's get going.'

Amaury was standing in front of him with a broad smile on his face. They hugged.

'Eh bien, it's good to see you. Tu as raison, we need to go quickly,' said Jacques, reaching for his son's luggage.

They hurried towards the car park, where Jacques had parked his blue Renault.

'We can talk on the way,' said Jacques. 'You can tell me all about Gordes.'

****

'Manchester is famous for its rain but this is ridiculous,' she thought, as Thom steered carefully along the Chester Road towards the Mancunain Way roundabout.

The rain was hammering so hard on the windscreen that the wipers could barely clear a hole in the film of water. Being half English one would have expected that Francine would have become used to the weather, but the city seemed to have a climate all of its own. Besides, she had been brought up as a soft southerner. Francine started to reflect on the eighteen years they had lived there. They had been some of the best years of her life, despite the weather. She smiled to herself. But, now that Thom, her baby, was about to leave for university she and Jacques would enter a new phase of their life. She looked across at Thom fondly as he negotiated his way through the deluge.

'This rain is awful,' she said.

'I think we need an ark, not a car,' he replied, wanting to talk but concentrating hard on the traffic.

'Yes a boat would be good,' she said with a smile, conscious of his need to focus.

The conversation gently sank back as the water hammered on the car; the noise of the bombardment dominating everything.

'It is getting worse,' thought Thom.

The incessant hammering of the rain on the windscreen seemed to be louder than ever. He could barely see where he was going. Francine was aware of the tension in her son as he drove. The queue of traffic in front had come to a halt. She was relieved to be stationary for a few moments. Francine's mind wandered back to some hours earlier. That morning her husband, Jacques was in one of his absent-minded moods. This was annoying because he seemed to have forgotten their big day. Then he walked into the kitchen with a small parcel and placed it next to her breakfast plate. She slowly unwrapped the parcel and opened the small box inside. She was savouring the moment. The pace was too slow for Jacques.

He was getting inpatient, as he always did. He wanted to see her expression when she saw the contents.

'Oh that's lovely, Jacques,' she said eventually, as she brushed an emotional tear from her cheek. 'I thought you had forgotten.'

'Ce n'est pas possible,' he replied, looking deeply into her eyes. 'Le plus beau diamant pour ma beauté précieuse.'

'I suppose you say that to all the girls,' said Francine.

'Only to the ones who I have married.' he replied.

'But it is supposed to be silver for the twenty fifth?' she said admiring the necklace.

'Oh, silver for my other wives,' he said teasing, 'diamonds for my lover.' He paused, 'Alors Francine, you know I am proud to be unconventional. I thought of the sparkle in your smile and I knew the diamond was yours. Besides, another thirty five years is too long to wait!'

He looked into her eyes. She found that he could still make her weak at the knees.

'Bien, for you it is time to get ready. For once, I have decided that the labs will not miss me, so I am going to be your escort for the day.'

'Where are we going? I've got a lot to do at work,' she asked, a little alarmed by the surprise.

'I have spoken to Gareth. He has given you the day off,' he said with an indulgent smile.

Francine was a project manager at the Centre for Fusion Research that was based just outside the city. Gareth was her boss and an old friend of Jacques'. Realizing she had been out-manoeuvred, she changed tack.

'What shall I wear?'

She was wearing jeans, sensible shoes and a turquoise top. These were normal clothes for her kind of work.

'Dejà, tu est belle. You can come with me as you are.'

'We are not doing anything formal then?'

'We shall see', said Jacques.

He had taken her to the old pub in little Bollington. This was where they had their first date and two years later where he had proposed.

Twenty-five years ago she was the only female electronics engineer in a class of fifty-seven spotty young men. Jacques had first seen her when some final year engineers had been allowed to trespass in the physics building. He decided to apply his cultured French image to the chase. But when he found out she was half French his plan was nearly derailed. Francine smiled at the thought of Jacques' "little boy lost" expression.

Being unusually attractive for an engineer (especially as all the others were male) and endowed with a sharp mind as well as other more obvious assets, Jacques was instantly attracted to her. To his relief she was not attracted to the other engineers on her course, so Jacques hoped she would find a young, French postgraduate physicist more interesting. In fact she did not. She seemed immune to all his attempts to get her to come out with him. Until eventually, through attrition, she gave in. The rest was history.

'Do you come here often?' he asked, teasing.

'Only with my lovers,' she said, paying back his earlier tease.

They had beer and beef and onion sandwiches. Jacques had said he would only eat raw onions if she did. They laughed. The rain had kept off so they walked in the park and onions or not, he kissed her, just like he had done those years before. It had been a wonderful afternoon.

The traffic in front of them started to move again. Thom let out the clutch and eased forward. She looked at her watch. Jacques had booked the restaurant at eight; it was seven thirty and they were not far from Piccadilly now. Jacques had arranged to pick up their eldest son, Amaury, from the airport. He had taken a flight from Avignon this afternoon. The middle son, Claude, was travelling up from London, where he was studying. He would meet them at the restaurant; it was only ten minutes walk from the station. Soon they would be altogether in the private room of a posh restaurant. Francine had never been there before, but she knew it would be lovely. When it came to restaurants, Jacques' taste was impeccable.

'We're making progress again,' said Thom, bringing her back to the present. 'Ten minutes and we'll be there.' He paused, concentrating on the road.

The traffic was heavy and they were moving steadily along the elevated section of the Mancunian Way, south of the city centre. The rain was still falling heavily making the road slippery. Thom was driving carefully.

Thom continued, 'It will be great to have all the family together for your anniversary. I'm looking forward to seeing Amaury and Claude.'

'So am I,' she said, reflectively. 'It doesn't seem so long ago since you were all so little and we were all at home together. Time seems to fly by.'

The rain had eased a little, so Thom was a little more talkative.

'Now that's a matter of perspective,' he said. 'To me it seems like Claude and Amaury have been gone for ages and from my point of view, they were never little.'

Francine laughed. Thom was quiet for a moment as they approached the Albion Street intersection.

'It's the next exit isn't it?' she asked, rhetorically.

'I think so,' he said, as they passed a series of huge car parks on their left. 'We'll have to find somewhere to park closer to the restaurant. It's too far to walk from here in this rain. I think there is a car park just behind the station. We'll try there. That is, if I can fathom the incomprehensible one-way system.'

There was a temporary break in the rain and the queue of traffic started to flow more freely as some traffic left the elevated highway at the intersection. The downpour resumed. Thom, his senses alert, noticed an armoured van on the inside moving towards the slip road. It was close. He could hear its engine above the noise of the rain as the driver changed into a lower gear. The van was now alongside.

'He's in a hurry,' said Thom.

The beard lit a cigarette. Francine could see him through the tinted glass of his window. She could make out his balding head before the lighter went out and he disappeared.

'You're right,' she said, being the protective mother. 'I'd keep your distance.'

The beard seemed to have changed his mind about leaving the fly-over. He was not going to exit here and he swerved into the gap between them and the car in front. Thom tried to move into the outer lane, but it was blocked with traffic.

'My God,' screamed Francine, 'what's he doing?'

'I don't know,' said Thom, annoyed. 'I'm going to pull off here anyway.'

He looked up at the sign marking the next exit.

'We're close enough to the restaurant and we'll get out of his way. He's crazy!'

Thom braked and took the slip road off the dual carriage-way. Someone blew his horn, but Thom was now focussed on his new route. The armoured van slid quickly by.

The beard ploughed on, forcing his way into the outside lane. He was now alongside his quarry: a blue Renault. He looked across and pulled sharply on his steering wheel. The armoured van responded violently and veered towards the small car. The driver of the Renault was alarmed. He braked hard, but the van mirrored his movements and swerved again. This time there was a bang as the vehicles made contact, pushing the front of the little car towards the traffic adjacent to the nearside crash barrier. The van and the Renault became locked in a duel as the bearded driver forced his target towards the vehicles travelling in the inside lane. No match for the larger vehicle the Renault began to skid, sliding into a gap behind the butane tanker next to him. But the tanker was being tailgated by an articulated lorry with a German registration. With the steering wheel on the left, the German had only a fraction of a second to react to the spinning car as it suddenly appeared in front of him. On a dry road he could have braked in time, but in those conditions there was no grip. The lorry slid as if in slow motion, its trailer starting to overtake the tractor.

'Scheis!' shouted the German artic driver, as he fought to control the skid. But it was impossible. The jack-knifed combination engulfed the small car like a shark swallowing a shrimp. There were friction sparks between metal and road as the colliding vehicles were no longer restrained by the rubber of their tyres.

'Good,' thought the beard, as he accelerated by watching the light show.

He pushed a button on a small box attached to his dash board. 'Better make sure,' he thought.

The Renault's petrol tank exploded, creating a hazy flash of light through the drizzle. Oblivious to the drama behind him, the driver of butane tanker slowed in step with the traffic ahead. The flaming Renault careered into the stationary gas tank, forced on by the unwanted embrace of a forty tonne artic. The second explosion was far more devastating than the first. Cars were tossed around like toys. Windows were blown out of nearby buildings. The motorway was in mayhem. There was no sign of the armoured van that caused the chaos. Having done his job, the beard glanced in his mirror at the fireball behind. Well clear of the carnage, he redirected the van into the inside lane and filtered left so he could take the next exit into the city.

****

From the moment the predatory van was in view, Jacques' adrenal glands were working overtime. Large quantities of the epinephrine hormone were pumping around his blood stream triggering high quantities of oxygen and glucose to enter his brain. Of course, at that moment, this was not what was occupying his attention. For him, time had slowed down. He was able to assimilate information and act more rapidly than ever before in his experience. This remarkable fact also did not attract his interest. In less than half a second he reasoned that their little car would be crushed between the artic behind and the tanker in front. If Amaury and he did not get clear of the Renault they would both die. He then made the decision that saved his son's life. In a swift movement, he undid their safety belts.

****

Francine was surprised that they had arrived before Jacques and Amaury.

'The plane was probably late,' she thought.

Francine looked about her at the décor of the private room that Jacques had booked. As she expected it was lovely. The room was a good size for the five of them, not too large or small. There were large Georgian windows on two sides and in spite of the dull weather; the room was light, airy and beautifully decorated. The windows were offset by long, cream coloured curtains and pelmets that blended with the pale walls and ceiling. There were paintings of classical style in ochre shades on the walls without windows. These emphasised the feeling of sophistication and taste. In the centre of an immaculate oak floor were five chairs and a mahogany table. It had been carefully laid out with silver service. The whole scene was exquisite. Jacques had chosen well.

'He must have spent weeks organising the anniversary dinner. I wonder what the food is like,' she thought. 'Mind you Amaury will give us his professional opinion I'm sure.'

Amaury was a chef in a hotel in Provence. She looked at her watch.

'Don't worry, Mum, they'll be here in a few minutes,' said Claude, guessing his mother's thoughts.

'Do you think I should call them?' asked Francine, starting to become a little concerned.

'Let's give them a few more minutes,' said Thom, calmly.

Five minutes passed then ten, then fifteen.

'Ok,' said Claude, 'you said Dad's driving so I'll call Amaury's mobile. They've probably been held up in the bad weather. The traffic must be awful out there.'

****

'Is that a phone ringing?' asked the traffic policeman.

'It sounds like it's coming from near the crash barrier,' replied the paramedic, as he was closing the ambulance door.

The ambulance pulled away with its cargo. The inspector had heard the phone too. He surveyed the burnt out wreckage. It was difficult to work out where one car began and the other ended. There was debris everywhere. He told the PC to find the phone. The copper moved towards the shrill ringing noise. The forensic investigation had not started, so the PC knew he should be careful about touching anything.

'It's coming from this backpack,' he said.

The backpack lay against the kerb. It looked pristine, as if it had been carefully placed there by its owner.

'It must have been thrown clear in the accident', said the PC.

The inspector nodded as if to signify the he should pass the bag to him.

Williams wanted to find out who was calling. The call may be relevant. He put on gloves and opened the bag and the ringing stopped.

'Oh well,' said Williams, 'it's best left to the liaison officer anyway.'

Williams started to look through the contents. He found a company photo ID card.

It read, 'Plasma Research Department, Department Head, Dr Jacques Degordes.'

The phone started ringing again.

'This is Inspector Williams, who is this?'

There was stunned silence.

'What's happened?' said an anxious voice.

'Who is speaking?' asked Williams, stubbornly.

'I am Claude Degordes. Why are you answering my father's phone?'

Williams paused, waiting for his training to kick in. This was a moment you could never adequately prepare for.

'Are you related to Jacques Degordes?' asked Williams, making no assumptions.

'I am his son,' replied Claude, irritated by the question.

'I'm afraid there's been an accident. A number of people have been taken to the Manchester Royal.'

'What has happened?' asked a woman's voice. Francine had taken hold of the phone.

'Are they badly hurt? How is Jacques? How is my son?' she asked, with rising panic in her voice.

Inspector Williams could not give any more details; in fact, if he had any more information he should not give it over the phone. That was the job of the liaison officer; face to face.

Williams continued, 'I'm afraid I have no more details. If you could tell me where you are madam, I will send an officer to speak to you.'

Francine's heart sank.

'We're in a restaurant, the Orchid, near Piccadilly. We're waiting for Jacques and my son. I must go to them now!'

'I understand madam. I will send an officer to pick you up immediately.'

Williams knew that the driver of the burned out Renault was not likely to have survived either the collision or the fire.

'He probably died instantly,' he thought. By some miracle the passenger had been thrown clear. The lad had head injuries and was in a bad way. The driver's body, if they ever found it, was probably burnt to a cinder in the mangled wreck smouldering underneath the white foam pumped by the fire engines. Williams was angry that the shit that had caused the carnage around him was nowhere to be found. He had disappeared into the stormy evening.

He glanced up at the traffic cameras on the gantry.

'We'll track him down easily enough,' he thought.

But there was something clinical about this accident that made him wonder. He looked at the carnage about him; twisted burned out metal, still smouldering from the intense fire.

'What a waste,' the thought, 'what a senseless waste.'

As before in his career, Williams knew he had become exposed to the beginning of a family tragedy. He had seen many accidents and a lot of victims. However this one was odd. He knew he must be detached. This was the only way he could do his job; emotion was dangerous. The liaison officer had arrived. He told her where to pick up the Degordes family. She would take them to the hospital, he wished her luck.

# Ten

## The Aftermath

What with joy riders out for kicks, careless day dreamers and rebellious young men who were angry with the world, Inspector Williams thought he could fathom the cause of every kind of accident. But this one was different; somehow it seemed premeditated. After the first few statements from independent witnesses, he had realised that no one noticed the armoured van until just before the driver aggressively wiped out the car next to him. This had seemed odd to Williams. Why, he wondered, would an invisible, and therefore safe, driver suddenly become aggressive? This is why he had called the CID in to investigate. The accident remained an enigma, but it had become someone else's puzzle to solve.

****

After two weeks CID had drawn a blank. The boss was frustrated that the trail had gone cold. The suspect had disappeared without a trace; the traffic cameras in the area of the accident and along the route had all gone faulty and showed no sign of an armoured van. It was beginning to look like the work of a highly competent killer, the kind that could be bought in South Manchester or Salford for a few hundred pounds. Whoever it was, he knew his way around Manchester. The boss could see no reason why Jacques Degordes would have been targeted. Dr Degordes was a popular man, a university academic with a distinguished record. The boss had always subscribed to the view that the simplest answer is usually right. The boss's approach had been a tried and tested formula for years and more often than not it had come up trumps. He had considered putting Francine

Degordes in the frame because murder cases usually involve people the victims knew. She was clearly a clever and resourceful woman and would be capable of careful planning to cover her tracks. But try as he might he could find no motive. If either of them had been unfaithful, this would have been a clincher. It was clear he liked the ladies, but there was no evidence that he was anything other than devoted to his wife and vice versa. He assembled his team in the incident room.

'Ok, we've looked at all the players and this Degordes bloke seems to have been one of the most well-liked people around,' said the boss.

'He must have pissed someone off,' commented the cynic.

'Clearly,' replied the boss with a withering look. 'It's probably a simple road-rage accident, or some South Manchester joy-rider looking for kicks.'

'What about an out-of-town killer?' asked the novice. 'Maybe it's got nothing to do with local villains.'

'Possibly,' replied the boss, without much conviction. 'But in my experience, the simplest solution is usually the right one.'

'Ah, Occam's razor!' said the thinker, smugly.

'What?' asked the cynic, bemused.

'The simplest solution that can account for the most observations, is probably right,' said the thinker.

'No offense Guv but it sounds like a cop out to me,' countered the novice. 'The failure of the traffic cameras is too much of a coincidence. I just can't see it; it looks like a planned hit to me'

'She's getting a bit lippy, this one,' thought the Boss.

'When you've got a bit more experience you'll find out that that murderers are usually stupid,' he said, putting the novice in her place. 'They often appear smarter than they really are.'

'What if it was the son, Amaury, who was the target?' she continued, refusing to be cowed.

'He was a French chef wasn't he?' the old hand chipped. 'I bet it was revenge for giving one of his customers a bad French pudding,' he continued cynically.

The rest of the team thought this was amusing. The boss did not.

'You can ask him when he wakes up. In the meantime cut the crap,' he said, looking at the cynic. 'I want someone to contact the hotel where Amaury worked in Gordes. Find out if they knew him, if he was up to anything and who were his mates.'

'Where is Gordes?' asked the cynic, seeing an opportunity for international travel.

''The South of France,' said the novice. 'It's a beautiful, ancient town on top of a hill in Provence. It's got an interesting history actually. There are some magnificent old buildings. Apparently…' her voice trailed off as she caught the boss's eye.

For the first time the cynic had become absorbed, visualising himself in a bistro sipping a beer with the sun on his back.

'Fascinating,' said the boss, his voice laced with sarcasm. 'Now can we get back to the case?'

'Sorry,' said the novice. 'I could phone the hotel, I speak a little French.'

'You'd better contact the local police as well,' said the boss as an afterthought. 'They may know him.'

'Ok, she replied. 'With a surname like his he must have been noticed in Provence.'

'Why?' asked the cynic, seeing his sojourn to the South of France receding.

'Degordes,' she replied, 'means his family came from Gordes.'

'Oh', he replied, pausing. 'Shouldn't we get on a plane and speak to the local police? A telephone call in schoolgirl French won't get us far.'

The novice looked hurt but O'Reilly had ignored the remark.

'When can we interview Amaury, the son?' asked the thinker, moving on.

'Amaury Degordes has been unconscious for over a week,' said the boss. 'He received head injuries when he was thrown from the car. He may be out for weeks even months.'

'Another cold lead,' said the cynic. 'This case is becoming a time-waster.'

The boss glared at him.

'Forget about any jolly to France,' he said, addressing the cynic. 'I want you to do the rounds in Salford and South Manchester. See if there is a sniff of any out of town hit-men operating on our patch.'

'That should clip his wings for a bit,' thought the boss.

The thinker smiled at the novice who tried her best not to look smug.

'Well, that's all we've got,' said the boss, with resignation in his voice. 'Any other ideas?'

'I've gone though Dr Degordes' diary,' said the thinker.

'Anything useful?'

'Not really. It's full of seminars, departmental meetings, lectures and a couple of international conferences. I can't find anything odd.'

'Sounds like a normal workload for an academic,' said the boss, behaving as if he knew what that was. 'Check out who was at the conferences and whether our illustrious doctor had annoyed anybody or presented anything controversial.' And as an afterthought, 'We have already interviewed his colleagues at the university. Let's see if you can find someone else who understands Dr Degordes' research work. Another perspective may give us something.'

The boss knew he was clutching at straws but he was beginning to suspect that this case would not just drop-out like most of his others. It was becoming far too complex for his liking. If they became bogged down in tedious grunt work he did not want to be the one who had missed an important insight buried in all the data. History was littered with disgraced detectives who had done just that. He turned to the thinker, who had been liaising with SOCO.

'Any news from forensics?' asked the boss.

'No DNA, no sign of bone fragments I'm afraid, the fire was too intense,' said the thinker. 'With the butane fire it burned hotter than the average crematorium. SOCO still haven't worked out how many were killed let alone who they were.'

'What about vehicle licensing records?'

'We have confirmed the drivers' names of the German artic and the butane transporter. They both died in the fire. The doctor's car was the only small vehicle to experience the full heat of the fire.'

'Shit, then he has disappeared into thin air or spontaneously combusted,' the boss paused 'We have an old fashioned missing person, assumed dead; that is until forensics find some sign of a human body.'

The boss did not like it when his job became difficult.

'Anything else?' he asked.

'They reckon the seat of the car fire was in two places: the engine and the petrol tank,' said the thinker.

'That's a hell of a coincidence,' replied the boss.

'Maybe not Guv, SOCO have found traces of calcium carbide around the engine block.'

The team looked blank.

He continued, 'Mixed with water it makes acetylene, which with an oxidiser will produce a very hot flame. I wonder whether there was some incendiary device that was triggered remotely.'

'Bugger,' muttered the boss, more to himself than the team, 'that rules out the Salford and South Manchester gangs then. Chemistry and sophisticated electronics are not their strong point'

'Traffic camera jamming, remote controlled chemistry; this is starting to look like the work of a competent assassin,' he thought. 'What the hell's going on?'

He reflected for a moment. Dr Degordes was a well-connected scientist. He must have mixed with lots of people with the know-how to do this. The question is who the hell did he annoy so much that they laid such an elaborate death for him?

'Whoever was responsible,' he thought, 'they are very dangerous.'

****

There had been a heart wrenching wait for the police to identify Jacques' remains, but they could find none. However the coroner assembled all the facts and concluded that it was most likely that Jacques had died in the fire. The prognosis for Amaury was as ambiguous as Jacques' identification. The doctors did not know whether he would ever regain consciousness. He had been lying comatose in hospital for nearly fifteen days. Up until the memorial service there had been an awful period of limbo. The service was a sombre affair, as they often are. Francine had wept, but it did not make her feel better. She thought that people talk about "closure", but she could not see how she could close anything given the uncertainty surrounding Jacques remains. She had been told that the service would be part of the healing process, but it was over and she continued to ache to the very roots of her soul. Francine had lost her true love, her closest friend. Her son, the eldest child had a special bond with his mother. He was stuck in a coma and unable to tell anyone the details of what happened on that awful day. She had been engulfed by grief, but the police were asking endless questions about whether her husband had had any enemies? Were things all right between them? Had they argued that day? She answered their questions in a tearful dream, understanding but resenting the implication of their enquiries. The coroner had been more understanding, but the verdict implied that Jacques and Amaury had been the victims of a road rage incident or something more sinister. That was over a month ago but the pain was still more than she could bear. Francine loved Jacques and Amaury so much. Her world was shattered. She needed to draw on all her reserves to get though the grief. She had to; Claude and Thom were in pain too. She had to be strong for them, she thought, but how? Francine remembered the death of her own parents. That too was painful but in a few years the ache had softened until it became a memory. Her sons were young and they would heal, but she would never get over the loss. Jacques' old friends had tried so hard to help her, particularly her boss, Paul, and Prama. She was grateful to them. It helped to talk about it, but there were too many loose ends about her loss, as the police were very happy to point out. Francine spent her time between Amaury's bedside and her work. She had hoped to be distracted by throwing herself into her job, but it did not help. She reflected that there were very few women in her line of work and most of her colleagues did not know how to handle someone grieving. Francine told herself, it was her grief not theirs. She should snap out of it. Francine longed to unload; to talk things through with someone who cared. She needed to understand why this had happened to her family and work out how to handle it. She needed explanation. Nothing about her loss seemed to make sense. Was it grief or was there something else? The police had got nowhere with their investigation. The case was still open. They were doing their best, but they seemed to have run out of fruitful lines of enquiry. What would be their next step? They did not seem to know. Francine was frustrated. Furthermore Francine's logical brain told her the contrary. The circumstances of Jacques' disappearance made it difficult for her to accept he was dead. She suggested that O'Reilly should look for a missing person, not a body. Francine realised that he would think that she was behaving irrationally or was hiding something. She was not. Given the circumstances of the accident, she knew her idea was far fetched but it seemed to be a valid possibility. O'Reilly was having none of it. Following their conversation he had her down as someone who could not accept the obvious. O'Reilly was only motivated by the obvious.

There was also tension at work. Francine's colleagues started to avoid any personal conversation with her. She had noticed some of them had difficulty looking her in the eye. If there had been certainty about the demise of Jacques, they would have consoled her and moved on but her lack of acceptance became difficult to handle. Her work-mates had stopped laughing and joking as she came into earshot, perhaps out of respect, or probably something else. The lack of closure had affected her colleagues also. Francine understood their difficulties, borne from misplaced sensitivity but their omissions had become like an impenetrable wall.

'What would Jacques have done?' she wondered. 'Use his resourcefulness and intelligence to get at the truth. I need proof, I need to know what happened,' she thought.

At that point Francine resolved to find who was responsible and call them to account. That was the only way to move on; for the sake of all her loved ones.

All of these thoughts were churning in her mind whilst she was sitting in front of the computer terminal on her desk.

'I must concentrate on my work,' she thought. 'I'm becoming a liability here.'

Her brain disobediently started to reflect on her healthy sons. Thom and Claude had responded differently to the loss of their father and the comatose state of their brother.

Claude went quickly back to university and absorbed himself with his studies. He took the loss of his father very personally. He was angry; angry with his family and angry with the world for letting this happen to them. His father had been his hero and his elder brother, who had always been there for him, may never wake up. He needed to be away where he could focus, he knew he should give his mother more support and he knew his reaction was selfish and unreasonable. This made him feel guilty and the guilt made him even angrier.

Thom on the other hand, looked at his mother and saw she was in pain. He didn't want to leave her in that state. He wanted to console her, but he knew there was nothing he could say or do to ease the grief. He was grieving also, but he could not believe that his grief was anywhere near the grief that his mother was experiencing. But she was determined that he would go to university as planned. Life must go on, she had said. He did as he was told.

Francine had shared so much with Jacques including a passion for achieving a goal; any goal, as long as he, or she cared about it. She supposed that was why she became a project engineer and not a super model even though Jacques used to say she was qualified for both. She smiled to herself at the thought whilst a tear started to form in the corner of her eye. Francine was frightened to have time to herself so she spent her waking hours between Amaury's bedside and her workplace. She was starting to realise it was not working. Normally she was good at her job, but at that moment she was going through the motions and not pulling her weight. Sooner or later her boss and colleagues would lose patience. The phone rang. She picked up the receiver. She hoped it was good news from the hospital.

'Hello, this is Francine Degordes,' she said, her voice brightening in anticipation.

'Hello, Francine, it's Prama. How are you coping?'

'Oh, hello Prama,' she said, finding it difficult to get the disappointment out of her voice.

Prama was an old colleague of Jacques and a good friend to both of them. She had just come back from her assignment in Japan and Francine was grateful that Prama was around to provide an understanding ear. She knew that Prama had cared greatly for Jacques. He was Prama's mentor.

'Sorry, I thought it was the hospital. I'm trying hard but I just can't concentrate on the project. Anyway,' she said, changing the subject, 'Have you got over the Japanese trip?'

'Yes thanks.  It was rather traumatic,' replied Prama.

'I was sorry to hear about Hideo. Did you ever get any news about him?'

'No, he just disappeared. He had become a good friend and I really liked him.'

'Another disappearance,' thought Francine.

'Anyway,' she said, her voice brightening as she changed the subject, 'I'm concentrating on the wedding now.'

'Of course, how are the wedding plans going?'

Prama was shortly to marry to Anil. This had been a difficult courtship, because of the different religious beliefs of their respective families.

'Let's just say it's complicated,' she said. 'It looks like we're going to have three ceremonies now, just to keep everybody happy.'

'At least it's not just a registry office jobby,' Francine said with a smile in her voice.

'Well, one of them is!' said Prama with a gentle laugh. 'That's the easy one.'

'You and the boys are invited to all of them. It will certainly be an experience.'

Francine fought back a tear, as she remembered that Jacques and she had already accepted the invitations.

'We'll do our best, Prama. I'm sure you'll have three wonderful days.'

Prama had been asked to clear out Jacques' office and although the police had been through everything, she did not want to touch Jacques' belongings without Francine's consent. She had sensed the pain in Francine's voice and was not sure how to broach the subject, so she decided to take a different tack.

'I wondered if you would like to have lunch in town tomorrow,' she said. 'It will get you out of the office and we could have a good chin-wag.'

'Yes, that would be lovely,' replied Francine.

****

'Any progress on the research expert?' asked the boss.

'Yes Guv,' replied the novice. 'We've found one of Degordes' ex – students. He is now a lecturer in London, a certain Dr Paul Dzibias. Dr Degordes was an expert in plasma physics and they have been working closely together for the last couple of years. Dzibias is an astrophysicist.'

'Is plasma physics the same thing as astrophysics?' asked the boss.

'I've no idea,' she replied.

'It's all gobbledy-gook to me,' the cynic chipped in.

'Everything is gobbledy-gook to you,' said the boss. 'How well did he know Degordes' work?'

'I understand they were working together on..,' the novice paused as she looked down at her notes, '..collimated, extraterrestrial gravitational wave radiation.'

'Oh great!' said the boss. 'So we're looking for an assassin from another planet who talks gibberish!'

'Well you said he might be from out-of-town,' said the thinker wryly.

He smiled at McKenzie. She returned the smile, enjoying the joke. O'Reilly simply scowled.

****

Prama and Francine met for lunch in a wine bar near Whitworth Street, next to the canal.

'Have you heard from Paul recently?' asked Prama.

Paul had also been mentored by Jacques. He was an old flame of Prama's, now married to Claire.

'Yes,' said Francine, 'the police have asked him to explain Jacques' research to them. He phoned to ask if I minded.'

'What do you feel about him doing that?'

'Oh, I have mixed feelings. The police don't seem to have made any progress, and I'm pleased they're still investigating. I'm sure I could do more to help, but O'Reilly now has me down as a loony who can't accept Jacques' death. I have no idea how Paul is going to explain what Jacques was up to. I don't even think Jacques knew.'

They smiled at each other; almost a laugh.

'That's better,' said Prama, 'It's nice to see you smile again.'

Francine's smile continued, but more reflectively this time, her eyes slightly distant.

'Prama, there is something I want to ask you.'

'Anything, just ask.'

'They never found Jacques' body you know.'

'I know.'

'I find it difficult to move on unless I can get real evidence that he was in that fire.'

Prama shuddered at the thought and waited for the question.

'Am I a loony? Is it mad to want to know what really happened?'

'No, you're not mad, but sooner or later you will have to come to terms with the facts you have.'

'Yes, but I'm sure there is more and I don't think the police are making much progress. I feel that they've been looking for obvious solutions and I think Jacques' murder is more complicated then that.'

'Murder?' said Prama, incredulously. 'Do they think it was murder?'

'Yes, they do. But they can't find a reason or lead to help them track down the culprit,' said Francine.

'Isn't that why they want Paul's help?' asked Prama.

'Perhaps, but there are things that Paul would never perceive the way I do; small things that don't tie up; things at the back of my mind. Half conversations Jacques and I had about his work. Inconsistencies that are almost, almost…' she struggled to get the right word, '…ephemeral.'

'Have you told the police?'

'Yes but I can't articulate the inconsistencies well enough. O'Reilly thinks I'm an irrational, grieving wife who can't see straight. He has stopped listening to me,' she replied, with a hint of frustration in her voice.

'Well, he's got you wrong,' said Prama.

Francine smiled a sad smile.

'All I know is that Jacques was dabbling in new ways of containing nuclear fusion. I didn't understand his idea as it was so revolutionary; in fact it was so revolutionary I told him it would come up against a lot of vested interest. There are some powerful people in that industry.'

'And you are wondering if he stepped on someone's toes by mistake?'

'I work with the nuclear power industry. Jacques thought the community was just the same as academia.'

'Isn't it?'

'At researcher level it is very similar, but I have met some very nasty ambitious, ruthless people at the top, who would do anything for money.'

'But surely not enough to kill someone!'

'Well, no, but I've never dealt with the huge commercial potential of a fusion reactor that actually works. You never know what people would do when the prize is counted in billions,' said Francine, ominously.

‘Anyway, while the police are not listening to me they could be missing a real lead. It’s driving me mad with frustration,’ Francine paused. ‘I want to do my own investigation. I want to put evidence before them that will make them take me seriously,’ she said, conspiratorially. ‘I just don’t know where to start.’

‘But none of this supports your belief that Jacques survived the crash?’

‘I know,’ said Francine sadly, ‘but I need to know for sure whether I have really lost my husband and why my son is in a coma in hospital. It’s eating at me.’

‘I will help you, but only if you agree to let it go if we find nothing. You can’t let it become an obsession.’

Francine paused again to collect her thoughts. ‘I agree,’ she said. ‘I have an idea. You know how I love delivering projects?’

‘Yes, you’re always happy bossing people around to achieve a gaol.’

Francine smiled again. Prama was a good judge of character.

‘Well, I have a new goal and I need to address it otherwise, as you said, it will become an obsession.’

‘That’s exactly what I’m worried about.’

‘Yes but I’ve been a project manager for years,’ said Francine, ‘I know that some projects become undeliverable and I know how to cut my losses.’

‘I see,’ said Prama. ‘Then who decides that it has failed?’

‘You.’

‘Oh’, said Prama, absorbing the implied responsibility. ‘And you agree to share all your findings with the police?’

‘For Jacques and my sons and for all the people who loved him,’ she said, ‘I will do anything.’

‘That’s also what I’m worried about,’ she said again, her eyes a little moist. ‘You’re determined aren’t you?’

‘I am,’ she said.

‘Alright, then how about starting by looking at everything in Jacques’’ office?’ Prama suggested. ‘We’ve been asked to clear it out anyway. Are you up to it?’

‘I think so,’ said Francine, a little nervously.

# Eleven

## Research into Research

As Prama opened the door into Jacques' office a scene of chaos and earlier frenzied activity met them. The room was furnished with two metal filing cabinets and a desk upon which was Jacques' computer. Underneath three full bookshelves there were tables pushed against the wall making a long work surface adjacent to the desk. Two chairs lay abandoned at jaunty angles in the centre of the room.

Francine looked at the familiar signs of where her husband had been at work. There was paper everywhere, stacks of books with yellow bookmarks, marking key points for further reference research, a half drunk cup of coffee, three waste paper bins full of scrunched up sheets of A4, scribblings on the whitespace of academic papers and his white board. Although there was no shortage of horizontal workspace, there was not a square inch visible to the naked eye. She felt a tinge of warmth as she pictured him frantically trying to take in as much information as possible from the sources around him. This turned to sad nostalgia when she realised that the actor in this scene was gone for ever. Francine stopped the thought.

'It looks like he had a conundrum he was working on,' said Prama.

'It does, doesn't it?' said Francine, distractedly.

Both of them knew that when Jacques had had a goal or puzzle, he became totally focussed and physical order was the last thing on his mind. His passion was to organise his thoughts, not tasks or his office. When his room was tidy, an unusual event, his closest friends knew that he was bored.

'I knew he was excited about something,' said Francine, 'but I had no idea he was so deeply into it.' She paused and continued regretfully, 'We used to chat about his ideas, but recently I've been so busy at work that we didn't get the time.'

'Francine, don't punish yourself,' said Prama, sensitively. 'If he was ready to talk it though with you, he would have. He was probably still making his ideas tidier.'

'But not his office,' said Francine, with a distant smile. 'You're right though. If he ever wanted my time, he usually made sure he got it. He was not the most reserved of men.'

Prama smiled, sympathetically.

'Where will we start?' she asked with a bewildered look.

With the nail of her index finger, Francine brushed away a tear in the corner of her eye.

'So you feel that you can help me with this?'

'What are friends for?'

'Alright,' said Francine, brightening. 'My job will be to follow the paper trail. The oldest ideas will be in his waste paper bins. I'll take those and see what scribblings he's thrown away. You follow the digital trail.'

'Yes maam,' said Prama. She paused, 'I don't have his computer security code.'

'It will be on a piece of paper in his right hand drawer. It's probably "FRANCINE" followed by forty-two or forty-nine. For some reason it reminded him of me and a hitchhiking holiday.'

Prama looked at her quizzically.

Francine continued, addressing the obvious question, 'I never understood why. He was very imaginative, but not with boring things like passwords. With those he tried to be enigmatic.' She paused, smiling to herself. 'He was usually unsuccessful though.'

Prama smiled as she pictured ebullient Jacques; a man with an insatiable desire to learn and then share what he had learnt. He never let trivia get in the way.

'He was too extrovert to be an enigma,' she said.

Prama moved over to the seat in front of Jacques' desk, sat down and opened his drawer. Sure enough the password was there. The computer was already powered up so Prama keyed in the code. It was as Francine had said and the monitor immediately filled with a picture of Francine and their sons.

'I'm in,' she said, slightly surprised about how easy it had been. 'You were right, the password was written on a yellow-sticky.'

But Francine was only half listening.

'Good work,' she said, concentrating on her own task. 'Now, get to work girl!'

Prama did as she was told. Francine had collected the waste paper bins around her. She sat down at one of the tables and cleared a space. She started smoothing a sheet from the first bin in front of her and read it.

Her quest had begun. It was the most positive feeling she had had for weeks.

****

Paul arrived at the police station in good time. He and Claire had left home before the sun had risen and caught the train to Manchester. Normally, he was not "an early bird" but he wanted to do everything he could to help Francine put Jacques to rest. As far as Paul was concerned his friend and mentor had been involved in a tragic accident. He had known Jacques for years and he owed it to him to help clear the air. But Paul was nervous. He had a nagging doubt. He knew it was ridiculous but he was worried that Jacques' death was somehow connected with their involvement in stopping the Tokyo experiment.

'I must calm down,' he thought. 'I don't want appear to be behaving suspiciously.'

Paul was not used to the police and he was not used to lying. He was not very good at it. His whole life had been geared to establishing truth - scientific truth. He did not intend to lie but to avoid discussing things that could put him into deep water. Besides, the incident in question did not have anything to do with Jacques' accident; or so Paul believed.

'Bugger I wish I was somewhere else,' he mumbled.

The sergeant at the front desk was phoning the detective who was leading the investigation.

Paul heard the clunk as the sergeant put down the phone. He had spoken to someone in the incident room.

'The chief inspector is busy,' he said. 'You'll have to wait a little longer.'

'Okay,' said Paul, relieved.

****

'This is interesting,' said Prama. 'He was working on a paper on gravitational wave solitons in plasma.'

'Pardon,' said Francine, distractedly, still focussed on the stack of wrinkled paper in front of her. She turned her head towards Prama. 'I didn't quite catch what you said.'

'I've found a partially written paper. It seems to be about a different approach to nuclear fusion that involves exploiting special kinds of waves.'

'Solitons?' asked Francine.

'That's right,' said Prama. 'His paper starts by saying that contemporary fusion programmes are going nowhere and researchers need to be more innovative.'

'Yes, he had a bee in his bonnet about that. I didn't know he'd written a paper though,' she said reflectively.

'Well even though it's not appeared in a scientific journal, he was very close to publication. This draft is virtually complete,' said Prama, scanning the pages. 'I wonder if he had submitted it for peer review.'

'Ready for publishing?' asked Francine.

Prama nodded.

'I'd no idea he was writing a paper, let alone submitting it to a journal,' said Francine, peering over Prama's shoulder at the document. 'He often said that the approach to controlled nuclear fusion had taken a wrong turn thirty years ago. He said that was why the projected date for having it on line kept moving out. I thought he was teasing.'

'He did that sometimes, didn't he?' said Prama.

'Yes he did,' said Francine, smiling reflectively, as a warm thought entered her mind. 'Anyway,' she said, switching back to the present, 'his alternative seemed too far-fetched for me. I hadn't realised he was treating his ideas as serious research.'

'What do you think about that, given your job is to help build a fusion reactor?'

Francine paused whilst her mind drifted back to a conversation with Jacques where he pontificated on her specialism. This was an area where Francine was the expert and not Jacques, but that did not deter him from offering his opinions. She would forgive him because he put on his little boy look that melted her heart. So she listened like a mother humouring her child.

'I believe that your tokamak will never work,' he had said.

This comment could have offended a person who had spent ten years of her career building a tokamak reactor, but this had been Jacques talking.

'But it does work,' Francine had replied, patiently.

'Ah yes,' he replied triumphantly. 'But is it stable? Can you get commercial electricity out of it? Can you get out more than you put in? Will it save the planet?'

Over the years they had had many conversations like this. Francine had handled all of them patiently and carried on with her day-to-day job. However just recently she was wondering whether he had been right. She returned to Prama's question.

'At first I thought he was just showing off, but as time has gone by and my project has met more and more practical problems, I was starting to think he had a point.'

'Well this paper seems to be based on the idea that a nuclear fusion reaction can be contained in a trapped gravitational wave field,' said Prama.

'I remember him talking to me about that, but I understood you could barely detect gravitational waves let alone focus them to control a fusion reaction. I thought he was clutching at straws'

'A few months ago I would have agreed with you, but after my experience in Japan and Paul's discovery of gravitum, I'm not so sure.'

'Paul's discovery?' asked Francine.

'Didn't Jacques tell you about Paul's experiment with the gravitational wave detector?'

'Oh yes, I remember,' said Francine. 'In fact he told me all about it. Didn't it destroy the laboratory and building that housed it?'

'That's right, an old fire station. Paul was mortified.'

'I heard,' she replied. 'Now you come to mention it, Jacques mentioned the discovery of a new compound that behaved unusually in a gravitational wave field.'

'Yes,' said Prama, 'and Paul called it Gravitum.'

'At the time, I didn't really understand the significance,' she said.

Francine was examining a crumpled sheet from one of waste paper bins. She moved over to the desk where Prama was working and smoothed it out in a space next to the mouse mat.

'Look at this,' she said. 'It looks like a sketch of a simple fusion reactor. There is an arrow pointing to the centre titled "Gravitum matrix".'

'Snap,' said Prama.

Francine looked over Prama's shoulder at the computer monitor.

'So what's gravitum got to do with nuclear fusion reactors?' asked Francine.

She cast her eyes over the text on Prama's screen to see if there were any other words that would jog her memory.

'When I returned from Japan, Jacques was trying to understand the plans of Hitzubishi's Gravitational Wave Rectifier,' said Prama.

'You mean the device that almost caused an earthquake in Tokyo?'

'Yes, that one,' said Prama. 'We were well aware that there is a huge flux of gravitational wave energy flowing though the Earth from space, but it is usually benign. Last year we found that two black holes were synchronised in such a way to provide a focussed beam, with far more intensity than normal.'

'Wasn't that predicted by Anil's computer program?'

'Yes, but none of us knew about the effect the beam would have on gravitum until Paul's experiment at the Old Fire Station. It turned out that Hitzubishi's Gravitational Wave Rectifier was using the same property to focus gravitational wave energy, but we never worked out what his device was for.'

'So Hitzubishi san was using gravitum in his equipment. Is this material easily available?'

'No, in fact we only know of six pieces: The crystal Paul used in his experiment and four crystals in Hitzubishi's rectifier that Hideo extracted from the meteorite sample.'

'So was Hitzubishi san trying to destroy Tokyo then?'

'I don't think so. Jacques believed that gravitational energy travels far more slowly though gravitum than other materials and that this distorts time and space in the area around the material. There could be a number of uses.'

'Jacques told me something about his idea but I thought one part didn't make sense.'

'I'm impressed, only one part!'

'It was such a basic point that if he explained it I'm sure it would have led to many more questions.'

'So you didn't ask?' said Prama rhetorically.

'Well you know what he was like. Once he started he wouldn't stop and I was preoccupied with troubles at work.' Francine paused reflectively, 'Now I wish I had asked him to explain.'

'So what didn't make sense to you?' asked Prama. 'Perhaps I can help.'

'Well he said that all these effects are triggered by gravitational waves that are usually very low frequency ripples in space.'

'Yes, that's correct and because the wave front travels at the speed of light, they travel a very long distance before they make one complete vibration.'

'That's what he said. The distance travelled by one wave crest before the next one comes along is about three thousand kilometres.'

'Yes, so if it was a radio wave, you would normally need an aerial at least one quarter of that to capture maximum energy from it,' said Prama. 'So it would need to be about seven hundred and fifty kilometres long. That's one of the reasons the latest gravitational wave detectors are many kilometres long. Even then they only capture small amounts of wave energy.'

'That's my problem,' said Francine. 'I don't understand how Jacques' gravitum crystal could capture any energy at all, given his crystal was about the size of a hen's egg.'

'We thought it was because the speed of gravitational waves in gravitum was incredibly slow, something like ten metres per second.'

'But that's ridiculous,' said Francine. 'Even sound travels many times faster than that.'

'That's true but we could find no other explanation,' said Prama. 'We just accepted it as an experimental fact and when Jacques stopped worrying about why the waves travel so slowly in gravitum, he started to work on what the consequences would be if it was indeed true.'

'Did he tell you any more?'

'Not really,' said Prama. 'I was working on other things.'

Francine thought for a moment.

'You mentioned you knew about six pieces of gravitum. You've only mentioned five, who has the sixth?'

'It's in space.'

Francine looked puzzled.

'It's in the Yakawa comet,' Prama explained. 'We think that the quantity of the gravitum on the comet is enough to absorb high levels of gravity wave energy and re-radiate it like a laser reemits light. The result is an intense beam of gravitational waves that regularly scan the Earth's surface. Both Paul and Hitzubishi used the beam that resulted as a trigger for their experiments. The other pieces come from a fragment that fell through the Earth's atmosphere in the early nineteenth century.'

'How can you be so certain?'

'Anil's software connected it to a tsunami that caused havoc in the Sea of Japan in eighteen twenty six. At that time, the beam's intensity had peaked. Also fragments of the comet fell in and around the same area. Last year, Hideo's survey vessel found one of the fragments near the centre of the tsunami, in the ocean to the South of Japan.'

'My God, so this stuff is dangerous then,' exclaimed Francine.

'It certainly looks that way,' said Prama. 'I still can't see a connection between Hitzubishi's device and nuclear fusion. Can you?'

'Not yet,' replied Francine. Perhaps if we pool our knowledge we may get somewhere. Where shall we start?'

'You can start by telling me about your project with nuclear fusion,' said Prama.

'Ok, the objective is to drive a steam turbine from the heat of nuclear fusion. This turbine then turns a mechanical generator.'

'It doesn't seem very efficient to me; going through two stages of energy conversion.'

'That's what Jacques used to say. Anyway, my project at the Centre for Fusion Research was based on tokamaks and plasma physics. As you know plasma is hot gas where the atoms are so hot that they have become separated from their outer electrons which move about separately from the rest of the atom.'

'Yes, I always like the example of a candle's flame.'

'You're right a flame, is plasma. The light of a candle comes from the electrons returning to charged atoms that previously lost their electrons due to the heat. Like children returning home to mummy.'

'Mummy being the atom,' said Prama. 'What's the tokamak for?' she asked.

'It is a device to hold the charged atoms, or ions, in a safe magnetic field. We heat them and crash them together to enable nuclear fusion. This then generates even more heat.'

'What, like an H bomb?'

'The fusion is the same but unlike a bomb, the fusion is controlled. I prefer to think about the reactions in the Sun. The idea of the tokamak is to control a tiny Sun inside a device that looks like a huge electric transformer…'

'You mean like the transformer they use in the electricity power grid?' interrupted Prama.

'Almost,' she continued, 'the magnetic field in the tokamak traps and energises the plasma.'

'How does it do that?'

'The transformers in the power grid have coils of wire called the primary winding that is powered by the generating source. A varying magnetic field created by the primary coil generates an alternating electric current in a second coil that is used to distribute the power that lights our houses and boils our kettles.'

'What's that got to do with the tokamak?'

'Our tokamak has heating coils and incredibly powerful superconducting magnets that behave like a transformer's primary winding. The secondary however, is not made of wire; it is hot gas, plasma.'

'And that lets you drive the plasma to temperatures that will cause atoms to bang together and cause a fusion reaction?'

'Yes, the fusion reaction gives off lots of energy. In theory we can turn the energy into electricity. There are other ways of generating the high temperatures needed for fusion, like powerful lasers, but my project involves a tokamak.'

'All of them convert the energy into electricity using conventional steam turbines and generators?'

'That's the idea, but to do this we must keep the energy flow constant and stable. This is where we have had problems.'

'I still can't see any connection to gravitational waves. They are all about "big physics" not the "microscopic world" of nuclear physics.'

'Big physics?'

'Stars, neutron stars, black holes and things like that,' said Prama elaborating.

'Well Jacques was never one to respect boundaries like "big" or "small",' said Francine.

'Do you think this is what Jacques was looking into?'

'I don't know,' admitted Francine. 'He had been prattling on about the weaknesses of the tokamak approach for years. I thought it was just hot air.'

'Was that pun intended?' asked Prama, sharp as ever.

'Not intended, I promise,' she said, pleased that she could talk about Jacques openly. She continued, 'I never thought his ideas about nuclear fusion were a real passion of his. I said earlier, I thought he brought the subject up to tease me.'

'Well, he could be mischievous,' said Prama, 'and that would have been typical of him, wouldn't it? But this looks like a serious piece of research. Shall I print it off so we can both read it thoroughly?'

'Good idea.'

Prama gave Francine a printed copy. They sat down and quietly read the draft paper.

****

The phone rang at the front desk. The sergeant answered it.

'Ok, I'll take him through,' he said.

He put the phone down and addressed Paul.

'I'll show you into one of the interview rooms,' he said.

'Here goes,' said Paul under his breath.

He followed the sergeant into a small room. It had a desk in the centre with chairs arranged at either side. He had been sitting down too long, so he decided to walk around the room to get the blood back into his legs. The door opened abruptly, making Paul jump.

'Detective Chief Inspector O'Reilly,' said the middle aged, balding figure in front of him. 'You must be Dr Dzibias.'

'Call me Paul, please,' he said, appearing more relaxed than he felt.

DCI O'Reilly was about five foot six and slightly too round for his height. He had a wide nose with tiny red blood vessels radiating out from the tip to the edge of his nostrils. He had the air of a man who liked a drink. He had small eyes but for all their diminutive status, they were cold and piercing blue. His clothes too, had seen better days. Paul hoped his talents lay in detective work and not sartorial elegance.

Paul held out his hand, but rather than shake it, O'Reilly made a gesture towards a chair behind a desk. The thinker was already seated on one of two chairs on the opposite side.

'Why don't you sit down,' he said.

Paul took his seat and waited expectantly for O'Reilly to start the conversation.

'If you don't mind, I'd like to ask you a few questions about Dr Degordes; the person.'

O'Reilly sat down next to the thinker.

'Of course,' said Paul, 'but I thought you wanted to hear about his work.'

'Yes, yes,' said O'Reilly impatiently. 'We can discuss his work later.'

'Alright,' said Paul, 'how can I help?'

'How well did you know Jacques Degordes?'

'He was a good friend,' he replied. 'I've known him for years. He was one of my supervisors when I did my doctorate.'

'How well do you know his wife and sons?'

'I have been a friend of the family for some years.'

'How often did you see Dr Degordes?'

'Last year we worked together on a big project that went pear-shaped,' Paul replied. 'Since then we've met a few times socially and exchanged loads of e-mails.'

'Socially?'

'As I said, Jacques and Francine are family friends. Claire, my wife and I have been to lots of barbeques and dinner parties with them. They are,' he paused, 'sorry, were amongst our closest friends. What are you getting at?'

'Oh, I'm just trying to get some background,' said O'Reilly, casually. 'Do you know of anyone who would want Jacques Degordes or his son dead?'

The question hit Paul like a bullet. 'So they think someone wanted to murder Jacques,' thought Paul, looking worried. He was suddenly in a quandary. Should he tell O'Reilly about his suspicions about Tokyo or would he be blowing things out of proportion? He decided to hold his line; for a while at least.

O'Reilly noticed the change in Paul's demeanour, but let it pass.

'No, I don't know anyone who disliked him.' said Paul, emphatically. 'He was a charming guy. He could be irritating, but always likable. Why would anyone want him dead?'

'That's what I'm trying to find out,' said O'Reilly, fixing Paul between the eyes. 'Did he have any enemies?'

'None that would want to kill him,' said Paul, quickly. 'He was an academic, his role was to challenge and enquire.'

'So he had disagreements with many people?'

'Yes, but that was his job. There is always conflict in academia, but it is no more than the sparring you find in a sport like tennis. The conflict is part of the process. Everybody understands that.'

'Bare knuckle boxing is a sparring sport that everybody understands but people can end up dead.'

'Well they say the pen is mightier than the sword, but I'm not sure it is meant literally.'

O'Reilly was not amused.

'I want you to think harder, Dr Dzibias,' he said, pressing Paul. 'Did Jacques upset anybody who would want him dead?'

Paul's brow became furrowed in thought. He realised that he could not hold out any longer.

'Well there was the Tokyo experiment but why Jacques?..,' he paused.

'Yes, go on.'

'I don't see how it could be relevant; Jacques was only one person in a team of half a dozen people.'

'Everything about Jacques Degordes is relevant. Now please go on,' his voice insistent.

'Okay,' said Paul, taking a breath. 'About six months ago, Jacques and I were members of a team that helped terminate a project in Tokyo.'

'Terminate?'

'Stopped,' said Paul elaborating.

'You mean sabotaged?' asked O'Reilly, rhetorically.

'If you like,' replied Paul. He went on, 'Anyway, as I said Jacques was an advisor to the team. Prama and my wife Claire were in Japan and the rest of us at the end of a telephone line in London.'

'This project you sabotaged,' said O'Reilly, beginning to smell a lead. 'Whose was it?'

'It was led by a Japanese guy called Hitzubishi san,' he replied. 'He was sponsored by a large Japanese energy company, based in Tokyo.'

'Where is he now?'

'I don't know. He disappeared straight after the experiment was aborted.'

'You mean the experiment you sabotaged,' O'Reilly corrected. 'Go on.'

'The experiment was very dangerous. It should never have been set up in a populated area like downtown Tokyo.'

'Why not?'

'Because, if it had gone ahead, it would have started an earthquake in one of the most populated cities in the world.'

'So you and your colleagues sabotaged it?'

'Yes,' said Paul. 'Hideo…'

'Hideo?'

'Sorry, Aoki Hideo. He is an expert on earthquakes and he found out what Hitzubishi san was doing and asked for Prama and Claire's help.'

'They brought me in and I asked Jacques to help me.'

'Why did they bring you in?'

'A few days earlier, I had done a similar experiment in my laboratory.'

'Where is that?'

'It was ten miles outside London,' said Paul. 'You see, the experiment created earth tremors that destroyed my equipment and the laboratory.'

'And this guy in Tokyo, Hitsob…'

'Hitzubishi san,' said Paul, helping.

O'Reilly continued, '..Hitzubishi san was doing the same experiment?'

'Almost the same,' said Paul. 'He was using a compound we discovered called gravitum.'

'You've lost me,' said O'Reilly, puzzled.

'Why is gravitum important?' asked the thinker, speaking for the first time.

'My experiment proved that if we put the compound under pressure, it could focus radiation from space and convert it to electro magnetic and acoustic energy,' said Paul.

'You mean radio waves and sound?' asked the thinker.

Paul was impressed. O'Reilly rolled his eyes.

'More specifically X-rays, light and sound.'

In spite of himself, O'Reilly decided to let the inane conversation continue. He sat back to let the thinker probe further.

'So you thought the Tokyo project would cause tremors and then an earthquake,' said the thinker.

'Exactly,' said Paul warming to him. 'My experiment was bad enough but the Tokyo gravitum crystal was much bigger and because their project was in an earthquake zone, it had to be stopped!'

'I see,' said O'Reilly, rejoining the conversation. 'I bet that pissed off Hisoboshi, whatever his name is, no end!'

'I expect so,' said Paul. 'But Jacques was only peripheral to the sabotage, as you call it. There would have been at least four other people ahead of him in the queue, including me. I can't see why Hitzubishi san would have targeted him in particular.'

Silence fell over the trio as they absorbed the implications of the discussion. The thinker broke the silence.

'Is this gravitum compound very common?' he asked, somewhat tangentially.

Believing that this question was borne of idle curiosity on the thinker's part, O'Reilly was about to stop the interview. The thinker gave him a look as if he had read his mind. O'Reilly sat back and did nothing.

'I only know of three known sets of gravitum,' said Paul.

'Could you explain?'

'Sure, the first was used in my experiment and the second in Hitzubishi san's apparatus,' said Paul.

'And the third?' asked the thinker.

'It's in space,' he said, 'in the core of the Yakawa comet. We believe the crystals used by me and Hitzubishi san were debris from a meteorite; maybe from the comet's tail.'

'So the gravitum crystals would be pretty valuable would they?'

'Well, they're very rare but only to a few scientists like me know they exist and who else would buy them?'

'Maybe a few mad experimenters in earthquake zones,' commented O'Reilly under his breath.

'Where did Hitzubishi san get his crystal from?' asked the thinker.

'Hideo discovered it when a seismology research submarine dragged it off the sea bed in the South Japan Sea.'

'Where is the Japanese gravitum crystal now?' asked O'Reilly.

'I don't know,' said Paul. 'Hideo took it into the country away from the city.'

'Where is Hideo now?' asked the thinker.

'I don't know,' replied Paul, slowly. 'He disappeared after we terminated the Tokyo project.'

'At the same time that Hitzubishi san disappeared?' asked O'Reilly.

The thinker was impressed at O'Reilly's improved Japanese pronunciation.

'Yes,' said Paul, 'about the same time.'

'Where did you get your gravitum sample from?' asked O'Reilly, beginning to understand where the line of questioning was leading.

'Jacques Degordes,' said Paul, thoughtfully.

'Where is your crystal now?

'I've got it,' he replied, slowly. Paul paused.

'Oh shit!' he said. 'It's on the mantelpiece at home.'

# Twelve

## Lateral Thinking

Francine and Prama had taken their time reading Jacques' manuscript. Absorbed in the content, they had not exchanged a word for over half an hour.

'Fascinating,' said Prama, putting the paper down.

'It certainly is,' said Francine.

'It seems his idea would reduce much of the complexity needed to control nuclear fusion, contain the reaction and generate electricity,' said Prama pausing, 'But he has proposed a device that is similar to the conventional approach.'

'You mean he has invented something that looks just like a tokamak?'

'Yes.'

'It certainly has some similarities. He proposes to uses strong toroidal magnets. These induce a feedback effect to hold the plasma inside the fusion reactor,' replied Francine, enthusiastically. 'But he controls the flow of ions around the core with gravitational waves. I don't understand how that would work.'

'I can guess but I don't understand why he doesn't need turbines or mechanical generators.'

'Jacques' theory seems to be that the energy from the fusion reaction can be taken away as electromagnetic energy in the primary windings. This would reinforce the magnetic field and in turn decelerate the fusion products. The process should keep the temperature of the whole system lower,' said Francine.

'So it stops it turning into a fusion bomb and you can draw your electrical power from the primary windings,' said Prama. 'Brilliant.'

'That seems to be his idea, but it can't work,' said Francine.

'Why not?'

'Because a transformer needs a magnetic field that changes with time.'

'An alternating current,' said Prama.

'Yes. It looks like his concept is based on your experiences with the Tokyo Gravitational Wave Rectifier,' said Francine. 'I don't understand how that makes the magnetic field vary with time.'

'You're right it seems to have something to do with gravitum,' Prama confirmed. 'When I got back from Japan, he told me that he believed Hitzubishi's project was far more sophisticated than either Paul or he originally thought.'

'In what way?'

'Paul and Jacques each had a schematic of the Gravitational Wave Rectifier.'

'How did they get those?'

'Hideo sent them digital copies when he wanted their help to disable the device.'

'Oh I see,' said Francine, reflectively. 'You said that Jacques thought the device had hidden sophistication?'

'Yes, he said that inside the device, in the middle of a matrix of gravitum crystals, was a small chamber. When Paul and Jacques first saw it, it didn't seem important because they had other things on their minds.'

'Like disabling the device?' Francine asked, rhetorically.

'Yes, but by the time I got back to Manchester, he had realised that if the crystal was exposed to intense gravitational wave radiation the area inside the chamber would be a closed system of time and space.'

'Which means?'

'He reckoned it would create an artificial black hole, where clocks slow down or stop and space bends back on itself,' said Prama, thoughtfully.

'So you think he has extended this idea to create a safe bubble to control nuclear fusion?'

'Yes, his design is based on an old idea thought up by an Oxford professor in nineteen sixty nine. He suggested that if you inject stuff into a black hole in a carefully controlled way, you can decrease the total mass-energy of the black hole.'

'I don't understand.'

'It means that if you have an explosion next to a black hole where some of the bits are sucked in and others aren't, then you can extract energy from the black hole.'

'So bits captured by the black hole increase the energy of the bits that weren't captured?'

'Yes their mass is used to speed up the charged particles, ions, that don't fall into the black hole.'

'So the electrical current around the black hole increases?'

'As I understand it,' said Prama, 'his idea is to simulate a small variable black hole by generating intense gravity fields. This bends time and space into a circle. He drives the ions around the centre of the circle by altering the phase of the gravitational wave pulses.'

'So instead of varying the magnetic field, he varies time,' suggested Francine. 'He's using gravitational wave pulses and not alternating electric current?'

'I think so. He extracts power by electrical induction from ions circulating near the black hole's horizon,' replied Prama. 'He's fooled the tokamak into believing it is truly an electrical transformer in the national power distribution system.'

'So he's used my tokamak as a simple transformer. If it worked, it would revolutionize power generation and produce electricity at a fraction of its current cost,' said Francine, feeling proud that the man she had loved had come up with such an idea.

They looked at each other in amazement, thinking about the consequences of such an invention.

'I'm confused. It seems such a brilliant idea,' said Francine, breaking the silence. 'Surely someone must have thought of it before?'

'There have been similar theories,' replied Prama. 'As I mentioned it was dreamt up in nineteen sixty nine. But the problem was where do you get the black hole from? They tend to swallow things up!'

'Sounds dangerous.'

'You could say that. This idea creates an artificial black hole by constructing a stationary gravitational wave. It's very clever.'

'What is a stationary wave?'

'The best example I can think of is a tsunami, but in this case it is more like a vortex. It's a wave that self-reinforces itself. It can remain stable for a long time.'

'But none of this will work without gravitum crystals?'

'Yes that's right, and it's not one of the most common substances on Earth! Our guess about Jacques' theory was right,' Prama continued. 'He didn't know why, but gravitational waves travel very slowly in gravitum. This means that the wavelength of gravitational waves is so small that a crystal can absorb many waves in a small space. By pressurising the crystal you can make it re-emit them.'

'It seems simple,' said Francine, impressed. 'Is it?'

'He needed four crystals arranged so that waves from one crystal trigger waves in its neighbours that, in turn, pass waves on to their neighbours.'

'And they keep doing that until the waves are trapped going round and round in circles, creating an artificial black hole.'

'The whole thing can be turned on or off by altering the pressure applied to the surface of the crystals,' said Prama.

'Well, there is one fly in the ointment,' said Francine, trying to control her enthusiasm. 'Where do you get the gravitum from?'

'Yes that could be a problem,' said Prama. 'Maybe it is in some of his notes.'

Prama looked at her watch.

'Oh,' she said. 'Look at the time. I've arranged to meet Claire. Do you want to come along?'

'Are you sure?' Francine asked, looking as though she would like to. 'I'm not very good company at the moment. I don't want to be a dampener.'

'Yes, I'm sure. She'd like to say hello.'

Francine took her copy of Jacques' manuscript and the wedge of paper she had collected from the bins and put them into a briefcase that Jacques had kept in his office. She moved into the corridor outside as Prama locked up behind them.

****

They met Claire in a wine bar near the university. She had travelled up with Paul for his encounter with O'Reilly. He still hadn't returned from the police station.

'Hello Claire.'

It was Prama who had spoken first.

'Hello Francine,' said Claire, with a sympathetic smile. 'I wasn't expecting you. I'm pleased you're here. How are you?'

'All the better for being with you,' she said.

'Don't forget me!' said Prama, in mock offense.

Claire gave them both a peck on the cheek.

'Why don't you sit over there,' said Francine pointing to an empty table. 'I'll get our usual three dry white wines,' she said and headed towards the bar to get some drinks.

'She looks a little agitated,' said Claire, perceptively.

'She's a woman on a mission,' said Prama, quietly. 'I'm a little worried about her.'

'Jacques' death must have hit her very hard,' said Claire. 'It seems to affect different people in different ways. I'm not sure how I would cope in similar circumstances.'

'I know, it must be terrible but there is more,' said Prama, with a frown. 'I don't think she believes he's dead.'

'Oh, I see.'

'She'll need all her friends to help her through this period. She's finding it tough.'

Before Claire could say any more, Francine returned with the drinks and sat down.

'So how did Paul's meeting with the police go?' asked Francine.

'I don't know,' she said. 'He's still there.'

'Well I wish I could say I'm surprised,' said Francine. 'He's very methodical and thorough but O'Reilly does take his time.'

'I've met him as well,' said Prama. 'He came to the university to interview Jacques' colleagues. He's rather blunt.'

'Well, I am a little worried about Paul,' said Claire, anxiously. 'He was very tense before the interview.'

'In what way?' asked Prama, with a concerned expression.

'He was worried about his part in sabotaging the Tokyo project.'

'But that wasn't sabotage,' said Prama defensively. 'We had to do it to stop an earthquake. You know that. You were there with Hideo.'

'That's what we all believed,' said Claire, 'but as Paul looked more deeply into Hitzubishi's plans he found that his device was more sophisticated than he had thought. Paul called Jacques a few weeks before he disappeared to compare notes. Jacques seemed to agree.'

'Oh,' said Prama thoughtfully.

'So Paul is worried he may have been responsible for stopping a perfectly legitimate experiment?' said Francine.

'I think so and he's worried that the police may think we broke the law by helping Hideo steal Hitzubishi's device.' said Claire.

'I don't think O'Reilly will care about an offence in Japan unless it has some bearing on his investigation,' said Francine.

'Paul shouldn't worry. O'Reilly's a pussy cat really,' said Prama, smiling.

'I suppose you're right,' said Claire, brightening. 'Anyway what have you two been up to?' she said conspiratorially.

Prama told Claire about the draft academic paper that they had discovered in Jacques' office and Francine explained a few of the practical implications. Claire was silent whilst she absorbed the information.

'What do you think?' asked Francine, enthusiastically.

'I'm sure Paul would understand, but I'm not sure I do,' said Claire apologetically. 'I'm sorry to be slow but I'm a biochemist, not a physicist. I'm just married to one and that's bad enough.'

'I know what you mean,' said Francine wistfully.

'Oh, I'm sorry Francine,' said Claire, touching Francine's arm. 'Comments like that must be painful. I didn't mean to be so thoughtless.'

'Don't be silly, Claire,' said Francine with a distant smile. 'You just reminded me of some lovely thoughts. I'm starting to move on now. Or at least I know how to.'

'You know how to?'

'I am going to apply myself to find out what happened to Jacques,' said Francine.

'This doesn't sound like moving on,' thought Claire.

She searched Prama's face for support. She returned a look that said, 'See what I mean?'

'I know what you're thinking Claire,' started Francine gently. 'I realise that Jacques is probably dead, but they haven't found his remains and perhaps they never will. But it leaves a question and if there is a tiny possibility he is still alive then I want to be there for him.'

This did not make Claire look any more comfortable. Prama looked at Francine sternly and nodded her head towards Claire to tell Francine that she was not finished.

'I have promised Prama that if she tells me I'm becoming obsessive, then I will stop and get on with my life.'

Claire looked at Prama for confirmation. She said nothing but gently nodded. Claire, her head slightly cocked, looked sadly at Francine.

Unsure of what to say, Claire continued falteringly, 'Paul and I were so heartbroken when we heard about the accident. I couldn't imagine what you were feeling. I was so sad for you and the boys. I don't know what I would have done if it had been Paul,' she paused collecting her words. 'But…'

'I know what you're trying to say,' said Francine, gently interrupting. 'You, Paul and Prama have all been such good friends to Jacques and me. You don't want to see me hurt even more by allowing me to live an unrealistic hope. I promise I will let him go,' she paused, her eyes moist, 'I will, but not yet. I can't bury him yet. Not whilst Amaury can't tell me what happened. Not whilst there are so many unanswered questions.'

'I hate to say this,' said Claire, a tear sliding down her cheek, 'but what if Amaury can't remember anything?'

'Or worse, he doesn't wake up at all,' said Francine interrupting again, to help Claire by voicing what she was thinking. 'I have turned all these things over in my mind again and again. Next to Jacques, you and Prama are my closest friends. If you tell me I will stop.'

She transferred her gaze from Claire to Prama and back.

'Look at us,' she said, 'I'll have you both in tears soon. Let's talk about what Prama and I have found out today. It's not sad at all, in fact I'm proud of what Jacques was doing. Perhaps we can give new life to his work if not Jacques himself.'

Francine took a tissue from her handbag and wiped her eyes. She put the packet of tissues on the table between them and smiled.

'Try one of these. They seem to help,' she said. 'I like to plan ahead. I thought we may need them.'

Claire and Prama took one each and followed her example.

'Once a project manager always a project manager,' said Prama, returning the smile.

'Ok,' said Claire, recovered. 'But as I said I'm no use to you. I'm a biochemist. I won't be able to understand anything Jacques was doing.'

'You may not be a physicist or engineer but you have one of the best analytical minds there is. Jacques used to say so,' said Francine.

Claire blushed.

'Ok I give in, tell me what you found out. But slowly please I want to have a few brain cells left afterwards.'

Prama and Francine explained what they had discovered about Jacques' last piece of research.

'You say it's a simple idea,' said Claire, with a frown. 'But that's just from your perspective. From where I sit, everything you have told me sounds horrendously complicated.'

She smiled at them and continued, 'But being a mere biochemist, I have noticed that without gravitum none of Jacques' theory will work.'

'She's not as slow as she pretends,' said Prama, teasing her.

'The only piece of gravitum I know about is on the mantelpiece in our flat,' said Claire. 'I keep asking Paul why he doesn't keep it somewhere else as it's so dangerous. He says it's perfectly safe at normal atmospheric pressures and I shouldn't worry. Then I remind him it was responsible for destroying his laboratory and shouldn't we wait until we'd paid for the flat before it was reduced to rubble.'

'Typical man,' said Prama, 'Didn't Jacques have it on a bookshelf in his office for years?'

'Yes he did,' said Francine, 'and before that he kept it in his study at home.'

'So Jacques has had the crystal for years?' asked Claire.

'Yes, I can't remember when I first saw it. I used to think it was just another piece of junk, like so many of the things he seemed to collect around him.'

Prama and Claire smiled fondly at the memory of Jacques' untidy office.

'Do you know where he got it from?' asked Prama.

'I've no idea,' said Francine. 'Probably a field trip somewhere or a gift from one of the international conferences he attended.'

'I wonder if anybody else knows where it came from,' said Claire thinking aloud. 'What about the article he was writing?'

'I'm sorry, Claire, I don't understand,' said Francine puzzled.

'Have you found out whether he had any co-authors?' Claire continued. 'Perhaps they would know about the origin of the crystal.'

Prama and Francine looked at each other.

'Why hadn't I thought of that?' they thought simultaneously.

'Surely, Jacques would have had one or more co-authors to help him refine his ideas. It would smooth the paper through the academic review before publication,' she said.

Francine pulled the paper out of Jacques' old brief case. There were no other names on it, only Jacques.'

'Nothing here,' she said, discouraged.

'Can I have a look?' said Claire reaching out for the paper.

Francine passed it to her.

'Some of the references are interesting. One of these may be a co-author. What do you think?' she asked handing the paper to Prama.

'Yes some of the names are familiar,' said Prama. 'I remember Jacques mentioning Dmitry Obukov.'

'That name rings a bell with me,' said Francine. 'Jacques mentioned a colleague called Dmitry. I think he was based in St Petersburg. Can I have another look, please?'

Prama handed the document back to her.

'Yes, that fits. He could be one of the co-authors.'

Claire looked at her watch.

'I'm afraid I've got to go and find Paul, I'm getting a bit worried,' she said regretfully, 'I hope they haven't arrested him.'

'I'm sure he'll be alright,' said Francine.

'Yes, but I must go. I'll tell Paul about everything. I'm sure he'll help as well,' she said, standing up and putting her handbag over her shoulder. 'I'll call when I get home.'

'It would be lovely if you could think about what we've said and call me back on your thoughts.'

Claire agreed and they made their goodbyes. She left for the train.

'It's time I left also,' said Francine.

'Oh, do you have to?' asked Prama, supportively.

'I'm afraid so,' she replied. 'You've been a dear. I don't know how I could have got through the day without your help, Prama.'

'I've enjoyed helping, what are our next steps?'

'I'm going to give our Russian friend a call tomorrow morning and see if he was involved in the early drafts. Have you the time to go through Jacques' e-mails and see whether he sent any early drafts to anybody?'

'Yes maam,' said Prama. 'I'll be back on the trail first thing tomorrow morning.'

****

Anatoly was waiting outside the professor's room as usual for his weekly tutorial. He was nervous because he did not fully understand the concepts of the electro weak interaction that were part of this week's assignment. He had been waiting for about five minutes, when his two fellow students came to join him. They were late.

'Has he turned up yet?' asked Viktor. 'I hope he's forgotten. I haven't got my head round this week's assignment.'

'I don't know about you two wimps, but I'm going in,' said Grigory, trying the door.

It was locked.

'That's strange,' said Anatoly. 'What's that funny smell.'

'Perhaps the old boy is bonking some old babushka!' said Grigory, mischievously. 'Was there a slow rhythmic noise with heavy breathing?'

'A babushka! I'm not sure he could even manage one of those at his age,' said Vitoria, confirming their belief that anybody over thirty was old and decrepit.

They laughed picturing the scene.

'I'm going find out where he is from administration,' said Anatoly. 'I've got another lecture in twenty minutes.'

'You're keen,' said Vitoria, disappointed that he may end up having the tutorial after all.

Anatoly marched off towards the admin office and returned with a severe looking lady brandishing keys. She unlocked and opened the door, whilst they waited outside. The smell became stronger.

The administrator entered. There was a loud scream. Anatoly peered around the edge of the door. The administrator was on her knees vomiting. The smell was awful.

'What the hell's happened?' he thought.

'Get out,' she yelled, hysterically, 'and fetch the police!'

He looked across towards the Professor Obukov's desk. Anatoly stepped back out of the room, his face white with shock.

'The professor has been murdered,' he said catching his breath. 'It looks like he's been dead for days.'

The administrator staggered out, her hand over her nose and mouth.

'Get the police,' she said.

They froze.

'Now!' she shouted. 'Go!'

# Thirteen

## Kindred Spirit

When Prama and Francine had seen the appointment in one of Jacques' old diary entries, they had not placed any special significance on his presentation to the Astrophysics Conference at the University of Osaka. The paper and transcript of his talk were amongst the hundreds of documents filed under the rather pompous title of Conferences and Symposia. Jacques had been a very popular presenter, his style being both charismatic and thought provoking. The organiser of the conference had known Prama during her eventful sabbatical at the Centre for Gravitational Research in Osaka and Jacques had been invited to the city under Prama's recommendation. The organiser wanted to break up the monotony of day to day updates on the results of experiments with something more imaginative. Prama could think of no one better than Jacques to rise to the challenge. Jacques had presented at many conferences like this one and had a wealth of material to draw from.  This time he chose a topic that was, in line with his reputation, innovative and challenging. Most of the more open minded of his audience loved it, but there were some who were irritated by the underlying criticism of a modern approach to science. Prama had heard later from one of her old colleagues that his presentation had gone down well. Jacques enjoyed being at the centre of controversy but it was not the content of his presentation that triggered later events; it was two of the delegates.

Jacques stood up in front of his audience and instantly the jet-lag from the long-haul flight disappeared. There was something about an audience that energised him and tired or not, this group was about to receive a performance. For some time Jacques had believed that many ideas are killed either because they come into conflict with someone's self-interest or there is a climate of cynical disinterest. Jacques had decided to speak on Non Linear Astrophysics. This rather dull title did not do justice to a topic which had remained outside conventional science for many years. He had chosen the subject because it illustrated that an idea that had been rejected by the establishment could turn out to give deep insight into modern physics when rediscovered many years later. As an anecdote Jacques gave the example of a young marine engineer, John Scott Russell, who in August eighteen thirty-four was examining the bow wave of a horse drawn canal barge when a rope that was connected to his apparatus came loose. Russell looked along the canal ahead of the barge and noticed that part of the bow wave continued without the pressure of the advancing vessel. He followed this solitary wave on horse back for some miles that in Russell's words, "travelled without change of form or diminution of speed". Had Russell been an eminent scientist, his observation would have been heralded as a great discovery. As it was, the establishment dismissed his observation as an aberration because it did not fit into the prevailing theory at the time. It was not until the late nineteen eighties when details of his ideas were revealed to students of physics. Jacques believed that this was an example of a plethora of missed opportunities that were suppressed because of vested interest or closed minds. Whatever the motives, the actions continued to hold the discipline back to that day.

'Now,' said Jacques, towards the end of his presentation, 'the theory of stationary waves, solitons, is an established concept that has importance in theories as diverse as the efficient transmission of light in optical fibres, the existence of Tsunamis, electrons and other elementary particles.'

He paused and looked around the room.

'What,' he said, 'would be the state of modern science today, if Russell's ideas had been accepted and available to the scientific and engineering community over one hundred years earlier? Would it have given us a head start on string theory, plasma physics and telecommunications? Would everybody have had internet access fifty years earlier, no matter where they lived?'

He concluded, 'Perhaps electricity from nuclear fusion would now be a fact not a prediction for thirty years hence. We owe it to the generations that follow us, to be more open minded than the generations before and to seek out negative self-interest and destroy it.'

In spite of themselves the establishment applauded as much as the up-and-coming. Jacques' presentation had gone down well and after the organiser had given Jacques a gushing thank you, several delegates came over to thank him personally. One member of the establishment was very keen to corner Jacques. He was a member of the old guard of Russian academics and had been a recognised authority in plasma physics long before many of the other delegates had been born.

'Ah Dr Degordes, he's the man who stretches his argument beyond the ridiculous to the outrageous!' he said in a raised voice to the lady standing next to him. His comment cut through the background noise and reached Jacques' ears.

Dmitry had devoted his whole life to understand how the physical things around him were connected; how they worked; why they responded the way they did. At an early age his teachers realised that he had a gift for science and although it almost broke his heart he was separated from his family and given the best education the soviet system could provide. This cruel action imprinted his character with self-sufficiency and solitary personality. This single-mindedness had enabled him to build his way almost to the top of his country's academic structure. Now white haired and in his early sixties, his natural intelligence was honed by education and brain exercise to be as sharp as a razor. He was respected by his colleagues and feared by his students. Dmitry had many colleagues but few close friends. His parents were long dead and there was no time left to build new human relationships. Without exception, those friends that he had were based on mutual interests. He had no time for self-interest, nationalism, politics, or causes. He was married to science or more specifically physics.

It was his passion and except for the occasional lecture he expended most of his energy with his experiments or gazing at the universe through the university's massive telescope.

Jacques expression became tense as he turned round ready for an argument. Then his face softened into a smile.

'Alors, do I see my old sparring partner Dmitry?' he asked, shaking the proffered hand warmly. 'I see you are the same old curmudgeon as usual. I hope you don't think the jet lag will stop me arguing. Are you sure you're up to it?' he teased.

The other people in earshot relaxed and were disappointed in equal measure, when they saw that these two giants of physics were not about to start an intellectual dual but were indulging in good-natured insults. Clearly they were old friends. Most of the delegates were surprised that Professor Dmitry Obukov had any!

'I'm not as young as I was, Jacques but I'm sure I can match you in a debate,' he said. 'However this time I found your lecture disturbing, engaging and unusually coherent.'

'Thank you,' said Jacques, thinking he had received a compliment. 'But disturbing?' asked Jacques, not knowing exactly what he meant.

'I believe I would call myself one of the establishment,' he paused, smiling. 'Mind you, given what has happened to Russian establishments over the last ninety years, I suppose I'm used to being disturbed.'

'Je comprends,' said Jacques, then remembering that Dmitry did not speak French, 'I understand. France too has had its fair share of revolution, but that's not what I was talking about. I support openness to ideas; ideas that should be shared and developed for all mankind. I think there is too much negativity and secrecy.'

'But surely many ideas are just crazy, others allow people to make a living and the rest are dangerous.'

'Dmitry, if you don't mind me saying; that's an interesting idea in itself. I think that if we publish all the ideas, including the dangerous ones, then the resulting shared knowledge is the best protection for mankind.'

Jacques paused aware that he was starting to lecture again.

'Je suis désolée,' he said. 'I am becoming a bore. Can I buy you a coffee?'

They had known each other for years and this kind of sparring was normal between Jacques and Dmitry. When they had first met they immediately respected each other's intellect and enjoyed the banter. In contrast with Jacques' personality Dmitry's appeared to be somewhat austere. However when he shared a bottle of vodka with Jacques, Dmitry's persona was transformed.

'I never asked you why you became interested in plasma physics Jacques,' said Dmitry over a cup of coffee, 'when there are far more glamorous subjects like particle physics.'

'Oh, you mean like the Large Hadron Collider project?' replied Jacques. 'Yes, I suppose that is more glamorous.'

'That's where all your European friends seem to be working.'

'Alors, my subject became a passion when I realised that most of the universe is plasma. I thought that the subject would give me plenty of scope for a lifetime of research. What's your excuse?'

'You mean, how did I get into plasma physics?' asked Dmitry. 'It became an interest when I was a child,'

Jacques looked puzzled and Dmitry realised his statement had been a little too enigmatic, so he decided to elaborate.

'Oh I can see I've lost you,' he said. 'When I was about nine, my grandmother told me a story that intrigued me.'

'One day as a child in a village near Lake Ladoga she was sitting at home looking out of the window at a thunder storm. Suddenly a bright glowing ball came out of the sky and bounced along the street. It did not seem to follow any rational path, it just rattled around like a pin-ball, scattering sparks as it collided with objects in the street.'

'What was it?' asked Jacques, trying to work out an approximate date when this could have happened, 'an incendiary or something?'

'Although there was brooding unrest in Russia, this was a relatively peaceful time, so I don't think so.'

'Anyway the people in the street panicked because they thought it was a secret weapon. It caused a riot that was put down quite violently by the authorities.'

'Did anybody find out who fired the weapon?'

'That's the point,' he said. 'My grandmother didn't think it was a weapon. She thought it came from the storm.'

'I see, you mean ball lightening,' said Jacques, the penny dropping. He continued dubiously 'Does the phenomenon really exist?'

'You ask me that after your presentation?' said Dmitry, in a mocking tone. 'I believe that a ball of plasma is formed due to the high temperature and the large electromagnetic radiation produced by the lightning'

'And the ball is formed into a bound stable state?' asked Jacques, chastened.

'Yes that's right,' he replied. 'My grandmother told her parents what she had seen and they told her she must have imagined it, her idea was dangerous and to forget about it. So for years she was too frightened to tell anybody else; until she told me. And the explanation of what she saw became my quest.'

'This is your reason for specialising in plasma physics?' said Jacques. 'So have you answered your grandmother's question?'

'Partially,' he replied. 'I have managed to simulate ball lightning in the lab. As you say, the phenomenon seems to be hot stable plasma, held in a self reinforcing electromagnetic field.'

'Like a soliton,' said Jacques, becoming interested in a new application of one of his pet subjects.

'Yes, and I create the ball by irradiating the plasma with strong microwave radiation. You could use a microwave oven and ions from a flame to do the same thing. Plasma balls bounce around inside the casing. My experiment creates plasma objects that are stable for many minutes.'

'Fascinating,' said Jacques. 'I've been looking into another aspect of plasma research where your ideas may be helpful..'

Jacques was just about to continue with his thought when the organiser of the conference appeared next to them with another delegate. The proximity of the newcomers broke Jacques' train of thought and the organiser took the pause in their conversation as his cuee to speak.

'Please excuse me Dr Degordes, I am Putyatin from the STKi Corporation. I am very keen to talk to you.'

An immaculately tailored businessman in his mid forties confronted Jacques. He was a slightly built man, shorter than Jacques at around five foot six. Putyatin wore wire-rimmed specs that did nothing to obscure his piercing cold blue eyes. His light brown hair was cut short and coated in some kind of coiffure's product that made him look as though he had just walked out of a Milanese fashion shop. Jacques had heard of STKiC. It was a secretive research company responsible for patenting many ideas that never saw the light of day. The corporation was engaged in just the kind of vested interest that he had just criticised. He was surprised that one of their employees would want to talk to him.

'Enchanté,' said Jacques, holding out his hand.

'Pleased to meet you,' said Putyatin, smoothly through his thin lips and returning a weak handshake.

Dmitry turned to see the newcomers. He appeared to recognise Putyatin and took a step back. For some reason, he did not want to be part of the conversation.

Dmitry turned to Jacques and said, 'Perhaps we can meet up later, and finish our conversation then?'

'Bien sûr,' said Jacques, keen to continue the chat with his old friend.

'I understand that you have an interest in nuclear fusion,' said Putyatin, completely ignoring Dmitry.

Dmitry drifted away.

'Only in as much as it involves the creation of high temperature plasmas,' he replied modestly.

'I have read your paper on gravitational wave detection. I was fascinated by your discovery of gravitum,' he said, with an insipid smile. 'Does it really exist?'

'To be sure,' said Jacques. 'but it was not my paper, I was just one of the co-authors. Paul Dzibias wrote it.'

'Of course, of course,' said Putyatin, dismissing the point. 'I'm sure you are aware that my company specialises in energy production, so fusion is very interesting to us.'

'I thought you were a natural gas company,' said Jacques, only partly interested in the conversation.

'Yes, that is true, but we have a large research programme related to other types of energy generation. We are looking for a new head of research.'

Jacques, realised that he was being propositioned and although he was flattered by the approach, he had heard some bad things about the ruthlessness of the STKiC.

'I am not very familiar with your company,' said Jacques, cagily. 'Where is it based?'

'Our European HQ is in Moscow,' he replied. 'The company is led by Mikhail Berezov. I report directly to him as, the head of the intellectual property division.'

'So you're a lawyer?' asked Jacques, rhetorically.

'Yes,' he said, with a condescending smile.

Now that his curriculum vitae were out of the way Putyatin seemed to feel he could get straight to the point.

'We have a number of patents related to nuclear fusion and we want to recruit a highly experienced plasma scientist to lead our push to dominate the fusion market. The job is to ensure we keep our commercial leadership position. I have spoken to Mr Berezov and he agrees that you are the best person for the job.'

For a moment Jacques was uncharacteristically speechless.

Putyatin continued, 'STKiC will find you somewhere to live, pay you an exceptional salary and bonus. We will employ your wife as well. In fact it is a condition that she either works for STKiC or not at all. We can't lose all our secrets to pillow talk after all,' he said, with an odd smile.

Jacques could not quite put his finger on it but there was something menacing about Putyatin. Although the man was outwardly courteous, Jacques felt uncomfortable. Putyatin was just a businessman, a manager, he had said nothing threatening. Besides how could he? Jacques had been offered commercial jobs before and turned them down. He had to admit that this one appeared to be very lucrative, but a voice at the back of his brain told him to be careful. He did not know why but he had taken an instant dislike to Putyatin. More tangibly, he did not like the thought of some of his best ideas being locked inside commercial patents, only to be revealed when an anonymous corporate bourgeoisie allowed them to see the light of day.

'Perhaps my French roots are showing,' he thought. 'I'll stall him'

'I'd like more information and a written explanation of the terms and conditions,' he said, quickly taking control of the conversation.

'I will put that in motion immediately. You have forty-eight hours to decide.'

And with that Putyatin, turned on his heel and left, leaving Jacques standing alone with his thoughts.

****

Jacques met Dmitry in the bar of the conference hotel.

'Do you know Putyatin?' asked Jacques, remembering Dmitry's earlier discomfort.

'No. I know about him,' said Dmitry cryptically.

'But you know more about him than I do!' said Jacques, probing for more information.

'He works as a lawyer for Berezov,' he said, thinking of how to frame the rest of his sentence, 'I think lawyer is a polite way of describing his profession.'

'I don't comprehend,' said Jacques.

'I understand that he learnt his law whilst working for the KGB. There have been many job opportunities for his kind over the last years, but they seldom result in defending clients in court.'

'I can only guess why STKiC wants to talk to you but Jacques you must understand; I do not like these people. You may think I am biased and old school but their plan is built on a US commercial model that goes against everything I stand for.'

'Comment?' asked Jacques, intrigued.

'They steal ideas and patent them.'

'Ah,' said Jacques, becoming very uncomfortable.

'They offered me a job as well, you know,' Dmitry volunteered. 'I refused their offer. STKiC did not push very hard because when they checked on my research, they decided that nothing I knew would damage their commercial interests. They left me alone after that.'

'They've offered me the job as their head of fusion research,' said Jacques, uncertainly.

'Be careful my friend,' said Dmitry, concerned.

'Do you think they are serious?'

'Oh yes, very serious, but I would not take their offer at face value,' he replied enigmatically.

'Dmitry, I have known you a long time. Do I have to get you drunk before you'll tell me everything that is on your mind?'

Dmitry considered Jacques' words for a few moments. He seemed to come to a decision.

'A drink could help,' said Dmitry, smiling. 'Mine is a vodka.'

They ordered four vodkas and sat down at a table out of earshot of the bar's other customers.

'They offered me a research job,' said Dmitry, after two glasses of vodka arrived for each of them. 'That's better,' he said taking a slug from the first one.

'And you turned them down?' he asked sipping his drink.

'No, I went along with them for a bit,' said Dmitry. 'They interviewed me about Paul Dzibias' gravitational wave experiment and asked whether I could repeat it.'

'What did you say?'

'I said I couldn't. Besides, I didn't have access to any gravitum crystals anymore and without them there was no way I could capture and focus the gravitational waves.'

'I'd forgotten you gave the Sky crystal to me. It was after one of our drinking evenings. You really should take more water you know,' said Jacques.

'It doesn't matter, even if I had the stone, I would never have come up with the idea of pressurising it.'

'So you think STKiC wants to use our gravitum idea to generate energy.'

'I believe that their reserves of gas will at some point run out. So they have developed a strategy to collect all the energy patents they can and make their business out of international royalties.'

'What do you know about STKiC?'

'Isn't it a Russian energy company based in Moscow?'

'That's what they want you to think but the first four letters of STKiC stand for of Shishi Toki Kyoudai Industries.'

'They're Japanese?'

'Japanese and Russian; they are part of a huge, private Russo-Japanese industrial corporation, that was formed in the late nineteenth century by disenfranchised samurai called the Shishi. They were members of a ruthless brotherhood who set up a business near Vladivostok.'

'What?'

'The company is privately owned. So there is very little published about them. I did some research. Shishi Toki Kyoudai means Shishi brothers over time.'

'What does that mean?'

'I don't know but given the history of the Shishi, it is likely to be sinister. I was happy to steer clear,' said Dmitry. 'But it is clear they are keen to use new discoveries in their patents. They really do sponsor pure scientific research.'

'That explains why they have such a large research budget. Normally that would be a good thing.'

'You would think so, except they spend as much on market research and patent lawyers. This ensures they catch germinating ideas early and no one else beats them to exploiting them. We academics are the most irritating, because when we publish an idea it becomes publically owned and STKiC cannot patent it.'

'You're telling me that they may have offered me a job to stop me publishing something?'

'That's very likely. My guess is that their marketing department has found a paper or article written by you that was very close to one of their un-patented research projects. They probably intend to pick your brains, patent your idea and let you go.'

'So if I join them, they cannot lose,' said Jacques, thinking aloud. 'They gain a patent and remove a competitor at the same time.'

'Exactement,' said Dmitry, displaying empathy with Jacques.

'What would you do?'

'That's a personal choice,' said Dmitry. 'Don't forget I'm biased. They can patent as many innovative developments as they like but I think scientific discoveries should be publically owned.'

Jacques, felt he had heard that sentiment expressed somewhere earlier that day.

****

Although Dmitry and Jacques had had rather a lot to drink, Jacques felt strangely sober when they finally parted company. The conference would end on the following day and Jacques was looking forward to going home to sleep in his own bed with Francine beside him. But as he walked back to his hotel, Dmitry's words about the STKiC kept returning to him.

'Perhaps Dmitry is just annoyed that they slighted him,' he thought.

Jacques started to go over the conversation with Putyatin. The man had made his skin creep and when put together with Dmitry's perspective; Jacques was starting to think that he was not being offered a job, but being told to take it.

He had arrived at the door of his hotel room. Still turning the day's conversations in his mind, he pulled out his card-key and swung the door open. On the floor in front of him was a large envelope. He turned on the light and could see the STKiC logo on the package. He moved into the room and dropped the parcel on the dressing table. He sat on the bed and studied the object from a distance.

'Alors, it does no harm to look,' he thought.

He reached for the package and tore the envelope flap open. There were glossy books about the company, two contracts of employment and a covering letter.

**STKi Corporation**
**Vladivostok**

**Dear Dr Degordes,**

**Contract Of Employment**

Please find enclosed your STKI employment contract. Sign the document and return it to me within thirty six hours. You will find the terms acceptable. The contracts cover both your employment and your wife's. As you will see the salaries are double the combined earnings that you currently accrue.

I will be very pleased when both you and Francine are my colleagues in the STKiC. It is a decision that you will not regret.

M K Berzov

**Mikhail Berezov**

**CEO STKi Corporation EMEA.**

Jacques read the letter several times.

'He never uses the words "offer" or "discussion",' he thought. 'It looks as though it's a done-deal!'

He looked at the salary details. Sure enough, the figures were exactly twice Francine's and his current salaries. He became alarmed.

'Who do they think they are that they believe they can give me an offer I can't refuse,' he muttered, to himself, 'and how the hell do they know our exact salaries? That information is private.' He gazed again at the letter. 'My God, these people are creepy'

****

After a restless night Jacques resolved to tell STKiC what they could do with their job. His opportunity came more quickly than he had anticipated as Putyatin appeared in the lobby as Jacques was checking out.

'Have you signed the contract?' he asked, after Jacques had taken his receipt.

'No,' said Jacques.

'Well you haven't got long,' said Putyatin, with his habitual smirk.

'I haven't signed it, because I'm not going to,' said Jacques, angrily. 'And I'd like to know how you got hold of my personal information.'

'As you will find out, when you join us, we are a resourceful organisation,' he replied, his smirk glued on firmly. 'You'd be surprised what we can do.'

'Mon Dieu, nothing surprises me about your arrogance,' said Jacques, drawing STKiC's envelope from his case. 'But you may be surprised when I tell you that I would not join you if you were the last company on Earth. So, if you excuse the Anglo-Saxon pun, you know where you can stick your job.'

Jacques held out the envelope for Putyatin. Putyatin did not move.

'That is unfortunate,' he said, with an amazingly resilient smirk. 'I suggest you reconsider.'

'Are you threatening me?' asked Jacques, so angry that he had become cold.

'Why would I need to do that?' he replied, turning away. 'We'll talk again no doubt.'

'Not if I see you first,' said Jacques.

But Putyatin had gone. Jacques, still holding the envelope stood aghast.

****

Whilst they shared a taxi to Osaka airport, Jacques told Dmitry about the contract and his encounter with Putyatin.

'You know, they even had exact details of Francine's and my salaries!' said Jacques.

'I'm not surprised they have probably accessed your tax returns. They seem to be able to tap into all kinds of secret information,' said Dmitry.

'Putyatin may have been in the old KGB where state information could be used for anything, but my tax records are held in the UK.'

'They are on a database aren't they and they can be accessed over the net. These guys have technology governments only dream of,' said Dmitry ominously. 'I told you. Be careful, my friend.'

'It's a shame you became a professor, Dmitry,' said Jacques, trying to lighten the conversation. 'You should have been on the stage. You could have been Boris Karloff's understudy!'

Dmitry smiled.

'I suppose it's the Slav in me,' he said, 'When we're sober, we have a tendency towards pessimism. Let's change the subject.'

For the rest of the journey they chatted about Jacques' paper on controlled fusion. Jacques felt guilty that Dmitry, the source of the original gravitum crystal used in Paul's experiment, had received no credit for the landmark papers that followed. When they had settled down in the airport lounge, Jacques suggested that he and Dmitry work together on his latest project.

'I would enjoy that, Jacques,' said Dmitry. 'What do you want me to do?'

'Well you could start by reading my draft,' said Jacques, pulling some sheets of printed-paper from his briefcase. 'Here's my first attempt. I have an uncomfortable feeling that Putyatin already knows what it says. You can read it on the plane and e-mail me with your comments when you get home.'

'It's a deal,' said Dmitry. 'By the way what happened to the Sky crystal I gave you?'

Jacques looked at him blankly. Then a light dawned.

'Ah you mean the gravitum crystal,' he said. 'Paul Dzibias still has it.' He paused. 'Why?' he asked.

'Well, I have its brother. It's slightly larger and darker blue. It has "Earth" in Chinese ideograms carved on it.'

'Earth and Sky,' said Jacques, musing over the words. 'It sounds like Ying, Yang mystical stuff.'

'It probably was,' replied Dmitry. 'I understand the stones were taken as booty from Peking when the European powers put down the Boxer rebellion.'

An announcement rang out over the public address system.

'That's my plane,' said Dmitry. 'I'd better run. Au revoir.'

'Au revoir, mon vieux.'

Leaving Jacques musing over the events of the last few days, Dmitry stood up and left for his departure gate. As Jacques watched him disappear, he noticed a pale, slight man with wire spectacles moving off in the same direction.

'I'm sure that's Putyatin,' he thought. 'What's he doing here?'

Putyatin, nodded to a man seated in one of the lounge chairs as if indicating it was time to go. The second man stood up. He was smartly dressed in a dark suit, tie and immaculately polished black shoes. He looked like an undertaker. He appeared to be well qualified for the role as it looked as though he could carry a coffin single handed; he was built like an all-in wrestler. A shudder went down Jacques' spine. At that moment he knew Dmitry was right. There was a voice in Jacques' subconscious, telling him that he had stumbled into something ominous. He took a breath.

'Jacques mon brave, grow up', he thought. 'Dmitry's obsessive mistrust has got to you.'

The public address broke his train of thought. He listened to the Japanese and then the English version.

'JL5051 Japanese Airlines flight to Paris is now boarding at Gate S34.'

Jacques got to his feet, picked up his bag and headed for the gate. All his concerns about evil international corporations had disappeared. His only anxiety was about making the connection in Paris for the Manchester flight. He was heading home to his wife and in a four days the whole family would be together to celebrate their wedding anniversary.

****

Francine and Jacques had a restful week-end at home, eating well and drinking good wine, whilst Jacques pontificated over the merits of generating power by fossil fuels, nuclear fusion, nuclear fission and his new passion, gravitational wave energy. Francine teased him that he was always more confident when he was talking about something he knew nothing about.

'You know me too well,' he said and kissed her.

They laughed and had another glass of wine.

'I missed you,' he said.

'Me too,' she replied.

Jacques was playing these scenes over in his mind as he sat at his desk at the university. It was seven o'clock on Monday morning and he was building up to doing some real work. He was not yet quite in the mood and was happy to procrastinate some more.

'I'll just check the arrangements for the party,' he thought.

He pulled out a list from his desk drawer. Unlike Francine who was addicted to lists, he rarely used them. There was something absolute about them. He was no absolutist. He liked flexibility. Conversely, Francine was a planner. For this reason he usually let her do the organising, after all she was good at it! However this time it was different. Jacques' list was a checklist of his secret arrangements for their wedding anniversary party, now only thirty-six hours away. Although he had taken a leaf out of Francine's book and produced a checklist, as usual he had a different approach. Francine believed in getting things completed. So her lists were full of nouns; things to be delivered. On the other hand, Jacques saw himself as an action man and his lists were full of verbs; things to do.

He ran his index finger down the column of printed text. He stopped about halfway down.

'Check the menu,' it said.

'I'll call the restaurant,' he thought.

He reached across his desk, but before he could lift the receiver, the phone rang.

'Allo,' he said.

'Is that you Jacques. It's Dmitry.'

'Yes, c'est Jacques,' he replied. 'How are you? Did you get home ok?'

'Yes I did thanks,' said Dmitry. 'I need to speak to you. I've had another visit from our friends. They tailed me after I arrived in St Petersburg airport. They followed me to my apartment.'

'They did what?'

'They tried to ask me some questions about you, and the gravitum.'

'What did you tell them?' said Jacques, hardly believing his ears.

'I told them nothing,' he said, 'but they kept asking about Earth and Sky and what we were planning to do with them. I thought they would get nasty.'

'What happened?'

'They left when a neighbour knocked on my door to return a DVD I'd lent her. It was as bad as the old KGB days.'

'Thank the Lord I don't live in Russia,' thought Jacques.

'How are you now?' asked Jacques, concerned for his friend.

'I'm okay,' said Dmitry, resiliently. 'I've had to deal with people like them all my life. You learn how to keep a low profile.'

'Alors, take care mon ami.'

'I phoned to tell you to be careful,' continued Dmitry. 'They have eyes and ears everywhere.'

'Surely not in Manchester?'

'Even in Manchester.'

'I will,' said Jacques, privately dismissing the incident as a hang over from the cold war. He changed the subject. 'Have you read my paper?'

'Yes,' said Dmitry, levelly. 'It's inspired. I have some ideas about how to test it experimentally. We will need to place Earth and Sky in the same laboratory though.'

'Sounds great,' said Jacques, relieved that his friend was able to shift to normal work. 'What kind of experiment are you thinking about?'

'Let's not discuss it over the phone,' said Dmitry, quietly. 'You never know who's listening.'

'Alors, can you put it in an e-mail?' asked Jacques, thinking that his friend's bout of paranoia was becoming chronic. 'You could send me a description along with your comments on the paper.'

'No,' he paused, as if deciding how much he should say. 'E-mail is not secure. My letter will explain. Don't worry.'

'What letter?' asked Jacques.

'I can say no more. Dasveedahnya,' he said with finality.

That was the last time Jacques spoke to Dmitry.

****

By the next morning Dmitry's obsessions and the arrogant employees of STKiC meant nothing to Jacques. His full attention was focussed on making Francine's day perfect. Their trip to the pub in the park had been wonderful and Francine looked radiant when they walked through the front door of their home in Altrincham. Their youngest son Thom was waiting for them just inside grinning from ear to ear.

'What are you grinning about?' she asked, smiling.

He gave his mother a kiss on the cheek and handed her a present.

'You'll see, mum,' said Thom.

As she unwrapped it, Jacques was on his way upstairs and in a few moments he returned dressed in a dinner jacket.

'Alors, cherie, It's time you got changed,' said Jacques. 'Something elegant, I think. I have a little errand to run. Thom will look after you.'

He kissed her, opened the door and walked towards his blue Renault that he had parked at the end of his drive. As he was opening the car door a courier drew across the drive. Jacques checked his step and looked towards the truck.

'Are you Dr Degordes?' asked the driver, who was standing right by him.

'Yes,' replied Jacques. 'Why?'

'I have a parcel for you. I need you to sign for it.'

Jacques was in a hurry, so without looking at it, he threw the parcel on the car seat and quickly signed the hand-held terminal proffered by the delivery man.

'Thanks,' he said and before Jacques had realised it he had gone.

Jacques saw the delivery van disappear up the street. He did not notice the other van parked discreetly a few metres away on the other side of the road.

# Fourteen

## Friends and family lives

After he had picked up Amaury and they made their way towards their rendezvous, Jacques noticed an armoured van in his mirror a couple of times but he thought nothing of it. He was elated to see his eldest son for the first time for months and between explaining his plans for the evening, he wanted news of his family in Provence.

'Did you get chance to see your uncle?' he asked.

'Yes I saw Uncle Yves and Auntie Maxime about a month ago,' replied Amaury. 'They live in a beautiful spot don't they?'

'Yes they do. Gordes is a lovely village. You've been before you know but I guess you've forgotten. You were only twelve months old.'

'You're right, I'd forgotten but I don't think even your memory goes back to when you were one year old does it Dad?'

'That's true,' said Jacques. 'My earliest memories are when we cousins played together at my grandparents' house.' There was a hint of nostalgia in Jacques' voice, or was it sadness? thought Amaury. Yves was in fact Jacques' cousin. Jacques never talked about his brother.

'Uncle Yves and Aunt Maxime took me to see your grandparents' house you know,' said Amaury. 'They told me that you and Uncle Yves still own it.'

The muscles in Jacques neck and shoulders became a little tense.

'It's very picturesque, on the plain below the village. The olive grove is overgrown though,' Amaury continued. 'But it's still beautiful. I'm surprised you never talked about it.'

'It has some sad memories for me,' said Jacques, reluctant to say any more.

Amaury did not notice the hesitation, thinking his dad was concentrating on his driving.

'Why dad?'

'Oh it's a long time ago,' he said, trying to deflect the question. 'I haven't been there for years. Yves looks after the house. It has been in the family for years. It's empty, but we haven't the heart to sell it.'

They were silent for a few moments. Amaury sensed he had touched on a difficult subject.

'How are Yves and Maxime by the way?'

'They're well. They send their love.'

'Yves is a real character isn't he,' said Jacques. 'Did you see his collection of old Solex mopeds?'

'Yes, some of them are over forty years old, but they are all immaculate.'

'Yes, they're a blast from the past,' said Jacques. 'That was the way we used to get around. I remember going out on the road for the first time at midnight on my fourteenth birthday.'

They were quiet for a few moments.

'How's mum enjoying your anniversary?' asked Amaury.

'I took her to the pub where I proposed,' Jacques replied.

'It hadn't been demolished then?'

Jacques smiled.

'Don't be cheeky. It wasn't that long ago,' said Jacques. He continued, 'It was like we were kids again.'

'Dad you're an old romantic,' said Amaury. 'I guess she's looking forward to the party. I know I am!'

'Un moment, mon fils,' said Jacques, looking in his mirror. 'There's a truck that's been behind us since the airport. He's driving badly. I need to concentrate.'

'Ok, dad. I'll sit quietly for a bit.'

Jacques had turned on to the Mancunain Way, he noticed the armoured truck a few cars behind. This was becoming more than a coincidence. They moved on to the elevated section and the rain was teaming down. He looked in his mirror. The armoured van's headlights came closer. Jacques had become totally alert; his subconscious had made the connection between Dmitry's fears and the aggressive driver behind him. Jacques looked about him. He saw the armoured van cut up a vehicle behind and drew up alongside Jacques' blue Renault. The van swerved towards them. Jacques had realised that the driver meant business. His mind racing, he looked about him. Jacques was ready when the armoured van made contact. But this time his subconscious had given him a head start; he could see how the inevitable accident would pan out.

'Mon Dieu,' said Jacques. 'Dmitry, tu as raison!'

'What?' said Amaury.

Jacques, reached over and undid Amaury's safety belt.

'Jump out when I get between these lorries,' screamed Jacques.

'Dad, What's wrong with you? Have you gone ma…'

The van swerved into them again; this time making contact. The Renault swerved into the inside lane.

Jacques, braked hard. The van shot past. He reached across Amaury and in one movement, opened the door and pushed his son out. The lorry behind swerved to avoid Amaury as he rolled on to the hard shoulder. But the driver could not brake quickly enough to avoid the collision with Jacques' car.

Jacques had managed to unlatch his safety belt and the driver's door. As the lorry behind hit him, the oblique impact caused the Renault to spin like a top. The centrifugal force threw Jacques out of the car like a rag doll. As Amaury lay unconscious on the hard shoulder away from the traffic, Jacques was thrown across the other carriageway. For a while the accident continued to play itself out as both Jacques and Amaury lay motionless by the side of the road. Dazed, not caring whether he had broken anything, Jacques stared towards Amaury's prone body. He took an unsteady step forward, brushing his foot against something. Dmitry's parcel still in the courier's plastic wrapping had landed next to him. Confused, he picked it up and looked again in Amaury's direction. Just then the butane tanker exploded. Still stooping from picking up the parcel, he was partially protected from the blast by the crash barrier. However there was still enough force to push him over the parapet to the ground twenty feet below. Still clutching the parcel, he fell, landing on a buddleia bush growing between the trees on the roundabout below the road. Perhaps if it had been a more pungent plant he would not have slipped into unconsciousness, but the aromatic aroma of the local flora was no substitute for smelling salts. Jacques passed out letting the parcel fall to the ground beneath him.

When Jacques came to, his first sensation was of being cold and wet. He tried to move but one of the branches, poked angrily at his shoulder. He gritted his teeth and rolled over. He fell painfully on to a bed of stinging nettles below. He tried to stand, but his head ached and he felt nauseous. The pain was so bad, he could not think properly. He looked around him in the half light. He was hidden from the street by the shrubs that had grown in the gaps between four large trees. Although the streets were well lit, little light could penetrate his position. He tried to see a way out, there wasn't one; only the way he had arrived.

'What the hell happened?' he asked himself.

Then a vision came back to him. He could remember Amaury's prone body in the road.

'Amaury!' he shouted, panic rising. 'Amaury!'

There was no reply, just the noise of the emergency services on the roadway above him, still clearing up four hours after the accident. Jacques' sank to his knees and cried.

'He's dead. My son, Amaury's dead,' he screamed, 'I killed him!'

But no one heard him.

****

Immediately after he had put down the phone following his conversation with Jacques, Dmitry set about collating the documents that he intended to send to his friend. He was sitting at his desk in the university editing the English translation of the documents he had promised to send to Jacques.

'Good they're all here,' he mumbled.

'I'd better check the diagrams to make sure I've converted the Cyrillic characters to Latin alphabet,' he thought.

'Good. That looks ok,' he said. 'Print and be damned.'

He selected an icon on the control bar and the printer, in the corner of his room, burst into life. By the time he had finished he had a wedge of paper some two centimetres thick. He quickly flicked through the pile to check if he had forgotten anything. Satisfied that everything was there, he set about composing a cover note. He decided at first write a long-hand draft in his mother-tongue. His dialogue with Jacques was always in English as this was their common language. However at that moment he felt that his vocabulary was inadequate to express the anxiety he felt about Jacques' safety. He knew that his friend thought he was being over sensitive, but Jacques had not lived through the bad old times when everybody in the Soviet Union was watching everybody else. There were many good things about the old ways; the education, health service and much more. But Dmitry remembered people like Putyatin. They were from the other side; ruthless and cruel and given the support of the state, no ordinary person could touch them.

He remembered that they used to joke. 'Just because you're paranoid, it doesn't mean they're not watching you!'

Like many Russian jokes it had more than an element of ironic truth about it. He cleared his mind and started to compose his letter. Now that he was scribbling in Cyrillic, the words were starting to flow.

'There, it is done,' he thought. 'Now I need to translate it.' Another thought struck him. 'How do I get the parcel to him?'

Dmitry lifted the receiver of his phone and dialled a number he had found on an unused envelope of a courier that he used from time to time.

'Zdrahstvooite,' he asked, 'can you deliver a parcel to Manchester, England by tomorrow evening?'

'You can,' he said relieved, 'and you can pick it up from the University today?'

'Excellent,' he said.

He gave the details of his room in the physics department of the university.

'You'll be here in fifteen minutes,' he confirmed. 'Excellent. Spaseeba.'

He put the phone down and returned to his translation.

There was a knock on the door. He had hardly started his translation. He slipped the draft into the courier's envelope along with the other documents.

'Come,' he said, his voice raised.

To his dismay Putyatin entered his room. But for his confident walk and piercing blue eyes Putyatin looked like a diminutive weed. However the man that followed him seemed to be his exact opposite. Dmitry thought that he was built like a shit-house door with brains to match. Dmitry did not see the third man until the "man mountain" had ducked under the lintel. He was also thick set but smaller with a slightly oriental look about him. Dmitry estimated that he was in his late thirties. His receding hair was compensated by a neatly trimmed beard. What hair he had, was trimmed closely to his head. He was menacing in a different way. He moved like a cat; appearing to be disinterested, but ready to pounce. Unlike the larger man there was a sharp intelligence in his feline eyes.

Dmitry slipped his parcel into his desk.

'What do you want?' demanded Dmitry, unsteadily. 'I told you yesterday to go away.'

He shuddered as Putyatin replied.

'We would like to know where the blue crystals are.'

'I don't know what you're talking about,' said Dmitry.

The beard rolled his eyes.

'Of course you do,' said Putyatin. 'Two blue crystals called Earth and Sky were stolen from the old Beiping Observatory. I want them back.'

'I know nothing about any robbery,' replied Dmitry, defensively. 'Besides, I don't believe you have any connection to an observatory in Beiping.'

'Perhaps not,' sneered Putyatin, 'but they were stolen and I know that you have seen them.'

Dmitry said nothing.

'I can see that you're not convinced,' said Putyatin. 'Explain will you Nikolas.'

The smaller of Putyatin's sidekicks stepped forward. Dmitry winced.

'Don't be alarmed. He's not going to hurt you,' said Putyatin. 'Not yet anyway.' Putyatin smirked.

'The stones have belonged to my family for years,' Nikolas said in English. 'They were captured during the Boxer rebellion by my ancestor when he was part of the allied army that put the rebellion down. I am his only heir. They belong to me.'

'So your ancestor stole them? You may have forgotten that we've had a revolution since then. The stone is now owned by mother Russia,' said Dmitry, amused and more relaxed when he saw it was becoming a legal, rather than physical argument. He continued, 'The stones have been with the university for years. They are no longer here,' he added, telling a half truth.

'Oh, we know that you gave one to Jacques Degordes,' said Putyatin. 'That was a big mistake that I will correct. In the meantime you have the Earth crystal and I want it returned.'

'You will have to take that up with the University authorities,' Dmitry replied. 'It is not in my power to return it to a group of ex-KGB thugs.'

The big man took a step forward. There was a knock on the door.

'It's like Red Square here today,' said Dmitry, calmer than he felt. 'That must be my ten o'clock meeting. I'm afraid you'll have to leave now.'

There was a second, more insistent knock.

'Hold on for a moment please,' said Dmitry, walking to the door. 'I must show my guests out.'

Dmitry opened the door whilst the courier stood aside to let Dmitry's guests file by. Putyatin's face was contorted in anger and frustration, as he could see, too late, that Dmitry's meeting was fictitious.

'We will meet again. Next time I expect you to be more co-operative,' he muttered, threateningly.

When he was sure they had gone, Dmitry went to his desk drawer and took out the parcel of documents.

'I haven't done the translation,' he thought. 'Too late it must go now.'

He sealed the package and as an afterthought wrote Jacques' home address, rather than the university on the label. He handed it to the courier and signed the credit card slip.

'Good luck, Jacques,' he thought.

****

Dmitry's package was on the ground in front of Jacques, but he was too confused with grief and concussion to notice it. He had remained in his kneeling position for some minutes, his mind playing partial images of the accident some hours before. He gazed up towards the parapet from where he had fallen. The sky above him was pierced by rays of blue and orange flashing lights, refracted by the water particles in the humid atmosphere. The smell of diesel fumes from recovery vehicles was starting to penetrate the choking smell of burning that had dominated the atmosphere for the past few hours. Jacques realised that he must get up there. Amaury could be alright. Perhaps the emergency people had got there in time. He had to get to his son straightaway. He tried to stand up, but he had lost the circulation in his legs. He stretched them out and in doing so kicked the parcel under the bush. He tried to stand but his ankle gave way.

'Mon Dieu, I've broken my ankle,' he thought, as a pain shot up through his left leg.

He sat down again, legs outstretched. The sharp pain gave way to a pulsating ache, centred on his ankle.

'Help!' he shouted but no one heard.

Since his fall Jacques had experienced a rollercoaster of emotions through his concussed brain. His grief had given way to hope that had now given way to frustration. Disabled by a damaged ankle he seemed to be stuck in this tiny nettled copse, with no way out. During his manoeuvres, he had flattened most of the nettles around him with the result that he had created a small nest surrounded by shrubs and trees. There may have been a way out, but in the poor light it was difficult to distinguish between hard and soft foliage.

'Pull yourself together, Jacques,' he said out loud. 'You're in the middle of a busy city. There's got to be a way out of here. Think! Think!'

For the first time he decided to give himself a physical check. In the dark he knew there was no way that he would be able to see any blood. But an open wound would be sticky, he thought. He could sense a wound on his temple.

'That accounts for the headache,' he thought.

He touched the wound. It was wet, but then everything was wet; it had been pissing it down. He remembered the rainstorm; until then he had hardly noticed that he was soaked to the skin.

Now starting to shiver, he systematically tested each limb, leaving his left leg till last. He could feel many scratches, bruises and stings from the nettles, but nothing that would make him immobile. Gingerly he felt down his left leg. He could feel that the ankle was swollen, but he could not find any bone sticking out.

'Ok,' he thought a sprain or ligaments. 'Let's hope it's just a sprain.'

He tested his ankle again.

'Well, that's not going to work,' he thought, as a pain shot up his leg for the second time.

His head throbbed.

'I need something to help me to my feet,' he thought.

His headache beginning to weaken, Jacques' eyes were functioning better. He could see the shadows of the shrubbery more clearly. He dragged himself the short way to the buddleia and felt for a medium sized trunk with dry leaves. He reached as far as he could up the stem and levered it against the root system. It snapped off at the bottom of the shrub.

'Good, a walking stick,' he said.

'My kingdom for a knife,' he muttered.

Deaf to the noise above him, he started to tear off the small twigs and sub-branches. Cursing and muttering as he whittled the branch down with his bare hands. Unable to snap the wood low enough for a walking stick he settled for a crude but serviceable crutch.

'Ok, now the big test.'

Being an accomplished skier, Jacques knew how to get to his impeded feet using a stick. He planted the stick in the ground in front of him and it slipped on something.

'What's that?' he asked, not caring whether anyone heard him talking to himself.

He spun round on his bottom and felt under the bush where his stick had slipped. He had found Dmitry's parcel. By now he had recovered his senses enough to realise its importance. He lifted it on to his lap and then wedged it in a branch above his head.

'I'll get to you later,' he said and with immense effort he forced himself to his feet.

Jacques could now see over the nettles and the shrubs and in a few minutes he was out on the open path. He hobbled over to a bench that was positioned under a streetlight in the deserted pedestrian area underneath the elevated road. He sat down, exhausted. He could see that traffic was moving on the carriageway above him.

'They've cleared the road,' he mumbled. 'Where have they taken him?'

He looked at the parcel. Illuminated by the sodium light above, he could just make out the sender's name, written with a thick felt tipped pen.

'Dmitry,' he muttered.

'The answer to why they did this to us is in this envelope,' he thought, tearing at the flap with his tired, dirty and bloodied fingers.

Several sheets of paper fell on to the ground in front of him. They were prints of digital photographs. Wearily, he picked it up. He squinted at the first one in the orange light, then the second and then the third.

'Merde,' he thought.

He looked around and saw a surveillance camera, trained on the pathway in front of him. He could feel tightness across his chest. He tried to control the panic before it gripped him.

'Merde, merde merde,' he said out loud. 'I must get out of here.'

'They're watching me,' he thought.

He returned the photos to the envelope and looked around his feet to make sure he had collected all the documents. Then he saw the black memory stick. He slipped it into his pocket, stood up and turned the collar of his torn jacket up to his chin.

'Don't run,' he said to himself, 'just walk gently.'

It was then that he realised that he could not go home until he understood what it all meant. He had to find somewhere to examine the other contents of Dmitry's parcel. It was the only way he could get out of the mess.

****

While Jacques and Amaury were leaving Manchester Airport, Dmitry was in his study frantically working at his computer. He was deleting files containing anything that was linked to the documents that he had sent to Jacques. The process of selecting which files was complicated because Jacques' parcel contained a conglomerate of many different topics. Although the original files were easy to find, there were many more that contained fragments of the same information. He was determined that none of it should fall into the wrong hands. Dmitry's task involved trawling through hundreds of archives that reflected years of his life as a research scientist. It was heartbreaking to destroy so much of his hard work, but extreme situations required extreme measures. At least he would not be disturbed, he was alone in the department; everybody else had gone home hours ago.

He heard a car draw up on the gravel below his study. He stood up and looked through his window. Two men were getting out. It was Putyatin and man-mountain.

'It's too late,' he thought. 'I haven't the time to be selective.'

He went back to his computer and made a different selection. He hit the left mouse button.

'Are you sure?' it said.

He clicked, 'Yes.'

The computer started to churn away.

'1%, 2%, 3%....,' it said, slow but sure.

The study door opened. This time they did not knock.

'Oh, no Nikolas this time?' said Dmitry, glancing at the computer's progress. 'Has he dropped his claim on the crystals then?'

'I'm afraid not,' Putyatin replied. 'He's running a small errand for me,' he continued with his habitual sneer.

'What do you want?' asked Dmitry. 'I'm busy.'

Putyatin took a step closer.

'I want all your work on gravitum.'

'You don't want the crystals any more?'

'That's taken care of,' Putyatin replied, brusquely.

'Where are your research documents?' asked Putyatin. 'Are they on that computer?'

'That's none of your business,' said Dmity, aggressively. 'Now leave before I call security.'

Putyatin took another step forward and picked up an ornate paper knife from Dmitry's desk.

Dmitry glanced at his terminal.

'81%, 82%...,' it said.

'Now get out of here and put my paper knife down,' he ordered..

'I asked you a question. Where are your research documents?' he repeated.

'Look at the workmanship in this,' said Putyatin, handing the knife to man-mountain.

Man-mountain ran his thumb along the point and grunted.

'Put that down and leave,' ordered Dmitry, reaching for the telephone.

'I asked you a question. I'm not going to repeat it again.'

'92%, 95%...'

'Which research documents,' said Dmitry, stalling. 'I have thousands.'

'You know which ones; the unpublished ones; the ones about gravitum; the ones from your friend Degordes.' said Putyatin, moving closer.

'97%, 98%…'

'Oh you mean work in progress,' he said, looking at the "finished" message on his terminal. 'They're deleted, gone. They don't exist.'

'What?' exclaimed Putyatin, reaching over the desk to turn the screen towards him. 'You idiot! You've deleted the files,' spitting out the words as he saw the message on the terminal. 'Then I have no more use for you.'

'The feeling is mutual,' said Dmitry, not realising that man-mountain had silently worked his way behind him.

Putyatin nodded to his henchman.

Dmitry felt a sharp prick in the back of his neck and then nothing else.

****

Jacques had never been worried by the appearance of street cameras before. Like so many people he had been pleased with their growth. It was okay to see the authorities watch everybody's movements if that meant they could catch bad people. Why should he care? He had nothing to hide. He thought that the people who asked, "Who watches the watchers?" needed to get a life. But he had not considered the possibility that bad people may have gained access to the systems. Even then, he would not have cared. What on Earth would they do with trivial information about his movements? However, now his perspective had changed. The fact that he and his family had been under surveillance for weeks and that surveillance provided the information to ambush him and Amaury on the motorway, changed everything. Jacques was now determined to find somewhere away from the prying eyes of traffic and security cameras. These cameras were no longer protecting him; they were the eyes of his enemy. When he had found a safe place he would work out how to stop these people. Having decided on his first objective, he needed to find the means. Manchester was littered with cameras.

'Every square foot must have a lens pointing at it,' he thought.

For a while he was devoid of ideas. Then it hit him.

'The canal,' he thought. 'There must be gaps there.'

A few years earlier Jacques had organised a family holiday on a narrow boat. It was the last time they had been together as a unit. He remembered that even in the middle of the city, parts of the canal system were like stepping into the eighteenth century. Jacques knew that some areas had been turned into trendy eating places and there was a good chance that in those locations there would be cameras on every corner. But the canals twisted and turned their way for miles around and under the city. He had to believe that there were unfashionable areas untouched by nosey electronic eyes.

'That's it,' he thought. 'I'll look for a bridge or tunnel. With luck, I can find a quiet secluded spot to shelter and regroup.'

The canal walk was less than a quarter of a mile from where he stood. That would give him access to the network. He could decide what to do when he got there. Transferring his weight to his makeshift crutch and gripping Dmitry's parcel under his arm, he started a secret journey; a journey where he would have no contact with his family and closest friends. STKiC was after him, not his family. Jacques had to play dead. So he decided to disappear for their safety.

It seemed longer but Jacques reached the tow path in less than fifteen minutes. Although he could see no cameras, he had arrived at a section of the waterway that was not as secluded as he wanted. He started to limp his way eastwards. His ankle was painful but he was able to keep up a reasonable pace. The rain had stopped, the clouds were thinning and a combination of light from nearby buildings and the full moon allowed him to find his way quite easily. The physical exercise was warming his body and he was beginning to dry out. However he knew he could not keep it up for long. He was tired and his head still ached. At some point he must find food and somewhere to rest. The canal was now shaded from the street lights; the steep banks blocking illumination from those businesses ambivalent to saving the planet. For a moment a rain cloud obscured the moon. The ambient light was much less intense. Although his eyes were adjusted to the dark, it was becoming difficult to keep his footing. He looked at the path in front of him. The cloud passed by and the silvery light from the full moon was reflecting off the mirror-like canal water. If Jacques had not been in such distress, he would have thought it was beautiful.

The footpath was now in shadow; the reflected light revealing areas where the bank had crumbled into the water.

'This is becoming dangerous,' he thought.

'I don't want to fall into the canal and drown, he muttered, 'and I'm not going to do their work for them,'

The irony of having a silly accident after surviving a murder attempt seemed to amuse him.

He looked up and saw that the canal was opening out. He had reached the fork where the Rochdale Canal branched north. He peered into the darkness and could make out four or five narrow boats moored on the left bank. As he got closer the space around him opened out where the canal ran alongside a large car park.

'I'm right behind Piccadilly,' he thought, picturing the streets above.

He could hear voices and the slamming of a car door. He glanced across to the other bank and saw someone ambling along, half cut. Jacques ducked into the shadows as the unsteady silhouette zigzagged by. He realised that he was near the restaurant where he had organised their anniversary party. Although it was less than seven hours since he had been heading towards the restaurant, he imagined Francine and his sons still gathered there waiting. The image switched to Amaury, lying hurt, damaged at the roadside. An overwhelming sadness nearly overwhelmed him, but he fought on; focussed, determined. He looked up at the sky, it was starting to lighten. Concerned about being seen crossing the open space, he increased his pace past the narrow boats and crossed the canal just beyond them so that he could continue east along the Ashton canal. Soon after he had left the junction, he felt as though he was in the countryside. In fact he was still very much inside the city limits. Jacques arrived at a lock and in the pound next to it four narrow boats were moored. It was just before sunrise.

'I must get under cover before dawn,' he thought, starting to become even more anxious.

Jacques could see that each of the boats had plywood covers over their windows. These were either protection against vandals, or the boats had been locked up for the winter. He instantly realised that this meant that the boats were not occupied and their owners may not return for weeks, even months. Jacques surveyed the scene around him. There were no surveillance cameras to be seen. The spot was quiet and isolated; except for the half million people in the city above him.

Jacques made his way to the first barge. Using his good leg and his crutch he stepped on to the stern platform. He put Dmitry's parcel down on the cabin roof as he looked around. In the increasing light he was able to see very clearly that this owner was very security conscious. He carefully stepped back on to the bank, nearly dropping the parcel into the water as he did so. Jacques climbed to the next barge.

'Still too secure,' he muttered, moving to the next one.

'Same again.'

Despondently he climbed on to the deck of the last barge and there on the roof of the cabin, he saw a windlass.

'That will do,' he said, almost elated. 'A makeshift crowbar.'

He levered the lock off the cabin door and he quickly went below, discreetly closing the door behind him. Jacques went straight to the galley and searched each of the cupboards. He found tinned food and drinks. Desperately hungry, he ate the contents of a can of cold baked beans and washed them down with lemonade. Within a few minutes of breaking in, he was asleep in the forward cabin oblivious to the world outside. However his sleep was not dreamless; his mind could not stop thinking of the last time he saw Amaury's face, his body prone on the verge of the motorway. Then suddenly his dream switched to a much earlier memory, one from his childhood, a memory he had tried to blank for years. When he awoke he found his crying was not a dream.

# Part 3

# Friends reunited

# Fifteen

## Conversion of a sceptic

After two hours of aggressive banter Mitzuko Hitzubishi and Hideo withdrew to a sullen truce. Having unloaded the Mitzuko's GWR Mark III from the Datsun, Hideo had nothing else to do except watch and wait. Now the device was in its new position Mitzuko's attention had turned to ensuring that it was installed so that no one else could sabotage it. They had placed it equidistant from the stone tower and the generator. Hideo waited patiently for an half an hour or so whilst Mitzuko tinkered with his apparatus. He was becoming bored.

'Are you going to be all day?' he asked. 'It's time I was going home.'

'You're going nowhere,' Mitzuko replied, without looking up. 'This is your new home. Get used to it.'

'You must be kidding. I'm not sleeping in that shack,' he said looking towards the shed engulfed in diesel fumes. 'Where's the toilet? Shall I use your tower?'

'Shut up,' said Mitzuko, sharply. 'I'm trying to repair the damage you did earlier.'

Hideo waited silently for a few more minutes.

'Ok,' he said, 'I'll shit here then.'

'Alright,' said Mitzuko, with resignation. 'Give me a couple more minutes to make this safe and I'll show you around.'

'You carry on. We don't want the rest of the mountain to fall on our heads now do we?' said Hideo, sarcastically. 'I'll just click my heels until you need piss as well.'

'Ok,' said Mitzuko, throwing a spanner to the ground. 'Follow me.'

He turned and headed for a small tunnel behind the stone tower. By the time Hideo had caught up with him, Mitzuko was levering the loose planks from across the entrance. Hideo stood behind him and watched.

'Help me then,' said Mitzuko. 'Do you want a shit or don't you?'

With a joint effort, they pulled the final plank away from the entrance. Mitzuko reached inside the entrance and switched on a bare filament bulb that revealed a rusty steel door.

'We haven't used this place for years,' said Mitzuko. 'I hope the door is not rusted closed.'

Mitzuko turned the handle and pulled the door open. After a few seconds of flickering, fluorescent lights lit a long corridor.

'Your room is the second door on the right. There's a WC in there,' said Mitzuko. 'I'll wait here.'

Hideo pushed past him through the doorway. The corridor was about thirty metres long with doors at regular intervals. The floor was carpeted and the walls whitewashed. Hideo could see a number of delicate Japanese paintings on walls. He walked to the second door and went inside. He looked around. It was almost as if he had stepped into a Tokyo hotel, not the international kind frequented by foreign visitors, but a traditional hotel, with cushions, a low table, paper partitions and a futon to sleep on. He moved into the side room where he found a Japanese style toilet sunk into the tiled floor.

'Do you want something to eat?' asked Mitzuko, when Hideo had re-emerged.

Hideo was fazed by Mitzuko's new politeness.

'Er, yes,' he replied.

'Follow me then.'

Mitzuko led Hideo into another room. Inside was a European style canteen with tables for five to ten people. The room was light and airy. The floor was spotless and there was not a trace of dust anywhere. Along one wall was a stainless steel counter that separated the eating area from the kitchen. Along an adjacent wall was an array of vending machines.

‘What would you like to eat?’ asked, Mitzuko, pleasantly.

Hideo did not reply.

‘I’m going to have a bento box and some tea,’ said Mitzuko. ‘Is that ok for you?’

‘Yes, that will do fine.’

Mitzuko pushed a couple of buttons on the machine and two plastic boxes appeared with rice and various sashimi delicacies. He put them on a tray and collected their tea from a second machine. He took the food to one of the tables and sat down. Hideo remained standing.

‘What’s wrong?’ asked Mitzuko. ‘You can sit on the floor and eat, if you want to.’

‘No, that’s not it,’ said Hideo. ‘You said that you hadn’t used this place for years.’

‘Yes.’

‘But there’s no dust, the food is fresh. How can that be?’

‘Technology,’ Mitzuko replied simply. ‘Technology.’

****

Hideo and Mitzuko had been living in the bunker for a few days and Hideo no longer felt like a prisoner. Over the period, Mitzuko Hitzubishi had convinced him that the GWR was perfectly safe and Hideo should not have interfered with it. Mitzuko showed him photographs of the Academy, now a pile of dust and explained that the police were after those who were responsible.

‘I now understand that you tampered with the GWR because you were misled by those foreign scientists,’ said Mitzuko. ‘Because of this I will not hand you over to the police.’

‘Thank you Hitzubishi san,’ said Hideo, meekly. ‘I am grateful.’

‘However, I suggest you lay low for a while. You can stay here a little longer if you want,’ said Mitzuko. ‘Your knowledge of seismology could help me ensure there is no risk of another problem like the one you caused at the academy.'

Hideo said that he was pleased to contribute. The longer he remained in the bunker the more he became convinced that his earlier conflict had been a terrible misunderstanding. His sense of duty told him that he should do something to make amends for his folly.

****

In the outside world nearly two months had gone by since Prama and Claire had taken their return flight to Heathrow. In that time they had returned to their earlier lives, Dmitry had been murdered, Jacques had disappeared and O'Reilly and Francine were well into their investigations. This was remarkable considering that Hideo's watch showed that only seventy-two hours had elapsed. Of course he did not know about any discrepancy. He could not see the sun rising and setting outside. If he had, the cycle of day and night would have seemed very fast. Hideo was not disorientated; he was disconnected. But as he believed that laying low was a sensible strategy for a fugitive from the law, he had no reason to suspect that the streets of Japan were operating at a different rate than the corridors inside the bunker. Hideo had put his trust in his new friend Mitzuko, who was clearly as honest as the day is long. Why would he expect anything untoward? He was not even suspicious when he finally found out that other people's days were much shorter than his. This revelation happened after the newcomers had arrived.

For the last few days Hideo had been working in the computer laboratory next to the canteen. In his job at the Tokyo Academy of Geosciences, Hideo had become an expert on the effect of seismic vibrations on buildings. This was ironic when one remembers that he triggered the earth tremor that converted his employer's headquarters to rubble. Whatever the merits of that disaster, Hideo was good at finding whether a construction was susceptible to p or s seismic waves. Mitzuko Hitzubishi wanted to tap into this skill. So he had asked his new friend to build a computer model that would simulate the effects of an earth tremor on the bunker. Mitzuko had given him plans of the bunker, the tower and the corridors. Whilst he was inputting the dimensions into the model, he noticed something interesting. Mitzuko was working at a computer terminal on the other side of the underground room.

'Mitzuko, can I speak to you for a moment?' Hideo called. 'I've found something unusual in the measurements.'

Mitzuko stopped what he was doing and made his way over to Hideo.

'What's the problem?'

'I've noticed that the plastered side of the roof of the main chamber is virtually a perfect parabola,' he said.

'Is it?' said Mitzuko, keeping his face expressionless. 'Why is that important?'

'I don't know, but it wouldn't happen by accident and whoever made this bunker must have had a reason,' he replied, puzzled. 'I wondered whether you would know why they did it.'

'Beats me,' said Mitzuko, innocently.

'There's another thing,' said Hideo. 'The focus of the parabola is at the base of the tower.'

'It's been like that for years,' said Mitzuko, wearily. 'I suppose the builders had their reasons. I don't expect we'll ever know what was going through their heads.' He looked over his shoulder as if he was keen to get back to his workstation. 'Anything else?' he asked, impatience starting to show.

'Yes there is one more thing,' said Hideo. 'Have you got that data on the characteristics of the plaster in the ceiling and the rocks used to build the tower and linking tunnels?'

'I've asked one of my associates to bring it with him. He'll be here very soon. Anything else?'

Hideo looked puzzled.

'I don't remember you mentioning any associates,' said Hideo, concerned.

'Didn't I? It must have slipped my mind,' said Mitzuko. Then seeing the concern on Hideo's face, he continued, 'Don't worry, he won't tell anybody that you're hiding here.'

There was a squeaking noise from the entrance to the bunker. The external doors were opening.

'Ah, good,' said Mitzuko, relief showing on his face. 'That will be Viktor now.'

'The name "Viktor" sounds Russian,' thought Hideo. 'That's odd.'

Mitzuko stood up and headed towards the entrance into the main chamber, leaving Hideo with more questions unanswered. Hideo was no fool and in the depths of his mind he had started to wonder whether Mitzuko was hiding something. He could hear the faint voice of reason, emerging from the left cortical hemisphere of his brain. It was saying, 'Mitzuko is not what he seems.' The seeds of doubt, dormant for the last few bunker days, were now germinating again.

# Sixteen

## Comeback

DCI O'Reilly was musing over some new information and wondering what relevance it had to his case. Chief Inspector Sokov of the St Petersburg police had phoned to ask about Dr Jacques Degordes. Apparently he was a close friend of a Russian professor who had just been murdered. O'Reilly told him about the accident.

'Do many professors get murdered over there?' asked O'Reilly, flippantly.

Given the demise of Jacques Degordes, the comment had not gone down well.

'Normally, this is not the way we lose our professors,' came the reply. 'It is not an occupational hazard in Russia. Is it standard practice in Manchester?'

Despite O'Reilly's flippancy, Sokov battled on stoically. The language difference could have made the conversation difficult but Sokov's English was good enough to get them through. Besides it was better than O'Reilly's Russian. O'Reilly soon realised that he had met his match and finally they agreed to pool their knowledge by e-mail. Not the most trusting of men, O'Reilly wanted to let Sokov go first and was relieved that Sokov agreed to open the dialogue by sending an e-mail within the hour. Half an hour later O'Reilly was waiting at his terminal.

'Ping!' went his computer.

'The first message,' he muttered.

He opened it enthusiastically and read the message. The last line caught his eye.

It said, 'I attach extracts from case notes. We are interested about individuals seen at the university when the murder happened. I attach photo-fits of three men. The security cameras not working during murder.'

'Faulty security cameras,' thought O'Reilly. 'This is becoming a pattern.'

He clicked on the first bitmap icon and looked at the picture. It was a drawing of a man wearing a baseball cap. It could have been one of a thousand people walking Manchester streets. He clicked on the second man and then the third. O'Reilly recognised none of them. But that did not surprise him. He would get the thinker to run the photo-fits through the image recognition software; maybe that would turn something up. He clicked on the fourth document icon.

'Oh Bugger! I suppose I deserve this,' he said, as the text was displayed. 'Why couldn't I have had a simple run-of-the-mill case like everybody else?'

He stood up and went to the door.

'Can anyone here speak Russian?' he shouted to the group.

Silence.

'Well find someone quickly,' he said, irritably, 'and make sure they can read the fucking Russian alphabet as well!' He paused. 'I want a briefing in half an hour,' he snarled.

O'Reilly went back into his room, slamming the door behind him.

****

Whenever she could Francine would try to be by Amaury's bedside. She would take a book and some of Jacques papers and read them; sometimes to herself and sometimes aloud. The doctors had told her that he could probably hear her, and her voice would help. It was mid afternoon and she was two hours into her daily vigil. No longer bandaged, he looked pristine in his bed. He looked well. He looked as he had always looked; except he was asleep. She had been holding his hand and talking to him about nothing in particular and there was not a flicker of a reaction. She opened Jacques' old brief case and pulled out some of her husband's documents.

'These were your dad's,' she said, continuing to talk to him. 'He was working on something important and I can't work out why, but I think it's connected to your accident.'

Amaury just lay there, his chest moving up and down, his eyes closed with no reaction, nothing.

She looked down at the first sheet of the document on her lap.

'There is something here, I just know it,' she said, starting to well up. 'If the clue is not here where is it?'

'The parcel,' said a distant voice.

Francine looked up sharply and gazed at Amaury's face.

'You said something,' she said excitedly, not sure whether she had imagined it. 'You said something. I know you did.'

Amaury's eyes flickered and then closed again.

'Nurse, nurse,' she shouted, 'he spoke, he opened his eyes!'

Suddenly people surrounded the bed. Francine continued to hold Amaury's hand tightly, as if she could not let go in case she lost him again. A doctor arrived. She gently took Amaury's hand from Francine. Opening his hand in hers she spoke to him.

'Hello, Amaury,' she said. 'If you can hear me, move your fingers.'

They all looked at his hand. Almost imperceptibly there was movement.

'He moved,' said Francine. 'His finger moved.'

She looked at the doctor for confirmation.

'Yes it did,' she said. 'Now Amaury move your fingers again if you can still hear me.'

They watched his fingers, nothing happened. His eyes flickered as if straining to control his hand. The doctor had noticed.

'Try again Amaury, move your fingers if you can.'

This time the finger moved conspicuously. Amaury was coming round.

****

Claire's mobile phone emitted a noise.

'dit dit dit, dah dah, dit dit dit,' it said, as they were approaching their front door.

'She really ought to update her alert tone,' thought Paul.

'You've got an SMS message,' he said, amused by the Morse code.

'So it would seem,' she replied, reaching into her handbag for the handset. 'What's so funny?' she asked catching his smile.

'Oh, just your SMS alert. You know it's Morse code don't you? It's a bit old fashioned.'

'So you keep telling me,' she said, 'but I'm not a technophile like you, so as long as it works I'm happy.'

Claire fiddled with the buttons on her phone as Paul fumbled for his door keys.

'It's from Francine,' she said. 'I'll read it when we get indoors.'

Paul put the key in the lock to their ground floor flat.

'Something's wrong,' he said.

'What do you mean?'

He could see through the frosted glass that things were not as they should be.

'Did your sister give you the key back?' he asked.

'Months ago,' she said. 'Why?'

'Someone's been here,' he said, cautiously. 'We've been burgled.'

'How do you know?' she asked, alarmed.

'Look at the living room door,' he said, pointing down the hallway.

It was slightly ajar. They always closed the doors before they went out.

'But the lock is not damaged,' said Claire, alarmed. 'Nobody else has a key. How could they get in?'

'I don't know but someone has got in somehow.'

'Be careful,' she said, quietly. 'They may still be here.'

'I'm going to check,' he said quietly, putting his finger to his lips to signal she should be quiet. 'Go next door and call the police. I think they may be after the crystal.'

'What the one on the mantelpiece?' she asked rhetorically.

He nodded.

His senses heightened, Paul peered along the hallway for signs of movement, straining his ears for the slightest noise. Claire stood silently beside him. He glanced over his shoulder.

'I thought I told you to go next door,' he hissed.

'Did you?' she whispered. 'I didn't hear.'

There was no way she was going to leave him to handle an intruder on his own.

They moved quietly down the hallway. There was nothing in the first bedroom or the second. There was no sign of a burglar or a burglary; the rooms were as they had left them.

Claire thought she heard a faint noise from the lounge. Gingerly Paul looked around the door frame he could see the mantelpiece. The gravitum was not there.

'It's gone,' he said in a faint whisper. 'The crystal's not on the mantelpiece.'

Slowly he made his way into the room. Claire was close behind. He could see a pair of feet sticking out beneath one of the two Queen Anne chairs in their lounge.

The feet moved. Paul quietly picked up an ornament from a side table.

'Right,' whispered Paul. 'Got you!'

'Be careful,' whispered Claire.

Paul moved closer. The person in the chair did not stir.

'I've already called the police,' said Paul in his firmest voice. 'Now drop what you've taken and get out of my flat!'

The body in the chair moved as if woken from a long sleep. Groggily the dishevelled man struggled to his feet.

'Enfin, vous êtes arrivé. Where the hell have you been?' he said, supporting himself on a rustic-looking stick. 'Do you know how dangerous it is to leave things like this lying around?' He held up a blue crystal with his free hand. 'It could have been stolen.'

'You're supposed to be dead', muttered Claire, an expression of shock across her face.

Paul said nothing. His mouth was open, but no noise came out.

****

There was a knock on O'Reilly's office door.

'What do you want McKenzie?' he snapped, still irritable.

The novice stepped timidly into his office.

'He's awake,' said the novice.

'Who?' he asked, thinking that the cynic had been caught napping.

'Amaury Degordes,' she replied. 'His mother has just phoned. He's come round.'

'At last,' he said, more positively, 'some progress.' He looked at the novice intensely as if waiting for something. She remained transfixed; like a rabbit caught in the headlights.

'Well, what are you waiting for?' he said, his irritation returning. 'Let's get down there. I've got a load of questions for him.'

'He hasn't spoken yet,' she said, frowning. 'They won't let us interrogate him for a while.'

'We'll see about that. Just bring the car round,' he said as she continued to loiter. 'Now!'

She scurried away, her hypnotic state broken.

****

'Where have you been? What happened to you? Why haven't you been in touch? Do you know they think you're dead? Have you contacted Francine? How did you get here?'

After a few moments their senses came back to them and questions came flooding out. Jacques stood, stick in hand, weathering the onslaught resiliently.

Then he said simply, 'Did you know the canal runs right behind your street?'

'What?' said Paul, exasperated. 'Have you lost your marbles?'

'You asked how I got here,' he said.

'What?'

'I stole a barge.' Jacques continued, 'You know canal travel is like stepping into the past, just peace, quiet and virtually no charged couple devices to be seen. It's amazing.'

The barrage stopped. Paul and Claire stared at him unable to interpret what their eyes and ears were telling them.

'Cameras,' he said, seeing their confusion. 'Surveillance cameras.'

Claire came to her senses first.

'You look awful,' she said, looking him up and down. 'Why don't you have a bath, whilst I put the kettle on.'

'Yes, you smell,' said Paul, somewhat unflatteringly, 'and you look as if you've been shaving with a penknife.'

'Do I?' he said, absentmindedly. 'I suppose I do.'

Jacques remained standing; motionless. A melancholy expression settled on his face. Paul wondered whether he had been too harsh about Jacques' appearance, but Claire could see that there was something else on his mind. He wanted to ask a question but he was not sure he had the courage. His eyes became moist. Over the last few weeks he had asked himself the question a thousand times. Now he was with people who might know the answer, he was afraid to ask.

'It's about Amaury, isn't it?' she asked gently.

'I, I, I must know,' he stammered.

'You must know what?' asked Paul, seeing the distress in his friend but not able to interpret it.

'I need to know….'

'You need to know that Amaury is alive,' interrupted Claire softly. 'He's in hospital and Francine is probably with him now.'

The change in Jacques expression was striking. His relief was palpable. It was as if a huge weight had been lifted from his shoulders. His eyes filled with tears as if he had been holding them back for an eternity.

'Thank God,' he sobbed. 'Thank God, I thought I'd killed him!'

'There is some bad news,' said Paul, hesitantly. 'He's unconscious. He's been out cold since the accident.'

Jacques' face dropped. His emotions had moved from depression to elation to fear in a few seconds.

Claire's phone beeped its Morse code message again.

'It's Francine again,' she thought, apprehensively. 'It could be important. Please let it be good news.'

Paul continued, 'He had head injuries when he was thrown from the car. He had a few bruises and scratches that have healed, so physically he's ok.' Seeing Jacques expression, he went on, 'The doctors say there is a good chance he'll come round soon. Francine visits him everyday and speaks to him. That's supposed to help.'

Jacques fell back into the chair. His head slumped to his chest.

Claire looked up from her mobile. Her eyes were sparkling with excitement.

'He's awake,' she shouted, with a grin.

'What?' said Paul, as Jacques raised his head.

'Did you say Amaury has come round?' asked Jacques, hardly able to cope with the emotional roller coaster.

'Yes. I've just read Francine's message Amaury has opened his eyes. Hold on,' she said, 'let me open the second message.'

The room was silent as Claire, her hands shaking, manipulated the buttons on her phone. She read the message out loud.

'A is talking. Says saw J after the crash. J alive or was A dreaming?'

# Seventeen

## Dangerous information

'I'm sure I saw dad after he pushed me out,' said Amaury quietly. 'He was standing on the other side of the road. He was holding a parcel.'

'What happened after you saw him?' asked O'Reilly.

'I don't remember,' said Amaury, his forehead wrinkling as if to squeeze out more memories. 'I just can't remember.'

O'Reilly waited.

'There was just a flash. Then nothing….'

'Must have been the explosion,' said the novice.

'Perhaps,' said O'Reilly, annoyed at the interruption. 'Come on Amaury, think. There must be something else.'

Amaury thought, his eyes watering.

'I can't remember anything else. I just can't.'

'Right,' said the doctor. 'That's enough. It's time you left.'

'Just one or two more questions,' protested O'Reilly.

'No. You've had long enough. He's tired. You must wait till tomorrow.'

'Ok,' said O'Reilly, reluctantly getting to his feet. 'I'll see you tomorrow Amaury. In the meantime try to remember will you?'

'I will.'

O'Reilly and the novice headed for the corridor.

'Do you think his mind is wandering with amnesia?' she asked. 'Perhaps Amaury imagined seeing his dad.'

'Possibly, but if Jacques is alive he must be hiding for a reason.'

'Do you think he's hiding from us or someone else?'

'I don't know. He seems to have been the victim in the accident. Why would he hide from the police?' asked O'Reilly.

'Unless he doesn't trust us; perhaps whoever tried to kill him is well connected,' the novice paused. 'Perhaps he's got mixed up with organised crime.'

'And pigs may fly,' replied O'Reilly, cynically, 'but more likely our young friend Amaury has imagined seeing his father and Dr Degordes is dead after all. You go back to the incident room and tell them there will be a briefing when I get back.'

'Ok, Guv. Are you staying here?'

'Yes, I'm going to speak to his doctor. I want to know whether Amaury could have dreamt it or not.'

****

After the news about Amaury and a bath, Jacques felt much better than he had for weeks. But then Paul told him about Dmitry.

'Of course you wouldn't know,' said Paul. 'They say that he was working late and someone walked into the university and stabbed him in the neck. The physics community has been chattering about it for days.'

'Mon Dieu,' exclaimed Jacques, his melancholy returning. 'I must find somewhere else to hide, and think. I'm putting you in danger just by being here.'

'That may be right,' said Paul, looking worried. 'But first we'd like to know what danger you're in so we know the risk. You haven't told us anything about why you've been hiding and who tried to kill you.'

'Jacques,' said Claire. 'Just look at you. You are tired and thin. You've done something to your leg. Whatever is wrong you need rest. Stay here and I'll phone Francine. She can be on the next train to sort you out.'

'No don't do that,' said Jacques, almost in panic. 'They have been watching her and me for months. As long as they think I'm dead, they'll leave her alone.'

For a short while they were at an impasse. They fell silent, each thinking about what to do next.

'You realise that the police now know you are alive, don't you?' said Paul, 'and that means they may make a public appeal.'

Jacques went pale as the implications of Paul's comment sank in.

'And if what you say is correct, that will put Francine in danger also,' said Claire, concerning showing in her eyes. 'You must tell Francine; to protect her.'

Jacques looked at both of them in turn as if trying to make up his mind. Then briefly focussing mid-distance he returned his gaze to Claire.

'Francine must disappear also. We must get her out of the glare of their surveillance,' said Jacques, not realising how paranoid he sounded.

Paul and Claire looked at each other doubtfully.

'Look Jacques,' said Paul, as if humouring a lunatic. 'Are you sure you're thinking straight? Where's the evidence that someone's after you and if they are, why would they want to kill you?'

The penny dropped. They were starting to believe he was having psychological problems.

'Who would blame them?' he thought. 'Everything I say must seem so irrational.'

'You think I'm having a mental breakdown don't you?' said Jacques, calmly. 'At first, I thought that was Dmitry's problem.'

Jacques hobbled over to the corner of the room and pulled an envelope from underneath his torn dinner jacket that was dumped like an old rag.

'Dmitry sent this to me before the accident,' he said, handing the envelope to Paul. 'I haven't been able to decipher all of it, but I understand enough to conclude I'm in danger.'

Claire moved next to Paul and looked over his shoulder as he opened the envelope. She noticed the letter written in Cyrillic handwriting.

'This letter is in Russian,' she said taking the paper.

'Yes,' said Jacques, 'That's the most frustrating document in the envelope. I don't speak Russian and I couldn't find a Russian on the Grand Union canal either.'

'Well the first line says,' Claire translated haltingly. 'Dear Jacques, Be careful.... They have eyes and ears... everywhere. If you don't believe me look at the ...photographs.'

Jacques fell silent, his mouth wide open. Paul gazed at Claire in admiration.

'I didn't know you spoke Russian,' he said.

'A little,' she said. 'It was one of my A-levels.'

Paul looked inside the envelope and pulled out the photos, now somewhat soiled from Jacques journey. Jacques watched their expressions as they examined the pictures. Their cynicism had gone.

'I don't know how he got them, but don't forget he sent them from St Petersburg and not from Manchester,' said Jacques. 'Have a look at the rest of them whilst I make myself a cup of tea. Do either of you want one? Claire, you could translate the rest of the letter whilst you drink.'

They didn't reply. Jacques moved to the kitchen to make the tea whilst they had time to absorb the contents of Dmitry's envelope.

****

'Ok you lot,' he said, as a preamble to his team briefing. 'We have some new information.'

The team shuffled into their positions as O'Reilly installed himself in front of the Perspex incident board.

'I assume you've heard,' he said, glancing at the novice, 'that Amaury Degordes is awake.'

'Has he said anything more?' asked the thinker.

'Only that he saw his father after the accident,' replied O'Reilly, 'but in my opinion there's a fifty-fifty chance he is recalling a dream.'

'What did the doctor think?' asked the novice.

‘She thought it was too early to know whether he can distinguish between what he saw and what he imagined.’

‘Is there another way to check,’ asked the thinker, ‘for example hypnosis?’

‘It’s an idea,’ replied O’Reilly, ‘but I’m pretty sure they’ll not let us anywhere near him for that kind of mumbo-jumbo until he’s a lot better.’

‘So let’s go over what *he thought* he saw,’ said O’Reilly, picking up a felt-tipped pen and moving to the Perspex board. ‘Amaury was found here,’ he said pointing to an “x” on a plan of the road some distance away from where the collision had occurred. ‘Where must Jacques Degordes have been standing to have survived the explosion and be seen by Amaury?’

‘Amaury’s line of sight would have been obscured by the other vehicles in the accident, so that limits the opportunities to see him,’ said the thinker.

O’Reilly drew three triangles on the plan; one behind Amaury, one along the verge in front of him and one looking across towards the other carriageway between the cars and lorries.

‘The lad said that his dad pushed him out of the car,’ said O’Reilly.

‘So he must have been in the car after Amaury landed on the deck,’ said the cynic.

‘That eliminates the possibility that Jacques was seen behind him,’ said the thinker, ‘leaving two options. Jacques landed on the same verge further up the road, or he was thrown across the road into the central barrier.’

‘Or,’ said the novice, ‘he was thrown across the central barrier to the other side of the carriage way.’

‘But oncoming traffic would have seen him,’ said the cynic.

‘Not necessarily,’ said the thinker, ‘There had been an accident earlier on the opposite carriage way and traffic was coming through at a trickle.’

‘Did forensics find anything on the opposite carriage way that was linked to Dr Degordes?’ asked O’Reilly.

‘There was a lot of debris from the explosion, but no sign of Jacques,’ replied the thinker. ‘I’m not sure they would have known what to look for.’

‘Amaury mentioned a parcel. I want you to check.’

'Ok,' said the thinker.

'In the meantime,' said O'Reilly, looking at the cynic, 'I want you, Wrigglesworth to examine the verge on either side of the Mancunian Way and see where our missing doctor could have wandered off to.'

'I'll need help,' said the cynic.

'All right, take McKenzie.'

The meeting broke up and each of the team set about performing their assignments. O'Reilly stayed put, ruminating over the possibilities of Degordes' survival.

****

By the time Jacques had limped back with his three mugs of tea. Paul and Claire had emptied the contents of Dmitry's envelope out on their coffee table. They were kneeling sifting their way through the papers.

'Who the hell are these buggers?' exclaimed Paul. 'There are photographs of you and Francine all over Manchester, in the street in Altrincham and shots of you on the motorway; they must have been taken by traffic cameras. How would they get them?' he said holding up the pictures.

Jacques sat down in the Queen Anne chair and sipped his tea; absent-mindedly picking up the gravitum crystal with his free hand whilst he watched them.

'Paul, look at this,' said Claire, picking up a document containing several stapled sheets. 'These are transcripts of their telephone conversations. One of them is between me and Francine.' She paused, thinking back. She continued, 'I remember it. We spoke just after Prama and I had got back from Japan.'

Paul reached across and took the pages from her.

'Shit,' he said. 'It's annotated with our name and address. Which phone did you use?'

'I think I phoned from here,' she replied, thinking back. 'Yes I'm sure. It was from that phone,' she said pointing to the land line in the corner.

'I can see how they could tap mobiles,' said Paul, amazed. 'They are radio systems, but to get calling number records from a land line implies a whole different kind of sophistication.'

Paul moved over to the window and peered across the street. He could see the green cabinet where their telephone wires would have been cross-connected. The street was empty. There was no sign of activity around the cabinet. He shivered, closed the curtains and moved back to his position at the coffee table.

'I thought of that,' said Jacques, reading Paul's thoughts.

'You thought of what?' asked Claire looking up from one of the telephone call transcripts.

'Paul was thinking that your line must be tapped by someone in the street,' he said, matter-of-factly, 'but that's twentieth century way of doing things. These people are a lot cleverer.'

'What do you mean?' asked Paul.

'What has all the surveillance information in front of you have in common?' asked Jacques, reverting to his university supervisor stereotype.

'I don't know,' said Paul refusing to play the student. 'What have they in common?'

'They are all connected to modern data networks,' said Claire, interrupting the testosterone stand-off.

'That's right,' said Jacques, 'and what's more, they have tapped into my tax records, my medical records and the university's employment database; to name but a few.'

'But how can they do that?' asked Claire, 'aren't these things secure?'

'Clearly not,' said Jacques, flatly.

'But I thought they used encryption systems that even with the fastest computers would take hundreds of years to crack,' said Paul incredulously.

'That's what they tell us,' said Jacques, with uncharacteristic cynicism, 'but even if you're right there was something in Dmitry's parcel that removes that problem at a stroke.'

'Where?' asked Paul.

'Here,' said Jacques, pulling a memory stick from his pocket, 'I think that the information on this caused Dmitry to be murdered and triggered the attack on my family.'

'What's on it?'

'Theory and descriptions about gravitum based devices,' said Jacques. 'Unfortunately most of the stick is encrypted. I think the key must be in Dmitry's hand written letter. Even so there was enough information in open text to make me realise how a ruthless commercial business may want to exploit them.'

'You've got to be kidding,' said Paul, doubtfully. 'We've read your paper on nuclear fusion. It's just a theory not a reality and the link to earthquakes can't have any commercial application surely.'

'I wish I was kidding,' said Jacques, 'But, if you excuse the pun, it was not my ideas on nuclear fusion that matter.'

'What does matter then?' asked Claire, trying to be open-minded.

'Whilst I worked on the fusion idea, I suggested that we could create a synthetic black hole. I sent Dmitry an e-mail outlining the principles. I think that e-mail was intercepted by someone who was either interested in the idea or keen to keep it secret.'

'I remember, you described the synthetic black hole in your draft paper,' said Claire. She looked at Paul who nodded. She continued, 'I didn't understand the principles but Prama and Francine told me that you were trying to bend space into a circle or something like that.'

'Sort of,' replied Jacques, 'except you not only bend space….'

'… you also bend time,' interrupted Paul, catching on.

'Oui, and Dmitry hooked on to this idea and found some earlier designs in the university archives that dated back to when the blue gravitum crystals were stolen from China.'

'Is that where the crystal came from?' said Paul, as he reached over and took the gravitum crystal from Jacques. He turned it over to look at the ideogram on its underside. 'That explains the Chinese calligraphy.'

'It does, doesn't it?' Jacques replied. 'Apparently, there were two crystals, that one called Sky,' he said, pointing to the crystal in Paul's hand, 'and the other one, kept by Dmitry, called Earth. For years he thought they were just useless rocks, but after your experiment proved that they were sensitive to gravitational waves, he decided to go back into the archives and see if he could find anything related to the crystals. '

'What did he find?' asked Claire.

'When the crystals were *given to*, or should I say *confiscated by*, the university, they came with a number of Chinese documents from the Beiping Observatory.'

'Modern day Beijing,' said Claire.

'Yes and these documents were in the form of correspondence between a Chinese mandarin and a woman who seemed to have been under the protection of a monastery in Korea.'

'What did they say?' she asked.

'They contained descriptions of experiments involving what we now call gravitum. She was performing the experiments and he was making suggestions and giving advice. Dmitry scanned the documents and their translations and put them on the stick. Unfortunately, they are encrypted.'

'Then you need me to translate Dmitry's hand written Russian to decrypt them?' said Claire.

'That would be nice,' said Jacques, smiling. 'I could work the characters out from my understanding of Greek symbols that we physicists like so much, but I still end up with Russian words.'

'Well I'm a bit rusty, but I'll have a go,' she said.

'What I don't understand,' said Paul bringing Jacques back to his story, 'if they've had these letters for so long, why did it take decades for anyone to realise that the crystals were important?'

'They were buried in the archives and, until your experimental results were published, no one thought of having them translated. Dmitry was the first European to ask a Chinese speaker to look at them. According to one of the unencrypted documents on the memory stick, that translator is now dead,' said Jacques.

'As is Dmitry,' Claire added under her breath.

Claire and Paul gave each other a concerned look as they realised that Jacques story was becoming more and more plausible.

He continued, 'Dmitry describes a device that creates two chambers, one to speed up time the other to slow it down. Perhaps the people who are after me want to recreate it.'

'Why would anyone want that information so badly that they would kill for it?' asked Claire.

'Imagine what you could do, if you put your computer in the "fast-time" room,' said Jacques, mysteriously.

'You could crack Dmitry's encryption algorithms for a start,' said Paul, joking.

'Precisely,' said Jacques, 'and whilst you were at it, you could scan the images from all the surveillance cameras you could find and locate every person on the planet.' He paused, watching his words sink in, 'and you could do it before most computers had booted up!'

'Bloody hell!' said Paul, softly.

'I second that,' said Claire.

# Eighteen

**Arrivals**

Although he had been concerned about meeting the new arrival, Hideo needed to get answers from someone other than his companion in the bunker. As soon as Hitzubishi Mitzuko had left to let the visitor through the security door, Hideo's brain went into overdrive. The potential appearance of an outsider suddenly made him realise how isolated he had become. Hitzubishi san could have told him anything and he would have believed it. But on reflection, there were some anomalies. He shivered as yet again he began to see himself as a prisoner.

'If only I could get to a television or phone someone for the news,' he thought. 'At least I would know for sure whether I'm a wanted man.'

His first thought was to play it cool by handling the newcomer casually. Hideo could wait in the laboratory doing his assigned tasks and listen to their conversation as he pretended to work on his computer model. But if Mitzuko was deceiving Hideo, he would have to be more subtle. At this point, his view of the whole situation had changed. Was he becoming paranoid again? Or perhaps he had come to his senses. Hideo was unsure. He decided to eavesdrop on the conversation in the main chamber. He could not expect the new person, Viktor, to be any more forthcoming than Mitzuko because he had made his way to the bunker on his own. If he knew that much, Viktor must be part of Mitzuko's gang, club, brotherhood… or whatever it was. As the newcomer was unlikely to be Hideo's natural ally, he would have to work at it. Hideo needed an edge. He resolved to befriend Viktor as soon as possible.

Hideo moved to the laboratory exit and glanced down the corridor to make sure the coast was clear. Somehow it looked different. Whenever

Hideo had entered the corridor before he was amazed at its length; its parallel walls coming almost to a point as railway lines do when viewed in perspective. He strained his eyes towards the white door into the main chamber positioned at the end. He knew that as he gazed towards it, the door usually looked like a point of white light. However on this occasion it was a different colour. It was black.

'The door must be open. He can't have put the orange lights on yet,' he thought. 'That's great. I should be able to hear without walking the length of the corridor.'

Hideo was banking on the fact that Mitzuko was meeting the new arrival in the large chamber. Its geometry when combined with the position of the corridor should have created an acoustic amplifier. This would mean Hideo could hear every word without moving closer.

He strained his ears to hear their conversation, but all he could make out were high-pitched squeaks, pitches so high he could barely hear them.

'Sounds like a dog whistle,' he thought. 'I'll have to get closer.'

He moved through the doorway and started to follow the corridor towards the main chamber where he expected Mitzuko would be meeting the newcomer. In the distance Hideo could see the rectangular black shape of the doorway at the end of the tunnel.

'Why hasn't he switched the lights on?' he wondered.

If Mitzuko had left the corridor door open, he would have expected an orange glow from the floodlights.

'He must be meeting them in the dark,' he thought 'How odd.'

He listened and was still unable to make out anything intelligible from the noises coming towards him. He made his way slowly down the corridor, listening carefully and desperate not to be seen. He paused by each side door just in case he needed to duck inside.

'If Mitzuko doubles back,' he thought. 'I'll have to drop into one of the other rooms to hide.'

He crept slowly towards the doorway. The rectangle appeared to have changed from black to violet.

'Weird,' he mumbled, rubbing his eyes. 'I've been down here too long.'

Although Hideo had walked up and down the corridor many times over the last few days, Mitzuko had always left the white adjoining door to the main chamber closed. This was the first time it had been ajar. Hideo noticed that as he walked towards the opening the violet light changed colour. It was turning to blue, then green. Although logic told him that he was witnessing some strange phenomenon associated with Mitzuko's experiments, his brain was not prepared to believe what Hideo was seeing. He paused to rub his eyes again

'What are they doing in there,' he thought, 'displaying a light show?'

He was beginning to wish he had paid more attention in physics lessons at school; although he had noticed that the colours were moving towards the red end of the spectrum, he could not work out why. Now stationary, he noticed that the background noise was different. The high pitched squeaks had dropped in pitch. He could hear something that resembled cartoon voices or people talking with helium in their lungs.

'I don't believe it. They're watching a cartoon,' he thought, preferring the obvious over the extraordinary.

Now even more curious about what his companions were watching, he moved further down the corridor. The cartoon voices continued to drop in pitch. The colour of the light shifted towards yellow. By the time he reached the entrance to the chamber, he could see that the light had become orange. The floodlights in the main chamber were now the only source of the doorway's illumination. The cartoon voices had dropped to the sound of two men talking. As Hideo hid just inside the corridor, he could hear Mitzuko and Viktor speaking together in English. Hideo did not know that he had experienced a phenomenon similar to the change of pitch when a train passes you by. In this case there was no train, just shifts in the passage of time.

****

'What have you told him?' asked Viktor.

'The truth,' Mitzuko replied.

'What,' exclaimed Viktor, 'You've told him everything?'

'Are you mad?' snapped, Mitzuko. 'I said the truth, not the whole truth. He knows very little except that the GWR is not a doomsday machine.'

Hideo cautiously peered around the door to get a better view of them. They were standing together next to a large van. Judging by the suspension, it was laden with supplies.

'That must have been hard to drive down the tunnel,' he thought, remembering his first and only encounter with the entrance to the bunker.

'He must be Viktor. As I thought, he's not Japanese,' he muttered. 'I wonder how Mitzuko knows him.'

Hideo was surprised; Hitzubishi Mitzuko was one of the most chauvinistic people he knew. It was not like him to mix with foreigners. Viktor was a thirty-something, fit looking European with a hint of the east in his face. His hair was thinning and trimmed close to his head. Hideo assumed this was to try to camouflage his baldness. His beard was trimmed neatly; short enough to look well-trimmed but long enough not to look like he had forgotten to shave.

'Sooner or later he's going to start asking difficult questions,' said Viktor. 'Why don't we get rid of him?'

Hideo froze, waiting for the answer and re-evaluating his plan to befriend Viktor.

'We need him,' replied Mitzuko, 'for the time being, anyway. I've had problems of acoustic leakage into the ground.'

'Why don't you do what you did last time and put it on the tenth floor of a skyscraper, designed to withstand earthquakes.'

'It doesn't work. Look what happened last time.'

'Yes but that was the idiot's fault,' replied Viktor. 'There would have been no problem, if he'd have left it alone.'

'That's what I told him,' said Mitzuko.

'So?'

'Well, it wasn't really the truth.'

'What do you mean, "It wasn't really the truth"?' asked Viktor, mimicking Mitzuko.

'I lied.'

'You lied?'

'Yes, I lied.'

'But you just told me you told him the truth.'

'I lied.'

Hideo's head was starting to spin. However he had confirmed one thing; Mitzuko was a liar.

'Enough of this,' said Viktor. 'What is wrong with the GWR III?'

'When the focused gravitational wave came over, the measurements of the energy being absorbed were one hundred times greater than I had calculated.'

'What?' said Viktor. 'That's not possible. We can't have got it that wrong.'

'We did,' replied Mitzuko. 'Remember the gravitation radiation is coherent and collimated, like a laser. It is far more intense than we predicted.'

'Amazing,' said Viktor. 'So it would have shaken the Academy to bits whether the idiot had moved it or not.'

Hideo, fidgeted; he was fed up with being described as "the idiot".

'That's right,' said Mitzuko. 'So he did us a favour. He got it out of the building and now I've reinstalled it here.'

'Brilliant,' said Viktor. 'So he's done his job. Why don't we do away with him?'

There was a noise as someone appeared from behind the tower. Startled, Hideo stepped back away from the door.

'We must do something about all this water,' said a female voice. She paused, 'Do away with whom?'

'The guy who sabotaged the GWR,' replied Viktor.

'Oh Viktor,' she said, condescendingly. 'You always want to do away with people. Let the mouse live, for a little bit anyway. You could always put him in the Fast Room. He'd be an old man in a few months and no threat to anyone.'

Hideo did not know what made him more annoyed, being called "the idiot", "the mouse" or the threat to kill him. Either way he now realised how much trouble he was in.

Mitzuko looked at her with admiration.

'You're brilliant,' he said. 'Put him in there with his computer terminal and he'll have finished the work in double time.'

'Actually a lot faster,' she said, correcting him.

'That's dangerous,' said Viktor. 'You can't keep an eye on him in there. You'll give him a lifetime to think of ways to stop us.'

'Not if he doesn't know,' she replied, smoothly. 'Besides, your lust for blood is becoming tiresome. Well, I don't want him dead, unless it's from old age. Understood?'

'Understood,' said Viktor, meekly.

'Right let's unload the truck,' she said, 'Hitzubishi!'

'Hai.'

'Fetch the mouse. He can help us with the supplies,' she ordered.

****

Hideo had just made it back to the laboratory in time and was still short of breath as Mitzuko entered the room.

'Hideo, my friend,' he said. 'We need your help to unload the supplies.'

'No problem,' he replied, sweat running down his back.

'Is there something wrong?' asked Mitzuko.

'No,' said Hideo, innocently. 'I sometimes find it claustrophobic in here, don't you?

'No,' said Mitzuko, flatly. 'Perhaps you're coming down with something.'

'Perhaps,' replied Hideo, pleased that Mitzuko did not seem to be suspicious.

'Don't worry,' he said. 'We have a recovery room on the other side of the tower. A stint in there would do you good.'

Hideo listened to Mitzuko's suggestion with a mixture of curiosity and terror.

'Do me good?' he thought, remembering the discussion about the Fast Room. 'I don't think so.'

'No need to worry,' said Hideo, standing up. 'I feel fine. Where are these supplies you want me to unload?'

'Come with me,' said Mitzuko.

Obediently Hideo followed Mitzuko down the corridor. This time the door was closed. There was no sign of rainbow colours or strange voices. Hideo put the phenomenon to the back of his mind.

A few moments later Mitzuko had opened the door and they were walking across the main chamber towards the van now parked neatly alongside the other vehicles. Viktor was busy unloading, whilst the woman looked on. They did not look round until Hideo and Mitzuko were within a few feet of them.

'Hi,' Mitzuko called, in English, 'This is Hideo.'

Viktor, nodded an acknowledgement and continued unloading. The woman turned towards Hideo and smiled. She moved towards him and made a slight bow. He returned the gesture. Unlike her companion, she did not look in the least European. She had a broad east Asian face. Hideo thought she was probably Chinese, Korean or Mongolian.

'Hello,' she said, holding out her hand, 'You must be Hideo. I've heard a lot about you.' His head still low; he took her hand and shook it. She continued, 'I hear you made quite an impression on the Academy of Geosciences.'

'More then just an impression,' muttered her companion. 'He wrecked it. Do you realise how much of our money he wasted?'

Hideo chose not to understand the question, so he ignored it. He was concentrating on the woman in front of him. Her hand was smooth and cold. He noticed that she was wearing expensive Italian black satin shoes.

As he lifted his head, he could see that she was in her late thirties to early forties. Her heels took her to about one metre eighty, about the same height as Hideo. She was immaculately dressed in a dark blue trouser suit and a white blouse. She had a necklace with a single large diamond hanging above her cleavage. Had she not arrived in a delivery van, Hideo would have believed that she had just stepped out of a corporate board room. Her manner and bearing were of extreme politeness that some people with power and influence display when they wish to win the trust of subordinates. He looked briefly into her green-brown eyes. They were unusually light for a Chinese person. He could see a cold hardness there. She frightened him.

'I'm very sorry,' said Hideo, looking away from her eyes, 'You seem to know my name, but I don't know yours.'

'Oh, I'm sorry,' she said, 'didn't I say? It's Lihua. My name is Lihua.'

# Nineteen

## Language overload

It was clear that if the police concluded that Jacques had escaped from the accident, then they would probably make a public appeal for him to come forward. If this happened both his and Francine's lives would be in danger again. Jacques was reluctant to use any communication that could be intercepted because this could have the same result. The three of them were at a loss to work out how to tell her.

'It must be done in person,' said Claire. 'I'll go and see her.'

'That could work,' said Paul, uncomfortable that it may put Claire in danger. 'I'll come with you.'

'No,' she said, emphatically. 'I must do it on my own. If two of us go it will look like a deputation. They may still be watching her. We don't want to arouse suspicion.'

'Perhaps we should go to the police,' said Paul, trying to find an alternative.

'I thought of that before,' said Jacques, 'but you realise many of these pictures come from police cameras. The moment, we tell them, they'll be sending e-mails, doing computer searches phoning people. They are not secure.' He glanced at Claire and continued, 'But, I agree with you Paul. I'm putting you both in danger. Claire must stay here. If you'll lend me some money, I'll go now and catch the next train to Manchester. I've become too comfortable in this chair, a train journey would do me good.'

Claire stepped over to her desk by the window

'It won't work, Jacques,' she said, gazing along the street. 'It has to be me. I can see two street cameras from where I'm standing. You were lucky that the canal is behind us and you broke in through the back door. If they are as sophisticated as you seem to think, you'll be identified within a few minutes of stepping into the street.'

She closed the curtains.

'I'll take my chances,' said Jacques.

'You can't,' said Paul, reluctantly. 'We need to know what you're up against. We know from the photos, that whoever is behind this has fingers everywhere, but we don't know if they have any weaknesses. Let's translate Dmitry's letter before we do anything.'

'You mean, let Claire translate Dmitry's letter,' she said smiling. 'You'd do anything to keep me off the streets, wouldn't you?'

Paul said nothing, he just looked at her desperately trying to think of another plan, but he could not.

****

Having had a frustrating conversation about lack of progress with his boss, O'Reilly felt he had to get out of the station. So he decided to check on the novice and the cynic. He was pissed off that his boss did not consider that Amaury's statement constituted progress.

'It wasn't you that woke him up,' his boss had said. 'He did that all on his own and now you don't know whether this is a murder investigation or a missing person case. You're going backwards.'

When O'Reilly had told him about the Russian murder, his boss was not impressed.

'You're making this case too complicated. This is Manchester not some exotic location in a spy story. Get real. Look for the obvious suspects and charge somebody will you!'

But in his heart of hearts O'Reilly was sure that this was not a normal domestic or local low-life murder. There was more to this. Unfortunately he could not find out what it was.

He was drawing near to the accident spot. As there was no way to park safely on the elevated section of the Mancunain Way, they generally parked in an area between carriageways beneath the flyover near the Princess Road roundabout. He pulled up behind McKenzie's small Ford and stepped out of the car. He opened the back door and took a bright green fluorescent waistcoat from the seat.

'Let's see if they've found anything,' he thought, as he headed off towards the closest slip road to the motorway above.

He had only gone a few paces when he saw the novice in her safety jacket leaning over the parapet above.

'What's she looking for?' he thought. 'There's nothing down here.'

'McKenzie!' he shouted. 'Oi, McKenzie!'

There was no reaction; the noise from the motorway above must have drowned everything else.

Then he caught her eye. He raised his thumb and little finger to the side of his face to make the international signal for her to phone him. She nodded. His phone rang.

'What have you found up there?' he asked.

'Nothing, Guv,' she shouted, over the background noise. 'But he may have….' Her voice was drowned by a passing lorry.

'Say again,' he shouted, even though it was quieter down below.

'He… have fallen …. the parapet,' she shouted.

'Come down here,' said O'Reilly. 'I can't hear you.'

'I can't hear you,' she shouted.

He made another unmistakeable hand signal and McKenzie started to make her way back towards the slip road. Within a few minutes she was by his side.

'There's nothing up there,' she said, 'except buckled sections of crash barrier that they haven't replaced yet.' She looked up towards the road above. 'The heat must have been incredible to bend steel like that,' she added.

'Yes,' said O'Reilly, disinterested. 'What did you say about the parapet?'

'Oh there's no evidence,' replied McKenzie, 'but the only way down is over the parapet. He could have fallen.'

O'Reilly looked about him. 'That's crazy,' he said. 'He'd have landed on the road. It must be a twenty to thirty foot drop to the concrete below. He would have to have been indestructible to walk away from that.'

'Not unless something broke his fall,' she said.

'Like what,' he said, looking along the lower carriageway. 'A moving lorry? A bit far fetched.'

'But he may not have fallen on the road,' she said, her eyes lighting up. 'We're right next to a roundabout full of trees.' Turning to look at the road in the other direction, she continued, 'And just over a hundred yards down there, there's another one that's even more overgrown.'

Under normal circumstances he would have ignored her far-fetched idea, but as he had nothing else to go on he decided to let it run on a little longer. He took his mobile and keyed the thinker's number.

'It's O'Reilly,' he said, 'Did SOCO examine the area under the motorway.' He listened to the thinker's reply. 'They did?' O'Reilly looked at McKenzie, doubtfully. 'Did they find anything?' This time the thinker's reply was short. 'Did they look at the wooded areas under the flyover?' The thinker had asked a question. 'The roundabouts, they're covered in trees.' O'Reilly hung up. He had his answer.

'Ok,' he said. 'Let's take a walk.'

He clicked his phone shut and put it back in his pocket.

They headed off towards a clump of trees immediately below the motorway with stinging nettles and a buddleia that had a few broken branches.

****

Claire had installed herself at the desk by the window, surrounded by her first attempts at Russian translation for many years. She had been working for over an hour on Dmitry's letter and had managed to translate most of the first page. There were a few key words she could not find in her dictionary and she was becoming frustrated. Paul was on his knees rummaging through the other papers, whilst Jacques sat in his favourite chair with a laptop, scanning the accessible documents on Dmitry's memory stick.

Claire picked up her latest translation and handed it to Jacques.

'This is as far as I've got,' she said, slightly disheartened. 'It's difficult to read some of his handwriting and some of the words must be technical terms that I can't translate.'

'This is wonderful,' said Jacques, scrutinising the page. 'The words in red are the words that you can't translate?'

'Yes,' she said, 'I've converted the Cyrillic characters to phonetic Latin letters, so you can work out what the words sound like. If they are common technical terms, you may recognise them.'

Paul, put down the document he was reading to look over Jacques' shoulder at the translation.

'The first one is easy,' said Paul. 'It says "geodesic".'

'Of course,' said Claire, sarcastically. 'That's obvious.'

'It means space-timeline,' said Jacques, smiling.

'That explains everything,' she said smiling back. 'I'd better go back to my translation. At this rate it will take me all night.'

Her translation skills were coming back and Claire was beginning to get used to Dmitry's handwriting. Within the next hour she had handed Jacques three more pages of her translation. She had one to go.

Jacques and Paul had to read the pages several times before they could decipher out the technical content that had caused Claire so much difficulty. Finally she handed them the last page. After a few minutes Paul and Jacques had filled in the remaining technical words. They sat in a huddle and read the whole document from end to end.

'Alors,' said Jacques, 'That explains how Dmitry got hold of the surveillance information. He tapped into the company's computer.'

'Who are "the company"?' asked Claire.

'He means the STKiC. They are the people who offered me a job. Dmitry was convinced they were behind everything bad. I thought he was paranoid. It looks like I was wrong and he was right.'

'They are a massive international corporation,' said Paul. 'I have no idea what nationality they are.'

'I understand that they are Russo-Japanese.' said Jacques. 'The people I met seemed to be Russian.'

'How does a Russo-Japanese company get so much power in the UK?' asked Claire, not expecting an answer.

'This could help us find out' said Paul, pointing to a section on the second page. 'There's useful information here.'

'You mean the details of how he hacked into them?' asked Claire. 'We could do the same thing,' she said, looking at the computer on her desk.

'Not from here,' said Jacques. 'They may be able to track us down.'

'That's probably how they knew Dmitry was on to them,' said Paul.

'And that led to his murder,' said Claire, thoughtfully. 'You're right we'd better be careful.'

They continued to read until they reached the end of Claire's translation.

'I can't see anything that looks like an encryption key, or password,' said Claire. 'Can you?'

'No, I can't,' said Paul.

'Nor can I,' said Jacques, despondently. 'Which means we still can't decrypt Dmitry's memory stick.'

They each took a sheet and examined each word as if it would jump out at them.

'There is a sentence here telling you to remember why you and he got into physics.' said Claire. 'What is that all about?'

'Oh, it's something we talked about at a conference. We told each other what made us specialise in plasma physics,' said Jacques, reflectively.

'Can I look at the extract again please,' said Paul, putting out his hand for the sheet Claire had been reading.

Claire handed him the page.

'It's odd,' he said. 'All the rest is about the company, references to documents on the stick and telling Jacques to be careful. This part is completely different, it's conversational; a completely different tone.'

'Perhaps he wanted to make the letter more personal,' said Claire.

'I don't think so,' said Paul, warming to his theme. 'The letter is in a staccato mode, with facts jotted down like a list; important things that he wanted Jacques to know. I think he was in a hurry. I reckon this paragraph contains a hidden meaning.'

'You think the encryption code is in here?' asked Jacques, leaning over to look at the sheet.

'No,' said Paul. 'He's given you a clue to some information you shared privately. By doing that he's avoided writing the key in open text.'

'Remind me,' said Claire. 'What does it say?'

Paul read the section out loud, 'My dear friend you must remember why we both specialised in physics. It will remain important to both of us.'

'What did you say at the conference?' asked Claire, 'Can you remember?'

'We talked about lots of things.'

'Like what?' asked Paul.

'The presentation, STKiC, the man who offered me the job, his grandmother, pet theories…'

'What did you say about his grandmother?' asked Claire.

'Mon Dieu, So much has happened since.'

Jacques' forehead wrinkled as he tried to take himself back to the conference where they spoke about their ideas.

'He said that his grandmother saw a natural phenomenon that she kept secret for years, because she was frightened people would not believe her,' said Jacques, picturing the scene. 'He said it was a lightning strike,' he paused, as more detail came to him. 'No, not a lightning strike, ball lightning. That was it! ball lightning.' Paul and Claire listened quietly, reluctant to break Jacques' train of thought. He continued, 'he said that he believed her and wanted to understand it. This was what made him interested in plasma physics.'

Jacques sat back relieved at his recall. He picked up the laptop, loaded the encrypted archive.

'Enter password,' it said.

He keyed in the word 'grandmother.'

Nothing happened.

He keyed in the phrase 'ball lightning.'

Nothing happened.

He keyed in other combinations of the words.

Nothing happened.

'Wait a minute,' said Paul, thoughtfully. 'Did you say that he was a specialist in plasma physics like you?'

'Yes he was,' said Jacques, 'and I told him that when I realised that most of the Universe was made of plasma, I made it my specialism. It was a way of always having a job… or something like that.'

'But in his letter, he says that you were specialists in physics, not plasma physics. Why did he omit the word "Plasma"?'

Jacques keyed it into the computer.

There was a beep noise and a new message came up.

'Enter encryption key,' it said.

'Try grandmother again,' said Paul.

'Enter encryption key,' it said.

'Try babushka,' said Claire.

'Enter encryption key,' it said.

'I'll try ball lightening,' said Jacques.

'Enter encryption key: Final Attempt,' it said.

'Merde,' muttered Jacques.

'Ok Jacques,' said Paul. 'Think back. You've forgotten something.'

Silence.

'What is ball lightening anyway?' asked Claire.

'What did you say?' asked Jacques, frowning.

Claire repeated her question.

He looked down at the keyboard. His hands were shaking.

Jacques keyed one word into the laptop. He closed his eyes as he hit the return key.

The machine emitted a series of beeps. Jacques opened his eyes. The screen was blank. Then the disk drive light started to flash. Paul and Claire move closer.

'What's it doing?' asked Claire.

'It's accessing the disc and not displaying anything,' said Paul. 'I hope it's not deleting everything!'

'Too late now,' said Jacques.

The screen suddenly burst into life. The word "decrypting" appeared at the top of the screen and was repeated until it filled the whole display.

'What was the key?' asked Paul, quietly.

'Soliton,' he said.

'Like a tsunami?' asked Paul, rhetorically.

'I think that's very appropriate,' said Claire.

'Why?' asked Jacques.

'Well, this information is just about as dangerous, don't you think?'

# Twenty

## No hiding place

Jacques, Paul and Claire had been staring at the scrolling text for a good five minutes before anyone spoke. It was Paul who broke the silence.

'There must be masses of data on there,' he said. 'Look how long it's taken to decrypt the files.'

The scrolling stopped and an emphatic "beep" came from the computer's speaker, like a small child seeking attention. The screen cleared and was replaced by a page of yellow folder icons. There was a text file called "Read me". Jacques clicked on it.

'Wow,' said Paul, when he had finished reading the document. 'That's incredible!'

'Which bit in particular?' asked Claire, a few paragraphs behind.

'He says that "blue crystals" have been known since the late eighteenth century,' replied Paul. 'I assume by "blue crystals" he means gravitum. The Koreans and Chinese had collected blocks of gravitum from earlier meteor storms.'

'Yes, but the mineral remains pretty rare,' said Jacques. 'Serious research started in the mid nineteenth century and STKiC has inherited most of the reserves and knowledge. Dmitry says that the company is desperate to keep all samples under their control.'

'I couldn't find out why,' said Claire. 'Perhaps it is like the diamond trade; a way of keeping the price up,' she added.

'There has to be another reason,' said Jacques, 'He's given us a link to another document. I'll open that.'

Jacques followed a link to a directory titled "Background" and opened a file mentioned in Dmitry's readme file.

'STKiC are trying to keep gravitum and its properties secret,' said Jacques, paraphrasing. 'So if they lock the stones away, no one can find out their full potential.'

'But surely it's too late,' said Claire. 'Paul's paper has been published. Gravitum is in the public domain.'

'That's true,' said Paul. 'They can't do it.'

Jacques scrolled on to the next page. He was now silently reading ahead of Paul and Claire whilst they stood behind him discussing STKiC's megalomania.

'Is there something else?' asked Claire, seeing that Jacques was completely absorbed.

Jacques didn't reply. He opened a new document, then another. His eyes scanned over one schematic diagram after another. They watched him for a few minutes, silently agreeing not to disturb him, until Paul got bored.

'Jacques,' said Paul, attracting his attention. 'Have you found something else?'

Keeping his eyes on the screen, he raised a finger to indicate that they should wait for him to finish.

'What is it?' asked Paul, impatiently.

'Mon Dieu,' muttered Jacques, to himself.

'What's wrong?' asked Claire. 'What have you found?'

'I understand their plan,' said Jacques enigmatically. 'They will discredit you Paul,' he said, pausing, '…and kill me.'

'What?' said Paul, whitening.

'Their plan was to steal all the gravitum that is not under their control and then challenge you to repeat your experiment.'

'But that will not be possible without the crystals,' said Paul.

'Précisement,' said Jacques. 'Nobody will be able to repeat your experiment, including you, and the scientific community will either condemn you as a fraud or put your results down to bad experimental practice.'

'But gravitational wave energy demolished Paul's laboratory at the old fire station!' said Claire. 'Isn't that evidence enough of the power of gravitum?'

Jacques did not reply. He was reading another page. Paul gazed at Claire absorbed in thought.

'Thanks for jumping to my defence luv,' said Paul finally, 'but you know as well as I do, that the experiment has to be repeated. Besides they'll probably say I dynamited the building.'

'Then they will destroy your reputation,' she said shocked, 'your career. We can't let that happen.'

Paul and Claire looked at each other devoid of ideas. Jacques continued to read. Simultaneously Paul and Claire caught each others eyes and spoke.

'Sky!' they said.

'Yes, Sky,' said Jacques, looking up at them. 'We must keep it from these people. It is our only hope.'

'And have an independent team repeat the experiment,' said Claire.

'Yes,' said Paul, enthusiastically. 'We could get another university to use Sky in their experiment. Then there is no point in attacking us.'

Claire looked at Jacques, trying to read his face.

'It is not that simple,' she thought.

'I don't understand why an experiment that detects gravitational waves should be so important to a company like STKiC,' she said. 'There has to be more to this.'

'I'm afraid you're right,' said Jacques returning his gaze to the laptop computer. 'We need to do more than repeat your experiment.'

'What do you mean?' asked Paul, puzzled.

'From what I have seen in Dmitry's dossier we have only seen the tip of the iceberg,' said Jacques, picking up Sky. 'This crystal has other uses we could only dream about. Not only is gravitum valuable, but the knowledge about how to use it is priceless. If STKiC allow us to experiment we may be able to find out what one can do with it. They want to keep that to themselves whatever the cost.'

'And they would kill to keep it to themselves?' asked Claire.

'I must have gone too far with my paper on nuclear fusion,' said Jacques. 'Dmitry says here, that they didn't want that technology to be publicised.'

'So they tried to kill you?' asked Claire.

'But you never published it,' said Paul. 'How did they know?'

'According to Dmitry, they tap all private e-mails.'

'What world-wide?' asked Claire incredulously, 'in all languages?'

'That's what he says.'

'That's not possible,' said Paul, confidently. 'It would take the fastest computer years to find key e-mails, let alone process and translate the words into anything meaningful. There would have to be a huge search engine, just to cross reference everything back to an individual like you, Jacques.'

'You would think so, mon ami,' said Jacques, 'but what if you put your computer in a room where time ran much faster?'

'I don't understand,' said Claire. 'Is that possible?'

'That's what Dmitry says,' replied Jacques, 'and he's given us parts of one hundred and fifty years of research to show how.'

'But what's that got to do with Paul's gravitational wave detector,' asked Claire, her head starting to spin.

'That's what was puzzling me,' said Jacques, pleased with himself. 'You see they don't actually care whether Paul's results are confirmed or not. Their objective is to stop all research into gravitum.'

'Why,' asked Paul, 'are they trying to corner the market in research grants?'

'They don't need the money, my friend,' replied Jacques. 'They have already found far more uses, beyond what we have discovered. If they permit anybody to work with gravitum, then they may find out what STKiC already knows.'

'What do STKiC know that's so valuable?' asked Claire, now convinced that her head had indeed completed a number of rotations.

'That's what I want to find out,' he said. 'Let's put the coffee on and print some of these diagrams out. It's going to be a long night.'

****

It had not taken SOCO long to find traces of Jacques' DNA in and around the buddleia below the motorway. O'Reilly was kicking himself for not thinking of it before.

'This opens the case up completely,' he thought. 'It looks as though he wanted to disappear.'

O'Reilly immediately suspected an insurance scam and assumed that his wife would be the first beneficiary. The idea of a felon faking his own death and turning up later in another place as someone else was not entirely new to O'Reilly. He was beginning to feel comfortable that the case was moving towards terra firma. Unfortunately when he accused Degordes' wife of being an accomplice, his whole theory fell apart. It turned out that she was the big earner in the house, a house incidentally that she had already paid for, and there was no financial gain by his disappearance. Francine then tearfully pointed out that her son was nearly killed in the accident. If he thought either Jacques or she were accomplices in that then he wanted his head examining. He left her house in a foul mood and not convinced of her innocence. It was just as she was closing the door behind him when the phone rang. It was Claire.

'Do you know what O'Reilly just said?' asked Francine, barely able to speak. 'He thinks Jacques and I faked his murder for the insurance!'

Claire was on her guard. Jacques and Paul had told her to assume that Francine's phone was tapped.

'That's terrible,' said Claire, then quickly changing the subject. 'I'm in town this evening. Do you want to meet?'

'Oh,' said Francine, taken aback, by Claire's tone. 'I'm not sure. I've got to think.'

'Just a drink,' said Claire, insistently. 'We'll meet at the place we met last time.'

'You, mean…'

'That's it,' said Claire interrupting. 'I'll see you there at seven o'clock.'

'Alright,' said Francine, confused.

'Bye,' said Claire.

The line went dead.

'How odd,' thought Francine.

****

'Do you think she will turn up?' asked Claire, 'I was a bit rude.'

'She'll turn up,' said Jacques, 'if only out of curiosity. You told me you met at the wine bar near Whitworth Street, didn't you?'

'Yes, it's next to the canal,' she replied.

'That's ideal,' said Jacques. 'If you walk west along the tow path you find there are no cameras. Look around and make sure there is no one in earshot and tell her the plan.'

'She'll think I'm mad,' said Claire.

Jacques scribbled something on a scrap of paper.

'Give her this. It should convince her that I'm part of the plan.'

Claire picked up her bag.

'Do you remember what you've got to say?' asked Paul.

Claire gave him a withering look.

'Well, I'm off then,' she said. 'Wish me luck.'

Claire kissed Paul on the lips.

Jacques wished her good luck and said, 'We'll see you in the cottage tomorrow.'

'Bye,' she said, blowing a kiss.

She closed the door behind her.

Jacques nodded at Paul to acknowledge the concern they both had for their loved ones. But they had more work to do. Now they understood the problem they had to focus on the solution. Paul and Jacques went back to work.

****

She was still coming to terms with her conversation with O'Reilly when she heard her doorbell ring. The noise startled Francine. Fearing that O'Reilly had returned to accuse her of something else, she eased the front door open. Preoccupied by Jacques' theoretical reappearance, she was confused by the mundane appearance of a man in overalls in front of her. She looked at him blankly.

'Gas,' he said.

'I beg your pardon,' she said, trying to assimilate his words.

'I've come to read the gas meter,' he said, brandishing an identity card.

'Oh,' she said, coming to her senses. 'The meter is in the garage. I'll get the key.'

She took a few paces towards the end of the hall, but before she opened the door into kitchen, where the keys were kept, something made her turn. Suddenly she realised that the man had stepped over the threshold.

'I said the meter is in the garage,' she said, sharply. 'Wait there please.'

He did not move.

'Is everything all right?' said a familiar voice from outside.

'Just come to read the meter mate,' said the gas man. 'I'm waiting for the lady to unlock the door.'

'Show me your ID,' said O'Reilly, coming into view.

The gasman handed his plastic card to him. He examined it closely.

'Looks ok,' he muttered.

'I can see you're busy madam. You can phone the reading in or do it over the internet,' he said, handing her a card. 'I can see it's not convenient at the moment.'

Francine, saying nothing took the card from him. O'Reilly could see that she was as white as a sheet.

'What's wrong, Mrs Degordes?' he asked, as the other man turned to go.

'Nothing,' she replied, watching the gas man's back as he retreated down the drive to his van. 'For some reason he frightened me. I'm just a little jumpy I suppose.'

'I see. Do you want me to put a WPC with you?' said O'Reilly, unusually considerate. 'You've been through a lot lately.'

'You wanted to ask me something?' said Francine, recovering her composure.

'Ah yes,' he said. 'I wondered if your husband had a second home or a regular holiday spot.'

'Oh you mean somewhere where he could hide?' she said. 'No, we liked to fly somewhere different each year. Is that it?'

'Yes, thanks,' he said politely, turning toward his car.

Francine closed the door behind him. She entered the living room and sat down. She was still shaking.

The moment the front door was closed, O'Reilly pulled out his mobile.

'McKenzie, I'm at the Degordes' house,' he said. 'I want you to get on to West Manchester Gas. Find out whether any of their employees have been reading meters in this area today.'

****

Paul and Jacques had installed themselves in the holiday cottage that Claire and Paul had rented last summer. It was in an isolated part of Dorset, away from prying eyes.

'This place is ideal,' said Jacques, as he unpacked Claire's laptop, 'but they will track us down eventually. I'll need to find an even more secure place to hide whilst I work out a plan.'

'Plan?' said Paul incredulously. 'Jacques Degordes plan. I'll believe that when I see it.'

Paul was carrying a large box of equipment in from the car. He put the box on the dining table.

'Anyway how could they possibly find us here?' asked Paul.

'Your car,' said Jacques.

'It's under cover,' said Paul. 'We smuggled you into the car through the flat's basement garage. Why would anyone make the connection between you and Claire's car?'

'When they realise I'm alive, it will be easy to make the connection from me to you and then to Claire. Then they can go back over old traffic camera footage and track you down.'

'Aren't you overreacting a bit?' said Paul. 'All that information would have to be stored on their computers. It's a massive amount of data, let alone the processing time needed to match us to this spot near the sea'

'You could be right,' said Jacques, 'but I think paranoia may be a healthy condition, don't you?'

'Perhaps, but there are no cameras round here,' said Paul.

'No but there were lots on the main road to Poole and don't forget you can get satellite pictures of this area on the internet.'

'I'm not sure anyone is that clever, besides everything is out of sight now. It's just as well this place has a garage,' said Paul.

'I'm still not sure we are secure enough for what I have in mind,' said Jacques, uncertainly.

'Do you have anywhere else in mind?'

'I'm working on it,' replied Jacques. 'I thought it may be a good idea to get off this island though.'

'Why?'

'Because it's the most photographed place on Earth,' he said. 'I thought somewhere in the South of France, where it's less populated,' he suggested tentatively.

'Your home territory makes sense,' said Paul. 'How do you plan on getting there?'

'I haven't worked that bit out yet.'

'A minor weakness in your plan, I would have thought,' said Paul harshly. 'You need a systematic person to help you.'

'Are you volunteering?'

'You've got to be kidding,' said Paul. 'I'd be useless. You need Francine.'

'You're right,' said Jacques, sighing. 'I need her more than you think.'

Paul was no longer listening. While they had been talking both Jacques and Paul were reassembling their computer equipment so that they could resume the investigation that they had started in the flat. Their conversation drifted away as they started to concentrate on Dmitry's dossier.

'Jacques, I've found something,' said Paul, excited. Jacques and Paul had split the work by copying the memory stick on to a second computer. Jacques continued to work on the laptop whilst Paul examined the second copy. 'Open the file GWR two. There's a drawing and some notes,' added Paul.

'Got it,' said Jacques,' it seems to be a Chinese document with some annotations in Dmitry's neat hand writing. At least he's used English and Latin script.'

Jacques examined the drawing.

'It seems to be some kind of cavity to produce a gravitational standing wave,' said Jacques, thoughtfully. 'I can't see how that's possible.'

'Why not?' asked Paul. 'It would resonate like a guitar string that vibrates with sounds that match the string's pitch.'

'That's right, but the cavity would have to be huge, because the frequency of gravitational waves is so low.'

'The frequency of the radiation from our infamous black holes is between fifteen and one hundred and fifty Hertz. That would mean that a half-wave cavity would have to be from a thousand to ten thousand kilometres long. I see what you mean.'

'It would have to be longer than the diameter of the Earth,' said Jacques.

'So the design can't work,' said Paul. 'I imagine even STKiC would have some technical difficulties building that!' Paul opened another document. 'Have you looked at the notes yet?' he asked.

'It's in Chinese,' said Jacques. 'Claire doesn't happen…'

'No she doesn't,' interrupted Paul. 'There's an English translation in the next document.'

Jacques opened the file and the English text was displayed.

'Voila!' said Jacques.

Both Paul and Jacques were now reading the technical explanation. Even though English was not Jacques' native language he absorbed the information much faster than Paul.

'You finished yet?' asked Jacques.

'Nope,' said Paul, glancing up 'You know me, I never read manuals. I'd rather just play with the gadget and see what it does.'

While he was waiting, Jacques reopened the drawing of the GWR two.

'Bloody hell,' said Paul, 'that's incredible!'

'Bien sur,' said Jacques. 'I think I understand how it works.'

'So do I,' said Paul. 'I'm not sure I can believe it, though.'

'They collect the gravitational wave radiation in the ceiling and focus it on the bottom of the tower.'

'Yes,' said Jacques. 'It looks like they have created a parabolic mirror using a mixture of gravitum and gypsum plaster.'

'Presumably they are able to bend the gravitational waves at the boundary between atmosphere and gravitum where they travel slower.'

'Yes I assume the gypsum is to adjust the concentration of gravitum to some critical value. Then "hey presto", the waves are reflected,' said Jacques, enjoying the magic.

'So they have built a reflecting telescope that works on gravitational waves instead of light.'

'It looks like a Newtonian telescope,' said Jacques, 'except there is no secondary mirror to divert the image to an eyepiece, just a group of gravitum crystals.'

'Yes, but that's the clever bit,' said Paul. 'The gravitum crystals are tuned to the hundredth harmonic of the incoming gravitational wave. That means they vibrate at a frequency one hundred times higher than we talked about before.'

'So the resonant cavities can be much smaller than we calculated!' said Jacques. 'You know what that means, Paul don't you?'

'Yes,' Paul paused, looked blank. He paused again, thought a bit and finally he said, 'well no not really.'

'It means that it can create a standing wave in the cavity.

'So?'

'These are longitudinal standing waves.... fixed areas of dense and sparse gravity.'

Paul still looked blank.

'Come on Paul think,' said Jacques, returning to his university professor mode. 'It's called a "Rectifier", remember!'

'Well I assume that's because it separates each half cycle of the vibration, like converting alternating electrical current to direct current.'

'Yes, go on.'

Paul still looked blank. His forehead wrinkled, probing for an answer, 'It means there are places in the cavity where the gravity field appears to be steady. One part will be more intense than the world outside and the other part will be less intense. Time and space will be bent differently depending where you are in the cavity.'

'Go on.'

Paul's face brightened then as if he had found enlightenment, he said, 'That means that time speeds up in some places and slows down in others!'

'That's right!'

'Bloody hell!'

****

Francine was annoyed.

They had met as arranged at the Whitworth Street wine bar. Without saying a word, Claire had handed Francine Jacques' note.

'What's this?' asked Francine, confused by Claire's behaviour.

'Just read it, Francine and don't comment on it until we are outside.'

Francine's pallor had changed from slightly pale to white.

'I feel giddy,' she said. 'Can we sit down?'

Although the bar was busy, there were a couple of spare chairs near a table occupied by a group of happy looking students. They sat down.

'Would you like a drink?' asked Claire.

Francine did not reply. She was rereading the short note.

'It's a dry white wine then,' said Claire, improvising.

'I'll kill him,' muttered Francine, scanning the last few lines for the third time.

The colour had come back to her cheeks. Claire disappeared, returning a few minutes later with two large glasses of wine.

'I'll kill him,' repeated Francine, not quite as aggressively.

'Someone's already tried that,' said Claire, under her breath. 'We can't talk here,' she added louder.

'Why didn't he tell me where he was?' she asked, angrily and too loudly for Claire's comfort. 'Doesn't he know what we've been through?' she added, staring at the note.

The wine bar was heaving with customers. Fortunately Francine was not shouting like everybody else and Claire could only hear fragments of words. She was able to understand by watching Francine's lips whilst listening. She remembered what Jacques had said about computer aided lip reading. It was originally designed to aid people with impaired hearing but it was no surprise that STKiC had improved the software and integrated it into their surveillance systems. She looked up and saw a darkened, inverted hemisphere of Perspex.

'A closed circuit camera,' she thought. 'I wonder how closed it is?'

'We must talk somewhere else,' she shouted.

Francine stubbornly remained seated. Claire was becoming desperate to get away from potential eavesdroppers. Then one of the students spilt a pint of beer over an innocent burley bystander. The student was drunk, the bystander was annoyed. An argument started.

'Time to move,' said Claire.

'Alright,' said Francine, hardly noticing the germinating rumpus.

They slipped away before a fight broke out.

****

By now Paul had rigged up a cottage network and Jacques had already taken advantage by printing off copies of the GWR II documents. Jacques then set about reviewing them as he would any other academic paper. In the meantime Paul was scribbling in a notebook that he habitually carried round with him. Jacques looked over to where Paul was sitting and watched him for a few moments.

'You have had another idea?' he asked.

'Not really,' said Paul. 'You've known me long enough to know I can only think with a pen in my hand.'

'Mon ami, for a young man, you are very old-fashioned,' teased Jacques. 'So tell me, what are your thoughts?'

'I suspect there is more to this than we reckon.'

'I don't understand,' said Jacques. 'Don't you think that an invention that speeds up and slows down time is important enough for you?'

'Well yes,' stammered Paul, pausing for thought, 'I mean no.'

'Make up your mind,' said Jacques.

Paul and Jacques were so engrossed with their conversation that they didn't hear the car pull up outside.

'From our perspective, the discovery is amazing, but if you think about it, it's ancient history,' said Paul. 'These diagrams are very old. I think that if this device really works someone built it long ago…'

'And since then they have had the opportunity to refine it and learn other applications,' interrupted Jacques, catching on.

'My point is that Hitzubishi's gravitational wave device is probably the state of the art and we don't know what it does.'

'I thought it was a system for containing nuclear fusion, but that was clearly wrong,' said Jacques, reflectively.

'That's right,' Paul responded, 'you were wrong.'

'Comment?'

There was a slight crunching of gravel outside as someone accidently stepped off the paving stones in front of the unlocked door. Paul looked up, but ignored it. He was on a roll.

'Hitzubishi san was not designing a system for generating electricity. He must have had another objective,' said Paul, thinking aloud.

'His device contained the same arrangement of gravitum crystals, but there was no resonant cavity and no parabolic mirror,' muttered Jacques, musing along with Paul.

'I know what we should do!' said Paul.

'What?'

'We should try to build one.'

'Build one what?'

'Build a replica of his device.'

'But we've only got one crystal,' Jacques objected. 'Are you suggesting we cut it into four?'

'There's no need,' said a woman's voice at the door, 'you only need to cut it in half. I've got Earth.'

Jacques turned, hardly able to believe his ears. He jumped up and forgetting his weak ankle rushed over to the door.

'Ma cherie,' he said, squeezing her in his arms. They kissed passionately. 'Oh how I wanted to speak to you, to hold you.'

They kissed again.

'Urrhum,' said Claire, clearing her throat behind them. 'Can you love birds let me in. I need a cup of tea.'

Still in a clinch, they moved aside. Claire struggled trying to carry two cases past them. Francine returned her attention to her husband.

'I told Claire I would kill you,' said Francine, breathlessly.

'Someone has already tried,' he said, squeezing her more tightly.

'That's what Claire said,' she replied, 'but that doesn't mean I won't finish you off.'

'That could be nice,' he said with a mischievous smile.

Francine glanced into the room. Claire and Paul were standing together watching them and smiling.

'Do you want us to leave you two alone for a while?' asked Claire diplomatically.

'Oh, yes,' said Paul shuffling uncomfortably. We'll get out of your way,'

'Hello Paul,' said Francine, noticing him for the first time. 'Don't worry. We'll just go outside and get some fresh air.'

'You could push me off the cliff,' said Jacques, jokingly.

'Don't give me ideas,' said Francine, taking him by the hand and turning. 'We won't be long.'

Paul and Claire waited until Francine and Jacques had disappeared towards the cliff path before they spoke.

'How did she take it?' he asked.

'She was furious.'

'I'm not surprised. She thought he was dead and then he turns up as right as rain. Did you manage to explain why he hadn't contacted her?'

'Yes, I managed to get her away from the wine bar and as we walked along the canal tow path.'

'Away from cameras as Jacques had suggested?'

'Yes but no matter what I said, she wasn't convinced. She said that the police believed Jacques was involved in some kind of fraud and now she didn't know what to believe.'

'So what changed her mind?'

'When we got back to the wine bar, she saw a man come out that she had seen earlier that day. He seemed to be looking for something or someone. She made me duck back on to the tow path.'

'Did she say who it was?'

'No she just said "that's the gas man" and her attitude changed. She looked very frightened,' Claire added.

'So what did you do next?'

'We waited until he had gone, got a taxi back to her house. She packed a bag and here we are,' said Claire.

****

During alternate scolding and affection, Jacques persevered with his story. Francine told him about Amaury's progress and he visibly relaxed.

'Mon Dieu,' he said. 'In my darkest times, I thought I'd killed him, just like Jean-Claude'

'You saved his life,' said Francine, looking into his watery eyes, 'and you didn't kill Jean-Claude either, that was an accident.'

Francine gently raised the palm of her hand to his face and wiped away a tear that was rolling down his cheek.

'But he was my little brother, I should have looked after him and I didn't. I didn't look after Amaury either,' he said, his head tilting away from her hand.

'You did, Jacques,' she said. 'You did. Amaury would not be alive now but for you.'

Francine's eyes were becoming moist in sympathy. She had never seen her husband in so much pain. She took his head in the palms of both hands.

'Now isn't the time to give up,' she said, gazing into his eyes. 'We need you more than ever. We need the Jacques who can think his way out of any problem, the Jacques who can apply himself to anything. We need the Jacques we all love. I need the Jacques I love.'

Tears were now streaming down both of their faces. She kissed him tenderly on the lips. He returned the kiss, as if the healing was beginning.

'Ma cherie, how I've missed you,' he said.

'I love you darling,' she said. 'Please don't disappear again.'

'I won't,' he said, 'though I'm afraid I can't do this by myself. We must find out what these people are trying to do. If we don't they'll never leave us alone.'

'I'm, scared too,' she said.

'I know,' he replied, 'but there is a way to beat them.'

'How?'

'We need to learn what they know and use it against them,' said Jacques, recovering his old resolve. 'Paul has given me the idea. I'm going to build a replica of Hitzubishi's gravitational wave device and see what it does.'

'Isn't that dangerous?'

'Only if it's built in an earthquake zone and I take no precautions.'

'We'll need a laboratory. Where are we going to do this? Here?' asked Francine.

'At my grandfather's house near Gordes,' he replied, noticing she had switched to first person plural. 'I'm not sure how I'm going to get there though and where I get the equipment from.'

Francine looked at him uncertainly.

'Are you sure, my darling?' she said, 'You haven't been there since the accident. Can't we do this somewhere else?'

Jacques looked into her eyes. They were almost pleading with him. More than anyone else, Francine knew how much pain his plan could cause. These old memories had been buried for years and he had found them too hard to face head on.

'No, I must go back,' he said, softly. 'Alone, over the last few weeks the image of Jean-Claude keeps coming back. I have to lay him to rest.'

'I understand,' she said, putting her arms around his waist.

'Merci, cherie,' he said. 'I don't deserve you.'

'You do,' she said.

His face brightened, his mind refocusing on the problem in hand.

'Did I hear you say that you have Earth; the other gravitum crystal?' asked Jacques.

'Yes, it arrived in the post after you left that morning. But you'll need more than two crystals to build a laboratory and start a research programme. You were always better at aspiration than delivery,' she said, recovering her decorum.

Jacques feigned taking offence.

'What you really want, young man is a research team and brilliant project manager,' said Francine, smiling.

‘And that would be you, I suppose.’

‘It could be if the job’s vacant. Mind you that’s only if you let me recruit some of our friends. I gather they’re keen to help.’ she said.

‘I don’t want to be responsible for putting more people in danger,’ said Jacques.

‘But they already are. They were in danger the moment Paul published his paper on gravitum,’ said Francine. ‘And they want to help,’ she added.

‘I can see why Paul would want to help,’ said Jacques. ‘If we don’t stop STKiC in their tracks they will destroy his career. But we can’t make Claire a target as well.’

‘You try and stop her,’ said Francine. ‘She’s like a vixen whose mate has been threatened. Besides she’s a brilliant researcher.’

They had reached the top of the cliff and had a magnificent view across la Manche. Jacques was silent for a moment, only the sound of waves breaking against the dark Jurassic cliffs below. He raised his eyes to the horizon. The channel was too wide at that point to see France. He strained his eyes on the line between the sea and sky. He could just make out a ferry returning on its cross-channel duties.

‘If only we could cross the water. You can’t do anything without someone watching,’ he whispered, as if he was worried someone would over hear.

‘You really are becoming paranoid my dear,’ she said. ‘You’ll find things much easier now you have an expert to help.’

She snuggled in closer and hugged his arm as they gazed out to sea together. A moment later Paul and Claire came to join them. Jacques and Francine had been alone long enough. It was time to work together. All four of them knew that they could not win unless they held strong. They were in this together. Both couples were under attack from a hidden malignant force. They had enough trust in each other’s abilities to believe that they could uncover and beat their tormentor. For a while, they stood together as a group of four.

'Beautiful isn't it,' said Claire, sharing the view as the sun glinted off the sea.

'Yes, it is,' said Francine.

'Have you decided?' asked Paul, quietly.

'Yes,' said Francine.

Jacques slowly turned to look into his wife's eyes as only a two people bonded in love can. There was an understanding, a communication tinged with fear. He shifted his gaze to Paul and Claire.

'We are going to take them on,' said Jacques, gently. 'Are you still prepared to join us?'

'Yes,' said Claire, simply.

At that moment the four became more optimistic than they had been for some time. They were aware that their opponents had eyes everywhere and had superficial knowledge of each of them, but the prying eyes could not get inside their heads, not yet anyway. This was how the four would take control; they were not prepared to be the hunted, they would become the hunters. Perhaps the four friends were naïve because they had no idea of the scale of their undertaking. How could they know that in taking the role of four Davids pitted against Goliatian opponents they were about to start a chain of events that would rattle through the economies of the world? Standing on a cliff-top looking out to sea, they had faith in their ingenuity and determination. For sure they did not know enough about their enemy but equally their arrogant enemy did not know enough about them.

# Twenty-one

**STKiC**

Being the last day of the nineteenth century the day had more joie de vivre than usual. It was the evening before the dawn of a new digit. Businesses were buoyant. Bankers were discussing a "prosperity panic". People were optimistic and celebrating and where better to celebrate than in one of the most vibrant outposts of the most powerful empire on Earth?

'I like this place,' said the young Chinese businessman, to no one in particular. 'It's so alive and exciting.'

'Is it your first visit to Hong Kong?' asked the stranger sitting next to him.

It was obvious that they were in the mood for a bar-room chat. Somehow each knew the other was from out of town, doing what many visitors do; find a smoky, sociable bar and have a drink. That day in particular was not a time to be on your own.

'Yes, my first time,' said the young man.

'Do you want a top-up?' the barman asked, always keen to keep liquidity in his business.

'Yes, and one for my friend,' said the businessman.

'Thank you,' he said. 'My name is Mitzuko.'

'Pleased to meet you,' replied his companion with a seated bow and holding out his hand, European style. 'I'm Kuang-hsien,' he said, using his family name as was usual with someone with his background.

His companion returned the bow and shook the proffered hand.

'And you?' Kuang-hsien asked.

'I've been here many times. I do a lot of travelling,' said Mitzuko. 'I work on merchant ship. She's a new iron-clad. We carry freight around the western Pacific.'

'Ah you're a Japanese sailor' he said, recognising the accented English.

'No, I'm the head cook, I am qualified to do much more but they like my fish.' Mitzuko paused, 'and you?'

'I've just started working for The Russo-Chinese bank,' he replied. 'I was educated in Beijing. They're so old fashioned. I couldn't wait to get out.'

'The Russo-Chinese Bank,' said Mitzuko, 'never heard of it.'

'The company is new,' replied his companion. 'The Czar has got a load of French money, but he needs people who know their way around the Chinese civil service. I applied for the job.'

'If you don't mind me saying,' Mitzuko started, looking at his companion for the first time, 'you look a little young to be a go-between for Chinese mandarins and a Russian bank.'

'I'm older than I look,' he replied, enigmatically.

Mitzuko held his gaze a little longer. His companion shifted his position as he became uncomfortable with the scrutiny.

'Is there something wrong?'

'I know you,' said Mitzuko. 'I'm sure I've seen you before.' He continued to examine him through the murky atmosphere. 'You were only a boy when I last saw you, but I know you,' he added.

'I don't think so,' said the young man, uncomfortably.

'Your name is Quon!' he said excitedly. 'You are Lihua's son.' He paused, 'That's right! She sent you to the Han-Lin Academy to improve your education.'

'How do you know that?' asked Quon.

'I was there. I was at the monastery,' he said. 'I knew your father. He was my comrade. I was one of the Shinto monks who came with the Shishi raiders.'

Quon's jaw dropped. He had finally found a link back to his father, his hero.

'You knew my father?' asked Quon, hardly able to believe his ears.

'Yes he was a great man, a patriot,' he replied.

'Where is he?' asked Quon, visualising a first meeting with his long lost parent.

Mitzuko could read Quon's mind. He decided to tell him the truth.

'I'm sorry, but he's dead. He died just after we tried to build fast and slow rooms, like the ones we had at the monastery.'

'How, did he die?' asked Quon, hoping for an honourable death.

Again Mitzuko could read Quon's expression. He decided to lie.

'He committed seppuku,' said Mitzuko. 'He died honourably. Your mother died broken hearted.'

'Why did my father have to commit suicide?'

Mitzuko decided to return to the truth. He was enjoying this game.

'He had promised his masters that he would build a time compression device that would be one hundred times more effective than the one he had seen in Korea. It would use a parabolic mirror to reflect energy like a Newtonian telescope.'

'You mean he wanted to build the device that my grandfather designed?'

'Yes, but the fast and slow rooms did not work, so he believed he had failed in his mission.'

Quon sat silently reflecting on the information. He realised that he was not sad about his father's death, just disappointed. However Quon was proud in the manner of his parent's departure. His chest filled.

'What was he like?' asked Quon.

'As I said he was a hero. He was a brilliant tactician as well,' said Mitzuko pandering to his new friend's vanity.

'At the monastery, they said he was a coward, because he did not commit suicide when your raid failed,' said Quon, desperately wanting a correction to the story.

'He was not a coward because his mission did not fail.'

'But you were all captured.'

'That was his plan,' replied Mitzuko. 'His mission was to obtain the secrets of the monastery and he successfully achieved that.' Mitzuko squinted at Quon to gauge his reaction. He decided to continue with the truth, 'He worked out that over time he could earn their trust, even as a reformed prisoner. Your mother was a great help to him.'

Quon's eyes widened like a child listening to an adventure story. The fact that Mitzuko's version seemed to be at variance with what Quon's mother had said, did not bother him.

'He knew that our band was too small to overwhelm Taoist monks schooled in martial arts. So he planned the battle so a few of us survived.'

'But the monks told me that my father, Jiro was just a low ranking samurai. He didn't have anything to do with planning the battle,' he said, acknowledging a contradiction for the first time.

'That's right, Jiro was a low ranking samurai.'

'But you just said….'

'That's because your father was not Jiro. Your father took his identity when Jiro was killed by a Taoist monk.'

'Who was my father then?'

'Your father was Okuba-sama, the leader of the Shishi band,' Mitzuko said, 'and I was not a Shinto monk. I was a young samurai.'

'But why didn't he take you with him when he escaped back to Japan?'

'He guessed that your mother may have forgotten to tell him all her secrets, so I agreed to stay behind.'

'You were a spy?'

'If you like.'

'But only recently after both your parent's death do I realise your mother did indeed keep something back. She used the wrong concentration of blue crystals in the ceiling. Now I know why the fast and slow rooms did not work.'

Oblivious to the celebrations going on around them, their discussion went well into the next century. They talked about time, money and edited exploits of Quon's father, mother and grandfather. Mitzuko told Quon more details about the bunker, and continued to lie about how Quon's mother had been treated.

'If only we could get back to the bunker,' said Quon. 'We could make a fortune.'

'They use it as a military bunker,' replied Mitzuko, 'and they've sealed the two time rooms up. There is no way we can get in there.'

Quon thought for a moment.

'There is another way,' he said.

'What's that?'

'We could build our own.'

'We don't have the plans,' said Mitzuko, doubtfully, 'and we don't have any blue stones.'

'Ah but I know were I can get both and I am the only person who knows where they are!'

'Where are they?'

'In the Beiping Observatory,' said Quon triumphantly, 'and my grandfather put them there.'

Before the sun had dawned on the new century and in the spirit of the time, they had worked out a charter for a new enterprise. They worked out ways of using the Russo-Chinese bank's money and their shared knowledge from the monastery to build a fortune. They designed an organisation where the executives and key employees would be recruited only from Quon and Mitzuko's descendants. They would not list their brain-child on any new-fangled stock market; they could get enough money from the Russians and embezzle it if necessary. This would be the way that Quon's grand father's research would be resurrected, but this time with a vision; a vision far beyond the narrow focus of Xu or the Shishi; something more global, something more international.

Their plans once laid would be implemented to perfection. The company would be able to avoid public scrutiny; sustaining their businesses through rebellions, natural disasters, world wars and revolutions. Like the dynastic elite who would run it, their company would remain an enigma. Remarkable by their longevity, little would be known about the families who ran the operation. However one thing was sure: the huge research budgets would have objectives much less altruistic than those of the ancient alchemist Xu and his daughter.

Satisfied with their plans only two gaps remained. The first was problematic, in order to start a dynasty, they would need wives. Neither of them was married and neither of them had much experience with women. The second gap was less problematical and the opportunity to resolve it dropped neatly into place nearly six months later.

****

On May 31st 1900, a detachment of three hundred and forty British, Russian, Japanese, Italian and American marines arrived in Beiping. They had been assigned to put protect a group of Chinese rebels calling themselves "The Fists of Righteous Harmony". The Western Powers call them "The Boxers". Their goals seemed to be very similar to the Japanese Shishi, so it is ironic that Quon and Mitzuko posing as Japanese officers were amongst the allied troops who were given the job to put the rebellion down.

Using the cover of military action, the two were able to take a platoon into the Beiping Observatory. After the "visit" the resident astronomers found that important equipment had been stolen. They checked their inventory for missing items and found that some of the most ancient, delicate astronomy instruments had been stolen along with half a dozen blue stones and some documents from the library. The theft of the instruments was so outrageous that they focussed all their efforts on getting them back. As far as they were concerned the loss of the ramblings of a long dead mandarin and some dusty rocks paled into insignificance. They had bigger things to worry about.

Quon and Mitzuko were now equipped to build replicas of the fast and slow rooms that Lihua had created at the monastery. Although the design of the bunker was amongst Xu's papers, they did not have enough space or blue crystals to build such a large construction; their ambitions had to be more modest. Noticing that world politics were becoming unstable they decided to spread their resources internationally; they prudently split their resources so that they could build two small facilities one in Japan and the second in Russia. Quon used his share of crystals, which included Earth and Sky, in the Russian device. Mitzuko set up a hidden base in a mountainous region of Japan on Honshu Island. There he experimented with four smaller crystals

The plan was to install laboratories in each of the two Fast Rooms and they would employ scientists and engineers to develop recent scientific discoveries into patentable inventions. Using the Russo-Chinese Bank to bank-roll them, they recruited some of the best brains they could find to work in the two laboratories. The employees worked on four day shifts, working and sleeping on the premises. The researchers were pleased to find that at the end of each shift only one day had passed in the outside world. This seemed to be a good deal as they were paid for four days. The system worked well and the owners of the company became rich from the royalties due from a myriad of highly original ideas. The proceeds of their business were paid into bank accounts all over the world, or squirreled away in the form of gold and silver bullion. Although Mitzuko never married, Quon did. He fell for the daughter of his chief engineer who had died from an aging disease. She was half Greek and half Russian and it was the cosmopolitan make up of his wife that first attracted him to her. They had three sons and a daughter who he would school in the arts of his business. There was only one fly in the ointment; the laboratory workers seemed to age very quickly. Interestingly the owners of the company never went inside the Japanese or Russian laboratories. By the outbreak of the First World War, the STKi Corporation was producing multiple inventions that it sold to the highest bidder. In terms of employees it was a tiny company run by small elite, but in terms of financial turnover over it was as big as a medium-sized European country. Everything was going well. Then disaster struck.

On the sixteenth of July nineteen eighteen, the majority of the Russian Imperial family was executed and Russia started to slip into civil war. Although Mitzuko was not affected by this incident, Quon and his family were. As their home was in the extreme east near Vladivostok, until then they had been insulated from the revolution. He and his family kept themselves to themselves and often used assumed Russian-sounding names, hoping that they could go about their business unnoticed. However Quon could not hide the fact that he was a well heeled foreign business man. Quon and his family became vulnerable and a group of local Bolsheviks made an opportunistic raid on his laboratories. At the time of the raid, Quon, and his four children were sleeping behind the steel door of the slow room. His wife, diligent as ever, would join them later after she had instructed a number of their employees on their next day's schedule. Seeing the facility as a symbol of the rich and powerful, the raiders were jealous and ruthless. There was a massacre. Quon's marriage was not founded in love it was more of a convenience than anything else. Except for his children, Quon had no love to give. So he did not grieve for long over his wife. However the raid had shaken him. He decided very quickly to decamp to the safety of Japan, where his partner had set up the other half of the business. After securing his international investments, he and his family took the next ship to Japan.

Quon was shocked when he saw Mitzuko. He had not seen his business partner for many years, keeping in touch through fairly formal mechanisms such as the telegraph and post. Mitzuko had not aged at all; although a little pale, he now looked younger than Quon.

'Mitzuko must have spent most his time in the slow room,' thought Quon.

'You look well,' he said, not as a compliment but as an accusation. 'Who's been looking after the business whilst you've been in the slow room?'

'I'm just very efficient,' said Mitzuko. 'My part of the business looks after itself.'

Quon was immediately suspicious that his business partner was hiding something. Has the old liar made a discovery and kept it to himself? He wondered.

Quon decided to probe.

'How's the research going, any new patents?' he asked, knowing that there had not been any for months.

'It's a bit slow, I've reduced the research staff,' replied Mitzuko. 'They are not as well trained as they used to be. I don't like wasting money.'

'But that's how our business works and I've looked at the bank accounts. You've been spending money like water,' exclaimed Quon, becoming annoyed. 'Are you stealing from me?' he asked, accusingly. 'Or is there something else?' he added to himself whilst holding Mitzuko's gaze. Mitzuko looked away. 'You have discovered something, haven't you?'

'What makes you say that?' asked Mitzuko, using his well rehearsed tactic of answering a question with a question.

Quon was having none of it.

'Answer the question damn you!' he said, 'and no lies this time,' he added menacingly.

Mitzuko was frightened of Quon because he was clever, ruthless and resourceful. He knew how Quon had handled employees who stepped out of line. Like his father, Quon was a cruel supervisor, more like a slave master than a boss. Wisely, Mitzuko decided to come clean.

'All right, Quon. No need to get shitty. I was going to tell you anyway It's just I'm not sure it will work.'

'Cut the crap, Mitzuko,' he snapped. 'Tell me now, or I'll have you dissected.'

Mitzuko blanched, not sure whether the threat was just words or real. He took a deep breath.

'I've found out how they work.'

'How what works?'

'The fast and slow rooms.'

'We know how they work, we've been using them for years!' exclaimed Quon, thinking Mitzuko was stringing him along.

'That's not true,' said Mitzuko. Seeing Quon bridle and thinking he should chose his words more carefully, he added quickly, 'A Swiss scientist called Albert Einstein has just published a work on general relativity.'

'I've heard of him. So?'

'It explains how gravity works and he has proposed something called gravitational waves.'

'What's that got to do with us?' asked Quon, irritably.

'He says gravity effects time and space and so does gravitational radiation.'

'What are you saying,' asked Quon, becoming interested, 'that our fast and slow rooms are phenomena of gravity?'

'I think our two rooms hold one complete cycle of gravitational waves. One half cycle slows time down the other half speeds it up. It's like a one way valve or a rectifier that splits the energy potentials of the wave into high and low areas of compression. I think Xu, your grandfather, knew that because he designed the bunker to collect more gravitational waves and focus them on a core of blue stones. I have built a prototype to test the principle but I don't have enough of the meteorite to make it work properly.'

'It's a shame we can't get into the bunker and test your theory,' said Quon, cynically.

'But we can,' said Mitzuko. 'That's where the money went. I bought it off the government. The military have moved out.'

Quon stopped his interrogation. Had he finally got the truth?

'And you thought you would hide this from me, did you?'

'I was planning to tell you when I got it working,' said Mitzuko, lying.

'If I catch you lying to me again, I'll stick you like a pig. Do you understand?'

'Yes,' said Mitzuko timidly.

'So what were you planning to do with it, out-live me?'

'Yes,' said Mitzuko, submissively with head downcast. 'I've been trying some simple experiments of my own. The theory works.'

'So that's why I'm older than you?'

'Yes,' replied Mitzuko, quietly.

'So, if the bunker worked, it would be far more efficient than our existing facilities.'

'That's what I think,' replied Mitzuko, still chastened but recovering some of his confidence. 'I think the bunker would be over one hundred times more effective. Imagine the opportunity!'

'I already have,' said Quon, now very much in charge.

****

Before his temporary retreat from Russia, Quon usually took the back seat and let his partner lead. However Mitzuko's underlying character was devious. Quon's was ruthless. Originally Mitzuko was the senior partner, but Quon would never allow him to return to his old status. Quon was wily enough to realise that the two were complementary personalities. From now on Quon would be the boss; after all, every important idea had come from Quon's family and the bunker belonged to his father. As Quon mulled over the last few weeks he realised that the events leading to their escape from Russia had been fortuitous. But for the Bolsheviks' raid causing the loss of Earth and Sky, his wife already forgotten, he and his children would have carried on in Russia. This would have allowed Mitzuko to swindle him. Quon was an expert at swindling people, but he was not prepared to be swindled. For the time being Quon knew he needed Mitzuko. He had the keys to the bunker. Without a fast room laboratory Quon's business would be on an equal footing with his competitors' and without a slow room he and his children would age far too quickly. Neither of these changes appealed to him. He was amused when he remembered

Mitzuko's expression when Quon and family unexpectedly arrived on his door step.

'He must have aged a little then,' he thought, chuckling out loud.

Quon's thoughts switched to the re-opening of his father's now derelict bunker.

'I wonder what state it is in,' he thought. 'What if the military have damaged the structure? If they have, I have a really bad problem.'

He considered bumping Mitzuko off as a punishment. He would think about it when the time came.

If Quon could finish the installation properly, the bunker would compress and rarefy time one hundred times more effectively than his old facility in Russia. With the device operational, they could lie low until everything settled down and walk back into the open air decades later. What's more, his children and he would be only one or two years older. If Mitzuko behaved himself, Quon would invite him to join them; his business partner did have his uses.

****

Renamed GWR II, they spent the next few months restoring Quon's parents' bunker to Xu's design. They loaded supplies for the equivalent of a round-the-world cruise and sealed the entrance from the curious passers-by. They laid low through the Great Depression and the late nineteen thirties. Finally Quon decided to investigate what was happening outside.

After several days examining their affairs, they found all was not well. Before they entered their self-imposed internment, Quon and Mitzuko had invested much of the company's fortune in banks, bonds, trusts, shares and some precious metals. To Quon and Mitzuko's amazement much of their money had disappeared along with many collapsed companies and banks. They were outraged that other businesses that seemed robust and reliable had been so incompetent and untrustworthy. So they decided to change their strategy. They knew that their key strength was that they were able to manipulate the passage of time. They were worried that because of discoveries by others, their competitive edge would no longer exist. What was worse, it looked like another war was coming and they would not be able to cash in. They had made most of their fortune during the previous war. Unfortunately this time, they did not have enough capital or seed investment. They needed another angle. They needed to know what was going to happen before anybody else did. They needed to take control of their fortune. They needed more power, more control and more foresight. But it was not Quon or Mitzuko who had the brainwave; it was Quon's youngest daughter. Quon knew from the very start that she was special. She had her grandfather's cunning and her grandmother's instinct for nature. That's why he had named her Lihua and that's why she was the one who worked out how to send messages back in time. The twin boys were the youngest of the family and too young to take part in the complexities of his business, but in time they would grow up each to become as formidable as their father and doubly dangerous. His eldest son however had other talents.

# Part 4

# Anyone got the time?

# Twenty-two

## Improving the odds

Her mind was on fire. They had attacked her husband and her child. She was angry. Like a she tigress she was relentless in the defence of her family. Francine was establishing the logistics for their confrontation with STKiC with a vengeance. The goals were established, the strategy was framed.

'That's it,' she said, sitting back. 'Now for the tactics.'

'Finished the strategy then?' asked Claire.

Claire was acting as a sounding board. The team recognised her as the individual who was the most effective at running a faultless laboratory; the expert. They had to use everybody's expertise to the limit if they were to catch up with an opponent who had a head start of more than a century. Francine was the natural manager, Paul the experimental scientist and Jacques was the theoretician; the dreamer.

'Are we ready to tell the other two?'

'Not yet,' said Francine. 'First, can I run it past you again, please?'

Francine was a professional; she was used to organising her thoughts and asking others to validate them; she was not proud. This was the most important project of her life. She must not get the strategy wrong. They all knew how important it was that all of them had a common understanding of their areas of responsibility. They relied on Francine to organise them into a competent team. Francine realised that the group, small as it was, had individuals with strong personalities. Without good coordination they could dissipate all their energies and achieve nothing. She had to create a careful balance that would make sure that every individual had the breadth of responsibility that would use each person's full capability without getting in each other's way and without leaving gaps. Either problem would result in failure. The goals had to be explicit not vague; realistic not stupid;

inspirational not trivial. If their goals were right, all else would follow. Before that day Claire had not understood why some leaders made such a meal of their planning; her boss at the university was a case in point. However she had noticed that what he planned usually happened; perhaps not the way that he expected, but there were fewer surprises, there was more control and they had time to correct course for the unexpected storm. Now having seen Francine at work, she was starting to cotton-on. Over the last few hours, Claire could see how Francine's experience would be invaluable if they were to take on such a formidable opponent as STKiC. To help her understand, Francine had told Claire about the founder of a famous Japanese electronics company.

"Keep the goals simple," he had said, "but not too easy."

To illustrate the point, he had dropped a cigarette packet on the table in front of his researchers. They gazed at it wondering whether they were about to go into the tobacco industry. He told them to make a tape recorder the same size. At the time tape recorders were the size of a suitcase.

'But that's impossible,' someone had said, but they did it. In fact the final design was much smaller.

Francine had produced some notes. She turned the first page and started to rehearse her ideas.

'Our goal,' said Francine 'is simple. It is to emasculate them. Our strength is our intellect; our weakness our physical exposure and our numbers. We are threatened by their ruthlessness and their ability to strike anywhere. Our opportunity is to strike back before they know we are a threat. Their strengths are their knowledge and global reach. Their weakness is their arrogance and need for secrecy.' She paused to gather her thoughts, she continued, 'Our strategy will be to use their technology against them, confuse their surveillance, make them not believe the things they see and hear, destroy their confidence, remove their technical advantage, create public outrage and attack their life blood – their money. This will be a war, unlike any other. Our battlefields will be laboratories, stock markets, public opinion and world wide data networks. Our weapons will be information, disinformation and publicity. Our soldiers will be theories and discoveries.'

For a few moments, Claire was speechless.

'What do you think?' asked Francine.

Claire recovered her wits.

'That's amazing,' she said. 'You sound like Elizabeth the First, sending her army and navy out to engage the Armada.'

'Oh you mean the famous "I know I have but the body of a weak and feeble woman; but I have the heart of a king," speech.' Claire nodded. 'Well they have certainly got me riled,' said Francine. 'It's a pity we only have an army of four though.'

'I suppose that's the bit I can't get my head round,' said Claire. 'I'd like to understand how so few of us can take on a multi-billion dollar corporation that can draw on tens of thousands of people.'

'It's impossible,' she said, 'but that's what they said to my Japanese entrepreneur. I have no idea how we're going to do it, but I believe between us we'll find a way.'

'Ok,' said Claire. 'It looks like it's time to involve the boys.'

****

Like Claire "the boys" were flabbergasted.

'I'm up for it,' said Paul. 'Aren't we a little outnumbered though?'

'It depends who you count,' said Francine. 'If you include only their executives, we are on a par with them.'

'So you're ignoring their thirty thousand employees?'

'Yes,' said Francine.

Jacques said nothing. He just looked at his wife with pride, grinning stupidly.

'What do you think?' she asked. 'Can we do it?'

'I have no idea,' said Paul, 'but I'm prepared to have a damned good try.'

Jacques remained in his trance state, still in awe of his wife.

'Mon Dieu, I'm so lucky,' he thought.

She smiled at him.

'If you agree to the goals, then we have some work to do,' said Francine. 'Claire and I cannot plan this on our own.'

'Come on boys, time you did some work too,' said Claire teasing.

Francine explained that all they had to do now was work out the how; the tactics. She had played some of the battles out in her mind, but she knew her limitations. She needed help. Francine explained that they should do everything they could to ensure the war would not involve anything more physical than transferring data. At all costs she wanted to avoid meeting the enemy face to face. If they did they would probably lose. As the other three absorbed the ideas, more questions came flooding out.

'How are you going to get the money out of the UK to fund the laboratory?'

'How are you going to withdraw money from the bank without either being seen or using an insecure internet connection?

'How are we going to get to Provence without being seen?'

'How do we stop STKiC watching us from satellites?'

'How do we prevent STKiC tracing us through our communications with the outside world?'

Jacques had trusted friends and relations in Provence. He had a cousin who owned a foundry. Paul could use his knowledge of amateur satellite communications to prevent their communications being traced. They could use a derelict family property that was surrounded by an olive grove thus giving them natural cover. They could use unregistered bikes for transport. One by one they answered their own questions. Their plan was coming together. To even up the odds, they would enlist the help of Jacques' family and old friends. These were people with old values who would close ranks to protect their own. The plan still had some gaps, but their ideas could work. Finally Francine was almost satisfied with the result.

'This is wonderful, but it leaves one large weakness,' she said.

'What's that?' asked Claire.

'Paul,' she replied.

Paul's expression changed from confidence to shock. Claire moved towards him as if to defend him.

'What do you mean?' she asked.

'If you analyse our plan, Paul is essential to three quarters of the work.'

'So why is he the weakness?' asked Claire, defensively.

'Paul is the most practical of all of us. He is critical to everything,' said Francine, 'and he has too much to do, in too little time.'

'I see,' said Paul, 'so you don't think I'm a liability.'

'You are very sweet taking on so much,' said Francine smiling, 'and you have more skills than I could dream of, but you'll have to pass some of the more straight-forward tasks on to the rest of us. Otherwise we'll watch you wear yourself out.'

'I understand,' said Paul, feeling better. 'You want me to delegate some stuff.'

'Yes please,' said Francine, then turning to the whole group, 'All that remains is that we stay hidden. No one must find us before we are ready to strike.'

There was silence as they pondered the enormity of the journey that they were about to take. They were frightened, excited and optimistic. Above all Francine's plan had given them hope.

'What's that?' said Claire, alarmed.

'Yes, I heard it to,' said Jacques. 'It sounded like car's tyres on the gravel outside.'

Francine moved to the window, and gently eased the curtain aside. She peered through the gap discreetly.

'You're right,' said Francine, urgently. 'It's a car. There's a man in the driver's seat, he seems to be taking something out of the glove locker.' She moved position to get a better view. 'He's getting out,' she said.

'Shit,' said Paul.

'Who knows we're here?' asked Jacques.

'No one knows about you and Francine,' said Paul, 'and only the owner knows about me and Claire.'

'Jacques, Francine. You'd better hide,' said Claire. 'Paul and I hired the cottage. We'll try to tough it out.'

'Paul, take my stick,' said Jacques, handing him his buddleia stem.

Jacques and Francine ducked into the kitchen. Jacques opened the kitchen drawer and took out the bread knife. Francine's eyes widened.

'What are you going to do with that?' she hissed.

'Protect my friends and family,' he said.

Silence fell on the cottage. They could hear the sea breaking on the cliffs. Then they could hear footsteps as the man crossed the gravel, the tone changing as he stepped on to the flag stones leading to the front door.

Paul's mouth went dry. His hand was shaking. Everybody froze.

****

Hideo was pretending to work on the task that Mitzuko had assigned him. Sitting quietly at his computer, he was straining his ears to eavesdrop on his companion's conversations. Occasionally he tapped a few keys to make it look as though he was working. He had not seen her leave the others, but he sensed her proximity next to him. He was simultaneously shocked and excited. He looked up. Lihua was looking down at him with her green brown eyes. He looked away embarrassed, quickly opening a complex screen to make his work look more meaningful.

I wonder how long she's been there, he asked himself. He knew it could not have been long; he would have known.

'What are you working on?' she asked.

He could smell her perfume, as she lent closer to look at the screen.

'It's a modelling tool,' he said. 'Mitzuko asked me to look at the effects of seismic p and s wave vibrations on the bunker. I'm just checking the dimensions.'

'We have a far more powerful computer next door you know,' she said, her voice soft and alluring. 'Didn't Mitzuko tell you?'

A chill went through Hideo's stomach, his mind racing.

'Err, I think I'm ok thanks,' he said. 'I've nearly done, besides I'd have to reload it. It could take days.'

'As you wish,' she said, losing interest.

She turned and headed towards the corner of the room where Viktor and Mitzuko were fiddling with some new equipment. His eyes were transfixed on her as she walked away from him.

'Don't even think it,' he thought. 'She's lethal.'

Hideo casually stood up and stretched. Mitzuko briefly glanced over to him and seeing nothing untoward, returned his attention to the equipment he was adjusting.

'Have you made much progress?' asked Lihua, in a supervisory tone.

Mitzuko and Viktor looked up instantly paying attention.

'I think we may have got it right this time,' said Viktor.

Hideo was finding it difficult to keep the balance between eavesdropping and appearing to be working on his own. This had meant that he had only been able to catch fragments of conversation and even then it was only when all three of his companions were in dialogue. For some reason whenever Mitzuko and Viktor talked to each other as a pair, it was in hushed tones. At first Hideo had assumed that they were determined to keep secrets from him but then he realised that it was Lihua that they were worried about. Now standing at a distance, he could see the body language. They were speaking in hushed tones because they did not want her to hear anything disrespectful. They were frightened of her. She was the boss.

'Interesting,' he thought.

There was a tea pot half way between Hideo and the point where the satellite group was talking. He casually moved towards it, watching them out of the corner of his eye.

'Father will be upset if you fail again,' she was saying, her voice soft and gentle.

'I'm confident it will work,' said Mitzuko, his voice more confident than his body language.

Viktor carried on working, adjusting something with a small screwdriver, whilst watching an electrician's meter.

'You know what will happen if you are wrong don't you?' she said in silky tones.

'Yes,' said Viktor, irritably. 'We'll have to go back to the old methods, open the Fast Room and fill it with stooges again and daddy would be really pissed off, wouldn't he?' he added defiantly.

'You should show more respect,' she said softly. 'One day that tongue of yours will get you in trouble.'

Hideo's kettle made a click as the water boiled. Lihua turned and saw him. He had the presence of mind not to turn towards her. He just poured water into the teapot and made his way back to his chair with his pot of tea and a small handleless cup.

'Do you think he heard?' said Viktor.

'It doesn't matter if he did,' said Lihua. 'He's going nowhere.'

****

It seemed as though they had been frozen for an eternity.

'Is anybody in?' said a deep voice from outside.

Paul opened the door.

'Fucking hell,' he exclaimed, 'you frightened the living daylights out of us.'

The tall intruder stepped into the room and gazed innocently at the startled woman in the corner.

'Hello Claire,' he said. 'Prama said you may need some help.'

'You do know how to make an entrance, Anil. I'm still shaking.'

'Sorry,' he said. 'Prama tells me I have that effect on women. I didn't believe her.'

He looked around.

'Where's the fugitive?' he asked affably.

'Doctor Degordes to you,' said Jacques exiting the kitchen, knife still in hand.

'You won't need that,' said Anil, smiling.

'Oh no, sorry,' said Jacques.

'Ah and this must be Francine,' said Anil holding out his huge hand.

'So you're the famous Anil?' she said, her hand disappearing into his.

He shook it gently.

'Have you brought her with you?' said Francine. 'Is she in the car?'

'No,' replied Anil. 'She's still in Manchester, doing as you asked, talking to Amaury.'

'How the hell did you find us?' asked Paul, suddenly becoming concerned. 'Did Prama tell you where we are?'

'She didn't know.'

'Then how?'

'Francine, you have not made any mobile calls, but you have left your phone on. I would turn it off now.' he said.

'Oh bugger,' said Paul.

'Paul, your car is parked in the cottages garage. It has an antitheft security device and even if it hadn't I tracked you from Poole by satellite after you passed the last traffic camera.'

'And Jacques you now have a very distinctive walk. I hope you enjoyed the view out to sea.'

'Oh heavens,' said Claire. 'How are we ever going to hide from STKiC if you can find us so easily?'

'Well, Prama said you would need help,' said Anil. 'So here I am and my first recommendation is that you need to get out of here.'

'How?' asked Francine, despondently. 'They can watch our every move.'

'I suggest a small electronic diversion may be in order,' he said, brightly. 'But first I need to know a few places where you don't want to go. So that's where they think you may be.'

They looked at him puzzled.

'One of these days, Anil, you'll get arrested,' said Jacques, the first to understand. 'You're dangerous.'

'From what I hear, I'm in good company,' he said looking at Jacques and smiling broadly.

****

The odds were getting better. They were no longer four; they were six. Prama and Anil agreed to help them on the outside. However they would need ways to communicate with each other without giving their locations away. Paul and Anil took up the challenge. They could not use plain old telephones, mobiles, or broadband, because they are too easy to trace and tap. Where possible they decided to use the post and dead letter addresses, but this would not be good enough to beat the fast response of their hi-tech adversary. Try as they might, they could not think of a foolproof way of stopping STKiC eavesdropping. Paul and Anil decided that the most important thing was to keep the location of the laboratory secret. Accepting the inevitable the pair agreed to use a data link using amateur radio satellites. This would be open to anybody who bothered to listen but Paul could make it difficult to locate the position of the laboratory's transmitter. The link would give the remote lab access to public information via a connection to the Internet at Anil's end. Having sorted out how they would wire things up, Paul and Anil started to think of ways to make their information more private. They armed themselves with copies of the fifth edition of The PC Manual for Thickies; one of a myriad of pointless publications that explained the bugs that had been found up until six months before printing, now fixed and replaced by new bugs. These volumes became the codebooks that they would use to encrypt their communications. The group split into two teams Anil went back to London and the four headed for a village outside of Gordes.

Whilst they headed to Jacques' home territory, the authorities believed that the four had scattered around the globe. Paul and Claire had gone on holiday to Singapore. Jacques had boarded a plane to Rio. A few days later he was spotted by a CCTV data stream entering a Sao Paulo museum, then caught by satellite leaving and finally driving a hire car west along the auto-estrada that cuts through the rainforest and coffee plantations to Sorocaba. Meanwhile Francine had followed a complex route via Mumbai to her destination in the Maldives where her image was recorded whilst she sunbathed on the beach. If that's what the authorities thought, for the time being so did STKiC. In reality the four had taken a ferry to Jersey, then onwards to the west coast of France. From there they split up and travelled by different trains to their destination in Provence. Francine knew that Anil's diversionary tactics should impede STKiC and the police in their search for Jacques. She reasoned that the authorities often had to balance their ambitions against their resources. She hoped the police would give up when they realised that Jacques was not a criminal, just a missing person. That left STKiC. She thought that they would behave differently. They would never give up. She was sure that sooner or later the four would be found. Francine hoped to God that they could stay hidden until they were prepared to take STKiC head on.

****

The novice knocked on O'Reilly's door. He looked up to see her hovering.

'What is it McKenzie?' he asked.

'I've just heard, Amaury Degordes has been discharged and is heading back to France to convalesce.'

'Do you know where he's living?'

'Yes he's going to stay with Jacques Degordes' cousin in Gordes. Amaury's planning to go back to work within the month.'

'Seems a bit quick,' said O'Reilly, absorbing the information. 'Don't forget to get their address.'

'Will do,' said McKenzie, turning to leave.

'Just a minute,' said O'Reilly. 'Where's Mrs Degordes?'

'Oh, apparently she's gone on holiday to the Maldives,' she replied. 'Bit odd I thought.'

'Interesting,' thought O'Reilly.

# Twenty-three

## Catching up with the past

The four had arranged to stop over at Jacques' cousin's ancient stone house in a village in Luberon en Provence. Francine and Jacques had figured that the authorities in the hill town of Gordes did not have the same preoccupation with watching its citizens as seemed to be the trend in the other parts of the world. Also the town had other advantages if one wanted to avoid being spotted by prying eyes from above. The streets were rambling and narrow. This made it difficult for a spy satellite to identify specific pedestrians who could keep out of sight by staying close to the medieval buildings that lined the streets. It was dusk when Francine alighted from the bus part way up the hill into the town. She struggled up the incline of the Rue Andre L'hôte and then along the steep cobbled ally leading to Yves and Maxime's home. Her case was becoming a dead weight and by the time she reached their front door, she was exhausted. She dropped her case and knocked. She heard voices and then the welcoming face of Jacques' cousin, Yves appeared from behind the opening door.

'You look worn out,' he said, holding out his arms to embrace her, 'but still as beautiful as ever.'

Francine returned the embrace, happy to be amongst friends. She could smell cognac on his breath. She was relieved; that meant Jacques had arrived before her. They had probably already drunk half a bottle.

'He's here then?' she asked rhetorically.

'About an hour ago,' he replied, taking her case indoors.

She followed him into the living room.

'Bonjour,' she said, crossing the room to Maxime and giving her a big hug. 'It's been so long, how are you?'

They kissed each other on each cheek.

'I'm well,' she replied. 'It's wonderful to see you. We're so grateful that you agreed to help us. We are in such a mess.'

'Not any more,' said Yves' voice behind her. 'When they attack one Degordes, they attack all of us. They have no idea what this family is capable of.'

'Well, I'm still grateful,' said Francine. 'Where is he?' she asked.

'The last time I saw him he was sleeping on a garden seat with a cognac in his hand,' said Yves. 'He never could take his drink,' he added smiling.

'How are Claude and Thom?' asked Maxime.

Jacques had already told her about Amaury.

'I spoke to them from a phone box yesterday,' said Francine. 'It was a risk, but I couldn't leave them believing that their father was dead. I hope you don't mind, but I expect you'll have two more guests in a few days.'

'It will be lovely to see them,' she said. 'I suppose they'll be all grown up now,' she added.

'Yes,' said Francine. 'They're young men now, but still my babies.'

Maxime smiled, she had never had any children of her own. Maxime gently touched Francine's arm.

'I feel that your boys are my family too. Amaury is such a lovely boy. I was so upset when I heard what had happened,' she said. 'When Jacques told us who was responsible, I became angrier than you can imagine.' She looked at Francine. 'I'm sorry, of course you can,' she added.

'No need to be sorry,' said Francine, smiling. 'You are right to be angry. These people must be stopped, but I don't want to get you too deeply involved. They are dangerous. We'll move to the farm as soon as we can. Then you'll be safe.'

'You don't need to worry about Yves and me. We will help as much as we can. Whatever you decide, we are with you. But tonight you stay here and that's an order,' said Maxime, firmly. 'Yves can take you to Sénanque tomorrow.'

'I see Yves and Jacques have taken up where they left off,' said Francine, changing the subject. 'Is it the homemade stuff?'

'I'm afraid so,' said Maxime, shaking her head. 'They're impossible. Thank god you're here. Perhaps we can control them together.'

'Hello, when did you arrive?' said Jacques, standing unsteadily in the doorway to the garden. 'You are as beautiful as always.'

'Flattery will not save you,' she said, sternly. 'Come on Maxime let's get the coffee on.'

'Good idea,' she said, as they moved towards the kitchen. 'When are the others arriving?'

'Amaury will arrive tomorrow morning and Paul and Claire in the evening,' said Francine.

'Has Jacques told you the full story?'

'Yes,' said Maxime. 'He says you are planning to go to his grandfather's farm.' Francine nodded. 'Are you sure that's wise?'

'Jacques says he must finally face it,' said Francine, quietly.

Maxime looked through the open doorway at the two of them, laughing at a joke that Yves had just told.

'The three of them were so close, you know. It hurt Yves as well. He's got over it now. It was so long ago.'

'But Jacques still blames himself,' said Francine, 'and it's been haunting him for years.'

'Well,' said Maxime. 'No one else blames him. It was a tragic accident. It could have happened at any time, whether Jacques had been there or not.'

'I know,' said Francine. 'I hope this time Jacques can accept that.' She paused, watching Jacques and Yves. 'It's wonderful to see him and Yves together again.'

Maxime nodded sympathetically.

'Alright, they've had enough fun,' said Maxime. 'Let's sober them up.'

You're right, said Francine. 'They have work to do. Are the Solexes ready?'

'Yes, Yves has fixed them all up. There are four serviceable mopeds in Jacques' father's old workshop. They're rather a slow form of transport for this day and age though, but they'll get you around.'

'Yes,' said Francine, 'and they're not registered. No one will notice or care about us coming backwards and forwards into Gordes, especially with helmets.'

'Well,' replied Maxime. 'It'll keep you all fit anyway.'

'Keep us fit?' queried Francine.

'The engines aren't powerful enough to get up the hill into Gordes without peddling.'

'Oh,' said Francine amused. She glanced over to Jacques. 'At least it will help him burn the alcohol off,' she said.

Maxime laughed. Francine joined in. They were still giggling as they delivered two large cups of hot coffee to their errant husbands.

****

The next morning Jacques' hangover hovering in the background, he could hardly believe his eyes when he saw his son walking up the steep cobbled street towards him. It took all of Jacques' will power not to go outside and meet Amaury in the street, but he knew he would have to wait indoors. When the door opened, Jacques' emotions overflowed. They spent most of the morning talking about what had happened and more trivial things. Jacques and Francine desperately wanted to stay in their son's company, but they both understood they couldn't.

Jacques and Francine had left for the house in the early afternoon. Less than half an hour later Claire and Paul arrived. Although they had travelled by different train routes, they had used the same bus on the penultimate leg from Marseilles. Impressed by Amaury's affection for the pair, Maxime and Yves fed and watered them like long lost friends.

'I need to get you to the farm,' said Yves, knocking back the last dregs of his coffee.

'Is it far?' asked Claire. 'Jacques and Francine haven't told us very much about it.'

'It's only about six kilometres from here on the road to the abbey,' said Maxime. 'We call it a farm, but it's only about two hectares, most of which is covered by olive trees.'

'That's about five acres,' said Paul. 'I would think that's easily big enough for us. The trees will help to obscure us from above.'

'It's also got a workshop full of machinery, including a forge and old lathe,' said Amaury. 'Dad said that would come in handy.'

'It certainly will,' said Paul, enthusiastically. 'Are they on mains power?'

'No,' said Yves. 'There's an old generator. I start it up every month and there's plenty of diesel. I'm afraid, it's a little unreliable though.'

'We'd better go,' said Yves, standing up. 'It's getting dark enough for you to go outside. We need to walk about one hundred metres to where I've parked the car.'

Paul and Claire said their goodbyes, collected their bags and headed off down the road with Yves to his car. They wound their way down the twisty streets towards the bottom of the town, catching glimpses of the incredible views across the plain below. Yves slowed down as he took a hairpin that gave a view to the northwest.

'The farm is over there obscured by the trees,' he said. 'If you look carefully you can just make out the Abbey Sénanque.'

Paul and Claire strained their eyes and could just make out the top of the Abbey's roof.

'It looks like an ideal place to hide a laboratory,' said Paul, enthusiastically.

'Let's hope so,' said Claire.

****

Two days later, from his position on the red tiled roof of the farmhouse, Paul could see the whole of the smallholding. The building on which he was perched was a single storey stone structure, positioned in the middle of a rolling four acre plot. It had two bedrooms in the loft; each of which had a dormer window. Paul had used one of these to gain access to the roof.

Joined to the main building was an extension that housed the workshop. This was where Paul planned to make the more intricate parts of their gravitational wave device. Yves had taken schematics of the other components to one of their cousins who had agreed to make them in his foundry. Except the gravelled area around the house and the drive, most of the plot was covered in mature olive trees. This meant that they could walk around most of the property, without being seen from above. To the west Paul could see that part of the olive grove had been cleared to make way for a small field. Overgrown with weeds, it looked as though at one time more productive crops had been harvested there. Now left fallow he could see a speckling of colour from the yellow and red wild flowers of late summer. At the far side of the field, overshadowed by a spreading Holm oak, was an old barn. When the smallholding was operational, the barn had been used by Jacques' family to press olives and bottle the oil. This was to be Jacques' new laboratory. Here they intended to assemble their GWR. On the first day, Francine had opened the barn door to find that the press and bottling machines were still inside, rusty and derelict. Leaving Paul to his list of jobs, Jacques, Claire and Francine had taken a full day to clear out the barn. It had been exhausting work, but now Claire was free to convert the building into its new role as a laboratory. Paul could see clouds of dust radiating from the barn doors. Claire and Francine had started to make the place spotless. Beyond the barn and the dark green foliage of the olive trees, the farm was surrounded on three sides by a forest of huge oaks and Aleppo pines. The fourth side was bounded by the road that took a twisty route past the Abbey to Gordes. The boundary of the Degordes property was delineated by a six foot dry stone wall that completely engulfed the smallholding. Having gaps only between the pillars of the entrance and a small gate leading into the forest path, Paul thought it looked pretty secure. The view to the north was blocked by trees but as Paul looked south the land fell away, giving him a view over the canopy of the forest. In the foreground, he was high enough to see the twelfth century Abbey Sénanque and the fields of blue lavender that stretched out around it. To the southeast he could see the buildings of Gordes hanging on to the hillside as if by their fingernails; the hill dominant on the landscape as it rose from the plain. If he hadn't been so worried about being seen from above, he would have spent hours absorbing the view. Even with his wide-brimmed hat, designed to disguise him from above, he had already been up there too long. He glanced towards the barn. Jacques, his limp almost gone, was walking towards his new laboratory. As Paul watched he noticed that Jacques seemed to have been startled by something in the trees. Jacques stopped and stared for a moment. Then, his gait quicker, Jacques made a detour off the gravel path into the open field and back towards the barn.

'That's odd,' he muttered. 'He seems to be avoiding something near the path.'

Paul strained his eyes into an area shaded by the Holm oak. At the edge of the path, amongst the trees, he could see an old tractor with a rusty agricultural machine attached at the rear. It looked as though it had not been moved in decades.

'It looks like an old tractor with a cultivator or tiller attached at the rear,' said Paul to himself. 'I wonder why it startled Jacques.'

Paul realised that as long as he was admiring the view, his task was not advancing. He was on the roof attaching a large microwave dish and guidance system to the stone chimney. This would become the communication system to Anil and the rest of the world. He had already run a cable into the workshop where he would test the system. If it worked, he would run the final cable to the barn where Claire and Jacques were currently working. Paul made a few final adjustments and satisfied with his work, slowly descended down the roof though the dormer window and back into the house.

'Now for the testing,' he said to himself.

He made his way back to the workshop and sat down in front of his computer. With the microwave dish in place, he would start to test the link between the farm and Anil in London. He looked at his watch. The amateur radio satellite was about to come overhead.

'It may be slow and illegal, but if it works, we will be in business,' he thought.

Paul was in the middle of his tests when Francine interrupted him.

'Fancy a cup of tea?' she asked, proffering a full mug, 'We're low on reserves, so it may be your last one for some time.'

'Ah thanks,' he said, 'just what I need.'

He put down an oscilloscope probe he was holding and took the mug gratefully.

'I'm not sure what's worse,' he said, 'being pursued by homicidal megalomaniacs or running out of tea.'

Francine smiled, pleased that he still had a sense of humour.

'How's it going?' she asked.

'Ok I think,' he said. 'The satellite is passing overhead now. We've received some fairly harmless data from Anil and it seems to be working.'

'You sound surprised,' she said.

'I am a bit,' he said. 'The whole thing is slightly Heath-Robinson, but it works, so I'm not going to complain.'

'Let's hope it's a good omen for the rest of the project,' she said.

Paul nodded. He put down his mug for a second and tapped a key on the laptop computer next to his oscilloscope. The display on the latter burst into life, the green line shaking as it displayed a signal being transmitted into the sky.

'There,' he said, 'I've sent our acknowledgement.'

He picked up his mug again.

'You said the satellite is passing over. Does that mean we can't communicate when it's not?'

'That's right,' he replied, concentrating on the oscilloscope trace, 'We are using a low orbit satellite. It's not overhead all the time.'

'I thought you would be using geostationary satellites. Like those used to transmit satellite television,' she said. 'Wouldn't that be better?'

'It would be simpler but radio amateurs can't afford them,' said Paul. 'Geostationary satellites are in much higher orbits, twenty two thousand five hundred miles to be exact. So it costs a lot of money to launch them.' He paused whilst he adjusted a component on the electronic board in front of him. The oscilloscope trace enlarged and became calmer. 'That's better,' he muttered. 'Where was I?'

'You were telling me about communications satellites.'

'Oh yes,' he said. 'There is another reason why low orbit satellites are good for us in particular. They have a smaller footprint. They are closer to us. Their orbit is only about five hundred miles from Earth.'

'Why is that good for us?'

'We are using instant messaging. If the eavesdropper misses the slot then he misses our message. Anil and I have to be on line, looking at the satellite at the same time. If someone wants to listen in, then they have to be within a small area of the Earth that encloses London and the South of France, simultaneously with us.'

'So because Anil's station is in London, that area includes most of France?'

'Yes,' said Paul, 'but that's better than half the world.'

'I see,' said Francine, thoughtfully. 'Doesn't that mean our communications can be relayed from France?'

'Very easily and we have to assume that they will do just that,' said Paul. 'The whole idea of ham radio is that everything is public. We can assume that hams all over France and the south of England will be listening in perfectly legally. We are the ones breaking the law just by encrypting the data, although hopefully they won't notice or care. Let's hope STKiC doesn't employ any radio hams.'

'So why are you going to all this trouble?'

'So they can't trace our uplink,' said Paul. 'We're using highly focussed microwave transmissions.'

'That's why you have a dish on the roof?'

'Yes it looks like a large satellite television dish, but actually it has a built in transmitter. We are vulnerable to being traced when we transmit.'

'Is that what you wanted the microwave cooker for?'

'That's right, I took the magnetron out. It produces powerful microwave radiation that I've modulated and routed to the satellite dish. I've added a tracking mechanism to follow the satellite as it comes over. It works really well,' he said proudly. 'There is lots of background radiation from other microwave cookers, so why would anyone think we're doing anything odd?'

'Impressive.'

'Actually it's a bit dangerous,' said Paul.

'What do you mean?'

'I've used the components from a commercial microwave oven and focussed all of its energy into a narrow, focussed beam. The beam is very dangerous to anybody who gets in its way.'

'Why?'

'It works at two-point-four Giga hertz. If you were exposed to the beam, the water molecules in the exposed part of your body would vibrate violently.'

'So the water in your blood and cells would boil,' said Francine. 'Can't you reduce the power?'

'I've reduced it to a minimum using the old control from the cooker,' he said pointing to a switch on the side of the tracking system. 'Even at minimum power it would cook any pigeon that flew into the beam's path.'

'What if an aircraft flew past?'

'They're made of metal,' said Paul. 'So they would be ok, but although they wouldn't be cooked we can be detected from above.'

'So they could find us from an aircraft or satellite?'

'Eventually yes, so we should use the link only when we need it,' said Paul. 'In the meantime Anil and I have included special key words that tell us that the messages we are sending are lies.'

'Disinformation?'

'That's the idea,' he said. 'For example you know that the word "get" in English is completely redundant.'

'No I didn't.'

'Well, anything you want to say that contains the word can be said differently without it.'

'So?'

'So, if any encrypted paragraph contains get, or a number of other key words, the message is untrue.'

'So you're assuming that they will not only eavesdrop on our communications, but they will also break our encryption.'

'Given the computer power they have available, I'm certain they will. It's a matter of time.'

Paul's laptop beeped.

'What's that?' said Francine.

'It's Anil's acknowledgement,' he said. 'We're in business.'

'Well done,' said Francine. 'I'd better get back to work,' she added turning to go.

A few minutes later she had joined Claire in the farmhouse. They were pouring over Francine's project plan, ticking off completed tasks. Claire seemed preoccupied; there was something on her mind.

'Francine,' said Claire, looking up from the network diagram to look at her. 'I hope you don't mind, there's something I'd like to ask.'

'Ok,' said Francine, waiting.

'It's about Jacques.'

'Ok,' she said, her voice trailing off cautiously.

'When I was working with him in the laboratory I noticed that he seemed worried about something in the trees.'

'I don't understand,' she said.

'Well,' said Claire, trying to pick her words carefully. 'He was startled when he saw an old tractor and machinery parked next to the barn. He looked quite shaken.'

'Oh,' said Francine, turning a little pale. 'I thought they'd taken it away.'

'What the tractor?'

'Yes and the cultivator,' she said.

Francine was quiet for a few seconds as if making up he mind what to say.

'You don't know about it do you?' she said.

'Know about what?'

'About the accident,' she said. 'It's the reason why Jacques hasn't returned here for over twenty years.' She paused. 'It was too difficult for him.'

'Oh,' said Claire, seeing Francine's discomfort. 'I don't want to interfere. If it's difficult, you don't have to tell me anything. I was just worried about him. I'll forget it, if you like.'

'I do wish they'd taken the machine away,' she said, not hearing Claire's words. 'It must have hurt him terribly to see it.'

'Oh I'm sorry, Francine,' said Claire, turning back to the plans computer. 'Let's get on with reviewing the project.'

'No you ought to know,' she said. 'This place has good memories for Jacques and a terrible one. If you don't know what happened, you and Paul will not be able to understand some of the ways he may react.'

Embarrassed that she had asked the question, Claire's eyes returned to look at her. Francine's face was sad and her eyes, focussed at middle distance, were watering. Claire waited patiently as Francine composed herself. Then Francine took a deep breath and started to tell her the story.

****

'They're trying to get me inside that Fast Room,' he thought, 'and she's as bad as them.'

He tried to remember the conversation when she first arrived.

'He'll be an old man in a few months,' she had said.

As he was only twenty-seven at the time this statement seemed odd. Now it seemed to have substance. Her words were threatening, frightening and annoying all at once. He did not want to get old yet, he wanted to see the world, make great discoveries, get married, have kids and do lots of other things.

'This isn't fair,' he thought.

When he first arrived Hideo had assumed that escape would be easy. Hideo had never formed a detailed plan, but the gist was to jump Mitzuko when his guard was down. But Mitzuko had persuaded him to stay, so his plan was forgotten. Now that his urge for freedom had returned, he did not know what to do. He was outnumbered and he did not have a clue what to do. There must be a way out of there. He had probably missed his chance when he was alone with Mitzuko, he thought. He racked his brains. Although Mitzuko had said Hideo could leave when he liked, he knew it was a lie. He could not unlock the bunker without knowing the combination. How could he get hold of the combination? Maybe someone had written it down. He thought about sneaking into their rooms at night. The idea attracted him as he thought of Lihua's room. But he did not know when night was. There didn't seem to be a routine. There was no night, or day for that matter; only the bunker and its flood lights. They all seemed to sleep at different times. It was hopeless!

The more Hideo thought, the more confused and desperate he became. He knew he could not hold them off much longer. The task that Mitzuko had assigned to him was almost finished. Mitzuko would soon be getting impatient. When it was finished, would Hideo be dispensable? Would Viktor dispense of him? Hideo could feel the panic rising inside him. Then he had a thought, he could watch as someone else keyed the number in. He resolved to spend as much time as possible in the main chamber; at least the exit was in there. All he needed was an excuse.

'Day dreaming?' said a voice.

It was Mitzuko who broke his train of thought.

'I'm not sure what day is anymore,' said Hideo, pitifully. 'It would be good to see the sun if only for a few minutes.'

'I'm not sure that's wise,' said Mitzuko, disinterested. 'How's the model coming along?'

'Oh,' he said, ready with an excuse. 'I made one or two errors in the measurements. I need to do them again.'

'You're an idiot,' said Mitzuko, irritably. 'I don't know why I put up with you. Sort it out and quickly. Time is money, particularly in here.'

'Mitzuko, I don't understand. Why "particularly in here"?'

'Just do your job and finish your measurements. Don't get involved with things that don't concern you,' said Mitzuko returning to his natural persona.

This is what Hideo wanted to hear; a direct order. It gave him an excuse to have another walk around the bunker. This time he would be more observant.

'I'll get on with it now,' he said, picking up the laser ruler.

'Where are you going?' said a second voice. It was Viktor.

'It's okay,' said Mitzuko. 'He's screwed up some measurements. He'll have to do them again.' Mitzuko turned to go. 'Idiot,' he muttered.

Trying not to run, Hideo headed for the main chamber.

'The key to my escape is in there,' he thought.

'I may be some time,' he shouted over his shoulder.

'Take your time,' said Viktor. 'Good riddance,' he muttered under his breath, 'you irritating little shit.'

As Hideo opened the door into the main chamber, he saw it in a different light. As before, it was bathed in the bright orange tint from sodium plasma floodlights. But this time he was more observant. He was looking at the shapes and the colours of the items around him from a different perspective. The tower, the roof, the tunnels all had symmetry about them. The bunker had been built like this for a reason. He recalled his journey along the road into the mountains. He thought of Prama's friends over six thousand miles to the west. They had helped him; guided him. Somehow this made things clearer. He wanted to find a way to talk to them. They were the only people whom he could trust. An image of Prama drifted into his mind. He remembered what a beautiful woman she was. Hideo knew he was a little in love with her. The memory made him feel warm and then cold; isolated in his captivity. He shook his head to force himself to focus. Prama's friend Anil could find a way of cracking the lock.

He was clever. Mitzuko had deceived Hideo into believing that they were fools. Hideo now knew Mitzuko was a liar.

'How can I talk to them?' he wondered. 'They understand these things.'

He scanned the chamber, looking for inspiration.

'I need help,' he thought. 'There must be a way of contacting them. How can I contact them?'

Over and over these questions circled his mind. He could see his old Datsun by the entrance, battered and dented, abandoned against the wall of the cave.

'Somewhere in this bunker,' he thought. 'There must be a telephone, a radio; something I can use to talk to them.'

But if he found a telephone how would he know what number to call. He couldn't just look them up in the yellow pages. He heard a door close in the corridor behind him. He pulled out his laser measure and note pad. He slipped quietly to the back of the tower where he had first seen Lihua. Hideo would be out of sight there and have a plausible excuse if he was caught. Slightly out of breath, he peered round the edge of the tower, as two figures came out into the chamber. He could just make out their voices over his pounding heart.

'He's not here,' said Lihua. 'He must have gone back to his room.'

'It's time we got rid of him,' said Viktor. 'He's no use to us now.'

Hideo sank to the ground, he was feeling quite ill.

'There are one or two things he must finish,' she said, soothingly. 'Be patient, little brother, we have all the time in the world,'

'I do wish you wouldn't call me that,' he said.

'Call you what?'

'You know,' he said.

She ignored his response.

'What are we going to do with the other little shit?' asked Viktor.

Hideo's ears picked up, his colour returning.

'Who are they talking about now?' he wondered. 'Do they mean me?'

He moved back to his former eavesdropping position.

'Oh,' she said. 'I don't know yet. I think he's quite cute.'

'I do wish you'd get your hormones under control,' he said.

'Like your temper you mean,' she said, smoothly.

'We all have our faults,' said Viktor. 'Anyway, you didn't answer my question.'

'He amuses me. You know he listens to everything we say?' she said.

'Yes, he's a creepy little shit.'

'Well for the time being he's mine. You can dispose of father's old friend when we know the GWR Three works,' she said. 'How did the test message go?'

'It went ok,' he said. 'We managed to send the message backwards by fifteen pico-seconds.'

'That's not enough,' she said, her voice sharp and aggressive.

'I know that,' he replied, impatiently. 'It must be longer than a second to anticipate the trader's computer software. I don't need Mitzuko's help to know that,' he snarled.

'One and a half seconds would be nice,' she said. 'That's enough time to anticipate the collapse of a national banking industry. This time we'll make a fortune, instead of losing one.' She smiled to herself, her eyes sparkling. 'If you could get me longer, I could trigger the collapse of the whole system and hedge without any risk. All those irritating people who annoyed us last time would be selling their shirts for a living.' She looked up at him, 'Prove yourself; get me a message that goes backwards for more than a second.'

'I told you. I'll do it,' he said, turning back to the corridor. 'Just get off my back and let me get on with it.'

'Of course,' she said sweetly, following him through the door.

Hideo heard no more of the conversation because they had closed the door behind them. Hidden behind the tower, he slumped in silence trying to understand what he had just heard.

From his position he could see his poor old Datsun.

'Shame about the car,' he thought. 'It's never going to be roadworthy again.'

He could see dents and the damaged paintwork where the car had banged against the walls of the tunnel leading to the bunker. The hatchback was still open where he and Mitzuko had unloaded his gravitational wave device, no longer shaking as violently as when Prama was trying to call Anil on his phone…. His phone. Hideo stood up and stepped out from behind the tower. He walked quickly to his car and peered inside. The backseat was still folded down where he had left it. He walked round to the offside passenger door. This is where Prama had got out of the car before making her way up the hillside to phone Anil. He lifted the catch and pulled. The door was jammed, damaged by one of the collisions with the tunnel wall. He pulled harder and with a loud screeching noise it came off its hinges and clattered to the floor. He looked around. The entrance to the living area was still closed. With luck no one had heard. The orange light threw strange shadows on to the upholstery. He lifted the backrest to its vertical position revealing the foot well. There was nothing there. He reached over to the other seat and lifted the nearside backrest. There was nothing in that foot well either.

'Mitzuko must have taken it,' he mumbled to himself, 'outwitted again.'

He hauled himself into the back seat and slumped, depressed. Something was sticking into his buttock. He was sitting on something. He pulled it out, from under him.

'Well there you are my beauty?'

****

'I don't know whether you knew but Jacques had a younger brother,' said Francine.

'No I didn't,' said Claire, softly.

'His name was Jean-Claude. He was six years younger than Jacques and devoted to his big brother.'

'About the same age as Paul,' said Claire.

Francine nodded.

'Did they live here?' asked Claire

'No they lived in Paris,' said Francine. 'Jacques and Jean-Claude's parents brought the boys up in Suresnes.'

'In Paris; near La Défense?' prompted Claire.

'Yes,' said Francine. 'When they were younger, the boys would come here and visit their grandparents during their school holidays. Their parents used to stay in Paris working and join them later.' Francine moved to the window and gazed out. 'They would play in that field,' she said. Claire joined her at the window. Francine continued, 'Jacques and Yves were about the same age and would race small motorbikes around the field. Jean-Claude was too young to race so he would help them maintain the bikes but just watch them go round and round. Occasionally they would let him ride one of the less powerful Solex mopeds.'

'When Jacques was about nineteen, he won a place at the Polytechnic in Paris. That winter his parents rented a holiday apartment in the Italian Alps. They travelled down early with Jean-Claude. Jacques was to join them later for their skiing holiday after he had attended a revision session. When they arrived the apartment seemed to be very comfortable. It had two bedrooms; one for the boys and the other for their parents. It was particularly cold the night before Jacques was due to arrive and Jacques' parents had the heater on in their room. They didn't know that the owner had not maintained the gas fire. By the time Jacques had arrived, his parents were dead and Jean-Claude was in hospital recovering from carbon monoxide poisoning.'

'What a terrible tragedy,' said Claire, quite moved by the story. 'Did Jean-Claude recover?'

'Yes he did,' said Francine, 'and he came to live here with his grandmother. She had been widowed many years before and lived here on her own.'

'She managed this farm without any help?' asked Claire.

'She was made of strong rural stock. She had help from the extended family but she was very independent,' Francine paused, reflectively. 'Most of the time she could get by alone, but she loved her grandsons and their parents so she was devastated by the tragedy. When it happened, Jacques was at university in Paris and Jean-Claude needed some stability; he had become a little reckless since his parents' death. Besides she liked the company.'

'So Jacques and Jean-Claude came to live here?' suggested Claire.

'For a few weeks but then Jacques took up his place at the university. Whenever he could Jacques came down to Provence to see his brother and grandmother. Yves and Jacques would race their bikes and use the workshop to tinker with the engines and make them go faster. Yves in particular was very good with machines. Jean-Claude was not allowed to ride the more powerful bikes, only the Solexes.'

'I suppose you couldn't come to much harm on one of those,' said Claire remembering the group of old bikes that Yves had parked up near the farmhouse.

'That's true,' said Francine. 'In his third year at the Polytechnic, Jacques didn't go to Provence to see his brother, but went on holiday with some of his college friends. Yves had got a job in an engineering company and was busy learning his new trade. Without his brother or Yves, Jean-Claude spent most of his time riding around the field on his moped, but when his grandmother wasn't watching, Jean-Claude borrowed one of the more powerful bikes from the workshop. Hearing the different engine from the house his grandmother saw Jean-Claude from the bedroom window.'

'Did something happen to him?' asked Claire.

'She could see him going round and round the field quite safely, but she wasn't happy so decided to stop him.'

'Did she?'

'Just as she arrived at the field, the front wheel of the bike hit a sharp stone. It punctured the front tyre and sent Jean-Claude's flying into the trees, behind the barn. He was wearing a helmet and normally he would have been alright.' She took a deep breath.

Claire was quiet, listening expectantly to the story.

Francine continued, 'She had forgotten that years earlier her husband had parked an ancient tractor behind the barn. Jean-Claude had landed on the trailer. It had dozens of steel spikes sticking into the air. He was impaled. He died instantly.'

'Oh, that's awful,' said Claire, horrified, 'and the machine in the trees is the one that killed him?'

'Yes,' said Francine.

'Oh how awful. Jacques must have been devastated,' said Claire, picturing the scene, the emotions. 'Jacques had lost his only brother so soon after the earlier tragedy with his parents.'

'Yes but he didn't find out until the French consulate in Barcelona tracked him down.'

'At first Jacques blamed himself for the loss of his brother.'

'Why did he blame himself?' asked Claire. 'It was an accident and he wasn't there.'

'That's why,' said Francine. Claire looked puzzled. 'He wasn't there; he had taught Jean-Claude how to ride a motorbike; he left the more powerful bikes in the workshop, lots of reasons.'

'Does he still blame himself?' asked Claire.

'The guilt is still there, but not as strong. He knows in his heart of hearts that it was a terrible accident. His grandmother was as distraught as he, but she was strong and helped him through his grief. Time is a great healer.'

'His grandmother moved back to Paris for a while and saw him though university. She died of old age a few years ago. She was a remarkable woman and very proud of him,' said Francine. 'I met her many times. Jacques loved her very much.'

'I understand now, why he was so upset by the tractor,' said Claire, recalling Jacques' expression. 'He looked so shocked. Poor Jacques, I suppose the visit here has brought it all back.'

'Yes, I can't understand why Yves hadn't had the awful machine towed away,' said Francine, distractedly. 'Perhaps he couldn't deal with it either.'

****

While Claire had been talking to Francine, Paul was assembling the equipment in the laboratory. Jacques, recovered from his shock, had been doing the intellectual stuff. He was using a computer in the workshop to read more of Dmitry's files. He was concentrating on Hitzubishi's design of the GWR. He could find nothing in the files that he did not know before he met Dmitry in Osaka. Jacques was about to give up when he found a folder called "GWR mods". He double clicked on the folder and found hundreds of documents. He opened the first document. It was a diagram of the GWR. It seemed to be very similar to the original diagram, giving no clue as to its purpose. His eye caught something new.

'What's that?' he asked himself.

He moved his cursor over the diagram and magnified a small section of the schematic.

'Interesting, that's new.'

He took his cursor back to the main folder and scanned the titles of the other documents. One in particular caught his eye. He opened it. He gazed at the diagram and then searched for the text document that described its function.

'Merde,' he cursed. 'It's in Russian.'

Claire had just entered the workshop. Francine wanted to find out how Jacques was progressing with his tasks and had asked Claire to check. Francine suspected that he might have digressed into something he found more interesting. She was right. Jacques looked up just as Claire the entered the building.

'Claire,' he shouted, relief on his face. 'Just the woman I wanted to see. Have you a few moments?'

'Of course,' she shouted back across the room.

Claire walked over to Jacques, suspecting that whatever he wanted to talk about it was not about the mundane tasks he had been allocated by his wife.

'What would you like sir?' she asked, 'a haircut, a manicure?'

'How about a translation,' he replied, smiling.

'No problem,' she said. 'Just let me fetch my dictionary.'

He touched her arm.

'See if you can translate this bit first,' he said, pointing at the first two sentences.

Claire examined the text.

'It doesn't make any sense to me,' she said.

'Try me,' said Jacques.

'Okay, It says' she replied, taking a deep breath, 'part X-two-one-six is designed to,' she paused, 'is designed to …'

'Display?' offered Jacques.

'Yes, display,' she continued. 'Then there are three Cyrillic letters that don't make a word.'

'What are their Latin equivalents?' asked Jacques.

'E,P,R,' she said.

Jacques was hanging on her every word.

'So it means. Part X-two-one-six is designed to display EPR messages.' She looked at him curiously. 'What does that mean?'

'It means, you are wonderful,' he said. 'EPR is short for Einstein, Polosky and Rosen, don't you remember your project with the Bee DNA?'

'How could I forget? The three of them put forward a preposterous idea that turned out to be true,' she paused remembering the details, 'something to do with an anomaly that involved going faster than the speed of light?'

'You are brilliant,' he said, standing up and kissing her.

'Careful, your wife's next door,' she joked, a little flustered.

'It doesn't matter,' he said, excitedly. 'I'm going to kiss her as well. In fact I'm going to kiss all of you.'

'Where's Paul?'

Claire looked at him doubtfully.

'Last time I saw him, he was in the laboratory.'

'I've got to tell him,' he shouted. 'I know what Hitzubishi's device does.'

'What does it do?' Claire shouted after him.

'It sends messages back in time,' he shouted back. 'It communicates with the past.'

'Bloody hell,' said Claire, not realising she had been infected by Paul's vocabulary.

# Twenty-four

## The magnificent seventh

When Hideo got back to his bedroom, he found that the battery in his mobile phone was flat.

'Shit,' he muttered. 'Why do things never work when you need them?'

He looked around the room for a way to charge the battery. He could see nothing obvious.

'I'll have to go back to the Datsun,' he thought. 'There's a charger in the glove locker.'

He put the phone in his pocket and padded it with some tissues so that there was no hard outline to his pocket. He was becoming more cautious. Hideo opened the door from his room and stuck his head into the corridor. There was no one in view but he could hear voices from the laboratory. He headed towards the main chamber. Walking as quietly as he could past the open door to the laboratory, he paused briefly to listen. He could not work out what they were saying and being too frightened to hover any longer, he hurried onwards towards the end of the corridor. He was just about to step into the main chamber when he heard Viktor's voice behind him.

'Where do you think you're going?' he asked.

'I left my laser measure in the main chamber,' he lied.

Viktor moved closer.

'I've just been out there,' he said. 'I didn't see it.'

'I just surveyed the whole chamber,' said Hideo, starting to sweat. 'I could have left it anywhere. I've one final measurement to make, so I need it.'

'You look worried,' said Viktor.

'You make me nervous,' said Hideo, truthfully.

Viktor looked flattered, but he was not convinced about Hideo's errand.

‘I don’t like you sneaking about here on your own,’ said Viktor. ‘I’ll search with you.’

Hideo went pale, but held his nerve.

‘Ok,’ he said. ‘Why don’t I look behind the tower? You could search the other side.’

‘No, we’ll do it the other way round,’ said Viktor.

Viktor started searching behind the tower. Hideo, surprised and relieved that his bluff had worked, quickly moved towards his dented car. He reached into the glove locker and retrieved the charger. He plugged it into the power socket. Nothing happened. The keys were still in the ignition. He turned them carefully so that that he didn’t turn the engine over. The ignition lights remained dark.

‘Shit, the battery’s flat,’ he thought. ‘Now what?’

‘What are you doing over there?’

Viktor had emerged from behind the tower and was walking towards Hideo.

‘Just looking,’ said Hideo, as calmly as he could.

‘Shit, shit, shit,’ he muttered, holding the charger as if it were a red hot coal. ‘If he catches me with this, I’m dead.’

Just as Viktor rounded the bonnet of the car, Hideo had managed to kick the charger behind the rear wheel. He could see out of the corner of his eye that some of the cable was still visible. He fought his natural instinct to gaze at the protruding wire.

‘Look at the state of my car,’ said Hideo, nervously.

‘Bugger your car,’ said Viktor. ‘What are you up to?’

‘Looking for my laser measure,’ he said. ‘Ah there it is.’

Hideo reached into his car and took it off the back seat, where he had left it earlier.

‘What’s it doing there?’ he said, as innocently as he could.

‘Good question,’ said Viktor, his eyes boring into him.

‘Viktor,’ said Lihua’s raised voice from the corridor’s entrance. ‘I need you now. What are you doing?’

'I'm over here,' he replied, 'keeping an eye on your pet mouse.'

'I told you. Leave him alone and come back to look at the GWR. It's urgent.'

Throughout the exchange, Viktor had not taken his eyes off Hideo.

'You're up to something you little shit. I know it,' he growled. 'When I find out, you'll regret you ever lived.'

Hideo said nothing. He was not able to. Viktor returned to the entrance, leaving Hideo as he stood, petrified, rooted to the spot.

It took Hideo a minute or so to recover his wits. He retrieved the charger from under the car and looked around. Mitzuko's pickup was parked in front of his Datsun.

****

Paul was in the workshop. He had broken off from working on the computer network and other communications systems. He needed to remake a component for their version of the GWR. One of the parts delivered from Yves' cousin did not fit properly. Paul had been concentrating on fixing a block of stainless steel into one of the machines in the workshop. It would soon become the replacement part. He was just about to fire up the milling machine when he heard an insistent voice from outside. A few moments later Jacques was standing next to him.

'Bien,' said Jacques. 'I've found you.'

'I'm glad you're here,' said Paul, looking up. 'The GWR is almost finished. I need to re-machine one small component and it's done. When I've finished that, I'll set up a data link between here and the laboratory, so we can monitor the equipment remotely. I'm going to lay an optical fibre cable across the field to the olive pressing barn – your laboratory. I may need your help.'

Jacques expression changed. He looked uncomfortable.

'Do you have to route it across there?' he asked. 'You can be seen from above. Isn't there another way?'

'Yes,' said Paul, 'but it will take more cable and I'll need to install a repeater. I don't have one. The route across the field is definitely the best option.'

'Alors, do we need a remote controlled link? I'm happy to work next to the equipment,' said Jacques. 'In fact I'd prefer it. I don't want to miss anything.'

'I can set up cctv cameras and all the telemetry you could imagine,' said Paul. 'You don't need to be in the lab. It's safer not to be. You remember what happened to the lab in my fire station.'

Jacques looked uncomfortable. He remembered Paul's last laboratory very well. The old fire station had been destroyed by a similar experiment. Jacques was desperate to stop Paul working in the field but he could not think of an alternative. Jacques did not want to unburden his soul. His pain was too deeply buried and Paul had enough on his mind.

Paul's computer made a noise, distracting him. He moved over to the terminal. Jacques seemed relieved that the subject had been dropped.

'Anil's sent us a message. It's too long for a test message,' he said. 'That's odd.'

The team had agreed to keep their messages short and use the system only when it was absolutely necessary. Paul knew whatever Anil was sending was important. He started the decryption software. Jacques was becoming impatient to unload his other news.

'Paul, I've worked it out,' said Jacques, excitedly. 'Hitzubishi's cylinder is an entanglement device.'

'What?' said Paul, still concentrating on the descrambling software.

'He was building a device to send a message backwards in time.'

'But that's impossible,' said Paul, only half listening. 'It violates general relativity, the speed of light and all sorts of other things.'

'Yes but quantum mechanics says different,' said Jacques. 'Are you listening to me?'

Paul turned round to see Jacques' excited face for the first time.

'You're serious aren't you?' said Paul, starting to engage. 'You're not talking about the EPR paradox are you? People keep thinking they can violate general relativity, but in practice, it never works out like that.'

'I have never been more serious in my life.'

'So how does it work?'

'It would be easier if we had Hitzubishi's original device but…'

'The one Hideo took into the mountains?' said Paul, interrupting.

'Yes, the schematics show that a laser beam is split into two paths. One half of the beam goes straight to a semiconductor detector, the other half circulates around the synthetic black hole until it is released and polarised.'

'So it could circulate for years,' said Paul, 'and the result on the detector would reflect the final polarisation, even though the polarisation was fixed much later.' He shook his head in disbelief. 'Bloody hell, that's clever,' he said.

'I don't think it works over years, more like a fraction of a second.'

'Either way it's remarkable.'

'If I could get my hands on the laser optics design,' said Jacques. 'I could confirm that the device uses entanglement of light photons sending messages backwards in time. But as we don't know where Hideo took the device, I'm stuck.'

'Perhaps not,' said Paul.

'What?'

'You could always ask him.'

'What?'

'Ask Hideo.'

'I don't understand.'

'Hideo's just spoken to Prama,' said Paul, calmly. 'He is in a bunker. A bunker that from his description, is just like Dmitry's diagram of the Chinese GWR two.'

Jacques' jaw dropped leaving his mouth wide open.

'It seems he's a prisoner, trapped, can't get out and he needs our help,' said Paul. 'The good news is that we can talk to him and he knows where Hitzubishi's device is.'

'Mon Dieu,' said Jacques, reverting to his native tongue.

'You know what Jacques?' said Paul. 'We have a seventh team member and he's on the inside.'

****

From Hideo's perspective he was not the seventh member of a team; he was on his own, alone in a weird environment with hostile companions. Sitting in Mitzuko's pickup, he had plugged the charger into the socket in front of him and pushed the "on" button. To his great relief, the mobile phone had lit up. He waited and eventually the mobile found a signal.

'Time must be normal in here,' he mumbled, remembering the trouble Prama had had trying to get a signal.

Hideo was ecstatic when she answered the phone. Prama gave him hope and shortly afterwards Anil gave him an escape plan. He sent a series of SMS messages to Hideo's phone that would help them break into the bunker's computers. Anil reckoned that these controlled both the gravitational wave devices and the door locks. Hideo had made his call from the pickup. Although he felt vulnerable there, his phone was not charged and he needed the power from the car battery to receive and read Anil's messages. They were still arriving thick and fast when he heard the door to the corridor open. Panicking, he ducked down below the dashboard praying that no one would see him. He heard Viktor's harsh voice.

'The last time I saw him he was messing about near his car.'

'Well he's not there now,' said Mitzuko.

'He might be hiding in his car,' said Viktor. 'Why don't you go and have a look?'

Hideo slid further into the foot well of Mitzuko's pickup, trying to make himself small and invisible. His heart was pounding. His breathing was deafening. He was sure they would hear him. He heard Mitzuko call back to Viktor from the Datsun.

'He's not here,' he shouted. Then his voice dropped. 'Oh there you are. I didn't hear you come up behind me.'

'You weren't meant to,' said Viktor.

'What do you mean?' asked Mitzuko.

'How old are you now? One hundred? Two hundred and fifty?'

asked Viktor, coldly. 'Time you had a rest, Mitzuko.'

'You can't. You need me,' Mitzuko paused. 'Don't please…'

There was a dull thud followed by the sound of a body sliding to the floor against the contours of the Datsun. Doubled up in the pickup, Hideo started to tremble uncontrollably. He felt the urge to scream. He forced his hand into his mouth. Hideo was a gentle man. He hated violence. He had never even seen a dead body before, let alone heard one being created. It was some minutes after Viktor's footsteps disappeared before Hideo could move. He was paralysed by fear. He had to draw on his last reserves of self control to not scream out.

'If Viktor knows I saw the killing, I'll be next,' he thought, a chill going down his spine. 'I must get back before they miss me.'

He struggled to free himself from his position under the dash. He rolled out of the pickup and landed in a heap on the ground. He tried to stand up but his legs gave way, having been constricted of blood for so long. His head was spinning. He was feeling nauseous. Struggling he managed to stand up, pins and needles running through his feet and legs as the circulation returned.

'I must get back. I must get back,' he thought, panic rising.

He reached into the pickup for the phone, stuffing it into his trouser pocket and accidentally wrenching it from the power cable that was still plugged into the cigar lighter socket.

'Shit,' he said, as he looked at the broken plug hanging on the end of the lead.

He looked towards the corridor entrance. The distance seemed immense. He felt exposed, naked. The orange light from above sliced through chamber like a malevolent gas. He shivered. Even though he knew his mind was playing tricks on him, everything still appeared distorted, eerie, frightening. He walked shakily around the back of his Datsun. The floor seemed different; wet, sticky, slippery. He looked down. Mitzuko's lifeless shell had a hole in the centre of its forehead from which was oozing a liquid; viscous and black due to the tint of the illumination. He traced the stream across the ground. He was standing in a lake at the end of the flow. Hideo's brain, his body rebelled. His eyes rolled, his stomach heaved. He sank to his knees and involuntarily released the contents of his stomach over his poor, dented, precious Datsun.

****

'I've just received another message from Anil,' said Paul.

'Ask him to ask Hideo….'

'Hold on, Jacques,' said Paul, interrupting. 'I can't work that quickly. I haven't descrambled the Anil's last message yet.'

They sat side by side watching the hieroglyphics on Paul's computer screen. Finally the decryption software had finished.

'He's lost contact with Hideo,' said Paul. 'Bugger.'

They read the rest of the message together.

'So the GWR Two is an underground bunker,' said Paul.

'Anil has found its position by tracking Hideo's mobile phone signal.'

'It's northwest of Tokyo,' said Paul. 'Hideo managed to get Hitzubishi's gadget well away from Tokyo then.'

'It looks like it,' said Jacques. 'Anil's sent Hideo instructions on how to open the bunker's network firewall.'

'That's great, Anil may be able to patch us into their systems,' he said. 'It would be great to browse STKiC's computer.'

'What an opportunity,' said Jacques. 'The problem is that Anil has not had an acknowledgement from him. Hideo might not have received the SMS messages.'

'Let's hope he has,' said Paul. 'In the meantime we continue with our original plan and build a copy of the GWR.'

'You're right,' said Jacques sighing. 'Let's make our replica. The sooner we start the better. At least we now know what it's for.'

'To send messages back in time,' prompted Paul, 'but we can't build it without a detailed design of an optical system to split the laser beam.'

'Absolument and I've not seen any details in Dmitry's documents,' said Jacques, 'We'll have to design our own configuration.

'Do you know how?' asked Paul, pointedly using the second person singular.

'No but now I know it's possible, I'm more likely to find a way,' said Jacques optimistically, 'that is unless you saw any hints in the files.'

'No. I've seen nothing that would fit the bill. It looks like it's the critical component of the GWR and STKiC have managed to keep that bit to themselves,' said Paul, not sharing Jacques' confidence. 'Perhaps that is really their big secret.'

'Amazing though it is that they have developed something that talks to the past,' said Jacques reflectively, 'I still don't understand why they would kill to keep the idea away from the rest of the world.'

Paul returned a blank expression.

'By the look of you, you haven't a clue either,' said Jacques.

'Nope,' said Paul. 'I think it's time we called in the cavalry, don't you?'

'As usual, you have an answer,' said Jacques. 'Come on, mon ami. Let's go to the house and pick Claire and Francine's brains. We need a touch of feminine intuition Besides it's dinnertime, I think it's my turn to cook.'

'My God is it?' said Paul standing. 'I'm not sure my digestion can stand it.'

Jacques clapped him on the shoulder.

'If I can eat your cooking, you can eat mine,' said Jacques, grinning.

'That's true, but I can't eat mine either!'

'Oh yes, I remember. You almost killed us with your chilli con carne,' said Jacques, with a chuckle. 'Did you actually use chilli peppers or were you being inventive again?'

'I'm not sure. I thought, the skull and cross-bones symbol on the bottle meant it was hot spice. I was just playing it by ear. Isn't that what all great gourmet cooks do.'

'Ah, that explains it! You taste your cooking "by ear". I think you need some advice from an old friend who has excellent experience in the finer arts of cordon bleu.'

'..and who would that be?....'

Their conversation continued in this vein all the way to the farmhouse. They were still laughing as they crossed the threshold.

****

Soon after he had regained control of his body's reflex actions, Hideo's rational mind kicked in. He took off his shoes and headed towards the corridor. There was no way he wanted to leave bloody footprints across the floor of the main chamber. With a shoe in each hand he was able to run down the corridor without making a noise. He opened his bedroom door and silently slipped inside. The toilet room door was open.

'Wash the shoes,' he thought.

He held his shoes in the low level toilet and flushed the blood away. Leaving his shoes to dry he went back into the bedroom. Hideo sat down on the edge of the futon to examine the messages stored in his mobile. The phone lit up but it had no signal.

'I'm underground so it won't work, but it worked in the main chamber,' he muttered quietly. 'Prama said it would not work if time was distorted. Maybe time is only distorted in here.'

He scanned down the list of the message headers already downloaded. At least twenty of them were SMS messages from Anil. He opened Anil's last message. It was complete, full of detailed instructions and what looked like computer programming code. Hideo's head was starting to spin again. He could feel the panic rising from his gut.

'I can't understand this. It's like a foreign language,' he sobbed. 'I'm not a programmer. I'm going to be stuck here for ever, or thrown into the Fast Room, whatever that is.'

His vision was starting to blur. He sniffed and brushed a tear away with the back of his hand.

'Stop it,' he said, scolding himself. 'They're out there trying to help.'

Hideo decided to start from the beginning. He wiped his eyes and opened Anil's first message. It was encouraging. He could understand it. Perhaps he may live to see his children after all.

# Twenty-five

### Entangled times

'So what's so funny?' asked Francine as Paul and Jacques stepped through the entrance.

'Paul's cooking,' said Jacques.

'It's not that funny,' said Paul, feigning wounded pride. 'I admit you've become a little strange ever since my culinary creation, but I didn't actually poison you. You survived. That's something.'

'You're the one who said your cooking was a joke,' said Jacques. 'Not me.'

'Oh yes,' said Paul. 'I admit it.'

'He's got other talents,' said Claire, supporting her spouse. 'I have to admit his cooking lacks a little refinement, but I can eat it,' she paused and added, 'if I hold my nose.'

'Ah not you as well,' said Paul. 'Traitor.'

'I think it's his way of getting out of cooking duty,' said Francine, amused by the banter.

'Ah, you've found me out,' said Paul. 'Would you like me to do tonight's dinner?'

'No,' they chorused.

'Alors, next time Paul's on cooking duty, I'm going to wait until he takes his first mouthful, then I'll take mine,' said Jacques, suppressing a laugh.

'Alright boys, settle down,' said Francine. 'What have you been brewing in that workshop?'

'Nothing alcoholic, I assure you,' said Paul, regaining control.

'We need your advice,' said Paul addressing Francine and Claire.

'You explain, Paul. I'll start the poison,' said Jacques, grinning and heading for the kitchen.

'Let's sit down,' said Paul. 'I need to pick your brains.'

'Sounds interesting, said Claire. 'What about?'

'Jacques thinks he understands what Hitzubishi's device was for,' said Paul.

'You mean the steel cylinder that Hideo, Prama and I took from the Tokyo Academy of Geosciences?'

'It seems that the Academy was a front for clandestine research sponsored by our friends STKiC.'

'Oh them again,' said Francine.

'Well, after you and Prama were left behind, it seems that Hideo was kidnapped and has been held in a bunker northwest of Tokyo ever since.'

'But we thought he died when the cylinder went out of control,' said Claire shocked.

'That's what we thought,' said Paul. 'Not only has Hideo survived, but so did Hitzubishi's gravitational wave device.'

'But how can that have happened?' asked Claire. 'He didn't know how to stop it vibrating.'

'It wasn't Hideo who stopped it. It was his boss.'

'What, Hitzubishi san?' asked Claire.

'That's right.'

'I've met him. He's a nasty piece of work,' said Claire.

'Well,' said Paul, continuing, 'he kidnapped Hideo and now he's holding him prisoner in STKiC's bunker.'

'That's one way to keep your employees close to you,' said Francine, ironically. 'I wonder which management training school they use.'

'The Academy of evil managers, I expect,' said Paul. 'Anyway Anil and Prama have managed to communicate with Hideo and he's told them that the device is a GWR Mark Three.'

'Mark Three?' asked Francine.

'That's the device that Prama and Hideo took out of Tokyo,' he explained. 'It looks like it was the latest of a series of gravitational wave rectifiers that went back many years.'

'With what purpose?' asked Francine.

'They manipulate time,' he said. 'The first device trapped gravitational waves and built rooms in dense and weak gravitational fields. The effect was what they called Fast Rooms and Slow Rooms…'

Jacques entered from the kitchen carrying a bowl of salad and interrupting Paul's flow continued, 'The bunker, where Hideo is held, is a GWR Mark Two. And depending which room he's been living in, he either thinks he's been there for few days or many years.' He placed the bowl on the table. 'Hors d'oeuvres. I'll just get some bread,' he said.

Paul resumed his explanation.

'But Hitzubishi's device was always an enigma to us. Originally, I thought that it was a system designed to extract energy from gravitational waves.'

'Then I thought it was a system to contain and control nuclear fusion,' said Jacques, returning with some plates and bread. 'It was still a good idea though,' he added, proudly.

'Let me guess,' said Francine. 'It was neither. It was something to do with time.'

'You're good,' said Jacques, 'you're very good.'

Paul continued, 'Jacques thinks that the GWR Mark Three creates an artificial black hole by manipulating gravitational waves. It also generates a laser beam that is split in half. The first half goes straight to a detector and the other half travels round the artificial black hole. It continues to circulate until the black hole collapses.'

'The machine then puts a message inside the half that went round the black hole,' said Jacques, taking up the story, 'by fixing one of its properties, like polarisation, or phase.'

'Using a theory called entanglement, the message will travel back in time to when the beam was originally split, then forward in time to when the first beam collided with the detector where the complementary measurement can be seen.'

'So the message on the detector was displayed before the property was fixed to the second beam. It would be only one bit of data, but if you kept doing it you could send text messages or even pictures back in time.'

'Very clever,' asked Claire, 'but why and who's the message for?'

'We don't know,' said Paul, 'but whoever they are then they would have to have quick reactions.'

'Why?' asked Claire.

'The messages would only be a fraction of a second from the future,' said Jacques. 'At most a few hundred milliseconds, they couldn't hold the artificial black hole together any longer than that.'

'A computer,' said Francine, who had been listening carefully to every word.

'Pardon,' said Paul.

'Claire asked, "Who's the message for?" If the period is so short, the message must be aimed at a computer,' she said. 'No human could react so quickly.'

'And money,' said Claire, thinking aloud. 'They are doing it to make money.'

'Why?' asked Jacques.

'Why would STKiC do anything else? Wealth brings power,' said Claire, still churning the idea round in her mind. 'Nowadays aren't most big money things controlled electronically?'

They were all quiet, waiting for her to speak. They could see there was something on her mind.

'You said a message from the future, didn't you?'

'Yes,' said Paul and Jacques together.

'You said short time frames?'

'Yes.'

'And where would you get those things together?' asked Claire.

They looked blank.

'On networks of trading computers,' said Francine. 'STKiC are running a huge financial scam. They are betting on certainties.'

'Paul, I told you they were good,' said Jacques, nodding towards Francine and Claire. 'But that's much more than intuition.'

'I'll second that,' said Paul.

****

For the time being Hideo's courage had returned. Unusually he had been alone in the bunker's laboratory for a long time. To his relief, Lihua had left the room over two hours earlier. She had gone quickly without acknowledging him; perhaps Viktor had done something that she had to correct. She would have her work cut out to correct Mitzuko, he thought. Hideo was relieved that he had not seen Viktor since Mitzuko's murder. He was terrified that he would give something away at their first encounter following the horrific incident. He fought hard to clear his mind of the memory of Mitzuko's body, leaking blood. He had to concentrate on his escape plan. He had read all of Anil's messages in his bedroom and he now understood the significance of the fast and slow rooms. Hideo realised that an hour in the laboratory would be much longer than in the main chamber, where time ran normally; although he was no longer sure whether "normal" had any meaning. Hideo was covertly following a series of commands that Anil had asked him to type into the bunker's computer. Hideo did not know how they worked, but Anil had explained that the commands would, amongst other things, allow him to control the locks to the bunker. With luck Hideo would be able to escape and lock the door firmly behind him, changing the combination in the process. With Lihua no longer watching him, Hideo had the opportunity to follow Anil's instructions still secreted in the mobile phone. Knowing that his homicidal companions might appear at any moment, he had hidden the phone under the work-sheets on which he had recorded the measurements of the bunker. The phone was not fully charged and he was worried it would not last long enough for him to complete Anil's instructions. Hideo was not a computer boffin. He could not commit the programming commands to memory so he copied them onto a sheet that he kept in the back pocket of his trousers. He was worried that he had not transcribed them correctly, so for the time being he was using the phone, only peering under his stack of measurements when he was ready to follow the next directive. He hoped the battery would hold out, now that the charger was broken.

'What are you doing?'

Hideo had not heard Viktor arrive.

'Oh just sorting out the data files,' he said, hoping that Viktor had not heard the tremor in his voice.

Lihua stepped into the room and walked past Viktor towards Hideo.

'You've been a naughty boy Hideo, haven't you?' she said with a menacingly sweet voice.

'Sorry?' he said.

'You will be,' said Viktor.

Hideo said nothing.

'What have they found out?' he thought. 'Do they know I've seen Mitzuko's body?'

'Look at him,' continued Viktor. 'He's as guilty as sin.'

'Where is it?' asked Lihua.

'What?' he asked.

'You know,' said Viktor, taking a step closer.

Hideo winced.

'You didn't think we wouldn't catch you out did you?' said Lihua. 'We see everything. We track everything. We know.'

'Know what?'

'Shall I break a few fingers?' said Viktor, 'or something more permanent?' he added with an unpleasant smile.

'Not yet,' said Lihua. 'I'm sure he'll hand it over, if we ask nicely.'

Hideo, now terrified dropped his gaze from her and made an involuntary glance to the papers on his desk. Lihua had followed every eye movement.

'There,' she said. 'I told you Viktor. You shouldn't be so impulsive.'

She moved over to Hideo's desk and lifted his papers.

'You're really not very bright are you Hideo,' she said. 'It's a shame. I thought you had promised to be a good boy.'

'I, I have,' he said, trembling. 'I can help, whatever you want me to do I can help,' he said eyeing his exposed phone.

'Look at the wimp,' said Viktor. 'He's not worth it.'

'Alright,' purred Lihua. 'I know how you can help me.'

Viktor glared at her amazed.

'How many chances to you want to give the little worm,' said Viktor outraged.

'Oh little brother,' she said. 'Do calm down.'

'I said don't call me that,' he said, his neck becoming red with anger. He reached for the phone and pointed accusingly with it at Hideo. 'This little turd has been nothing but trouble. I'm going to get rid of him.' He raised the hand with the phone and brought it down violently onto Hideo's right hand that was resting near his keyboard. Hideo screamed as pain shot up his arm. The force of the blow shattered some bones in Hideo's right hand, the phone disintegrating with the force. Viktor then struck Hideo across the face with his other hand. Hideo spun round in his chair, and fell stunned to the floor. Viktor went to his prone body and started to kick him.

'Stop it, you fool we needed to know what was in that phone!' shouted Lihua. 'Stop it!'

Viktor ignored her and continued to kick Hideo, now in the embryo position on the floor. She looked at the pieces of Hideo's mobile scattered around them. She could see it was beyond repair.

'Stop it,' she shrieked. 'if you kill him we'll never find out what he's done.'

There was a sharp retort; they turned towards the laboratory door as it slammed shut. A greying, thickset man was standing glaring at them.

Everything stopped.

Viktor froze, his face purple with rage. He looked over towards the laboratory door, ready to vent his anger on anybody who got in his way.

'What's going on here?' said a commanding voice from the entrance.

'Hello father,' said Lihua, sweetly. 'Oh it's just Viktor. It looks like his anger counselling is wearing off.'

Quon alias Mikhail Berezov took a few steps into the room. Hideo remained motionless on the floor, unconscious in a ball.

'So I see,' he said. 'I've just stepped over a body in the main chamber.' He glared at Viktor, whose anger had subsided, replaced by petulant contrition. 'I assume it was my ex-partner.'

'Yes,' said Viktor. 'Lihua said I could.'

Quon glanced at Lihua for confirmation. She nodded.

'Is he dead?' asked Quon.

'Who Mitzuko or the worm?' asked Viktor.

'What worm?' asked Quon.

Lihua nodded towards Hideo.

'I see,' he said. 'I was asking about Mitzuko? He looked dead but I've never trusted him.'

'Yes, he's dead, father,' said Lihua.

'Good,' said Quon. 'You saved me the trouble.'

****

Although Hideo had not had enough time to key in all of Anil's computer script, he had done enough to give Anil an electronic foot into STKiC's system. Prama who had travelled down the night before to give Anil moral support, was sitting next to him sipping a cup of coffee. Anil was concentrating on the screen waiting to see if his last attempt to break through had worked.

'Anything?' asked Prama, leaning forward to get a better view.

'Another dead end, I'm afraid,' he said. 'Ok, let's try a different approach,' he added with new resolve.

Anil's method was a combination of inspired guesswork and systematic probing for weakness in STKiC's security. Depending on how successful he was, the work could be laborious or exciting. At that moment it was laborious. He was grateful for Prama's company.

'Hideo must have keyed my IP address into the firewall,' he said.

'That's good is it?' asked Prama.

'It gets me on to their intranet, but I still need to hack into their servers.'

'So you're halfway there,' said Prama, hopefully.

'Only a little way really; STKiC have hundreds of servers and have secured each one differently,' he said. 'I've broken into their intranet. It's like a private version of the Internet and now I need to work out which of the company's thousands of PCs contain information that's useful to us.'

'Oh, that sounds like it may take a long time,' said Prama.

'It's not that bad. Hideo and I have managed to send messages between our terminals so we don't need the mobiles anymore. I've rigged up the links so my messages appear to come from inside their company. That should make it less likely they suspect they've been hacked.' He held up his right hand, his middle over his index finger. 'Fingers crossed,' he added.

'That's great,' said Prama. 'It was always possible that STKiC could tap into his mobile calls and make Hideo vulnerable. He should be safer without his phone.'

'That's true except I've lost contact with him,' said Anil. 'I have tapped into his screen and I've been watching every keystroke he has been making.' He turned the monitor towards Prama and tapped a few keys. 'Look,' he said. 'This is an image of what he's been working on. He was typing in the commands I sent him, and he was adding the information he had discovered from within the bunker. I could tell that he's not very familiar with computers because he was very typing incredibly slowly but some time ago he paused and I'm not sure if he's going to finish.'

'How slowly was he typing?'

'About ten times slower than me; it was as if he had to search for each key on the keyboard before typing it.'

'He must be in the Slow Room,' said Prama, thoughtfully.

'What?'

'The Slow Room,' repeated Prama. 'You know time moves slower relative to us. From our perspective his hands are working slowly, but for him, he's typing normally.'

'They put a laboratory in the Slow Room,' said Anil. 'That's weird; you'd think they'd want to complete their research faster, not slower.'

'I see what you mean,' she said, reflecting on STKiC's motives. 'Perhaps they work in there when they are waiting for something. I wonder how slow the Slow Room is.'

'The problem is that I don't know whether Hideo is going to finish the script I gave him, or he's just gone to the loo,' said Anil. 'If he's not coming back I should start breaking into their systems without him.'

'Why don't you do that anyway?'

'It's more risky,' Anil replied. 'I've disguised my IP address, but I'm still working through their firewall. If they see unusual traffic and get suspicious, then they could track me down.' He looked at Prama, seeking inspiration. 'We don't want STKiC knocking at our door do we?'

Prama and Anil were silent for a moment, deep in thought. They both knew that STKiC were unlikely to bother with a polite knock. Prama smiled. She had thought of something.

'What?' said Anil, returning a warm smile.

'I've seen Hideo work,' said Prama, casting her mind back to her time in Japan. 'He's not as fast as you but, as a user, he's pretty proficient on the keyboard.'

'So?'

'If you normally type twice as fast as him then for every character he keys you key two.'

'Ok,' said Anil, not sure where this was leading.

'So correcting for your speed, in the bunker he was five times slower than you.'

'Which means the Slow Room is slowing time by a factor of five,' said Anil, catching on.

'It's very approximate but yes,' said Prama. 'When did he stop typing?'

'Just over two hours ago,' said Anil, 'which means he's been out of action for twenty-four minutes, bunker-time.'

'If you remember how approximate our calculations have been, let's say anywhere between fifteen minutes to half an hour,' said Prama.

'So he could be at the loo, or he could have been disturbed,' said Anil, looking at the screen. 'But why would he stop in the middle of a word?'

Prama gazed at the point on the screen where Hideo had stopped typing, the cursor still flashing, very, very slowly.

'Let me see if his phone is on line,' said Anil, tapping a few keys. The terminal responded.

'OFF LINE,' it said.

'I'm going to assume he's not coming back,' said Anil, with resolution.

Prama nodded her head sadly.

'That means he's probably been caught trying to sabotage them,' she sighed. 'Poor Hideo, he's such a gentle person. It never works out for him.'

'He's certainly not very lucky,' said Anil, 'but if they've worked out what he was doing, then it's a matter of time before they block my access. I've got to work quickly.'

'If they're working in the Slow Room, you'll have time on your side,' said Prama. 'That may be their mistake.'

Anil nodded and returned to his computer.

Prama looked at her coffee mug. It was empty.

'Fancy another coffee?' she asked.

'Good plan,' he said. 'We may be here for some time.'

****

After eight hours of frantic keying, Anil had managed to gain access to over five hundred servers on STKiC's private network. He had compiled a list containing names of databases, addresses, and security details. He glanced over to Prama, she was asleep in the chair next to him. He reached across and brushed a wayward lock of hair away from her temple. Sleeping lightly, she yawned and stretched. Her head made a tiny movement towards Anil's hand responding to his touch. Her eyelashes flickered revealing her sleepy eyes. She smiled as Anil's face came into focus.

'I've done it,' he said, gently.

'I knew you would,' said Prama, her smile still in place.

Anil clicked on a button on his screen marked "Send".

'There,' he said. 'I've sent Hideo extra instructions to his terminal in the bunker. Let's hope he reads them. I'll just copy them to Paul.' He clicked the mouse a couple of times, 'There, they're on their way.'

'It's time we went home,' said Prama suppressing a yawn.

'Good idea,' he said as he logged out.

It was at that moment when Putyatin and Nikolas walked into the university's foyer on the ground floor below them.

# Twenty-six

## Entangled friends

Paul was at the other side of the workshop when Anil's message came in. He was working on a lathe making the finishing touches to the replacement component of the GWR. He did not hear the musical chord from the computer warning him of an incoming message because the machine tool was making a piercing, screeching noise against the stainless steel rod that Paul was turning. Paul winced, as the noise seemed to irritate every nerve ending. He quickly turned the handle on the old lathe to retract the tool post and the sharp tool that was cutting the stainless steel. He reached down beneath the saddle of the lathe and pushed the red button. Gradually the chuck stopped turning. He leant over the lathe to look at the tool.

'Bugger,' he said.

'Using your wide vocabulary again I hear,' said Claire's voice behind him.

She had been curious about the awful noise, so she had wandered into the workshop to find out what was happening. Paul turned and stuck his tongue out at her.

'Ah, I see you're using your wide repertoire of gestures also,' she said teasing.

He decided to stick to the facts as he could see she was in a mischievous mood and he would lose.

'The tool is broken,' he said. 'It's scored the surface. I'll have to change the tool and start again. This machine is ancient and my skills are a bit rusty.'

'They're not that rusty,' she said.

The double entendre was not lost on him and as she was within range, he reached out and wrapped his arms around her. She pushed at him.

'Get away,' she said. 'You're filthy.'

'I am aren't I?' he said, continuing in the same vein.

'Oh, I give in,' she said, her resistance subsiding.

'Was that you screeching?' said Jacques' raised voice from outside.

Jacques stepped into the workshop. Seeing them in a clinch, he stopped and grinned.

'I see the Mediterranean air has got to you,' he said.

'The screech wasn't me, honest,' said Claire, giggling into Paul's shoulder.

'What's this; a worker's refreshment break?' said Jacques with a chuckle.

'I'm certainly refreshed,' said Paul, with a slightly embarrassed grin.

Jacques was amused by his friend's English reserve. Paul released Claire from his embrace. She looked disappointed.

'My tool broke,' said Paul, returning to Jacques' question.

Jacques gave him a sideways look. Claire burst into fits of giggles.

Paul looked embarrassed.

'Or rather, the lathe tool broke,' he said, blushing.

'As I see,' said Jacques, enjoying Paul's embarrassment.

'It's the last component,' said Paul, regaining his composure. 'And you can wipe that smirk off your face Degordes,' he added.

'Alors,' said Jacques, keeping his face as straight as he could. 'So you've nearly finished.'

'Yes, all but this last part are laid out on the bench over there,' said Paul. 'We're nearly ready to put it together.'

'Amazing,' said Jacques.

'He is isn't he?' said Claire, refusing to be sidelined for a gravitational wave device.

A flicker of a smile passed over Paul's face as she winked at him.

'I'd better be going and leave you two boys to your toys,' she said, turning to leave and blew Paul a kiss as she exited through the doorway.

'She's in a good mood,' said Jacques, watching her go. 'You're a lucky man.'

'I know,' said Paul. 'Anyway,' he continued returning to the GWR, 'if you start carrying the components over to the barn. I'll join you in about half an hour with the final piece.'

'Ok,' said Jacques and with that they started the final stage of their race against STKiC to build a working replica of Hitzubishi's gravitational wave machine.

****

Hideo woke up wondering why he was still alive. He checked his limbs, his body, and his head, to make sure he was not mistaken. The pain from the broken index finger of his right hand suddenly shot up his arm. He tried to roll over. He could feel pain from bruises over his back. His kidneys ached.

'Yes,' he thought. 'I am alive.'

He raised his right hand so that he could see it. His index finger was as a strange angle to the others.

'It's a good thing I'm left handed,' he said to himself.

He had heard about people who had set their own bones. He took his broken finger in his left hand. The pain nearly caused him to pass out.

'I'll do that later,' he thought, 'when I've got my courage back.'

Hideo had realised long ago, that when under pressure, his personality alternated between paralysing fear to absolute recklessness. At that moment he was in neither phase; he was somewhere in between.

Still disorientated, he worked out that he had been dumped on the floor just inside his room in the bunker. Avoiding putting any weight on his right hand, he struggled to his feet. The effort was so immense that he nearly fell over, grabbing at the door handle with his good hand for support. The handle held his weight. It was rigid, locked.

'Shit,' he muttered.

He staggered over to the futon and sat down on the edge. He looked down at his right hand. It made him angry. He would not give in to the bully Viktor. He knew he was out-matched but the anger gave him courage. He took his right index finger in his left hand and wrenched. It clicked. He fainted.

Semi conscious Hideo was aware of other people in his room.

'He's still unconscious,' said Lihua's voice

'It looks as though he crawled over to the bed and passed out,' said Quon. 'At least he's not dead. We'll question him when he comes round.'

'What could he possibly know that we don't?' asked Viktor, in his most arrogant voice.

'You can be a fool, Viktor,' said Quon. 'I wonder sometimes if you really are my son.'

'Viktor didn't know about the surveillance, Father,' said Lihua, trying to diffuse the conversation.

'That doesn't alter the fact that by his stupidity, he has nearly jeopardised our entire mission.'

'How?' asked Viktor, defiantly. 'The worm is harmless.'

'The worm, as you call him, has been in contact with his friends outside,' said Quon, angrily.

'He spoke to them on his mobile,' spat Viktor, defiantly. 'So what?'

'He didn't just speak to them, Viktor. They sent him messages, instructions. That would get them into our computers,' said Lihua softly, encouraging him to calm down.

For a moment, Viktor was speechless.

'But now we know that, we can block them can't we?' asked Viktor hopefully.

'Yes by closing the whole network,' said Quon, losing patience, 'and if we do that we miss our time window.'

'Window?'

Quon made a low guttural noise in his throat as he stared at Viktor in disbelief. Lihua decided to enlighten Viktor.

'In two days, there is a global meeting of finance ministers and central bankers,' she explained. 'That's why we've been marking time in the slow room labs. We disrupt their communications and launch our attack on their currencies when they are distracted.'

'It's a good thing that someone in the family has brains,' said Quon, smiling indulgently at Lihua. 'Why couldn't you think up a plan like your sister?' he continued, returning his penetrating gaze to Viktor.

'Sorry father, do you know who the worm talked to?' ' he said contritely. Without waiting for the answer he continued, 'I can eliminate them if you wish.'

'No need,' said Quon. 'Your brothers have traced them to London. Their elimination is in hand.'

****

She had been using Paul's network to download some information from the internet. Francine's eyes were tired so she decided to stretch her legs and check on Paul. She had just walked into the when she saw a flicker on the computer monitor.

'Paul, it looks like you've got a new message,' she said.

'Pardon,' said Paul, switching off the lathe and removing his goggles. 'You said something?'

'I said you've got a new message.'

'That's great,' he said, moving to join her at the computer screen.

He bent over to read the icon on the taskbar.

'It looks like it's an update from Anil,' he said, wiping his hands on his overalls.

Francine watched him wipe his hands.

'Do you want me to open it for you?' she asked. 'Your hands are still oily.'

'Yes please,' he replied.

She clicked the mouse and Anil's message came up.

It said, 'Hello.'

'The message is in the attached multimedia file,' he said. 'It's encrypted and embedded in the video.'

'That's clever,' she said.

'That's Anil for you,' he said, 'and you can even play the video back.'

'Wouldn't it be distorted with hidden messages in side?' asked Francine.

'Just a little fuzziness around the edges of sharp objects that's all,' he replied. 'As you said it's clever.'

'Can you drag the attachment to this icon,' he said pointing at a blue symbol on the screen.

Francine did as she was asked and a message appeared.

'Enter key.'

Paul reached behind the monitor and retrieved his copy of "The PC Manual for Thickies".

'Could you open the original message for me again, I need to see the time and date of Anil's message,' said Paul.

Francine clicked on the window, now hidden behind the encryption message. Paul read the header and thumbed through his book, leaving a few smudged fingerprints as he did it. Francine watched curious, but silent. Seeing her expression, he smiled.

'This is our codebook,' he said. 'Anil and I have agreed that the encryption key depends on the date and time of his message. There are one or two other rules like if the line contains certain words, we go to the next line; things like that.'

'You never cease to amaze me,' she said.

Paul was concentrating.

'Ok,' he said, 'if you could open up the encryption window, the key is: "LOADED AND WHAT SERVICES ARE RUNNING THIS FEATURE….",' he paused. 'Sorry, I should ignore the last word.'

'What "FEATURE"?'

'Yes,' said Paul. 'It's a private joke; Anil says the operating system's features are usually bugs, so we swap the word.'

'So I key in "BUG"?' she said.

'Yes,' he said, 'then "SHOULD GREATLY.'

'It doesn't make any sense,' said Francine.

'It's only one line out of the book,' he said. 'Besides, this manual doesn't normally make sense.'

Francine clicked on an icon titled "Submit".

The computer played a tuneful chord and displayed a new message.

'Password?' it said.

The cursor waited patiently for Francine's response.

'Hold on,' said Paul, adding a few more oily smudges to the pages of his book. 'IPCONFIG,' he said.

'Can you spell that for me please,' said Francine.

He leant over and pointed at the word with a dirty fingernail. Francine keyed the word in and waited.

After a few seconds, the screen came alive.

'What's all this?' said Francine.

'It's a list of STKiC's servers and their security details,' said Paul. 'Anil's a genius.'

'Look there's one called trading server,' said Francine.

'So there is,' said Paul. 'It looks like you and Claire may be right. They're in the middle of a financial scam.'

'What's that at the bottom of the screen?' asked Francine pointing to a flashing icon on the task bar.

'It looks like Anil has sent us another message,' he said. 'Can you click on it and check the time.'

Francine obliged.

'It was sent twenty seconds after the other message,' she said. 'It's marked as urgent.'

'That's strange,' said Paul. 'Why didn't he include it in the first message?'

'Maybe something happened immediately after he sent it.'

She looked at her watch.

'They were both sent just over twenty minutes ago,' she said.

'I was working on the lathe,' said Paul. 'I guess I didn't hear the messages come in. Can you open the message please?'

Francine double clicked on the message. This time there was no attachment, just free text in the e-mail.

'We agreed he wouldn't send any free text unless they had hacked us,' he said, nervously looking over her shoulder. 'It looks like he's used our manual code. It's not the quickest way to encrypt one of our messages, and it's not as secure.'

'Perhaps his computer was off line and he didn't have access to the encryption software.'

'…and he encrypted it manually whilst he waited for his computer to boot up,' said Paul.

'Yes they sometimes take an eternity to wake up,' she replied. 'If that's true then Anil must have been in a real hurry. He would have keyed the encoded message into his terminal as soon as it came to life and then immediately sent it to you.'

'Maybe, either way something's wrong,' said Paul, 'very wrong.' He looked worriedly at the words in front of them. 'Can you print it for me, Francine? I need to decrypt this by hand.'

She hit the print button. They both stood over the printer watching as it fussed over the sheet of paper. They were apprehensive, tense and a little frightened, and justifiably so.

****

As was becoming normal around this time of day, his headache had returned. He was no stranger to stress-related headaches, but this one, just like his current case, did not want to go away. In spite of O'Reilly's preference for a simple answer, he had decided to follow up on Degordes' involvement in the sabotage of the Japanese experiment. O'Reilly had pulled every string and used every form of international co-operation to track down the Japanese saboteur and the boss – Hitzubishi. There was nothing; not a dicky-bird. The saboteur, Aoki Hideo and his boss did not exist. They never existed. Their project did not exist. The company that was supposed to have sponsored the research was squeaky clean. O'Reilly was confused and annoyed. Either Paul Dzibias was pulling his plonker or someone was very good at covering their tracks. Whatever the reason, O'Reilly knew that he must get Dzibias back in for questioning. Having worked out that Jacques had landed on a Lancastrian buddleia bush in the middle of the city, O'Reilly and his team were reinvigorated; they had finally got the breakthrough they needed. Their next task should have been easy; retrace Degordes' movements after his fall from the parapet of the Mancunian Way. Surely a man who had just fallen over twenty feet into an herbaceous border, must have shown some signs of wear and tear. The area around Canal Street was normally busy throughout the night and at the time of the accident it was no different.

'Someone must have seen Degordes,' he thought.

However there was a problem; Jacques battered, bruised and bloodied, clad in torn dinner jacket would simply not stand out. Like most nights, it was party night. The streets had been teaming with people behaving bizarrely in all kinds of strange attire. They were having a good time, or not as the case may be. After hours of questions, scanning CCTV footage and a public appeal, there was nothing. It was as if Jacques had simply vanished, or more likely he had blended into the background with all the others in fancy dress. Then he got a breakthrough. A narrow boat that had been stolen from its moorings at Ducie Street Junction, had turned up a month later in the London's Paddington Basin, right next to where Dr Dzibias lived. O'Reilly sent the novice to interview him only to find Dzibias and his missus had disappeared as well. O'Reilly was becoming quite frustrated. He could cope with suspects being murdered, but to keep disappearing like this was outrageous. His next "breakthrough" was no better either. He reckoned that when Francine Degordes had disappeared to the Maldives, his case was solved. Just as his instincts had told him, he thought she had arranged a rendezvous with her mythical husband. Much to the displeasure of his boss, he had flown out to confront them. But they weren't there; they had never been there. Now both of them had vanished. His head was starting to throb as he thought of the dematerialisation of the rest of the Degordes clan and everybody connected to them, or maybe that would be a good thing. O'Reilly was beginning to wish that his team had never been assigned to the damned case. His discomfort was compounded by the repetitive question, 'Any progress?' from his boss; to which his answer, 'Not yet', appeared to have triggered a disease in his superior's epiglottis requiring an insistent guttural throat-clearing noise. The team were assembled in front of him. Completely devoid of ideas, he decided to share his pain with the rest of them. He would feel much better if they had headaches as well.

'Right, we're in the shit,' he started. 'We are nowhere with this case. Has anybody anything new, or have I got to do all the work?'

A phone rang. An expression of irritation crossed O'Reilly's face as he glared at the novice. It was her phone, somehow his eyes had communicated that it was her fault that it was ringing. The novice lifted the receiver quickly and whispered into it.

'As I was saying,' O'Reilly continued. 'Has anybody any ideas?'

He looked at each blank face in turn.

'Come on,' he said 'There must be something, think!'

Silence; O'Reilly was good at applying pressure through silence.

'What about his mates?' said the thinker, fumbling in the dark.

The novice was still whispering to her caller. O'Reilly glanced at her, his irritation still evident.

'What do you mean?' he said, addressing the thinker.

'Dzibias told us that there was some problem with the Japanese experiment…'

'You mean the one that never happened,' interrupted O'Reilly. 'The one where our only witness has disappeared,' he added.

'That's just it,' said the thinker. 'He told us that his wife was in Japan when it happened.'

'In case you've forgotten, she's disappeared as well,' said O'Reilly, in frustration.

'Yes but there was someone else in Japan with her…'

'..Prama,' said the novice, putting the phone down. 'She was a friend of Dr Dzibias' wife Claire and Francine Degordes.'

The whole group turned to look at her.

'What do you mean was?' asked O'Reilly. 'Who was that on the phone, McKenzie?'

'It was the Met,' she said.

There was a knot in O'Reilly's stomach, to balance his headache.

'What did they want?'

'They want to know if we know what's happened to Dr Paul Dzibias and his wife Dr Claire Dzibias.'

'Why?'

'Because they are missing and two of their friends have been found,' said the novice, 'Prama and her fiancé Anil.'

'Found?'

'The report says that they were both shot through the head.'

'Oh bugger,' said O'Reilly, his headache now firmly entrenched.

'Oh bugger,' said the thinker.

****

Some minutes after Quon and his off-spring left, Hideo had continued to drift in and out of consciousness and when his senses were finally restored, he was not sure whether he had dreamt the conversation over his bed or it had been real. Whatever had happened, it was as if a hypnotist had implanted the words in his mind for later recall. Although the information was fully embedded, he did not understand the significance. Why should he? He was a seismologist, not a market trader.

Hideo swung his legs over the side of the low futon and although his head started to swim, he was determined to struggle to his feet. He stood for a few moments whilst his head cleared, but like O'Reilly, his nervous system insisted in relaying a constant throbbing sensation to his brain. He stumbled to the bathroom and filled a glass with water. He gulped it down, spilling much of the contents over his chest. He felt better, he took another glassful, and this time drank it more efficiently. His eyes clearing he looked at his surroundings with new purpose. Whilst he had been in the bunker, he had often thought of escape, but now he was locked in his room, he felt trapped, cornered. As his mind cleared, he found he was seeing new opportunities. He could use the cable from the table lamp and wire up the keyhole so it would electrify the next person who unlocked his door. He could set fire to his futon and set the fire alarms off, maybe the bunkers systems were designed to automatically unlock the fire escape doors as in the offices back in Tokyo. He looked at his windowless surroundings.

'Perhaps that is not one of my better ideas,' he thought.

'If only I could get access to the computer,' he muttered, thinking of Prama and Anil.

Then he remembered words from his sub-conscious. Someone had said, "Their elimination is in hand"

Hideo shuddered. For the first time Hideo looked above him. He could see that the ceiling was tiled with panels of gypsum plaster like those in the main chamber. He moved to a dressing table thoughtfully installed next to the adjoining wall between his room and the corridor. He clambered on the table and carefully avoiding his damaged finger, stretched towards the ceiling tile. He found he could lift it a little.

'It's a false ceiling,' he muttered. 'I wonder how big the space is above.'

He stepped down from the table, almost falling as he weak, bruised legs took his weight. He placed a chair on top of the dressing table and climbed back on. Soon he was peering into the space above the ceiling. The corridor wall extended to the rock above.

'Shit,' he said, despondently. 'It's hopeless.'

Preparing to descend, he took hold of the framework that supported the ceiling tiles. He felt the steel structure flex and creak under his weight. The framework appeared to respond differently in the direction away from the corridor wall. His head still above the level of the tiles, he turned to look in the opposite direction, towards the area above the bathroom. It was too dark to see more than a few metres of empty ceiling space. He thought of climbing up into the roof space, but realised that the steel structure would not support his weight. He clambered down again, this time being more careful in his decent. After a few seconds thought, he dragged the table and chair into the bathroom, creating a screeching noise that made him wince. He recreated his plinth against the wall furthest from the corridor and clambered on top. Gently lifting the closest tile he peered into the space above.

'Thank you God,' he said to himself. He was not sure why he said this as he was not a believer.

The steel framework was resting on the wall, leaving about one and a half feet between the ceiling structure and the top of the wall. If he could squeeze through, he would be able to escape to the room next door. With herculean effort, he hauled himself through the hole where the ceiling tile used to be. The steel structure became bent and distorted as it strained under his weight. He eased his body over the wall. As he shifted his weight onto the ceiling tile of the room next door, the bathroom ceiling, no longer weighed down by Hideo, let out a groan as it flexed to its equilibrium position. Unfortunately one room's relief was another's burden and Hideo soon found himself falling as the ceiling of his new abode gave way. But all was not lost. He had landed in a pile of gravitum-doped plaster dust on a futon; a futon that had not been used for many years, as it was in the dangerous "Fast Room".

# Twenty-seven

## Dangerous locations

All four of them had repaired to the farmhouse. Paul was sitting at the farm table with the open codebook and Anil's encoded message in front of him. His audience was standing in a semicircle behind him, apprehensively watching every gesture of his shoulders, his hands, his pen.

'Anil and I agreed not to write any software that would encrypt or decrypt certain messages,' Paul explained. 'The algorithm is in our heads. So if someone stole our computers they would find nothing to help them. We agreed to use the same codebook, though.'

'What if someone got hold of the codebook?' asked Claire.

'Then sooner or later they would crack our codes and everything we communicate would be as visible as if we had shouted the messages from the roof tops.'

'How long would that take?' asked Jacques.

'Well as you can see, even if you know the algorithm, it's still a laborious task. The idea was to give us a head start of maybe a few hours,' Paul replied. 'The algorithm is asymmetric.'

'Asymmetric?'

'You can encrypt messages very quickly, but is laborious to decrypt.' Paul paused and wrote a few more letters. 'That's it,' he said.

He smoothed out his worksheet in front of them.

The message read,

**We have unwanted visitors. They have traced us. They are downstairs now. We're going to leave for home. They will get hold of our codebook. They will be able to locate you when Hideo's messages are cracked through whatever method they choose.**

**You can't get access to their servers, because I was too slow and the addresses are all wrong. You will not be able to help Hideo by getting into their access control systems. The details I gave you got corrupted, so Hideo is lost and cannot escape. He will not be able to get you the information about which systems they are using in their scam because the security codes I sent him were wrong. Get out of the house and get into the secret room in the workshop. Put all equipment in there. Hide. I expect they will be with you soon.**

**Good luck my dear friends, Prama and I must leave now.**

'Merde,' said Jacques. 'We've lost. It's over.'

****

He was completely exhausted by the physical exertions that were needed to lift Hideo's tired bruised body into the crawl space and over the partition wall. In the half-light of his refuge, his mind and every sinew and muscle told him to rest, sleep or just lie still. If Hideo had known where he was, he would have realised that there were some benefits to landing in the Fast Room. One of these was that if he lay quietly for fifty minutes in the Fast Room, only ten minutes would have ticked by in the outside world and less than a minute in the Slow Room. This would mean that by the time Viktor had made himself a cup of tea Hideo would be fully recovered. Even though he was not yet aware of this gem of information, Hideo had his rest anyway. After an hour or so he opened his eyes and looked up at the hole through which he had fallen. This seemed to be the source of the only light in the room; a bright blue light. He tried to picture in his mind where the light was coming from.

'It must be reflected light from his old room,' he thought. 'Light that is bouncing off the roof of the crawl space.'

But he could not remember any blue illumination in his bathroom. He remembered that when he was in the roof space that surface above him had been painted white. It now looked blue. There was no light only a heater on the wall.

'Why blue?' he muttered. 'Why does the colour of light keep changing in here?'

One would have thought that at that moment he had more important things on his mind, but Hideo was not ready to face the other realities of his situation and he was content to muse. He remembered the weird lights when he had looked down the corridor of the slow room towards the main chamber. He was no expert but he felt it was something to do with shifts in time. He wished he could ask Prama, she would know. If he ever got out of this he would ask her for a date. She was brilliant. If he could have spoken to her she would have told him that his guess about time was right; his eyes were seeing the reverse effect of a red-shift; red light was changing towards the blue end of the spectrum because of time shifts between the Slow and Fast Rooms. In fact the blue light that he could see in the Fast Room was not visible in his bathroom because it was coming from the heater. It was infrared and below the range of the human eye. Whether he understood the physics or not, Hideo had deduced that clocks would run differently where he was. It was a matter of perspective. Suddenly Hideo had an insight. He sat up quickly; he had realised where he was. He was in the Fast Room and he remembered Lihua's words.

'He'd be an old man in a few months and no threat to anyone,' she had said.

'Shit,' muttered Hideo, 'why does nothing ever turn out right?'

If not exactly rejuvenated but feeling slightly more human, he struggled to his feet. It was then he heard a noise. Someone or something was in the room with him.

****

'It's not good, but it's not as bad as you think,' said Paul.

'Comment?' said Jacques.

'I see what you mean Paul,' said Francine, gazing at the decoded text. 'Anil has used your disinformation code.'

Claire and Jacques looked at Francine quizzically.

'That's right,' said Paul. 'He's used the word "get", "got" or "getting" several times. It means that we should reverse the sense of the sentence.'

Claire peered over Paul's shoulder to take a closer look at the message.

'So his message means that they have been discovered by STKiC but Anil has kept the code book safe.'

'That's right,' said Paul. 'But Anil reckons they'll crack our encryption through other means.'

'With all their computer power I'm not surprised,' said Jacques, 'and presumably he believes that will lead them to us.'

'I suspect he's right,' said Paul, 'but now he's warned us, it gives us a head start.'

'The rest of the message is not as it seems either,' said Francine.

Claire interpreted for them, 'He's telling us that the addresses he's given you for STKiC's file servers are correct and you can get access to all their computers including their access control systems.'

'I assume he means the door locking system in the bunker?' interrupted Jacques.

'I think so,' Claire continued, 'So that means Hideo will be able to help us find out which systems they are using for their scam and we will be able to release him from the bunker. Anil and Hideo have managed to find out all the security codes that we need.'

'That works only if we can communicate with Hideo,' said Jacques.

'That may be a problem,' said Paul. 'His second sentence says that they have traced Anil's location, so we must assume they will found out about our microwave link. That would give them an extra way to trace us. I'll need to think of how else we can access the Internet without being traced,' he added, pensively.

'What does this last sentence of the "get" paragraph mean?' asked Jacques, reading ahead. 'Secret room? What does he mean?'

'It's disinformation for STKiC when they crack this code,' said Francine. 'He's telling them that there is a secret room in the workshop and they will find us there, because that's where we will be doing the experiment.'

'But there is no secret room,' said Claire.

'To be sure, that's true, but he's telling us to move out of the workshop because they will look for us in there,' said Jacques. 'I think we should "hide" somewhere else.'

'We should set a trap,' said Paul, quietly.

'Comment, mon ami?' said Jacques.

'If we know they will come for us in the workshop, we can set a trap in there,' said Paul, elaborating on his thoughts.

'What blow it up or something?' asked Claire, warming to the idea.

'I wasn't thinking of anything so drastic,' said Paul, amused. 'All the buildings have strong steel shutters. I could rig up servos to lock them in when they go inside.'

'But these people are killers. They are dangerous,' said Jacques. 'They killed Dmitry. They tried to kill me.'

'That's right but we're not killers,' said Paul. 'We hold them prisoner and call the police. I'm sure the police would like to talk to them about why they were attacking us on private land and about Dmitry's death.'

'It's very risky,' said Jacques. 'What if they don't crack Anil's last message? What if they don't fall for his diversion?'

'The shutters are strong on all the buildings we'll lock ourselves into the farmhouse,' said Paul. 'It's a stone building with a slate roof. We can control the equipment remotely. It could take them days to break in.'

'We can't give up now, my darling,' said Francine. 'We have come so far.'

'But Francine, have you seen Anil's first sentence?' asked Jacques. 'STKiC has found them. Even if Anil and Prama made it home, they are still in danger? We must call the police and give ourselves up. The police will come quickly because we're fugitives. It is the only way to stop this before anybody else is killed.'

'They'll arrest us and then we'll never be able to stop STKiC,' said Francine.

Francine looked into her husband's eyes, her head cocked, looking for inspiration. But it was not there. Jacques had battled on and on, but he was now exhausted. He had no more to give. A tear rolled down Francine's cheek.

'It's over, my love we have lost. All we can do now is defend ourselves.'

Jacques looked back at her. They had all read the first paragraph of Anil's message and although they had not talked about it, each of them desperately hoped that Anil and Prama had escaped the STKiC henchman. But Jacques had had personal experience of their efficiency and in his heart he knew they were lost. He had come such a long way to fight this enemy, but he knew she was right. STKiC were too strong. He must protect his family and friends. They must give themselves up and hope the police could protect them; that is if they believed them.

****

It took a good ten minutes for him to find the door to the Fast Room corridor. Now out of the bedroom, there was no light at all. In the pitch black he fumbled his way along the walls until his hand brushed against a door handle. He turned it and felt his way through the door. He stepped though the entrance into a new room. He could not see anything, but he could sense that wherever he was, it was a large space; this was no bedroom. Hideo ran his hand up and down the wall. He flicked the switch.

'Finally, some good luck,' he mumbled, as the room became illuminated. It was full of computer equipment.

'Now we're talking,' he said to himself.

He turned one of the computers on. It started to boot up.

'Now,' he said. 'I wonder if I can download Anil's latest messages.'

****

Paul had brought his laptop into the farmhouse. It was still connected to the microwave link by a radio system built into his PC: a WiFi link. Out of the corner of his eye he noticed a flash on the task bar. Jacques and Francine were still preoccupied with their thoughts.

'What is it?' asked Claire, under her breath.

'I think we've got a new message,' said Paul.

Francine and Jacques turned to watch Paul as he reached over to his laptop. He started to decrypt the message.

'But their last message implied they were leaving,' said Jacques, relieved that they were still sending messages.

'It's not from Anil,' said Paul.

'Who sent it then?' asked Francine, more worried than relieved.

'It's from Hideo,' said Paul.

****

Hideo's ears had tuned into the sound. It was a whirring noise, like the sound of an electric motor stopping and starting.

'I'm becoming too twitchy,' he thought, turning his gaze towards the noise. 'It's only a faulty cooling fan or something.'

He turned back to the computer terminal in front of him. Although Hideo was not a computer expert, with Anil's guidelines and enough time he could work things out. In the Fast Room, time was something he had in abundance and slowly but surely he had figured out what Anil was asking him to do. Now armed with a new understanding, memories of the conversation over his semiconscious body and a clear head, Hideo had managed to complete all of the tasks that Anil had assigned him. In fact he had been able to do more. By accessing STKiC's Intranet Hideo had interrogated the computers of each of STKiC's subsidiaries. He had obtained a mass of interesting information that served to confirm that the words embedded in his subconscious were true. He put all of this into a message and sent it to Anil. Now very satisfied with his work, Hideo sat quietly in front of the terminal and waited for the reply. With luck Anil would soon unlock the doors and he could escape. Hideo knew that Anil's response might be slower than normal, because of the different rates of time between the Fast Room and the world outside. So he knew he had to be patient. Unfortunately Hideo did not know that Anil was no longer taking messages and at that point Hideo was completely alone, isolated; there was no cavalry to save him. However before he and Prama headed for the exit, Anil had managed to do one thing that would improve Hideo's chances of staying alive. Hideo did not know that the delay may have cost Anil and Prama their lives.

There was a noise in the corridor.

'Shit,' he said. 'They've come in after me. I'll have to hide.'

He moved quickly to the light switch. The room did not go completely dark. His computer monitor was generating a soft light around the room. Before he could get to the off switch the door started to open. He ducked behind one of the computer cabinets.

****

'How could we? We almost forgot about Hideo,' said Claire. 'If we give up now, he'll never escape.' Only Claire and Prama had met Hideo in person. They had both grown to respect the timid young man who, when the chips were down, showed amazing courage and determination. 'We can't leave him to fend for himself,' she continued. 'We're the only friends he's got. By the time we've convinced the police that we're not completely mad, he could have been murdered. If we think we're outnumbered, think about how he feels.'

'But what can we do for him now?' said Jacques, in an uncharacteristically tired voice. 'They have us trapped.'

'I'll tell you one thing,' said Paul lifting a sheet of paper from his printer. 'He may be a prisoner but he's battling on. What's more, he thinks we're still working with him. I've decrypted his message. He's found out what STKiC are up to.'

'What does it say?' asked Jacques, unconvinced.

'He says that the scam is based on a number of international banks dotted around the world.'

'We know this Paul,' said Jacques. 'Claire and Francine worked out that STKiC were setting up a financial scam.'

'Yes, but we didn't know what kind of scam,' said Paul. 'There are lots of different trading systems around the world. We had no idea which ones they were interested in.' Paul stopped to re-read part of Hideo's message. 'I'm not sure I understand this part. He seems to be talking about markets and trading systems. It's all double-dutch to me.'

'May I have a look,' said Francine reaching out for the message.

Paul handed her the printout. She scanned the section that had confused Paul.

'So that's what they're doing,' she said.

'You understand it?' said Paul incredulously.

'I think so,' she replied. 'Hideo has not only told us which market is involved, but also which trading systems and which banks they intend to hi-jack.'

'Hi-jack?' asked Claire.

'Yes, hi-jack,' Francine repeated. 'They want to channel their illegal trading through a number of banks. They are all banks based in countries with favourable fiscal systems.'

'Tax havens?' said Claire.

'That's right,' said Francine, 'and STKiC has selected systems within these banks that have one thing in common.'

'What's that?' asked Jacques.

'Currencies'

'What do you mean currencies?' asked Paul.

'I mean foreign currency. They all specialise in currency trading,' said Francine. 'Their plan is to place bets on currency deals, except they are not really betting. They know the outcome before they start. They intend to connect the GWR Mark Three...'

'Hitzubishi's original device,' interrupted Claire.

'Yes, the steel cylinder that you, Prama and Hideo took from the Academy of Geosciences,' she replied. 'I think they have connected the machine to their trading systems so that it will respond to the details of future currency prices.' She paused, 'Is that possible?' she asked directing her question to Jacques.

'In theory yes,' he replied, 'but it's a big step from sending a simple EPR message back from the future.'

'Bloody hell,' said Paul.

'Well,' Francine continued, 'if I'm right they will transfer their holdings from one currency to another and get a profit on every deal.'

'But isn't that how trading systems normally work?' asked Claire. 'Don't they already have systems to predict future values?'

'Yes,' said Francine, warming to her newly acquired subject, 'but normally trading systems predict future values by extrapolating trends. If the trend is upwards, they will buy the currency that is rising and sell it before it falls. However it doesn't always work and there is lots of room for human error. Markets can be very unpredictable. Everybody plays to the same rules, so the system usually remains stable.'

'Unless they all do something stupid,' said Jacques. 'Like lemmings over a cliff.'

'Like lending money to people who can't pay it back, you mean,' said Paul.

'STKiC have taken the principle to the next level,' said Francine. 'They are working on the basis that money has no intrinsic value. It's just paper or more correctly bits and bytes. For them it's just a tool to get power.'

'You know a lot about currency trading all of a sudden,' said Jacques, impressed.

'While you've been building laboratories, I've been reading,' said Francine.

Francine knew that the team were not familiar with trading systems; a few days before nor was she. But after Paul had given the team fixed times of the day when they could gain access to the internet, she had used the timeslots productively. She had downloaded a wealth of information and used every spare moment to read up. Even though her version of how things worked was probably polluted by errors from well-meaning sources, she decided to give the little group a tutorial.

'Anyway,' she continued. 'STKiC are not working on historical patterns and predictive trends like other trading systems. They want to use the GWR to build a table of currencies that records the actual prices of the Pound, the Euro etcetera. If the trader had only had that information before the table was created he would never make a mistake.'

'So they'll get GWR to send the results back in time,' suggested Paul.

'It would need to look far enough into the future to allow the transactions to be properly accepted and logged, but yes,' she replied. 'My guess is that it must look around one second into the future.'

'Even longer if the trading computers were connected over satellite links,' chipped in Paul.

'If you say so,' she said. 'It's all about timing.'

'But from my calculations they would be lucky to hold the artificial black hole for a few hundred milli-seconds, let alone a second,' said Jacques.

Francine looked disappointed. She had no answer to this point. They were silent for a few moments. Then Paul's eyes lit up.

'You're right Jacques, but Hideo has sent details of a modification,' said Paul. 'He reckons they are testing the GWR with messages almost a second into future. If STKiC's computers need at least one second to do their scam, they are nearly there. It all fits.'

'I still don't see how it works,' said Claire.

Francine explained, 'I'll give you an illustration. If a currency trader had a traditional list of probable prices from a computer prediction, he may say, "I'll buy Euro's using my spare Dollars, but just in case it's wrong I'll spread my risk by keeping some of the Dollars and buying some Yen." He would do this because the computer prediction is normally only a guide. It is often wrong so there is a human intuition involved in the transactions. STKiC will remove the need for intuition.'

'How?' asked Claire.

'The GWR **is** the trader. No human is involved. It would send a list of currency values from the future to the trading system one second earlier. The computer would instantly transfer money from the weakest currencies to the strongest.'

'That would create a time anomaly?' said Jacques. 'I thought basic economics say that the future value would change because of increased demand.'

'That's right. You are saying STKiC will create a demand that wasn't there in the message sent back from the future,' said Francine, 'and this should change the message from the future.'

'Yes,' said Jacques. 'Making the first message wrong and creating an anomaly.'

Francine was stumped. Claire's head was starting to spin, but Paul was becoming intrigued.

'I assume the currency transactions would only affect future prices after the trade had gone through,' he said.

Francine nodded.

'I doubt whether this would happen within the one second time frame,' he said, 'Global networks tend to slow things down.'

'By which time the GWR would have moved on to its next trade,' said Francine.'

'So there would be no anomaly,' said Jacques, thoughtfully.

Francine went on, 'By continuing this process over a whole week the value would grow geometrically. They could convert a few dollars to billions in an incredibly short time.'

'Because they never make a mistake,' said Jacques.

'I think STKiC reckons that all governments have been printing millions of tonnes of paper money to shore up their economies,' said Francine. 'There is simply too much paper in the system. That's fine as long as it sits in vaults or keeps going round and round. STKiC intend to use this to their advantage. Their plan is big.'

'How big?' asked Claire.

'Thousands of trillions of dollars,' said Francine. Her audience gasped. 'Their last act is to dump the profits back on to different trading markets by buying, oil, gold, silver copper, silver, weapons… whatever has the highest intrinsic value. The result is that they engineer the devaluation of most international currencies.'

'But if they do that currencies all over the world could collapse,' said Claire, 'and it could start a financial crisis like we have never seen before.'

'It'll put a lot of bankers and accountants out of work,' mumbled Paul.

'Paper money would become just that; paper,' said Francine, 'and as with all financial disasters someone will come out on top.'

'Mon Dieu,' said Jacques. 'Because they have the GWR Mark Three, STKiC will know who that is and be a step ahead.'

'And they will bet on the winner,' said Francine. 'At the end of the crisis, STKiC will be holding all the right things: things with inherent value or currencies that survived the collapse. I told you their plan was big.' She paused, adding, 'Their plan is to run the world economy.'

'But what kind of economy would STKiC be running?' asked Jacques.

Claire had been listening to the conversation intently. She was absorbing the information, extrapolating and working out the implications for the average person.

'One based on barter,' said Claire, almost reflectively. 'If you have nothing of value to barter, you starve,' she added, horrified, 'and if the bulk of the population is starving, there will be billions of desperate people rioting, stealing and looting.'

'Anarchy,' said Jacques, turning to Francine. 'I was wrong, we cannot give in. If STKiC are not stopped billions more people will starve or die.

'That's right,' said Francine. 'STKiC would have assets to back up their wealth. They will produce bonds or certificates, which could be issued by their subsidiaries. Like a huge chain of pawn shops for those who have things to pawn. Because the certificates could at any time be converted into gold, silver or other things, people would trust them and they would be exchanged for goods in the outside world.'

'This would create a new international currency,' said Paul.

'And STKiC would run it,' said Claire, horrified.

Jacques and Francine looked at each other without speaking, but there was communication. They did not need to put their thoughts into words; they had been together long enough to understand. Francine's eyes acknowledged a movement of Jacques' head, an almost imperceptible nod. Without saying a word they knew that they had to carry on, even though it would continue to place their family and friends in danger.

# Twenty-eight

## Melt down

Zakhar Putyatin was not particularly attached to his name as he had so many alternatives. Although his younger brother was equally unattached to names, he did have preferences. Nikolas Karpin was a good handle for an assassin, in that it was ordinary, but unusual in being Russo-Greek. He liked the classical feel to this alias. He would have been perfectly happy to use any one of his other favourites; all of which had subtle twists. At heart Nikolas was a rebel. He liked to demonstrate his individuality. This was probably a reaction to having a twin brother whom he labelled an idiot. In spite of Zakhar and Nikolas' ambivalence to nomenclature they were very careful to make sure that the names on their tickets matched their Russian passports. So for the time being the brothers would continue to use their assumed monikers. Still glowing from their father's praise for a job well done, they had been assigned the next task. Being the eldest and leader by default, Zakhar in particular was pleased. He had to admit that the removal of the two problems in London had gone very well, even though they had not been able to track down their confederates very quickly.

'Well no harm done,' he thought, 'We know where they now.'

Nikolas' thoughts were different. He had met two of the next targets before and they knew him. They were resourceful and determined. There could be no room for mistakes.

Like most of his family Nikolas had been given a wide and comprehensive education. Because the whole clan had access to Slow and Fast rooms they could rest and study very efficiently. Unlike his twin Viktor, Nikolas was extremely intelligent and took to education well, but in common with most of his siblings he had a cold ruthless streak. Some years earlier Nikolas' father had sent him to a university where it was rumoured that one of the blue stones was being analysed. His father wanted it back and Nikolas, posing as a student, was tasked to find it. He enrolled as normal and was allocated a laboratory and tutorial partner: Paul Dzibias. Their tutor was a young post graduate called Jacques Degordes. It was obvious from day one that Paul and Nikolas would not get on, but Nikolas tried his best to make the relationship work by ruthlessly attempting to dominate Dzibias. Nikolas was used to being top of the pecking order and Paul, a free thinker, would not yield to Nikolas' obscure demands; many of which were designed to help Nikolas track down the blue stone. He still blamed Dzibias for singlehandedly thwarting the first important assignment that his father had given him. His feelings escalated into outrage when years later he found out that the blue stone had been on a book shelf in a tutorial room all along. Degordes had been using it as a book stop! Nikolas' twin brother Viktor took great pleasure in reminding him that the stone had been under his nose for months and Dzibias had nothing to do with Nikolas' failure. This moved his feelings for Dzibias and Degordes towards irrational hate. In his mind this new assignment gave him the opportunity to correct an old wrong. He was elated to find out that they were on their way to Provence to eliminate two of his most hated enemies. The elimination of their wives would be a bonus.

'What joy,' he thought.

****

'Now we know what they are planning,' said Claire. 'How do we stop them?'

'Whatever we decide to do, we'd better do it quickly,' said Jacques. 'We can assume they will be walking up the drive in a few hours or so.'

'We don't have much time anyway,' said Francine. 'They are planning to start the currency trading when the G-however-many-they-feel-like-inviting ministers meet this week.'

'Why,' asked Paul, 'are they hoping to catch the governments out of the office?'

'I think the idea is that when the global economy goes into meltdown, STKiC can put some "really helpful suggestions" to the governments of eighty percent of global trade,' said Francine, 'and do it when they are together in the same room.'

'Won't they respond badly to blackmail?' asked Claire, 'and bomb them or something.'

'They don't think that will happen,' she replied. 'They are going to argue that STKiC have been prudent with their investments and have become multi-trillionaires by sheer hard work and good fiscal management. STKiC will help only if the various governments want it.'

''Which they will, of course,' said Jacques.

'I expect so' said Francine. 'They'll have no choice. By the time the offer comes in their currencies will be worthless. The G-countries will be bankrupt.'

'So what's the answer to Claire's question?' asked Paul. 'How do we stop them?'

Nobody spoke.

'Is the clue in how far they look into the future?' asked Claire.

'Go on,' said Jacques.

Claire turned to Francine.

'Did you say that they looked into the future for only one second because it was too short to affect the future currency values?' she asked.

'I don't know that for sure, but I think so.'

'It makes sense to me,' said Paul. 'Even though the markets are run by computers, it would take longer than a second for the impact of a single transaction to alter the currency value.'

'What if we looked further into the future?' asked Claire.

'Then it's possible the valuation systems of some systems could respond and change the future. The message would then be wrong, creating a time anomaly.'

'Didn't you say that they plan to keep repeating the process moving their money between currencies in a one-second cyclical process?'

'Yes,' said Francine.

'What are you getting at?' asked Paul.

'Well, what if we made our system send one message back one second and another one and a half seconds from the future every second?' asked Claire.

'I'm not sure that's possible,' said Jacques.

'Yes, but if it was,' said Claire. 'We would know what STKiC know and things from half second more into the future.'

'How is that useful?' asked Paul.

'I don't know,' said Claire. 'I'm not the trading expert.'

They all fell back into silence.

****

From his point of view, it did not matter whether he was in the Fast Room or not, to Hideo it felt as though he had been hiding behind the computer cabinet for a lifetime. He peered discreetly around the edge of his hiding place. He could hear the whirring noise again, but this time it was moving around the room. The light from the screen was not enough to illuminate the space around the doorway. He was frightened and puzzled. There was definitely something in there with him but he had no idea what.

'To hell with it,' he thought.

He jumped out from behind the computer cabinet ready to confront his assailant. There was nothing there except the whirring noise.

'Come out and show yourself,' he said in his most macho voice.

There it was again; the whirring noise.

'Who ever it is. I'm armed,' he bluffed.

Again the whirring noise, a little closer, a little lower.

He looked down and there it was.

Hideo collapsed to the floor. He could not contain himself. He burst out laughing. He was looking at a robotic vacuum cleaner, just doing its rounds. Unfortunately he did not realise that the cameras on its lid were watching his every move.

****

'I've got it,' said Paul.

'Don't keep us in suspense,' said Francine. 'Speak.'

'If we adjust our replica GWR so that it works exactly in step with the one in the bunker, we will know which currencies they are intending to trade.'

'How does that help us?' asked Claire.

'It's all about timing,' said Paul. 'The trading systems are all over the world and because of the fixed velocity of light and the speed of the computers its takes some time before all the trading systems are aligned. So when they make their trades there will be a delay before we can respond to it.'

'Because the bunker is in Japan and we are in the South of France,' said Francine.

'Right,' said Paul continuing, 'If we knew the contents of their list, we would know which currencies they were trading. We can reverse their transactions at about the same time.'

'But we don't know how much currency to buy,' said Claire. 'Surely that's a decision they will make in the bunker.'

'That's where your idea comes in,' said Paul. 'We won't be able to find out how much money they put into dollars, the pound or anything else until the systems across the world get back in step.'

'So that's why we need to look further into the future.' said Claire.

'But wouldn't that cause the anomaly that Jacques was worried about?' asked Francine.

'There is only an anomaly if we affect the contents of a future message, by fiddling with the past,' said Paul. 'We can put anything in our message we like. So if our future message only sends back how much they traded then nothing is different.'

'Paul, that's brilliant,' said Jacques. 'If we make sure we don't include any information about currency values or any trades that we have made, then our compensating corrections will not affect the message.'

'So the net result is that STKiC make no money. They break-even,' said Francine. 'For every currency they buy, we sell it just afterwards.'

'That's right,' said Paul.

Jacques withdrew for a moment, reflecting. The others sensed he was about to say something controversial.

'Enfin, STKiC will still have the GWR and the same resources they have now,' he said, hesitantly. 'These people have attacked me, my family, you, our friends, killed an old colleague and forced us into hiding.' Jacques paused, choosing his words carefully. 'They will not give up until we are destroyed and they can do it all over again. We will not be safe.' He gazed at Francine. She met his gaze understanding.

'You are suggesting we break them aren't you, darling?' she said.

'I am,' he said. 'We should not reverse their transactions. We should reverse their logic and make them lose money on each deal.' He paused again, knowing that his suggestion would affect not only STKiC's ruthless owners but also their twenty-five thousand employees. There was pain in his eyes. Destroying others did not come naturally to him. 'We have to break them. We bankrupt them. We have no choice.'

'Ok,' said Paul, simply. 'We'd better get on with it then.'

****

The three and a half hour journey by Eurostar to Paris was infinitely better than the plane, for several reasons. By the time you had factored in the tedious wait in airport lounges and the taxi ride into Paris, it was quicker. Uncharacteristically for regular business travellers, the indignity associated with invasive security did not bother Zakhar and Nikolas in the slightest. They enjoyed the challenge. It amused them that the train service had decided to emulate airport style security; security that was unable to detect two professional assassins who were just earning a crust by going about their normal day to day business. Zakhar and Nikolas were proud of their professionalism and were more than a little miffed when their father had insisted that they bring in muscle to assist them in removing the irritants in Provence. He had told them that Degordes and Dzibias had outwitted them in the past. He was not going to allow it to happen again. In some respects, Nikolas was a sensitive soul. Sensitive in that he was embarrassed that he had not managed to acquire the blue stone and he had not managed to eliminate Degordes in the fake Mancunian accident. He knew exactly which incidents his father was referring to and he was even more annoyed than Zakhar about his father's comments. Nikolas was not petulant like his twin brother Viktor. He kept his outrage to himself. However outraged he was, he would not allow his father or Zakhar to screw things up by lumbering him with hired help. Their father had set up a rendezvous with mountain man and his associate at the restaurant in the station where they would board the train to Avignon. By the time Nikolas and Zakhar had stepped out of the Gare de Lyon Metro station onto the SNCF concourse, Nikolas had his own plan for the mission. There was no way he was going to allow these clowns to make him fail again.

****

'This is all very well,' said Jacques, 'but our GWR device can't send messages back one and a half seconds from the future! At the moment we can only manage a few milliseconds. And that depends on the level of gravitational wave intensity from space.'

'Hmm,' said Paul, taking Jacques' comment on board. 'Hideo has sent us details of their modification, but that will only get us to one second in the future.'

Paul loaded the schematic on his laptop and sent the image to the printer. While they were waiting for the print Jacques examined the image on Paul's screen.

'It looks like they've changed the geometry of the gravitum crystals,' said Jacques. 'They have arranged them in a perfect tetrahedron. We'll have to cut Earth and Sky crystal in half.'

'If you do it carefully,' said Paul. 'You could end up with bigger crystals than Hitzubishi's device. Perhaps that's enough to get the extra five-hundred milliseconds.'

'Bon,' said Jacques, 'Let's do it. I'll need your help. Paul.'

'Ah,' said Paul. 'I can't. You'll have to do it on your own.'

'That's not possible, Paul. I'll need help,' said Jacques, confused by Paul's reluctance. 'What's the problem?'

Paul began, 'We have to assume that STKiC have decrypted Anil's message.'

'So?'

'He put disinformation in the message to deflect them towards the workshop,' he continued. 'I need to install cctv in the workshop and remote control locks. The steel shutters must be welded closed so anybody inside cannot get out through the windows.... I am going to turn the workshop into a trap.'

'How long will that take?' asked Francine.

'A couple of hours,' said Paul. 'Then I intend to secure the farmhouse in the same way. We'll seal ourselves in and control things safely from there.'

'So you'll take all the essential equipment out of the workshop and install it in here?' said Francine.

'Yes,' said Paul. 'Unfortunately the shutters on the barn are wooden, so it is not as secure.'

'What about Hideo?' asked Claire.

'I've worked out the bunker's access codes. I'll send him a message as soon as I can. He can let him self out and make a run for it.'

'You've got so much to do,' said Francine. 'Can I help?'

'Definitely,' said Paul. 'You can help me with clearing the workshop.'

'Ok,' said Francine, thinking, planning. 'There's another problem.'

'What's that?' asked Jacques.

'We can assume that if they have decoded our messages then Paul's microwave link is now compromised. We need to find another way to get access to STKiC's trading computers.'

They were silent for a moment. When no ideas were forthcoming Francine started to become worried that they could be foiled so quickly. Jacques was looking disheartened. Claire was looking desperately into her husband's eyes, willing him to come up with something.

'Come on, Paul,' she said. 'You're so innovative. There has to be a solution.'

Paul's forehead furrowed, the pressure making it harder for him to think. He looked around the room for inspiration. His gaze fell on the laptop.

'How do I make you talk to STKiC?' he mumbled. 'How, how?'

'What are the alternatives?' asked Claire, trying to prompt his brain. 'wires, microwave radio, light, gravitational wa…..'

'I've got it,' said Paul. 'When I set up the wireless link between the farmhouse and the workshop, I noticed that several other wireless networks are active in the area.'

'You mean the Abbey?' asked Francine.

'Perhaps, or a neighbouring farm,' said Paul. 'I'll try to hack into one of them and use their internet connection. That would give us onward connection to STKiC's servers.'

'Is that possible?' asked Claire. 'Are these things so insecure?'

'They can be broken,' said Paul. 'Of course it's harder if they've used a complex key, but I have enough computer power here to break the normal algorithms within a few hours. I'll write the code and leave it running whilst I do one of my other jobs.'

'It looks like you're busy,' said Jacques. 'But the fact remains that the modification to the GWR is a two man job.'

'Is that "man" the race or "man" the gender?' asked Claire.

'Are you volunteering?' asked Jacques.

'You've got me whether you like it or not,' Claire replied.

****

While Paul wrote a program to break the encryption key of one of their neighbours' WiFi networks, the others started to prepare for their attack on STKiC's banks and the arrival of some bad people. Two and a half hours later, a train from Paris rolled in to Avignon. Four men made their way to a shop that hired out motorcycles. Now equipped with one BMW and three Kawasaki off-road motorbikes, they began their thirty-one kilometres journey to the Degordes farm. Within twenty minutes they had arrived at the farm. The sun was setting. Night was drawing in. They regrouped on the road outside the gate. Paul and Francine had finished their preparations in the workshop and farmhouse. Claire and Jacques were still working on the GWR modifications. The preparations were well advanced, but not quite finished.

# Twenty-nine

## Show down

It took Hideo a few seconds to notice the camera on the top of the robotic cleaner.

'Shit,' he mumbled. 'They know I'm here. I need to move fast.'

He did not know that his companions in the bunker were not interested in the output from the cleaner's camera. They thought Hideo was still locked in his room. They did not know about his escape. If they had been watching, they would see him moving incredibly quickly. Hideo had used his time in the fast room well. For the first time in his life he had taken his time to read a computer manual; even the pages marked "This page is intentionally blank". At least he understood those pages, most of the rest were barely intelligible but in time he had gleaned enough from the book and Anil's instructions to find his way around the bunker's systems. He looked at his watch. He'd been in the fast room for nearly forty-eight hours.

'I wonder what that is in real time,' he thought.

'I need those access codes,' he muttered. 'Anil must have sent them by now.'

He logged in to his newly created e-mail account. There was one message in his intray. But it was from Paul Dzibias not Anil. He opened the message. A surge of euphoria shot through his body.

'The codes,' he shouted. 'I've got the damn codes.'

But Hideo did not jump up and run to the door.

'Now to get my own back,' he muttered. 'I'll change the code. Now let's see how they like being prisoners.'

He tapped in some new numbers.

'This is when they regret abusing a seismologist,' he mumbled.

He clicked on a computer program; a program he had written. He keyed in the word "Execute". Hideo then stood up and walked to the door. He made his way out of the Fast Room, into the main chamber and across to the exit. He keyed in his new code. Hideo left the bunker and closed the door behind him. A few minutes later he was in the open. Looking up at a cloudless sky; a sky he had not seen for months.

****

'What was that?' said Paul.

He was looking at a CCTV monitor.

'Did you see something?' asked Francine.

'I'm sure something moved by the entrance to the drive,' he said. He zoomed in to the front gate. 'There are four motor bikes parked by the entrance.'

'My God,' said Francine. 'They're here.'

'What are they waiting for?' he asked, more to himself than Francine.

'The sun has just set,' said Francine. 'Perhaps they're waiting for dark. I hope the GWR will be ready in time.'

'Bugger,' said Paul. 'Claire and Jacques are trapped. I've got to warn them.' He raced to the corner of the room. 'Quickly, turn the lights out,' he added.

Whilst Paul reached for the intercom link to the barn, Francine leapt towards the light switch, plunging the farmhouse into near darkness. Although it was twilight outside, with the windows shuttered, the interior of the farmhouse was virtually black, illuminated only by Paul's computer screen and the CCTV monitor.

'Do you think they saw the lights?' asked Francine.

'I hope not,' said Paul.

His eyes not quite adjusted to the low level of light, he fumbled for the intercom receiver, linking them to the barn. He pushed the buzzer.

'Hi handsome,' said Claire. 'What do you want?'

'They're here,' he said. 'Turn off the lights quickly.'

Through a crack between the shutter doors of the farmhouse Francine saw the lights of the barn go out. Claire's voice returned to the intercom.

'I'm frightened,' she said.

'I know love,' he said. 'You have to lay low. They won't see you if you don't leave the barn.'

'Oh my God,' she said, her voice trembling. 'Jacques is next to me. What should we do?'

'Keep the lights out, keep quiet and stay put,' said Paul.

'What if your trap doesn't work?' said Claire.

'It will,' said Paul, with more confidence than he felt. 'I love you,' he added.

Claire replied in kind. Jacques came on the line.

'We've nearly finished the modification,' said Jacques, another couple of minutes and we'll be trading.'

'Well, I'm afraid you'll have to do it in the dark,' said Paul. 'They're parked at the end of the drive.'

'Merde. We can't stop now,' he said. 'We'll work by torch light.'

'Be careful Jacques. Don't flash the torch about,' he warned. 'It's getting dark outside. If the light beam catches a hole in one of the barn's wooden shutters, you'll stand out like a sore thumb.'

'I'll be careful,' said Jacques.

'I'll call you back when I've trapped them in the workshop. Keep Claire safe for me,' Paul added.

'I will,' he said.

Paul hung up and went over to the crack in the shutters. He peered out towards the barn where Claire and Jacques were trapped. The barn looked dark enough. He moved across to his computer. Francine followed him.

'I can control the workshop's lights and doors from here,' he said. 'I'll turn the lights on so they think we are in there. I'll keep them at low intensity though. I'll put the radio on as well.'

Paul clicked a button on the screen.

Francine moved over to the window and peered through a crack in the shutters.

'The workshop lights are on and I can hear muffled voices from the radio,' she said. 'I can't see the workshop entrance though.'

Paul flicked through the CCTV images.

'Bugger,' he said. 'I forgot to adjust one of the cameras. There's a blind spot between the end of the drive and the workshop door.'

'I intended to fix it earlier,' he said,' but they've caught me off-guard. There is no way I can spring the trap without a view of that area.'

'Why don't we move upstairs?' said Francine. 'We can get a view of the whole area from the dormer window in the bedroom.'

'Ok then we'd better move quickly,' he said. 'We'll set up in the bedroom. Can you take the laptop and plug it in upstairs. I'll carry the CCTV link panel. I can view the images though the lap-top.'

One of the advantages of a small farmhouse is that everything is close to everything else and within five minutes they had repositioned the equipment with a good view of the workshop and the drive. However five minutes was more than adequate for the sun to go down and for the short motorbike ride to the workshop door. Whilst Paul was finishing his manoeuvres in the dark, Francine heard motorbike engines. Paul was plugging in his last cable when Francine saw them park up.

'I thought you said there were four of them?' said Francine, alarmed.

'I did.'

He joined her at the window. He could see the three Kawasakis parked in front of the workshop. The riders, dressed in black protective gear, were standing in a group looking back down the drive. All were brandishing pistols.

'My God where's the fourth one?' asked Paul.

He scanned the images from the various cameras. There was no sign of him.

'Are there any more blind spots,' asked Francine.

'Only on the public road,' said Paul. 'Perhaps he's waiting for them there.'

'They're moving towards the workshop,' said Francine.

'Ok,' said Paul. 'We'll have to assume the fourth one was a passer by.'

Francine looked doubtful.

****

Nikolas was not waiting in the road. He was an action man and waiting was not his forte. As soon as he had heard who the marks were, Nikolas had done his own research and produced his own plan. A quick search of satellite images on the Internet was enough to tell him that there were two entrances to the Degordes plot. There was a woodland path leading to the back of the property. With a robust off-road bike, he could make his own assault on the property from the rear. He knew Dzibias and Degordes. They were his enemies, but they were not stupid. There was no way he was going to drive up to their front door and attack them. He would have to be more devious. His plan kicked in as they waited by the front gate of the farm.

'It's dark enough,' said his brother. 'Let's start up.'

The starter motors of the four engines turned over and all but the BMW fired into action. At the time, Zakhar thought that was rather strange because BMWs are supposed to be very reliable bikes.

'What's up,' he asked his younger brother.

'I don't fucking know,' he said angrily.

It was a lie, he did know. Hidden under his glove, he had switched the red override switch off.

'Forget it,' said Zakhar. 'Get on the pillion.'

'Fuck off,' said Nikolas. 'I'll get it started.'

He switched the red switch back on. After a few splutters, from clearing the flooded cylinders, the engine fired.

'Right let's get going,' said Zakhar.

They slipped their helmets on. The four bikes started off towards the workshop, the BMW at the rear.

Suddenly the BMW engine cut out. Zakhar looked over his shoulder. Nikolas waved at him to continue as he tried to restart the unreliable engine. Zakhar shrugged and the trio followed the drive around the farmhouse towards the workshop. Once they were out of sight, the BMW's engine made a remarkable recovery. Nikolas turned round and headed for his alternative route.

****

'You'll have to be my eyes,' he said. 'I can't watch them at the window and operate the door locking system at the same time. Tell me when they are all in the workshop.'

It was now quite dark. Francine peered though the window.

'Here take these,' he said, handing her a pair of binoculars. 'They're night vision.'

Francine put them to her eyes.

'I can see them clearly,' she said. 'They are just outside the entrance. The smallest is slowly opening the door…..

****

Zakhar and one of his henchmen, their pistols pointing upwards were crouching against the hinged door jamb. Mountain man was at the other. Zakhar made a hand signal to Mountain man who slowly reached for the door handle. All was quiet except for the radio emitting muffled accordion music into the night. Zakhar raised four fingers and started to count down. His last finger retreated back to his palm.

A bang echoed out into the night as the door almost flying off its hinges flew open. The three sprang into the room like uncoiled springs. Shots reverberated though the night drowning the accordion music. In the half light the attackers could see four bodies collapse to the floor. But something was wrong, there was no twitching, no blood. Zakhar looked over his shoulder towards the doorway, their only way out. He saw the black entrance suddenly change from the black of the night to silver grey as a steel shutter screeched its way downwards to the floor. He dived towards the space at the bottom. He managed to get his hands under the bottom strut. He pushed, staining against the motor, whilst his companions gaped at him their mouths wide open. But the motor was too strong. Relentlessly, progressively the shutter closed. Zakhar could get no purchase. He slipped his fingers out just before they were crushed. Finally they were trapped.

****

Paul and Francine had seen the whole incident on the laptop. Paul punched the air as the door finally shut them in.

'Will the doors hold?' asked Francine.

'As long as they're not carrying explosives,' he said. 'Their pistols won't make any difference to those shutters. I'll switch the lights off, just to disorientate them until we call the police.'

'Are there other ways out?' she asked. 'What about the roof?'

'I've put a steel grid above the ceiling. They're stuck until we decide to let them out,' he said with confidence.

A couple of shots rang out followed by curses.

'I think one of them has just fired at the door,' he said. 'Not very clever really, the bullet would ricochet off the steel. They could kill themselves. Do you think I should tell them?'

'It may be a good idea to settle them down,' she said, 'but don't taunt them, they still have guns.'

'Let's see their reaction,' he said. 'I'll switch the cameras to night vision. Do you want to speak to them?'

'Ok,' said Francine.

He pushed the button and signalled for her to speak. Their images appeared on the laptop screen.

Francine started to talk to them, 'You cannot escape, so there is no point trying,' said Francine. She paused to watch their reaction. All three looked startled. The smallest had taken his helmet off. He produced a torch from his pocket and was scanning the room. She continued, 'We have been expecting you. All the exits are shuttered with steel doors. You cannot open them from the inside, so you may as well sit down and make yourselves comfortable until the police arrive.'

One of them responded to her words with a single finger sign. He then let off a shot in what he thought was the direction of the speaker. Paul typed in a command into his laptop. He signalled for Francine to carry on. This time her voice came from another direction.

'I wouldn't recommend you firing guns in there,' she said. 'It could be dangerous. Please settle down and we may put the lights on for you.' Francine's tone was sympathetic. Oddly she was starting to feel sorry for them.

Whilst Francine was speaking to her prisoners, Paul was starting to check the communications links for their counter attack on STKiC's banks. He glanced at Francine who was still watching the three trapped men.

'I'll call Jacques and Claire to find out whether they are ready,' she said, 'and tell them that your plan worked.'

'Ok,' said Paul. 'Can you ask Jacques whether we are ready to call the police? We can use our mobile phone now, as STKiC clearly know where we are.'

'I'm on it,' she said, already half way down stairs.

'You can tell them it's Ok to come out now, as well,' he called as she disappeared below.

'Ok,' she called back.

Paul satisfied that all his communications were working decided to have a look at the images from each CCTV camera. He quickly flicked from one image to another satisfied all was all right. Then he saw something that should not have been there. He saw the fourth motor bike.

'Francine,' he shouted. 'Stop!'

He could hear Francine's voice downstairs.

'Hold on,' she was saying, 'Paul's saying something.'

She was too late, they had hung up. Grabbing the night binoculars, Paul rushed towards the stairs, almost falling into the room below.

'It's the fourth rider,' he said. 'He's outside the barn.'

****

In spite of the impediment of working under torchlight Jacques and Claire had managed to complete the modification to the GWR. It was ready to go. They had been sitting silently in the dark for nearly half an hour as the events unfolded less than one hundred metres away in the farmhouse and workshop. They had heard the music, the gunshots and when the intercom's buzzer sounded, they nearly jumped out of their skins.

Claire was closest to the receiver.

'Hello,' she said. Then addressing Jacques, 'It's Francine.'

He nodded in the dark.

'Thank God. Are you and Paul ok?' she asked. 'Paul's plan worked,' she said to Jacques.

Jacques breathed a sigh of relief also.

Claire listened for a few more seconds and then switched off the intercom.

'She says, you can start the GWR up and we can go back to the farmhouse,' said Claire.

Wonderful,' he said. 'Now it's STKiC's turn to worry.'

Jacques stood up and crossed the room and turned the lights on. They were dazzled as the bright light reflected off the replica of Hitzubishi's GWR.

'It looks magnificent, doesn't it,' said Jacques.

'It looks just like the one Prama, Hideo and I stole in Tokyo,' said Claire. 'I'm not sure magnificent is the word. More like terrifying. If you remember it destroyed the building where it was installed.'

'Mais Oui, this is the new improved version,' he said, smiling.

Not in the least bit comforted, she said, 'I'll be happier when we're in the farmhouse. Can we go yet?'

'Yes,' said Jacques, looking at his watch. 'The gravitational wave intensity should be high enough.'

He flicked a switch and the device made a hissing noise, followed by the sound of hydraulic oil being forced into a pressurized container. The GWR started to vibrate. Jacques watched it for a moment.

'That looks ok,' he said. 'It will vibrate a little, but we've added extra damping and it will be much more stable than the original version.'

'I believe you,' said Claire, uncertainly. 'Can we go now.'

'After you madam,' he said, gesturing her to the door.

Claire lifted the latch and opened the door. The light from the barn flooded out into the night.

He was half way up the pathway to the workshop when he saw it. He turned and saw two figures silhouetted in the doorway. He recognized one of them instantly. He drew his pistol.

'Stop where you are you tricky bastard,' he shouted, as he let off the first shot.

****

Paul threw the farmhouse door open in time to see Claire fall.

'Hey shit house,' Paul shouted, using one of the parked Kawasakis for cover.

Nikolas turned.

'All my dreams come true,' he shouted, recognizing Paul's voice. 'You're next, you devious bastard.'

'Fucking hell,' said Paul. 'Is that you Nikolas?'

'That depends,' he replied, referring to his many aliases.

The point was lost on Paul.

'I'll see to you after I've finished Degordes and your wife off,' said Nikolas.

He turned and headed back towards the barn. Jacques had dragged Claire inside and slammed the door closed. He knew it would not hold long, but he was pushing boxes against it to barricade himself in. Jacques glanced over his shoulder. The GWR was vibrating violently. Claire was bleeding from the gunshot wound. He knew Nikolas could easily fire through the wooden shutters whether the door was barricaded or not. They were sitting ducks. He could hear Nikolas's footsteps as he was moving in for the kill. Panic was starting to grip him. He remembered how Francine always ran her projects.

'When there's too much to do, decide on your priorities and do that first,' she had said.

He tore off his shirt and went to Claire. I must stop the bleeding. His back exposed, he lent over her prone body and started to apply a tourniquet to the wound in her arm. The wound did not look serious but she was in shock and shaking. He held her closer, to warm and comfort her.

****

Francine always took her own advice. Her priority was to protect her husband and her friends. She had had enough of these thugs. She ran upstairs and climbed through the dormer window on to the roof. She clambered up the tiles until she reached the microwave dish. She searched for the switch that Paul had pointed out earlier.

'He told me it would fry pigeons,' she said, the tigress coming to the fore. 'Well wretched little man you're no pigeon, but you're going to fry.'

She wrenched the microwave dish round so that it was no longer pointing at the sky. She aimed it at the evil man in black, who was walking towards the barn. She switched the power switch from "Low" to "Maximum" and turned it on.

****

Paul continued to shout abuse at Nikolas, but he would not turn and face him. Paul's anger was rising. He jumped astride one of the Kawasakis and hit the starter button. It fired up. He had not ridden anything bigger than a scooter before. He found a gear and let out the clutch. The front wheel lifted as he applied too much power. He did not care. There was so much adrenaline pumping in his system, it seemed to help his balance. He aimed straight for Nikolas.

Suddenly Nikolas screamed. The pain from Francine's microwave boiling radiation had shocked him. He turned round. He could not see what had caused the pain but through watery eyes he saw Paul bearing down on him. He raised his pistol and aimed between Paul's eyes.

****

Francine was angry; angry at the man who was trying to kill her husband, angry at Paul because the pigeon had not been fried. She took aim again; this time she could see the villain's face. The beam hit him right between the eyes.

Nikolas temporarily blinded, was not going to be beaten that easily. He could hear the bike. He aimed and fired. The engine raced as its rear wheel was no longer providing traction.

Almost ecstatically, he shouted, 'Got the bas….'

****

The tourniquet now applied, Jacques was ready to take their assailant on.

'Go, they need you,' said Claire.

'You're sure?' said Jacques.

'Just go,' she ordered.

Brandishing a steel rod, like a sword. He swung the door open ready to attack. He saw Nikolas taking aim as Paul headed towards him.

'Don't shoot him,' he shouted. 'It's me you want.'

But it was too late. The shot rang out, but it did not hit Paul. It burst the front tyre of the bike.

'Oh bugger,' shouted Paul, as he flew through the air into Nikolas. The impact took both of them some twenty feet into the trees. They landed together in the spot where the Degordes' ancient tractor was parked. Their two bodies impaled on the sharp, steel spikes protruding from the trailer. The light through cracks in the barn doors illuminated a pool of blood that was collecting beneath the bodies.

A few minutes later Francine found Jacques on his knees. He was sobbing. She put her arms around him and sobbed with him.

'Not again,' he repeated again and again and again.

'I've called the police and ambulance, my love,' she said. 'Come on we must see to Claire now.'

****

'I don't understand,' said Lihua. 'Our revenues are falling.'

'They can't be,' said Quon, 'The plan was fool proof.'

'I bet the little shit's done something,' said Viktor. 'I'm going to question him. Don't worry father I'll sort the problem out.'

'Maybe you're right, my son,' said Quon. 'It's time he was eliminated. Bring him here I'll help you.'

'You'd better be quick,' said Lihua, impatiently. 'At this rate we'll have no money left.'

Viktor disappeared along the corridor and was back in a few minutes. He appeared to be agitated.

'What's wrong, Viktor?' asked Quon.

'He's gone, there's a hole in the bathroom ceiling. He must be in the Fast Room.'

'What?' shouted Quon. 'Then get him out.'

'Where, from the Fast Room?'

'Yes, where do you think? Idiot,' said his father, exasperated.

'I'm not going in there,' said Viktor.

'You're useless,' said Quon.

He transferred his attention to Lihua. She nodded. He handed her his pistol.

'Kill him,' he said. 'I'll find out what he's done.'

'Yes father,' said Lihua, taking the pistol, checking the magazine and switching the safety catch off.

****

'For God's sake will someone get me down from here?'

Jacques looked towards the tractor, the image blurred because of his tears. He rubbed his eyes, thinking he must be dreaming.

'Is that you Paul?' he asked.

Jacques and Francine stood up. They could see Paul lying on top of Nikolas' body. He was talking to them.

'Who the bloody hell do you think it is?' asked Paul.

'Aren't you hurt?' asked Francine, incredulously. 'You don't sound hurt.'

'Well I will be if you don't get me down,' said Paul. 'Where's Claire?'

'She's in the barn. Her arm is cut where a bullet grazed her,' said Jacques. 'I've stopped the bleeding.'

'Will you bloody well get me down,' said Paul becoming annoyed. 'I want to see her.'

'I'm here darling. My God you're hurt!' she said, starting to panic.

'No I'm not,' said Paul, I'm stuck. 'The bastard below me was not so lucky. The first layer of Kevlar didn't save him, but the second layer saved me.'

'Alors mon ami,' said Jacques. 'It'll take the fire service to get you down from there and we've only called the police and ambulance.'

Jacques smiled, then he chuckled, which developed into a raucous laugh. They were still laughing when the emergency services arrived.

****

Hideo had no idea of the events in the South of France. However he was still curious about what would happen when his bunker companions decided to leave. He was sitting cross legged on the ground on a hill on the other side of the valley from the bunker. He was enjoying the sunshine and smiling to himself.

'It can't be long now,' he said to himself.

Hideo was curious whether his self taught computer programming in the Fast Room would work. He had written a simple little programme that connected the access control locks to the GWR Mark Three. If it worked he would be rather proud of himself. When he was assigned the task to survey the bunker, he had found that there was a fault line in the ceiling right above them. He was quite pleased when Hitzubishi had accepted Hideo's suggestion about the safest position for the GWR Mark Three. Unfortunately for his companions in the bunker, he had lied. It was not the safest position. In fact it was a very dangerous position and if the GWR Three vibrated as much as it had in Tokyo, it could bring the whole mountain down on them. The other part of his idea was equally inspired. He had found out how Hitzubishi had controlled the dampers in his device. With a little bit of programming code learned from Anil, he had worked out how to take control of the hydraulics. These were responsible for controlling the intensity of the focussed gravitational waves and the vibration that resulted. Hideo reflected that before setting out on this adventure, he had known nothing about general relativity. He now wondered how he could live without it.

'I wonder who'll crack first,' he said out loud. 'I do hope it's Viktor.'

****

It was indeed Viktor. His sister engaged in the Fast Room and his father preoccupied in tracking through Hideo's computer logs, Viktor decided it was time for him to leave. He keyed in the door lock code and nothing happened; nothing to the door that is.

****

Hideo felt the ground rumble beneath him.

'That's interesting,' he mused.

He could see an opening in the hillside on the other side of the valley. There was a tiny puff of dust.

'Okay,' he said, 'time to go home.'

He uncrossed his legs and stood up. He was humming a song that he did not know he knew. Somehow it reminded him of an old friend.

'So I'm sitting at a bar in Guadalajara…..,' he sang.

# Perspective of Matter

## by

## David C. Fletcher

It is 1826 and distrust between Captain Jefferson and his Chinese trading partner leads to the theft of an unusual object desired by a Beijing astronomer. The loss of the object at sea, creates one of the most devastating natural disasters in the nineteenth century.

Paul, who is a recently out-of-work physicist, joins a research team which specialises in looking for signs of primitive life in space. He teams up with Claire, a rather attractive biochemist, who has discovered bizarre characteristics in an extraterrestrial DNA sample. As they search for an explanation, they realise that they have stumbled on a far larger conundrum which leads them back to the events in the Japanese Pacific over one hundred and eighty years before. As they investigate further, their colleagues' and their own lives become more interesting and dangerous.

**A Wise Grey Owl Publication**

www.ingramcontent.com/pod-product-compliance
Lightning Source LLC
Chambersburg PA
CBHW030821310726
48980CB00006B/580/J

* 9 7 8 0 9 5 6 1 5 7 4 4 7 *